# STRANGE FRUIT

# STRANGE

# FRUIT

## BY LILLIAN SMITH

### FOREWORD
### BY FRED HOBSON

BROWN THRASHER BOOKS

THE UNIVERSITY OF GEORGIA PRESS • ATHENS

The paper in this book meets the guidelines for
permanence and durability of the Committee on
Production Guidelines for Book Longevity of the
Council on Library Resources.

Printed in the United States of America

94  93  92  91  90      5  4  3  2

Library of Congress Cataloging in Publication Data

Smith, Lillian Eugenia, 1897–1966.
Strange fruit.
Originally published: New York: Reynal & Hitchcock,
1944.
"Brown thrasher books."
I. Title.
PS3537.M653S8      1985      813′.52      84-28073
ISBN 0-8203-0779-3 (pbk.: alk. paper)

*To Paula*

# FOREWORD

LILLIAN SMITH WAS a phenomenon—the most courageous, outspoken, and uncompromising white southern liberal of her generation. "A modern, feminine counterpart of the ancient Hebrew prophets," Ralph McGill once called her; the William Lloyd Garrison of the South, Virginius Dabney wrote; and numerous other southerners added both their praise and their amazement.[1] For no other white southerner in the first half of the twentieth century was so truly committed to the cause of racial justice as Lillian Smith, and no other was so bold in his criticism of a white South. Rare indeed was the southern liberal who had decided against racial segregation by the 1930s, rarer still the southerner who would announce such a decision, but Smith had both decided and had begun to speak out boldly against that "evil," segregation, by 1936. Her career from that time until her death

1. Ralph McGill, "A Matter of Change," *New York Times Book Review*, February 13, 1955, p. 7; and Virginius Dabney, quoted by Morton Philip Sosna, "In Search of the Silent South: White Southern Racial Liberalism, 1920–1950" (Ph.D. dissertation, University of Wisconsin, 1973), p. 309.

in 1966 was a sustained act of very personal truth-telling unsurpassed by that of any other white southerner of her time.

If Smith is generally assumed to have been a southern liberal, she in fact belonged to no official school of southern thought. Certainly, she was not an official liberal spokesman, as McGill, Dabney, Hodding Carter, and other southern editors were presumed to be in the South's crucial midcentury. In fact, the power and depth of these men's truth-telling about the South were restricted by their roles as prominent spokesmen—and as southern leaders who could not leave their followers too far behind. Smith called them "racial thumb-suckers" who regressed to childhood prejudices during times of stress. But Smith herself was bound by no institutional ties, restricted by no role as official voice. She possessed a freedom to attack southern ills in a manner they did not because of her position outside the liberal establishment—and also, she felt, because of her sex. Removed from southern political and economic life, the southern woman, Smith believed, was able to concentrate on the moral and the religious. And if she came from a prominent southern family, as Smith did, she was given a particular license to utter certain truths that few other critics, southern or nonsouthern, could voice and get away with.

Such were the truths that Smith expressed in her first novel, *Strange Fruit*. It was a novel that shocked, that challenged southern thinking—and not only disturbed white southerners but was determined to be so dangerous to the status quo in general that it was banned in Boston and condemned by other right thinkers outside as well as within Dixie. It was a sensational novel, one that sold six hundred thousand copies its first year, eventually sold three million copies, and was both proclaimed the best novel of 1944 and denounced as one of the worst of any year. It not only painted a devastating picture of southern society—and racial segregation, wherever it might occur—but it was also sexually explicit, at least for a time in which American publishing had not fully broken free of the genteel tradition. The story of a love affair between a young white man and a young black woman was bound to sell—and bound to generate controversy. "The most interesting novel I have read for a long time," Malcolm Cowley wrote in the *New Republic*; a new "Uncle Tom's Cabin," wrote Edward Weeks in the *Atlantic*. Other reviewers agreed. *Strange Fruit* was a "problem novel . . . a very good one," Diana Trilling wrote in *The Nation*; the *New York Times* called it "one of the most rewarding first novels to come out of the South in years"; and the reviewer in the *Christian Century* declared, "It can claim to be the most important novel of the year." According to *Commonweal*, Smith had "made us know again that the South is stained with racial evil; that it is foul and sick; and that each of us is troubled with its foulness and its sickness." Some reviewers, however, charged that Smith had gone too far in her graphic description of southern ills. Her novel, wrote the *Catholic World*, "sins against good taste so grossly as to make her story quite unfit for general circulation. It seems curious that [she] should recur with such fond frequency to the subject of urine and privies and should employ phrases which decent people regard as unprintable."[2]

Few of the reviewers, favorable or not, alluded to Smith's earlier work as an outspoken essayist and social critic, although in fact *Strange Fruit* is a novel that cannot be viewed

2. Malcom Cowley, "Southways," *New Republic*, March 6, 1944, p. 320; Edward Weeks, "Strange Fruit," *Atlantic* 173 (May 1944): 127; Diana Trilling, "Fiction in Review," *The Nation*, March 18, 1944, p. 342; William DuBois, "Searing Novel of the South," *New York Times Book Review*, March 5, 1944, pp. 1, 20; Cecelia Gaul, "Srange Fruit," *Christian Century*, July 19, 1944, p. 855; Francis Downing, "Strange Fruit," *Commonweal*, April 7, 1944, p. 626; and Joseph McSorley, "Strange Fruit," *Catholic World* 159 (May 1944): 182.

in isolation. For it was the product of the author's early life, her earlier thinking and writing about the South and about racial and sexual roles in general. She had been born in 1897 in the north Florida town of Jasper, a predominantly Negro town that served as the model for Maxwell, Georgia, the setting for *Strange Fruit*. Her father was a prosperous businessman, her mother a cultivated southern lady, and the Smith children had advantages not available to most other inhabitants of the town. Lillian Smith attended a small college in Georgia one year, studied piano for four at the Peabody Conservatory in Baltimore, and then taught music for three years in a mission school in China. Her parents, her early education, and the detachment with which she saw her native South while living in China all served to give Lillian Smith a somewhat different view of Dixie.

When she returned to America in 1925, Smith began to run the summer camp for girls that her father had founded in the mountains of north Georgia—but she also found time to read (particularly Freud), to write a novel based on her China experience (which was rejected by publishers as too controversial), and, in 1936, to begin a little magazine, first called *Pseudopodia*, then the *North Georgia Review*, and finally *South Today*. For the next ten years Smith and her friend Paula Snelling put out a magazine that was, by far, the boldest editorial voice in the South. In it Smith emerged as southern moralist, a role she was to fill for the rest of her life. She wrote of the "profound guilt for our treatment of the Negro" and "the rationalizations by which the white man eases his guilt." The South was an "intelligence-drained region," and the southern way of life was "hideous in its effects" upon blacks and whites alike.[3]

3. See Lillian Smith and Paula Snelling, quoted in Helen White and Redding S. Sugg, Jr., eds., *From the Mountain* (Memphis: Memphis State University Press, 1972), p. xii; Smith, "Act of Penance" (Spring 1938):

It was during her co-editorship of *South Today* that Smith wrote *Strange Fruit*, and many of the concerns in her essays and editorials assume dramatic form in the novel. The book, under the title "Jordan Is So Chilly," was rejected several times before it was accepted by the New York publishers Reynal and Hitchcock, who asked Smith to change the title. She suggested the eventual title because, she later wrote, she saw southern society as the "strange fruit" of racial prejudice. The strange fruit was not so much miscegenation and lynching (the "strange fruit" that hung from southern trees) as it was "the white man himself and his children and his Tobacco Roads and his own wasted life."[4] The picture Smith painted in her story was indeed of a South benighted and savage, ignorant and cruel. The Harris family, the leading white family in Maxwell, was based to a great extent on her own family. The Harrises are racial moderates, as the Smiths had been. Tom Harris owns the town's sawmill and turpentine works, as Calvin Smith had. He builds a mill village for his workers, as Calvin Smith had. The Harris family, like the Smiths, has nine children, and one of them, Harriet, resembles Lillian Smith. Harriet is "always protesting . . . what other folks took for granted"; she is sharply critical of her town and is "too ambitious, too restless to stop at Maxwell." Harriet concludes in the novel that white southerners are paranoid, a conclusion Lillian Smith had already reached in her editorial columns. In Harriet Harris and in another sensitive, artistic, out-of-place character, Laura Deen, Smith wrote herself into the novel.

---

67; Smith, "Dope with Lime" (Fall–Winter 1938–39): 11; Smith, "Wisdom Crieth in the Streets" (Fall 1937): 42; Smith, "Are We Not All Confused?" p. 106; Smith, "Putting Away Childish Things," p. 133. All in *South Today*, reprinted in *From the Mountain*.

4. Lillian Smith, in *Chicago Defender* (1949), quoted by Louise Blackwell and Frances Clay, *Lillian Smith* (New York: Twayne Publishers, 1971), p. 42.

But *Strange Fruit* was far more than veiled autobiography. In fact, the central incident of the novel—the love affair between Tracy Deen and Nonnie Anderson, and the subsequent tragic happenings—was based on no specific incident but rather on similar events that had taken place, or could have taken place, in the South of the early twentieth century. The novel at first seems to belong to that subgenre of southern social realism that had flourished in the 1920s but had declined by the 1940s. The leading practitioner of the southern realistic school was T. S. Stribling of Tennessee, and the violent, religiously fanatical and culturally barren south Georgia town that Smith depicts has much in common with the Tennessee and Alabama hill towns of Stribling's imagination. One finds the stock Stribling characters—the evangelist, the town radical, the rich, eccentric bachelor, the educated, angry young black man. The other townspeople are depicted as malicious, petty, and extremely limited in vision. Smith's is, at first appearance, the kind of fiction that focuses more on the type than on the individual.

But what distinguishes Smith from writers like T. S. Stribling is that Smith does not write satire. What Stribling often saw as targets for ridicule, Smith feels all too deeply. If her characters at first appear as types, as abstractions (and some remain so), the best of these characters—Dr. Sam, Bess Anderson, even to some extent Tracy Deen, his emotionally repressed mother, and the not fully realized Nonnie Anderson—emerge as individuals, living painfully day by day, suffering but usually enduring. Smith's novel is a tragedy of separation, of barriers people create, of humanity denied because of race and, to a lesser extent, class and sex. Smith's earlier novel about China had been entitled *Walls*, and *Strange Fruit* could as easily have borne that title.

If *Strange Fruit* qualifies as tragedy, however, it is of the deterministic variety, for the characters seem trapped by the society into which they are born. Smith later wrote that the segregated southern world "began destroying its children long before they were born"—that segregation "almost smothered the goodness in us"—and her novel illustrates her premise.[5] Her characters are anything but free agents: they are trapped by social forces, by patterns of conditioning, and their actions are nearly predictable. Tracy Deen at first appears genuinely to love Nonnie Anderson, but his society prevents his acknowledging or even fully realizing that love. He may use Nonnie for sexual gratification—the culture permits that—but he can never marry her or even love her outside marriage in anything approaching a mature, reciprocal relationship.

Determinism is at work in several ways in the novel. The Negro is an abstraction—without individuality, without personal identity—and the action of Smith's mob late in the novel demonstrates the Negro's invisibility as fully as the events of Ellison's *Invisible Man*. So does, perhaps, the name Smith gives her leading black character. Nonnie, also called "Non," is precisely that—a non-person. Climate—the oppressive heat—influences individual conduct. So do economic forces. The story takes place in August 1920 when times are hard: cotton is down and black field hands are scarce because many Negroes had left for the North after the war. Because the white inhabitants of Maxwell are frightened and vulnerable, the religious revival that runs throughout the story is assured a bountiful harvest. The revival also provides relief from the monotony of life in a town that offers nothing in the way of cultural activity or entertainment: Mencken was not far off when he said that revivals—and lynchings—took the place of plays and symphonies in backwoods southern towns. Finally, one finds a sort of psychological determinism at

5. Lillian Smith, *Killers of the Dream*, rev. ed. (Garden City, N.Y.: Anchor Books, 1963), p. 133; and Smith, *The Journey* (New York: Norton, 1965), p. 34.

work in *Strange Fruit*: Tracy's preference for black women to white is another product of the society into which he has been born. The white child of a privileged southern family, Smith wrote elsewhere, naturally preferred his warm, vital Negro mammy to his own rigid, repressed mother—and the black woman he wanted for sexual pleasure was his mammy in another form.[6] Nonnie is hardly a vital mammy type: she is refined, reserved, a graduate of Spelman College—and her skin is light. Nonetheless, she is a Negro, and Tracy has always had his emotional needs filled more by blacks than by whites.

One of the pitfalls of naturalistic or deterministic fiction is that authors often create characters that exist more as products of forces than as flesh-and-blood people. Naturalism presupposes that characters cannot truly make choices, or in any case meaningful or significant choices. Such is indeed the case with Smith's black characters—options for Nonnie Anderson are extremely limited—but with Tracy Deen there is at least the *illusion* of choice. If he is drawn into the relationship with Nonnie through something he himself cannot understand, he is capable of extricating himself from that relationship with more courage and honor than he demonstrates. He is, as Smith depicts him, even weaker and more pathetic than other white characters in the story. At first something of a rebel who rejects the conventional thought and the narrow religion of his town, he later becomes easy prey for the white-only muscular Christianity of Dunwoodie. He faces a situation similar in some respects to that of another fictional white boy whose closest companion is black and whom society tries to "civilize"—Mark Twain's Huckleberry Finn. But Huck rejects the institutions of his society and does right by appearing to do wrong—by vowing that he will never

6. Smith, *Killers of the Dream*, pp. 97–119.

betray his runaway slave friend Jim, that he will never turn him in, although he believes that would be the *right* thing to do. Tracy does wrong by appearing to do right—by accepting sanctioned southern values, joining the church, asking a respectable girl to marry him, and rejecting Nonnie. Unlike Huck, he could never say, "All right, then, I'll *go* to hell." He puts his faith in his society's institutions and, Smith knew as fully as Mark Twain, those institutions were corrupt.

But—even if he has the illusion of choice—Tracy could never, like Huck, light out for the territory, certainly not the unexplored territory of deep personal moral responsibility. And that, Smith believed, brought the burden back to southern society. As several critics have pointed out, Tracy is little more than a symbol of the white South: crippled (he walks with a limp), confused, tied to his past, unproductive, and preoccupied with the Negro, all the while refusing to acknowledge him. Racial segregation, Smith wrote elsewhere, produced "a way of life so wounding, so hideous in its effect upon the spirit of both black and white" that it destroyed the southern spirit. There was much in the South, she insisted, "that reminds one of mental illness." Southerners had "split their lives in a way shockingly akin to those sick people whom we call schizophrenics." They suffered "delusions of persecution." For herself, writing *Strange Fruit* was "therapy" that "removed a long amnesia about my hometown." "I wrote down things I did not know were true until I saw them staring back at me on the page."[7]

7. Blackwell and Clay, p. 45; Smith, "Putting Away Childish Things," p. 133; Smith, *Killers of the Dream*, p. 184; Smith, "Humans in Bondage," in *The Winner Names the Age*, ed. Michelle Cliff (New York: Norton, 1978), p. 38; and Smith, letter to Maxwell Geismar, January 1, 1961, in *The Winner Names the Age*, pp. 214, 216.

The year after *Strange Fruit* appeared Lillian Smith assessed in *Saturday Review* the reception the novel had received. "By even the most generous of white critics," she wrote, "it was not treated as literature—not even as bad literature." Smith overstated her case—many reviewers had seen her book not only as literature but as good literature—but, in general, her assessment was correct. Malcolm Cowley, in perhaps the most astute review of the novel and a generally favorable one, conceded that Smith lacked the "specifically literary gifts of William Faulkner or, let us say, Carson McCullers," and predicted that Smith's talents would "lead her eventually into some field other than the novel."[8]

Cowley was correct—and prophetic. *Strange Fruit* was far from a flawless work of art—the narrative point of view shifted from character to character, the dialogue was sometimes contrived, and the author's use of the stream of consciousness hardly approached Faulkner's in artistry—although it is clear to the reader today that the whole of the novel is much better than its parts. Like Dreiser, Smith was able to overcome certain literary deficiencies with power and with conviction. But Smith herself soon realized that conviction could better be channeled into other areas—particularly so, perhaps, after her dramatization of her novel failed on Broadway—and after *Strange Fruit* she was to write only one novel. What she did write was a series of essays and books in which she could speak more directly to the reader. *Killers of the Dream*, published five years after *Strange Fruit*, was her most honest and heartfelt book—perhaps the boldest, most starkly revealing portrait of the South by a notable white southerner since Hinton Rowan

8. Smith, "Personal History of *Strange Fruit*," *Saturday Review*, February 17, 1945, p. 9; and Cowley, "Southways," p. 322.

Helper's *The Impending Crisis of the South* (1857) nearly a century before. Her next book, *The Journey* (1954), was as close to being a spiritual autobiography as Smith would ever write. An attempt to come to terms with pain and suffering and human tragedy, it was also, in a deeper sense, an attempt to deal with her own mortality. Racial segregation she continued to attack with a fury until her death. Those southerners, such as the Nashville Agrarians, who she felt were betraying the southern cause by giving comfort to the enemy, she attacked with equal fury. "No writers in literary history," she wrote of the Agrarians, "have failed their region so completely as these did."[9] But Smith was involved in the 1950s and 1960s not only in writing about the South but also in serving as a crusader for the civil rights movement. The woman who for three decades had been calling for the end of legalized racial segregation saw many of her dreams fulfilled just before her death.

Demonstrably, then, *Strange Fruit* was of a piece with nearly everything else Lillian Smith wrote. In it, as in her other works, she tried to find a way out of the South's "dark tangled forest full of sins and boredom and fears."[10] If it was a "sociological" work, as some of the Agrarians charged, it was a work that went even deeper and painted an even more dismal picture of the American South than those notable sociological examinations that had preceded it—Frank Tannebaum's *Darker Phases of the South* (1924), John Dollard's *Caste and Class in a Southern Town* (1937), and Gunnar Myrdal's *An American Dilemma* (1944), as well as the works of the southern sociologists Howard W. Odum and Arthur Raper. It was, in many respects, a novel that offered dramatic proof of that "savage ideal" de-

9. Smith, *Killers of the Dream*, p. 199.
10. Smith, *Killers of the Dream*, p. 100.

scribed by Smith's friend, Wilbur Cash, three years earlier in *The Mind of the South*. In their work the social scientists had diagnosed and ministered to Dixie's physical ills. Cash, in his classic work, had explored the depths of the southern mind. But Lillian Smith, in *Strange Fruit* as well as her other work, plumbed Dixie's very soul.

FRED HOBSON

# STRANGE FRUIT

# ONE

S H E   S T O O D at the gate, waiting; behind her the swamp, in front of her Colored Town, beyond it, all Maxwell. Tall and slim and white in the dusk, the girl stood there, hands on the picket gate.

"That's Nonnie Anderson," they would tell you, "that's one of the Anderson niggers. Been to college. Yeah! Whole family been to college! All right niggers though, even if they have. Had a good mother who raised her children to work hard and know their place. Anderson niggers all right. Good as we have in the county, I reckon."

"Stuck up like Almighty, Nonnie Anderson," some colored folks said, "holding her head so highty-tighty, not like Bess. Bess common as dirt, friendly with folks."

"You forgot Ern Anderson's ways?" others said. "Spittin image of her pappy in her ways. Shut-mouth jes like him, dat all. Pity ain mo like her! Too many folks lettin off their moufs bout things they don know nothin about, pokin their noses in—"

"Biggety thing," white women said, "I wouldn't have her in my house with all her college airs." But most said it enviously, for women on College Street and the side streets knew

1

that Mrs. Brown's servant Nonnie was the best servant in Maxwell unless it was her sister Bess. And so good to little imbecile Boysie. Everybody knew how good she was to the little fellow.

"Sometimes I wonder," Mrs. Brown would say, "how I ever did without her! She's so good to the baby, Frank! He cries so in this hot weather and she never gets cross with him. You can tell a good nurse by her hands. Way she touches a baby. No matter how bad the poor little fellow is, Nonnie's never rough with him. Always so easy, picking him up. Wish we could pay her a little more. I'm afraid she'll leave us."

"Nonnie's a good nigger, all right," Frank would answer, "good as we'll find, I reckon. You pay her enough, three dollars plenty! Already more than anybody else on College Street. You'll have the women on you if you start raising wages."

"Her shy as a little critter," Tillie Anderson used to say, long ago. "Won't talk to nobody. Who got yo tongue, Nonnie? Come out from behind my skirt, can't spen yo life apeekin from behind yo Ma! You know dat, honey!"

And white boys whistled softly when she walked down the street, and said low words and rubbed the back of their hands across their mouths, for Nonnie Anderson was something to look at twice, with her soft black hair blowing off her face, and black eyes set in a face that God knows by right should have belonged to a white girl. And old Cap'n Rushton, sitting out in front of Brown's Hardware Store as he liked to do when in from the turpentine farm, would rub his thick red hand over his chin slowly as he watched her wheel drooling, lop-headed Boysie Brown in to see his papa, sit there watching the girl, rubbing his hand over his chin, watching her, until she had gone back across the railroad and turned down College Street.

Nonnie pushed her hair off her face as she looked across

2

White Town. Strange . . . being pregnant could make you feel like this. So sure. After all the years, sure. Bess wouldn't see it. You hated to try to explain. Bess would feel disgraced. Ruined. The Andersons ruined, Bess would say. You live in a dream world, she'd say. Sometimes I almost think you're crazy, Non! she would say. I almost wish you *were* crazy, she'd say in her bitterness.

Sharp words rattling like palmettos.

Nonnie sighed.

Across the town came the singing. A white singing to Jesus. An August singing of lost souls. A God-moaning.

August is the time folks give up their sins. August is a time of trouble.

*Whiter than snow . . . yes whiter than snow . . . oh wash me and I shall be whiter than snow.*

Her thoughts swung with the Gospel tune.

Around the curve from Miss Ada's, where the trees open up, clearing the path, she could see him coming. A drag of left foot, a lift of shoulder, half limp, half swagger. Limp, swagger . . .

She would tell him, now that she felt certain. Though she had known since that night at the river. Somehow she had known since then.

He would say, "You all right?" and look at her as if he saw her for the first time. And the sound of it would hurt in her throat. Funny, how you don't get used to things.

He had said it first when he picked her out of the sand-spurs, long ago; so long, it seemed now as if she must have dreamed it. She had fallen when Nat pulled up her dress, pulled at her underpants. Nat's freckled hand had reached out for her and she had jerked away from him, but more from the look on his sallow face, new to six-year-old eyes. His words already old. Words scrawled on circus posters, on priv-ies, on fences, said with a giggle, carrying no more meaning

3

to her ears than the squawk of guineas running crazily along ditches in search of worms.

"You all right?" Tracy had said; and then, to Nat, "Beat it. She's not that kind. And don't let me catch you around here again."

"Haw, haw, haw," Nat showed tobacco-stained teeth and lolled his tongue. "I didn't know she was yourn."

"She's not mine," Tracy said and reddened. "Now git— before I knock the liver-an-lights out of you."

Nat Ashley put his hands in his pockets, sauntered slowly away to show he wasn't afraid of nobody! Increased his nonchalance by jumping a gallberry bush. Grew in manliness by shouting to the boys on the distant ball ground, "Hi, how about some shinny?" Faded from their sight and from their lives.

The swamp had thrown deep shadows. Hounds barked in Nigger Town and beat the dust with their tails. The smell of scorched cloth from shanties clung to the sweet, near odor of honeysuckle in her hand.

Slowly she took a step toward him. "I *am* yourn," she whispered, and held out the grubby flowers.

Twelve-year-old Tracy took them. "You'd better run home," he said. "Your mama oughtn't allow you to run round alone. What were you doin, anyways?"

"Picking flowers and—" She hesitated.

"And what?" he probed.

"And visiting." She stooped, pulled a sandspur from her foot, pushed her toes deep into sand.

"Visiting? Who?"

"Everywheres. The swamp, mostly."

He spat and studied her face. "What you do in that swamp?"

"Nothing. Just goes." She paused. "It says, 'Come here, come here, come here.' "

He squinted his eyes.

4

"You hear it?" she whispered.

"Nope. Nothing but frogs croaking, and dogs."

She smiled, pushed her black wavy hair from her face, drew in a deep breath.

Tracy spat again, looked away. "Silly way to talk," he chided, "it's silly. You've got no business going near that swamp. You might get lost. Who you belong to?"

"I'se Tillie's child."

"Tillie?"

She searched for a meeting ground. "She's Miz Purviance's cook."

"Yeah, I know. Now run on before it's pitch-dark."

"Who is you?" Voice shy in its first social exploration.

"I'm Tracy Deen. Dr. Deen's son."

She looked at him gravely.

"Now run along! Ought to tell your mama on you."

She started toward the old Anderson place, walked a few steps, stopped, watched him cut through the gallberry bushes. In the dusk she could see him limp a little, could see his shoulder twist. He stooped over a bush. When he went on again his hands were empty. She sighed, began to run hard, dreading the scolding her sister Bess would give her for staying out so late.

In the dusk he stood now before her, tall, stooped. Took her hands from the gate, held them. "You all right?" His eyes searched her face, moved from her hair to her eyes, to her throat.

"Of course." She laughed softly.

"Cool. Your hands are cool, and it's hot as hell."

"I know. Boysie's cried all day."

"Boysie! How do you stand the slobbering little idiot day after—"

"I don't mind. It's a fine job for a girl like me," she said and smiled at the white man.

5

Tracy did not smile.

"Come in," she said. "I'll fix you something cool to drink. It's better in the arbor."

"No, I promised Mother—promised a lot of people—to go to the meeting tonight. Think all Maxwell is praying for me. Goddam em."

He opened the gate, came inside. Slim and white she stood there before him in the dusk. He pulled her behind a spirea bush. "I'm too hot to touch you," he whispered. "Sweet and cool . . . always sweet and cool . . . you smell so good to me. Non," he said unhappily.

"I'm glad."

"All right. Tell me quick. What's happened?"

She looked up at him steadily. "I'm pregnant, Tracy."

She felt his hand tremble on her arm. "And I'm glad," she whispered.

"Glad? You can't be!"

"I'm glad."

"But—"

"You see," she spoke quickly, "I want it. I'll have something they—can't take away from me." Voice low, hard to hear the words.

"What do you mean?"

"It's like thinking something for a long time you can't put into words. One day you write it down. You always have it after that."

His face eased into the old quick grin. "Might have been better this time to have written it down, Non."

He frowned, ran his fingers slowly over the fence pickets. "Let's don't think about it," he said.

"All right," she whispered. She looked at him and smiled, and he stared into her eyes as if he had not heard a word that she had ever said. "I wish you were glad," she said and felt her body shaking against his in sudden betrayal of her calm.

6

"Reckon we ought to talk about it, or something—" He looked out toward the swamp, forgetting his words. *In the dusk she's as white as Laura. God, if she weren't a nigger! Lord God what a mess . . .*

"No, we don't need to talk about it."

"Well, good-by, honey." He touched her hair, turned away, stopped, faced her again. "It's Mother. She—you know how it is! Nothing I've ever done has pleased her, as you know." He laughed abruptly. "Now the damned meeting's got her worked up. After dinner she—I don't know what's happened. Seems—well, she said—lot of things—about joining the church, settling down. Other things—Laura's lack of interest in church—seems disappointed in her children." He laughed. Non waited. "Nothing new as far as I'm concerned. First time I ever heard her put Laura in the red." He laughed again. "Well . . . better be going."

He stared into the evening. Turned suddenly, opened the picket gate, closed it. "I may come back tonight late. All right?"

"All right," Nonnie whispered, knowing he would not come.

# TWO

E D  F I N I S H E D the mullet, took a swallow of coffee from the thick hot cup, mopped his face. He laid a quarter on the counter, leaned toward Salamander—same old dried tobacco leaf he was five years ago—shouted in the old man's ear, "You keep it at the boiling point down here."

—same old place—same old roaches—

7

"Sho."

—same old dirt—same old window full of Bruton snuff—

"Been like this all summer?"

—same old Coca-Cola signs—

"Sho."

—same old rag in Salamander's hand—

"Hotter than Washington, and that's something. How're things?"

—same old spit—same old stink—

"Tollable." Salamander put the quarter in his pocket, leaned over the counter, peered into his customer's face. Blue lips puckered, sniffing, laying his rag down on the counter, sniffing again. "Who it be?"

"Ed Anderson."

"Sho, sho," staring at the light brown Negro, sleek in Palm Beach suit, cocky in white straw hat. "Sho," he repeated and rubbed his gray-woolled head.

Ed stood on the sidewalk. In front of him was the garbage-heaped alley of stores facing College Street. He could have been looking into a back alley of Washington, New York, anywhere. To the right of him four stores separated Salamander's Lunch Counter (Colored) from the white people's Deen's Corner Drug Store. Now he looked straight into Georgia. White girls in cars blew horns, ordered cokes, laughed, crossed their legs, uncrossed them, stared through him as their line of vision passed his body. He was a black digit marked out by white chalk. He wasn't there on the sidewalk. He never had been there . . . he just wasn't anywhere—where those eyes looked—where those damned eyes—

So this was his home town. *You've never had a home town!* Where he was born. *You've never been born!* Maxwell, Georgia. *You know the word!*

He'd dreamed its deep sand paths hot to bare feet, spat-spat of rain on palmettos, old rickety house pushed against the swamp; dreamed hot unmoving nights when moss hung

8

heavy against his face and his heart; dreamed its smooth hot days blazing against the eye; dreamed it still had something to do with his blood and his soul.

Well, he didn't want it. Wouldn't have it! Not a goddam bit of it! Why on earth Bess and Nonnie lived on in this dirty hole—

He turned toward Back Street, paused near the town water tank. Its drip-drip beat on his memory. He was delivering groceries on a bicycle, stopping under the tower, leaning under the drip, letting it spatter his hot face and run into his mouth and down his neck, feeling its sudden coolness slide like ice on his skin—racing Al back to the Supply Store, jamming his wheel hard into crates and coops, while little Mr. Pusey clucked, "Not so fast, boys, not so fast," and scampered out of the way as bicycles and boys piled on top of each other in a tearing shriek of scraping metal and laughter. Little Mr. Pug Pusey would stand there, pulling his pants up, pulling his lips down in a pout, until boys and wheels had righted themselves; then he'd march into the store in silence, his little pudgy hips quivering in disapproval.

Ed laughed, pushed his hat over to one side of his head, walked on. Felt better somehow. Better.

Somebody black said, "Hi, Stranger." He grinned, gave a brisk salute. At the back of the Stephensons' big white house he paused, looked down the yard for Bess, turned away. She'd be home by now. Had to talk to Bess. Relieved that he didn't have to do it now. Dreaded a talk with Bess. Like talking to God. End up by her knowing all about you. With Mama dead, bet she bosses Non like Mr. Almighty himself. Well . . . he was taking Non back. That's what he'd come for. And time! Rotting away in this place. Last night, tried to put a little life into things. They'd just sat there. Just sat. Be like Miss Ada next, just sit staring out into the graveyard. All they did was go to work, come home, go to work. Seemed enough. Enough for niggers in Georgia . . . sure! And after

9

all Mama had done to give them all a start. If she weren't dead, she'd take a stick after—

Mama dead. You said the words. Like scuffing sand against your shoes, watching the grains fall away again. You said them. You couldn't believe them. Last night as you stood there with your bags in your hand waiting for the train to pull in, waiting for it to stop, you'd said the words. And something had tightened in your throat. And you were afraid when you saw Non and Bess, afraid when you saw your sisters standing there, afraid you'd show how you were feeling. But you didn't. As you swung off the coach, you knew suddenly that they were not thinking about Mama, for Bess said something and laughed and Non was smiling. It shocked him to see them laughing and carefree, standing there under the station light, when last he had seen them was at her funeral, weighed down with her death. Under the station light they stood apart from the white people, waiting. Non tall, a little thin. Bess short, plump. Little Jackie in front of them, looking at the train, darting away toward the white coach.

"This way, Jackie, the coach is down this way," Bess's words rang out clipped and swift, like pebbles pouring on the ground. And Jackie turned and ran toward the Colored coach as he swung off the steps.

"Hi, boy." The kid had grown.

Jackie, suddenly shy, ran quickly to his mother. And they all had laughed and he had kissed his sisters and rubbed his hand over the boy's curly head, and then they had stood and looked at each other, searching for the word that starts the old family rhythms beating again.

He'd taken Non's arm and his fingers felt the bone through the flesh. "You're thin, Non," he'd said. And she had smiled and answered in that low voice she never bothered to raise, "About the same, I think."

"Can't say the same for me," Bess laughed. Keep on talking about weight. You can always do that.

"Afraid not. How much more? Ten pounds?"

"Not quite. But bad enough."

Say something else about weight. Good thing to talk about—

"How about me, Uncle Ed?"

"You're fine, boy."

"I reckon you've bringed me a little something?"

*"Brought,* Jackie. But I wouldn't ask if I were you."

"You bet. And it's not so little."

"Den it's a wagon."

"Right. And how you know?"

"That all I want dat's big cept a automobile," Jackie said quietly.

"Aiming high, old man."

"He's like Jack. Every penny goes into savings—for something big, some day."

Saying the things everybody says when they come home to their family—to keep from thinking other things.

They had laughed, walked on through the streets, quietly through the business blocks, not talking much there, down Back Street.

"Things look about the same," he'd said. Nothing's the same. Nothing's like it used to be!

"About the same."

"Anything happened?"

"Afraid not."

"How's Sam?"

"Working hard. Lot of fever. Otherwise he's all right. Anxious to see you."

They had come to the old ramshackly house on the edge of town and the girls had hurried in to put supper on the table. He'd stood on the porch, looking out toward Miss Ada's, toward White Town, hating to go inside, hating to go up to his old room, hating to face an old life so empty and so goddam full of things! Feeling a little sick. Afraid now to

11

pick up the old threads that in Washington he'd been home-sick to get his fingers on. Wondering now what made him change his mind and come home when he had planned all year not to come—

And then Jackie had called him to supper. "It's a fine supper," the kid said. "Let's hurry."

Ed cut through the gallberry bushes on the old Negro ball ground, picked up the broad path that led to the graveyard. Near the African Methodist Episcopal Church clustered a group of girls. Black. Pitch black, most of them. It made him feel queer. Couldn't remember feeling that way before he went to Washington. Couldn't remember so many pitch-black girls—couldn't remember color—couldn't remember getting color on your mind and not being able to rub it out—

Hopping across the sand road like a jack-rabbit a little somebody in a bright pink waist and black skirt collided with him, stopped with a stumble of high-heel pumps and a twist of her torso.

"Hi, kid."

"Hi, Mr. City Man."

He saw a pert face the color of pine cone laughing into his. He saw a full mouth, slender neck, tipped-up breasts. He saw big laughing eyes that looked as if they would grow solemn any minute, under a hat with three red roses flopping on it, perched on the side of her head.

"See you later, kid," he said, and listened with surprised pleasure to her laugh.

"You don eben know ma name," she giggled.

"It don't matter," he whispered, grinned, raised his eyebrow, started on.

"I'll find you," he called back; laughed as she switched her little tail in answer and ran toward the titillated cluster of girls. Nice little rumps, hard from chopping cotton, light, bouncy, India rubber.

12

"Why, Dessie," somebody said, "ain't you shamed?"

"Is I done some'in bad?"

"Is you! You knows you is," said a jealous voice.

Ed chuckled. Felt good. Walked with old careless rapidity in spite of the heat. Over to the right was the Evergreen Cemetery. He began to whistle. Stopped. Laughed at the strength of his boyhood habit. Consciously resumed his whistling. He hadn't seen Miss Ada. Wonder if she's crazy as ever. Wonder if she still walks around in her wedding dress. How she'd scared you once—

Under the ancient rows of cedars in front of Miss Ada's old house, Ed came face to face with Tracy Deen.

Both men stopped short.

"H'lo, Ed."

Be goddam if you'd call him mister. "H'lo, Tracy."

"Didn't know you were in town."

"Came in yesterday."

"Here long?"

"Week or so."

"Still in Washington, I suppose?"

"Still there."

They looked blandly at each other, having exhausted all but one conversational possibility.

"Damn hot weather."

"You're right."

"Well, so long."

"S'long."

Ed's mouth felt dry and his breath came fast. He stopped, wiped his face, wiped it again. "So," he whispered. "So," his mind echoed. "So," three hundred years shouted back at him.

He stood at the gate. Wiped his face. "Non," he said, and wet his lips. "Non."

She turned quickly, smiled at her brother.

13

He watched her push her hair off her face, the old gesture; he watched her swallow as she kept smiling.

"Non, what are you doing!"

"Listening."

"Listening?"

"The swamp—the night," she'd always said things like that, "trying to—get—things straight." Now what did she mean—

"You can't get things straight down here!"

Brother and sister stood there, hands on the picket fence. In the dusk Ed's face was dark, Non's startlingly white.

"You're going back with me. Next week! You hear! To live decently!" Voice pressing like a blade through dirt. "Like Mama intended you to. Four years in college—and this—"

She did not seem to hear.

*Someone far from harbor you may guide across the bar—*

It sounded as if the tent was full of people tonight singing—

"I've always wanted you. Ought to have taken you back last winter when Mama died. I— Up there you can be somebody—you can be somebody, Non! You can—" You wanted to say it over and over. You wanted to scream it in her ears— you wanted to take the words and drive them into her flesh with your bare hands—

*Brighten the corner where you . . .*

You kept your voice low and soft. "Non . . . you don't know what you're doing!"

She said, "Let's go in. Bess has a sick headache. May need something." She turned quickly toward the old house.

# THREE

BESS LAID the wet cloth across her eyes. Coolness drove the pain into her neck, gave blessed relief. She must go get little Jackie. She turned instead, tried to fit her body to the old leather sofa, lay listening to the evening sounds, knowing them by heart. Sometimes for weeks she did not hear them. Then her mind would grow quiet, like this, and there they would be. It was like picking up an old tune. Nonnie had notions about swamp sounds, but to Bess they were like Mama's picture above the mantel, the old ramshackly house they had lived in all their lives, Pap's overalls hanging on a nail in the closet since his death fifteen years ago. Nail . . . picture . . . sounds . . . things you hang your life on . . . fill your life with. Sometimes living seems a quick going from thing to thing to thing to thing—and then a slow coming back to them.

Into the evening sounds came a deeper note. That voice. Bess sat up. Lay down again. What's the use! Sometimes you thought you'd go crazy at the sound, stealing through your life like an old sin you could not name but felt a guilt for. Talking . . . What did they have to talk about year in, year out? What did a white man gallivanting with your sister have to say! Fooling with a nigger gal. That's what it meant to him. All it meant. Anybody would know but Non! Anybody! Try to get that girl to see. Try to get her to see anything she didn't want to see! It made you almost glad Mama was dead.

Bess took the cloth from her eyes, dropped it in the bowl. From the way the light slanted across Tillie's picture she knew the sun had set behind the swamp trees. She could scarcely make out the full-bosomed black silk waist or its prim high collar, but the face above was clear, honey-colored

15

like her own. Bess looked into Tillie's eyes. Only since death had she felt at ease with her mother. Lately she had slipped into the habit of coming to Tillie's room, stretching out on the old sofa, looking at that face, until the enlarged tinted photograph had become something her mother had never been to her. Though it was the same face you would always remember. The same guarded jaws, full mouth pursed in grim respectability, eyes that could bore through you when you were little. She must have seen so many things and had not grown scared in the seeing. Or maybe she had, and her children had not found her fear.

Sometimes you wondered how she could have helped seeing this thing. Sometimes you almost thought she pulled her old straw hat down on her head and shut the sight out. Though you knew better.

You'd seen them sitting under the grape arbor . . . heard voices . . . you'd seen them walk down the path toward Aunt Tyse's cabin. No more. Slivers of memories, sticking in you. Once you had been near them.

It was at Aunt Tyse's old cabin, when Nonnie was fifteen. Long ago. A laugh drew Bess closer than the path led, startled, excited. She had been fishing. Grown too big to work out longer she had taken the summer off, lazying around waiting for Jackie to be born . . . alone, not lonesome, though Jack was on his Pullman runs and home so little. She heard that laugh, knew it was Nonnie, though she did not know more. She put down her catch of fish, crept near the shack. Carefully. Somehow knowing she would see something she must not see.

The cabin seemed empty. She crept nearer, found a crack. Darkness. Again that laugh. In the dim light she began to see: Non's face, bleached white against dark walls, hair falling around her shoulders, hands cupping his face, eyes searching his eyes, blouse loosened until her breasts showed as she knelt on the floor. *Who is it?* The question crawled like a

16

slimy thing in her mind until he turned. *That Deen boy. Non mixed up with a white boy!* And how used to him she seemed! As if it's been going on all her life. Now she leaned down, kissed him, turned away. A laugh barely creeping over the threshold of sound crashed against Bess's eardrums. She started to cry, "Non! You crazy little fool!" and only hushed her mouth by pressing her face against the weather-beaten wall.

When she looked again, his head was in Non's lap. Her hand rubbing his forehead, slow-moving, easy. Fingers moving over temple, back of ear, neck. Fingers moving through his hair, lifting it, letting it fall, lifting it. Like breathing.

He was talking. Bess leaned to hear. "I've thought maybe I could do something with machinery—don't know—what do you think, Non?"

She'd smiled. "That is one of the things you know so much about. I know so little," she said, "but it seems right, somehow."

Lord Jesus—white man come out to a nigger girl to talk about machinery!

"Mother wants me—Dad hopes I'll be a doctor. Mother wanted me—to be something everybody in the world would hear about, I think. She's down on me since I quit college. You down on me too?"

She'd lifted a piece of his black hair, laid it over his eye, her lips moving in that slow half smile.

"You're not, are you?"

Shaking her head.

He turned and softly she adjusted her body to his turning.

Why does she look so old? As if she knows all in the world a woman can know about a man—

She stooped and kissed him.

He was looking up at her, studying her face, lines easing around his mouth. Heavy lines for a boy twenty-one, and he must be around that, for he was older than Ed. Studying her

17

face. What did he see there that he couldn't take his eyes off! Non was pretty but she wasn't so pretty that you couldn't bear to stop looking.

The old cabin wall was lined with newspapers and now a breeze caught a sheet, pulled it slowly as if a hand held it. They turned and watched it, and Bess watched too as the slow tearing continued on, on, on, filling the whole room with the thin cutting sound, until the piece of paper was loosened, fluttered to the floor. "Don't like it," Tracy said. And now they were laughing in that uncontrollable way folks do without cause, until tears were in their eyes. He caught Non to him.

"Coming back to the machinery business—" after a silence which seemed full of words, "what you think of my telling the family I'm going into an automobile factory? And meaning it this time." He grinned. "Oh I don't know if that's what I want," he moved restlessly, sliding his fingers along a plank of the floor, up, down. Bess had seen that hand moving in her dreams sometimes. White, with black hairs across it—touching the dirty floor, touching her sister.

"We'll find it," Non's voice was deep now, as if it had roots down in a million years of knowing. "We'll find exactly what you want to do."

"Some day?" He laughed, took her hand. rubbed it across his lips.

The sun made its way through the half-opened shutter, moved across Non's face, stripping off the maturity which had been there in the dim light, tendering wide full lips, until you knew you were looking at a kid—a fool kid who doesn't know what she's doing! Who hasn't got the faintest notion . . .

Bess found herself running. Mama must do something! She *had* to do something! And quick! Angered now. Mama thinking little Biddy so good—well, she'd tell her how good she is! The sneaky little— Bess had run under the grape arbor

18

and through the back door, to the front porch to wait for her. And as she waited she saw her mother in the clearing near the cedar trees, coming from work, walking cautiously on the sides of her feet to ease her bunions. Once she paused, shifted her bundle from one arm to the other, limped on, took off her straw hat, fanned her face as she neared the porch, stopped to pick a dead bloom from her spider lily, paused once more to examine the front of the old house, puckering lips as eyes moved relentlessly from peeled wall to peeled wall. "Some day fo I die, Gawd willin, I'm goin tuh splash it fum top tuh bottom, befo and behin, wid de snowest white paint I kin lay ma hands on." Bess had heard it a hundred times.

Tillie eased down on the step. "Honey, pull yo old ma outen her shoes."

Bess laid the fish down, knelt beside her mother. She'd tell her now. Tell her of Non's sly ways.

"We'll paint it, you and me, maybe, by time little Biddy git married. Ef she gits! She don seem tuh care a speck fo menfolks." Tillie chuckled contentedly.

Bess tugged at the shoe.

"Bess, you's big enough tuh be totin two pairs of twins stid of one. You looks plum lak a little fat sow." Tillie laughing in good-natured teasing now until big flat breasts jounced against her body like two old bags. "Hit must be near yo time, ain't it?"

The foot was freed from its binding.

Tillie sighed in comfort, unmindful of her silence.

Bess rubbing hot old feet, pulling damp stockings off, massaging flesh.

"Wheah's Nonnie?" her mother gathered up vigilance like a garment dropped off in fatigue. "Wheah's Nonnie, Bessie?"

"I sent her back for one of my fishing poles," Bess said quickly.

"You oughtn't tuh have done it, so late in the evenin. It's

19

near black dark, Bessie. Some'in might happen to the child!"

Bess did not raise her head.

"Things can happen." Her mother sighed. "Sometimes I think you is outgrowed yo careless ways and then lak this, yo seems— Sister, you must learn tuh think ahead! I don know what'll become of you ef you don learn tuh think." Tillie sighed again.

Bess rubbing toes, each joint. "I'll get some water to wash your feet," she'd whispered.

Tillie laid her hand on her daughter's bowed head. "You is a good girl, Bessie, ef you *was* born plum careless—lak your po' pappy."

Bess ran quickly up the steps and to the pump, and no one heard the quick sob which the rasping of the pump drowned out. And Bess herself had been surprised, and not certain why she cried.

She had not told. No. And soon Non had gone to Spelman, and then the war came. A war can change anything, Bess said to herself those years, trying to ease her worry. But he had come back. God yes . . . some folks always come back!

Silence out there. He had gone.

A sharp, more urgent sound. Eddie . . .

You wondered why he had come. Hating Maxwell, hating everything about Maxwell. Last winter at Mama's funeral— even then—when he was broken up over that, he'd got upset about Maxwell. What did he expect of Maxwell? She'd asked him that. What you expect Maxwell to do for *you?* Because you've had a college education, that doesn't mean Maxwell wanted you to have it. Remember that, Eddie! she'd said. Eddie had always hated the place—as if it were somebody. Once when he was sixteen, almost ready for college, he'd had one of his spells. Sassed Mr. Pusey down at the store. If it had been any other white man in town, Ed would have landed in the calaboose or chain gang—or worse—for his

20

words. But Mr. Pug Pusey turned and walked in the store without a word. And later talked to Mama. "Better get your boy out of town, Tillie," he'd said, "the boy's itching for trouble. He's not a bad boy—just restless." "Like a young billy goat," Mama said, pursing her lips, and sent Ed out to the Rushtons' plantation to chop cotton. "You to chop until you learns yo manners," she'd told the boy. "No matter what, you learns to get along wid white folks. Member dat!"

Yes, if you had dared tell her—why hadn't you? I don't know . . . sometimes I don't know! Bess turned restlessly. Mama would have done something. She'd have gone to whomever you go to about such doings and scotched the thing—long ago. There were things Mama wasted no time about.

Once, when they were little, Bess and Ed, Non tagging along, had been in the field hoeing the okra. Mama was home from work that day, bothered with her rheumatism. It was so hot that they had flung away their straw hats, choosing the blaze of the sun to the heat steaming against straw and skin. Sand burning feet but unmindful of it, Bess and Ed were playing a game, swinging their hoes between the chopping, to a tune they had made up, clashing the blades against sound, swinging hoes up as they moved down the rows. It was a gay game, and the heat was forgotten as they twisted their bodies between hoe and song and earth, stepping along. And then by a hill of squash the next step away lay a big cottonmouth, stretched out gold-brown-black and shining against the sand, eyes on them, unmoving.

They turned their song into such a wild scream that their mother had come running. She'd taken Bess's hoe and cut that snake to pieces, beating its head to a pulp against the sand, and then beating its body until it was nothing you could say you knew the name of when she finished with it.

"Hit's nothin but a cottonmouth," she'd said, handing the hoe back to her daughter and wiping her face. "Nothin to

21

go screaming about," wiping her hands on the corner of her apron.

But her children stood there, a killing in their minds, staring down at it, fitting blood and pulpy flesh back into the long gold-brown-black skin that had lain there a moment ago, so smooth in its shining length, so threatening, now gone forever.

Tillie looked from one half-opened mouth to the other and the other. Followed their eyes to the sand. "Tain't nothin but a cottonmouth. Nothin to make such a whoop-doodle over," using words to take that look off their faces as she would have used her apron to wipe their noses.

"But they kill folks," Bess whimpered.

"They can't kill you efn dey don strike you. Member dat. Jus mind where you puts yo feet. All of you, you hear!"

Ed had not taken his eyes off the blood and pulp in the sand. He looked up at his mother. "I woulda kilt it if Bessie had let me," he said. Wiping his face now on his sleeve, spitting vigorously.

"You durned little liar! You little old chickenhearted story-teller. You couldn't kill a roach. You too scary to kill a roach even! You too . . ."

"Bessie! Mind yo manners! And don go calling yo family names!"

Ed turned sullenly from the sound of her voice. "I just don like dead things," he said, and deliberately pulled up an okra plant.

"I don like um neider," little Nonnie quavered.

"Well, I don't like em neither!" Bess screamed. And now she and Eddie were glaring at each other, hoes raised, and quickly, hardly knowing why and without taking her eyes off her brother, she gave Non a hard push, toppling her over in the squash vines.

"Hush yo moufs, all of you! Us Andersons don raise voices.

22

We belong, you hear! Hurt one of us, you hurts us all. Member dat. Now git to yo hoein."

But the hoeing seemed hard to get to. For Nonnie had wandered off into the squash rows during the talking and was bending over a vine, sticking blooms in her hair.

"Look at her, Mama! Pulling all the squash blooms!"

Mama, inexplicably, seemed pleased. "Ain't she purty as a picture?" Tillie stood there, mouth a little open, lines easing around her eyes. "Bessie," she whispered, "ain't she a purty little sight!"

Bess was finding it hard to breathe. "Ain't I pretty a bit?" she squeaked.

"Yes, Bessie," Mama never took her eyes off the yellow blossoms flopping over Non's ears, shadowing the child's pale face. "You're real purty. Eddie's all right too. All my chudren fine, upstanding chudren. But purty is as purty does. You all member dat!" The moralist looked her family in the eye.

They had stood there in the hot blaze of a summer sun: Tillie and her children. Squash and okra and tender pea vines and corn and children growing together in the South's hot summer, drawing their life from its dark soil. A wind came out of the swamp, slapping young stalks of cane together, bending corn tassels, ruffling big squash leaves, plumping a tomato to the ground, cooling hot faces; as quickly left them to their quiet growing. And Tillie's children looking up into the brown strong sweating face above them, listening to her words, thrust their roots more firmly into that soil out of which they had come.

"Now, Eddie, git yo hoe an help yo sister. And next time you all sees a snake, go atter it. Don come callin me. An next time you wants to holler at each other you to stop still. You hear! You to stop and swallow your spit five time, you hear! And you ain to say it. Whatever hit is, you ain to say it!

23

Nonnie, come out of dat brilin sun. You is too little to set out in the sun all day. Come along."

And Tillie had turned toward the old house, planting each foot firmly on the deep warm earth, pressing every grain of sand in place. You'd felt it wouldn't dare move, not one little grain would dare, after Mama had put her foot down. But *you* had dared hiss, too low for her to hear, "Throw dat squash bloom away!" You'd put a threat in your voice which Non's ears heard. "Chunk it down." Bess remembered to this day the way Non had turned and looked at her, chin shaking, eyes swimming in tears, making no sound. Slowly she took the blossoms out of her hair, chunked them to the ground, ran down the field after her mother. Bess had watched Non's slim heels prick the soft sand furrows and the scrawny tendons move in the back of her knees as she ran, until the glare of midday blended them with the light and the field. And then in puzzled misery she and Ed slowly picked up hoes, went back to their weeding.

If she had dared tell Tillie, she would have taken a hoe and driven that white boy plumb out of their lives. And would have done it in the right way, minding her manners in the doing.

Bess turned on the sofa, looked at Tillie's picture. It was too dark now to see more than a blur but she knew what was there. Why hadn't she been able to do it! She'd never been able to talk to Non, either. Bess had a feeling that if she said it aloud, if she once put words to it, all she feared would come true. But if she didn't say it, maybe it would be something she had made up—like so many of her worries. A laid fire that would never burn if you did not strike a match to it with your words. You're such a damned fool, she groaned, turning her body to make it fit the old slippery sofa.

Yes . . . you wish Ed hadn't come. But he'd come. And now there was nothing to do but make the best of it. They

24

had taken for granted his vacation in New York or at one of those beaches where Negroes can go swimming, as he had always done before. You wouldn't have thought he'd choose to come home, way he felt about the town, and with Mama gone. His letter had surprised them. Worried her. But then it was one of her worrying days. He's lonely. When your mother goes, you try to hold on to what's left. That's what brought him back. Ed ought to get married.

Fix me up some corn and butterbeans and okra, I'm on my way home, he'd written.

Last night they gave him corn and butterbeans and okra, fried chicken and watermelon pickle. They watched him eat, and she and Non ate more with him than in months by themselves or at their work. And little Jackie was so excited that he did not eat at all but ran around and around the table until he fell against a chair and bumped his head and then cried long and hard and at last fell asleep in Non's lap.

They had sat there talking. Ed pushing his plate from him as he talked of Washington; bending his head to one side—trick of his, for he heard as well as anybody—as they told him about Maxwell, and Sam, and themselves; rubbing his thumb against the edge of the table, moving his chair, gray eyes darting around the room, when she mentioned Mama. He'd sat there in his thin summer suit, black hair plastered tight to his head, shining in the lamplight.

"Let's have a fish-fry," he said abruptly. He leaned forward, looked at her, at Non, laughed, moved his hand over the table, smoothing the cloth. What long, pale hands he had! As if he had never chopped cotton or worked in the slab pile. "How about it?" And they laughed with him, and Non said in one of her rare moments of teasing, "And a cane-grinding? Would you like a hog-killing, and boiled pinders, and how about a little crackling bread, and chitlins?"

He laughed, reached over, took her hand, as quickly sat back in his chair. "You're not funny. Don't try it."

25

"Tell you . . ." he went on, "let's have a fish-fry. Let's have one big week, shall we? Let's forget all our troubles—if anybody has any—and have a big time. Make Sam ease up and play with us. Now . . . what else? What else can we do?" He got up, walked to the fireplace, walked to the window, opened a drawer in the old sideboard. "Drawers stick," he'd said. He seemed to have forgot what he was talking about.

"You can fix that," Bess's words were a little sharp. "We need a man around for a few days."

He seemed not to hear. Walked again to the fireplace, lifted the screen, put it back . . . Shook the floor. "There's a weak sill under here, Bess," irritable now.

"There's a number of them," she'd laughed. "Don't shake the house so! We want it to last out your vacation."

"Let's have a big time, hmm?" as if he'd said nothing at all. "Let's have a fish-fry and how about a party? Any girls?"

"The twins. Roseanna's twins."

"Good God, the babies!"

"Ready for Spelman."

"Lord help us. Preacher Livingston cough up money for college? How he's making so much? Bootlegging? Are they pretty?" not waiting for her to answer. Now he was walking around the room. Studied a calendar on the wall. "1917. We don't believe in changing things, do we?"

Bess had laughed. "House too old, we handle it gently." Began to feel angered. All this getting on nerves, somehow. "Don't find so much fault, Eddie!"

"Fault? I wasn't finding fault. Only . . . wish we could fix things up a little better."

"Like a Coca-Cola?" Non said, in her easy soft way, "like a dope?"

"Dope all you got?"

He'd stopped again, smiling now. Old Ed, looking gay now, eyes laughing, throwing his head to one side.

"How about a real drink? A little corn?"

26

Teeth shining as he laughed. Mustache helped his mouth.

"Let's celebrate. Let's have a big time, hmm? How about a little drink? I've some new records. How about a little music and a little drink? I'll show you the steps they're dancing. More Bess's style than yours, Non." He laughed again. Rubbed his hands over his face. Looked up gravely. "Where do you get the stuff?" he said in a tired voice.

They told him. At Snooks'. "Be back in five minutes," he'd said.

He was soon back, came in slowly, put the bottle down on the table. He looked as if he had gone a long way. Stood at the table, rubbed his fingers on the bottle. "It's probably poison." He laughed. Singing now, bringing in glasses and a corkscrew, breaking ice, dividing it among the three glasses.

Then Sam had come. And Non gave him her glass and opened a Coca-Cola for herself.

They sat there, the four of them, drinking slowly, not much, nobody wanting the stuff. Sitting there. Sam, big, stolid, heavy-eyed. Been going hard for weeks. Sam Perry, M.D., Colored. Bess said the words to herself, half smiling, turned to Sam to ask him about the fever.

Sam was looking at Non as if reading a book he'd been wanting to get to for a long time. He rubbed his chin, softly sighed. They were like tones of a scale. Non pale, Bess a golden yellow, Ed light brown, and Sam darker than the Andersons, the lamplight picking up red in the deep brown of his skin.

Bess turned away, feeling restless. Looked now at his clothes. Rumpled. She'd have to remind Aunt Easter to keep him pressed up. Looked at his shoes. Worn out. She'd have to tell him. And assuming the old job of looking after somebody gave Bess an ease that she had not felt during the evening.

"Sam," she laughed, for the thing had become a ritual as the years passed, "it's about time, unless you're going barefooted, to take an hour off and go to the store."

27

Sam took out his big blue handkerchief, dusted his shoes off, looked up at the three of them, down at his feet. Smiled a little foolishly.

"Leave him alone. Maybe he wants to go barefooted."

"I thought they were doing pretty well, Bess. You surprise me."

"I know. But only once a year."

They said no more, each drinking a little, setting the glass down, picking it up again.

Sam studied Ed's face until Ed turned quickly.

"You look fine, Ed. How do you do it?"

"Fine? Why not? Sure I'm fine. Everything's fine," he said loudly. "We're having a big time this week. We're having a fish-fry. What else? A party. Yeah. That's right. What else can we do? What's your idea?"

Sam set his glass down.

"How about going with me on my calls in the morning? We ought to have a lot to get out of our systems."

"Good! That's fine."

Sam was standing now.

"You've just come, Sam! You can't go yet." As if he couldn't be left alone with them!

"It's late. Had to run by for a look at you. Better be getting along. It's great to have you home, old man. Do us all good." He laid his hand on Ed's shoulder, looked at the restless face. "It's the same old Maxwell, Ed," he said quietly. "But it's not so bad. You ought to have a pretty good time if these girls feed you the way your mother used to feed us."

They stood there, the three Andersons, and their lifelong friend, Sam Perry. Out across the back field, up in the cleared place in the hammock, where colored folks bury their dead, Mama's grave lay. They could see it there, in their minds.

Ed ran his hand over his hair. "They can't do that. But if tonight's a sample, they'll do well enough."

28

"We tried to find you to have supper with us. Mrs. Perry said you were delivering a baby."

"Out in the country all day. Yes, Aunt Easter fixes excuses even when I don't want them. Well, good night, everybody." He turned to go, turned back. "Non, you haven't said a word. Are things all right with you?"

And they had all looked at Non for a curiously tense moment, until she said in her low voice, "Yes, Sam, I'm always all right."

"Good!" he'd smiled, laid his hand for a brief moment on her shoulder. "Bess," he'd turned with the old half-laughing glance, "O.K.?"

"Perfect," making a face, "temperature perfect."

And this morning she had wakened with a sick headache, after dreaming all night—crazy things.

They were coming in. They would be asking her how she felt. She dreaded their questions so much that her voice met them halfway.

"Supper, Ed?"

"Ate at Salamander's. Sorry you're sick."

"I'll be all right. Not much to eat at Salamander's. To-morrow night I'll have you some hopping-john. Go out with Sam?"

"No, missed him. Somebody dying somewhere. He had to leave early."

Something's wrong. Ed looks stubborn, as if he's been in an argument. Rubbing his thumb against the side of the chair—you could hear the sound of it.

Bess looked at her brother, and though the room was almost dark she could see enough. Yes—feeling sudden pride —he's good-looking and clean and neat. How proud Mama would have been after all her work to see her boy turn out to be such a gentleman! Talked well. Black hair brushed back tight and slick, clipped mustache, nose a little turned

29

up, betraying his dignity. She laughed. "I approve of the mustache."

He seemed not to hear. He was looking at Non, who looked down at her lap, rocking a little as she sat there.

Maybe he's found out. *Don't be silly! How could he find out!* Maybe somehow in this one day he's found out! *Your headaches make you a fool. Don't imagine so much. Plan a party. Plan a party and make him go fishing with Sam.*

After a time Non said, "I'd better run get Jackie."

"Still let him stay at Miss Ada's?" He turned to Bess.

"Yes. It's all right, Eddie."

"How you know it's all right?"

Don't get mad. He's nervous. "She's just a silly old woman. And kind. I pay her old mother a dollar a week to give him his—lunch, we call it. They need that money."

"How you know it's all right?"

Keep yourself together now. "Because I've run in and checked. It's the best I can do anyway, with both of us working!" Yes, she had worried. Of course she had! But time and again she had run off from work and slipped in on them. One night she dreamed about Miss Ada and her Jackie, not a good dream, and the next day she went over in the middle of the morning to see what the half-crazy white woman was doing with her child. Well, they were playing under the magnolia tree, stringing the red seeds, and she was telling him fairy stories. Nice, white fairy stories. And they both looked peaceful and happy. "It's all right, Eddie. Her old mother is there, to watch out for him. Her wits are all right."

"No white woman's wits are all right who'll let her daughter nurse a colored child."

"Miss Ada is different . . . you know that, Ed. She's just different!" Trying to pick a fuss with her. As he used to do. Hold on now. Don't fuss back.

They sat for a time, in silence.

"Bess, you mind talking with me a little?"

30

Act easy and casual. "Of course not. Like to have a chance to, after so many years." Out of character. Too polite. "Bet you're broke—that it?" She laughed. That's more like it.

"No, believe it or not, I've saved a little. Bought a bond." They forgot to laugh.

"Bess—it's about Non." Two shadows talking in an unlighted room.

"What about her, Eddie?"

"She looks bad."

"I know. Heat's enough to make anybody look bad."

Ed rubbed his thumb against the cloth of the chair. It made your flesh crawl. "Bess, I want to take her back with me. I'll get an apartment. Maxwell's no place for a girl like Non. I can't leave her here, I've made up my mind."

How about me? It's good enough for me. Always he'd wanted things better for Non. Always everybody had wanted things different for her. Bess's head began to throb.

"What you think?"

"I think it's a fine idea. Jobs are hard to get. You think she can find one?"

"I'll find her one. Until she gets one, I'll look after her."

"That would be fine."

"Bess—you'll help me persuade her?"

"She won't need persuasion. Jump at the chance, probably." Keep your voice sure now, bright, casual.

"I don't know." Ed stood up, walked to the window, turned quickly. "It's this goddam town! Never saw such a hole! How you stand the place! It gets on my nerves. In twenty-four hours it gets on your nerves until—makes you—"

"Ed," take it easy now, "Maxwell's no place for you. You always hated it. When you were a boy you hated the dump, as you called it. Don't you remember how you felt when you came home from college? When you come back now, it brings back—things. Makes you jumpy. Folks' nerves get on edge, they imagine all kinds of things—that aren't so. Things that

31

just aren't so!" Don't stress it too much. "Once I got like that," she eased her voice until it was casual again. "Began worrying about Jack on his runs. Afraid some white woman would—scream or something, when he answered her bell. One day, I went down to speak to him as his train came through. Saw a woman in the Pullman, got on in Jacksonville probably from the way she was dressed, had bright red hair—I remember yet how she wore it—had quick, hungry-looking eyes, black as huckleberries. And I began to think, that's the kind of woman, that's the kind of old dope who would do a thing like that. And thinking it, I believed it. All night I thought about it. All night long, I lay there. I could hear her bell ring, see Jack lay his book aside, walk easy down the aisle. Everybody sleeping. Hear her scream when he touched her curtains. I waited all night for somebody to come tell me that they'd—got him." She laughed, found her hands wringing wet. "Crazy! Sure I know! But things get you like that."

Ed was standing now. Walked to the window. Back to his chair.

"Maxwell doesn't hold any good memories for a Negro, Eddie." Voice quiet. "Now that Mama's gone, there's nothing to keep you here."

"Then why do *you* stay? Non stays because you stay. Why don't you move to Washington? It's the other end of Jack's run. Why do *you* stay?"

Why do I? She was furious with him and surprised at her fury. "No rent," keep your voice steady, "the house is here, costs nothing to keep up. Too ramshackly to try to keep up. I have a good job and need it. Jack's saving every penny he makes for New York. You know he wants to move us there when he's able. You know that!"

"Then let Non go!"

"I'm not keeping her, Ed!" Voice hot. Angry now.

Non was in the hall. Jackie, talking. Thank God!

"Mama, hi's—"

32

"That's right," Non prompted softly.

"Hi's your head, Mama?"

"It's all right, Sugar. How're you?"

"Fine," the prompter said.

"I'se fine. Hi you, Uncle Eddie?"

"I'm fine. How's your wagon?"

"O.K."

Jackie came in, stood before them, while Non brought a lamp. He put his hands in his overalls, stood with his feet apart as he had noticed Ed's, looked at Ed, looked at his mother.

Face thin, forehead a little wrinkled, something tight around the kid's temples. Like an old man. "Give him a big supper, Non. I know the wagon's made him hungry."

Bess and Ed sat in silence, while Non put Jackie to bed. Listened to his shrill questions; her low answers. Heard him turn restlessly on his cot, slapping at mosquitoes, in an attempt to continue vicariously the intercourse with his world which had begun and ended, so abruptly.

Nonnie put the lamp on the hall table.

Ed said, "Think I'll mosey over to Sam's. See if he's back."

"Take Nonnie with you." At Non's silence Bess grew insistent. "Go on! Do you good! You need some fun."

Nonnie smiled at her sister, "I'll stay here, but I'll walk to the gate," she added, and smiled at Ed.

"Nonnie," Bess heard him say, "what under God's heaven is the matter? You're not yourself—you . . . Remember the fun we used to have? Remember Net and Howard? They're still in Washington. They often ask about you. They've got a nice little flat—" It was as if he were trying to rouse her from a bad dream.

"Of course I remember." But Nonnie said no more. And in Bess's straining ears was only the slur of their feet in the sand.

Across White Town came the scream of Brother Dun-

33

woodie's voice, calling white folks to God. Like calling hogs. Hogs so fat from devouring their black fellows they'd lumpishly rush into the sea and be drowned rather than heed the warning. Bess turned on the couch, feeling satisfaction. She liked having thought that.

"More cold cloths, or are you ready for a lemonade?"

She must have dozed. "A lemon and salt. Non—" how would you say it!

Non brought the lemon, waited while her sister sucked it.

"Non," she began again and did not look at her, "something's upset Ed. It's Maxwell," she added quickly. "He's always hated Maxwell. Wish he wouldn't come back to it. Gets him upset about—things. Non . . . let's don't—do anything to bother him while he's here. He misses the way things used to be, feels—let down, with Mama gone. Let's don't *worry* him while he's here."

"Of course not, Bess." Non hesitated, "I'm going out to the arbor, where it's cooler."

"Non, please!"

The whine of the screen door answered her. Bess listened to the blub-blub of its rebound, heard the rattle of loose plank as Nonnie touched the step, heard, in her mind, her sister walking in the sand under the arbor. Going straight out there to wait for that white man, as if you hadn't said a word. Lord God, what's the use!

White Town was quiet. Singing had stopped. Only sounds torn out of context drifted in, made her aware that beyond Miss Ada's, beyond the mounded, shafted silence of the graveyard, there were black people; beyond them, white people, still awake, moving about in the same old ways. Black people . . . white people . . . black . . . white . . . black . . . white . . . it could drive you crazy—if you let it; if you let it, she sighed. Nonnie always smiled and called her a "race" woman when she tried to tell of this flux of feeling, this

34

shifting rage and pride and despair that swirled and back-washed around her. Nonnie would smile; and smiling, seemed to lift her skirts above troubled waters, to withdraw to a remote and secret place of safety. It was as if she had shut out this world she'd been born into, insulating herself by soft denials of it. If she said it didn't exist, it didn't exist. It was this invulnerableness which angered Bess, this giving the lie to her fears. And sometimes she hated Non for her superiority to hurt as she had hated her, when they were children, for her bright skin.

No use to think of all that. No use to get it on your mind, tonight.

She went into the kitchen, took a jar of mayhaw jelly, laid it on the table. Ed used to eat half a jar at a time, in the old days. Mama always said the boy had a tapeworm; no other way to explain such appetite and such thinness. She mixed flour, baking powder, salt, sugar in a bowl, laid out two eggs. *Milk and butter in ice box,* she wrote on a scrap of wrapping paper, *make your batter thin. Melt a tablespoonful of butter and put in it.* She measured coffee for the percolator, added water. Put the iron for hot cakes on the oil stove. That's done. Breakfast will be no trouble for him. Don't forget to fix him some hopping-john tomorrow. Think about the little things—hang your life on things—this and this—Bess rubbed her head.

Across the hall, the cot creaked and squealed like a little caught pig. *You must go see about Jackie.*

"Why do *you* stay here! Why *do* you stay!" Words licked the edge of her mind, burning her peace.

She sat down at the kitchen table, rolled an egg softly back and forth with her thoughts.

You don't know why you stay in a place where you were born. How can you be sure! There're a thousand reasons why it's easier to stay than to go. "Maxwell holds no good memories for a Negro." You'd lied. A thousand good memories.

35

*Name them, girl!* All right. I'll name them. Moss . . . trailing in your face when you're little . . . you'd make great pillows of it, flop deep down in them, feeling luxurious and rich. Oak trees you couldn't reach around. You'd try, and some other child would try and your finger tips would touch against rough bark and you and that other human being, separated by slow ancient years of giant growth, finger tips touching around a hundred years, would giggle, feeling you'd encircled, in some strange way, grown-up knowledge that children should not know . . . Thickets of yellow jessamine . . . and violets . . . fly-catchers in low marshy places, looking so pretty, spreading their yellow fingers through the grass, smelling so bad when you put your nose to them . . . sand . . . everywhere sand—

She wanted to laugh—and to cry. *So those are your memories. That the best you can do? Sand . . . That the best you can do?* Sand is sand until you step on it . . . let it ooze between your toes, burn you on hot days . . . sting your eyes . . . It's more than sand then, it's you then . . . some of you you couldn't leave behind, forever. *Come on! Be honest. That's not why you stay in Maxwell—sand and moss!* There's cypress in the spring . . . you'd lie and look at it . . . blowing green feathers to the sky . . . lie and look at it, look up in the sky until you were dizzy with the light, with the blowing greenness, and then your eyes would slowly slide down the gray trunk to bulging knees, spread out in the swamp water, ugly and misshapen, making black splotchy shadows on brown water. *You stay for that? Cypress and branch water, sand and wild flowers?* There's an old ghost story all Maxwell children know about the woman whose arm was torn off in a train wreck down near Ellatown. She'd lived for a while without her arm and then she died and was buried. But night after night, she came back. You could hear her when the wind blew hard at night, you could hear her then, crying, catching her breath in deep strangling sobs,

36

searching for her arm, looking everywhere for it . . . That's the way you feel about the place where you were born. Always looking for it. Always staying or coming back, searching for the you that you left there . . . *So that's why you stay?* There's Sam—*Now, you've hushed your lies!* There's Sam. There has always been Sam. You'd leaned against him so long, be hard to put your weight back on your own feet. Most colored folks leaned on him. Like an old oak tree. Big, solid. Trouble could come, bending you to the ground, but Sam would be standing there, unshaken by the fury. Standing there between you and trouble. Not between you and Jack. No, you'd never thought it before, but that is right. *You think you love Jack?* Of course you love him! Reckon it's love when your whole life is tangled up with another's like a mess of briars! But when trouble comes Jack expects *you* to tend to it. You've wondered sometimes where Sam gets his strength. Some folks who believe in such things say you get it from God. Tillie used to say, pursing her lips and rolling her eyes, "The Lord gives you strength," but you knew she didn't mean it. She'd say it just to be on the safe side. Mama didn't depend on God for a strength that she could draw out of her as you'd draw endless buckets of water from a deep cold well. If Sam believed in God or even thought about God, he'd never mentioned it. Whatever it was, wherever it came from, folks felt it in him. White folks said, "Yes sirree, Sam Perry's one nigger a college education didn't ruin." They listened to Sam. "Sam Perry knows his place," they'd say.

Bess smiled. Wonder if he knows his place with me. And other women. Wonder if he ever thinks of a woman . . . since Ella.

One of the eggs rolled to the edge of the table. Bess caught it, laid it on the wrapping paper.

Strange . . . how everybody had forgot Ella. No one mentioned her name any more in Maxwell. But there was a time when they had talked. When Sam went off to Philadelphia to study medicine and left Ella behind, tongues wagged. Not only black but white ones. And when she died of galloping consumption the next spring, they all knew the answers. If he'd kept his job at Harris's sawmill instead of traipsing up North, trying to be one of them dichties, Ella wouldn't have died. Even Mama, who usually saw why folks wanted to better themselves, was silent when Ella died and Sam did not come to the burying. Mama laid Ella out, and came home and sat on the porch a long time, not saying a word; sat there rocking, looking off toward White Town, pinching her lips up tight, as she did when she had no use for a person or a thing. You'd wanted to tell her. You wanted to tell her what Ella had told you, but you'd promised the nasty little thing you'd never breathe it long as there was life in your body. And it would have been hard to tell your mother such a thing. You wondered sometimes what kind of thoughts Sam must have when he remembered Ella's name.

Well . . . no use to think about dead folks like Ella. Plenty of live ones to worry about. You'd better go see about Jackie.

She went in the room, felt her way to Jackie's cot, felt for his body, found him squatted in his sleep, pounding his head against the wall. She lifted him up, pulled his pajamas straight, laid him on the cot. Her hand touched his warm damp neck, moved over face, open mouth, lingered on his wet tight curls. The turn of his moist body and the loosening of his night clothes released a human familiar scent. Bess's eyes stung with sudden hot tears. In her ears roared a train in the night. Into her mind flashed a picture of Jack, sitting in a dim Pullman, dozing or reading under the night light, educating himself in some serious book, climbing from one idea to another idea—up, up; or answering the buzz of a wakeful passenger's bell, working for her and her child, night after monotonous night, saying his thank-you-mams, his yessirs, swallowing hurt pride, saving his tips for that fine life they were to live up North some day, when they had enough money. She saw him stripped of familiarity, cleansed of old connotations. She tingled with awareness of him as from the impact of a wholly strange and desirable personality. And as she stooped over the cot of their son, her nostrils quivering with the scent of childish sweat glands, this husband of hers took on stature, grew to an heroic size and for one brief exquisite second she accepted these larger dimensions, and her heart expanded in a great throb of pride and recognition.

Tremulous, she felt for Jackie again, seeking to hold by tactile reiteration this new reality, needing to hold it tonight; but as she touched him, as inexplicably as it had come the image collapsed, there was nothing there to hold but vague approximations. Hands groping in the dark. She stood beside the cot, uncertain, vexed, as if Jack had snatched this experience from her.

Ed's talk. What *was* she going to do about the kid! Getting so big now. *She* knew he shouldn't be at Miss Ada's so much. But what would you do! What would you do when you worked all day! And Jack left it *all* to her! Everything to her. All he thought about was his books and those ideas folks put in books. Eh, Lord . . . Jack had ideas. You wished sometimes he'd have one idea about his own child.

She pulled the top sheet off Jackie's bed, laid it on a chair. Padded barefooted to the back door. She had made up her mind. She was going to hear what words this white man was saying to Nonnie, what words after all these years he was still saying, and then she'd say a few herself. She might as well face this thing. She had to tend to it. And now before— *Now go out there and say it. And be sure you say plenty!*

She eased open the door. Moonlight splotched the ground. In an orange crate which she and Jackie had nailed, long ago, against the fence, a hen rustled. Beyond the twisted trunk of the old grapevine where the branches let the light through, Non sat in the wicker chair. The box where he always sat was empty.

Bess walked softly down the steps. Maybe now she could prove to Non that this was the way all white men did a colored girl. Treating her like secondhand clothes! She'd go right now and say what she should have said six years ago. She'd—

A breeze set in motion a grape leaf, swinging a shadow across Non's cheek. Bess watched it move, back and forth, back and forth . . . grow still. There was a look on Non's face as if you'd slapped her down. "Non's hurt," Bess whispered, and felt sudden ease.

She turned to go in the house, not wanting to say a word. Unable now to say it. Feeling a flood of pity for herself and her young sister sweep, with indiscriminate power, over her. Paused at the step to scrape a grape pulp from her foot. "Poor Non," she whispered, "poor kid—" wanting to cry now, wanting to cry a little.

A rustle of cane stalks, Non had risen. The noise stopped. She stood for what seemed a long time, sat down.

The empty box was a symbol now of white men and black women. Bess was shaking with fury. How she hated Tracy Deen! Every white man. All men! Yes, God help her, even poor old Jack. She turned the hall lamp out, slipped into bed. The sheet felt hot to her skin, the mosquito net a thick wall. You can't stay in bed on a night like this.

She went to the window, leaned out, touched the moist leaves of a vine. There was something human in their yielding, cool softness. The night was soft too. You wish you could enjoy it.

From where she stood she could not see the arbor, only cane whitened by moonlight, but she knew Nonnie was there. Waiting. Waiting all night. All her life! For what? What was she *after?* What was the fool kid after! Oh if she could just get her hands on that white man! If she could just get—

Her brown fingers flexed, fell to the window ledge. She sighed. Sometimes it seemed to Bess the only way she had of loving one person was to hate another more.

There was a step at the front door, a fumbling, a match struck. Eddie. At Sam's all this time. Talking. Four hours with Sam should do something for Ed. For anybody. Going upstairs. Good. That's good. Thought them asleep.

Bess tasted a tear, knew she was crying, knew she was crying about Ed and Nonnie and Jack and Sam. Knew suddenly that she wanted her mother, that they all needed their mother. Knew she wanted to be held in Tillie's arms as she had seen Nonnie held so many times. Knew she was mortally tired of having to look after Non and Ed, of worrying about Jack and little Jackie's future. Knew she wanted Mama to come back home and look after the family.

The courthouse clock struck two. She turned away, shamed, perplexed; laughed, wiped her nose on the sheet she had draped over the chair, tucked it around Jackie's cot, crawled into her bed. Work at six-thirty—and the evangelist invited to dinner. Mrs. Stephenson had asked her to be sure to get Mrs. Brown's corn fritters recipe from Non. She'd forget it sure! Yes, she'd forget it and then she would have to face Mrs. Stephenson, not her anger but her forgiveness, for Mrs. Stephenson believed in being kind to darkies. Was—God help her! Well, she didn't care. This very second she had to go to sleep.

She turned over, pressed her face resolutely against the mattress, closed her eyes. She sighed, got up, fumbled around in the dark, tied a string around her finger, crawled back into bed.

The back door clicked softly as Nonnie went to her room upstairs.

41

# FOUR

TRACY TOOK OUT his cigarettes, tapped one slowly up from the others, lighted it . . . forgot to smoke it. Across the street a light was on in the far room of the Pusey cottage. Dottie was undressing. He had never seen Dottie undress and had no desire to, but he knew how she would go about it. She would take off each garment carefully, gently, as if she were taking off a part of herself. Dress would be examined for spots, shaken out, hung up; slip would be shaken out, hung up; brassiere—

Tracy smiled. The Pusey cottage across from the big yellow house had always caused smiles in the Deen family, for little Pug Pusey was the kind of man on whom funny stories gather like barnacles, and after the years, only the stories stay in the mind, the man being lost beneath them. But Tracy's smile as he thought of Dottie was different. He felt about as you'd feel if your shirt were caught on barbed wire and you could not unsnag it. You wouldn't feel desperate at first—it would be merely worrisome—but it might occur to you after a time that you'd hate to stay snagged there forever. He had the feeling that Dottie might let him set the date but the decision of marriage itself had been made by her long ago, maybe in high school or when he took her to her first party. It seemed as old, as familiar as that. He had taken Dottie to her first party; after that, he had always taken her.

Now the light was off. Dottie was saying her prayers. In a moment she would lie in her bed, cool, clean, composed, all of her life completely contained in the rigid little box which shut the right way to do things away from the wrong. Dottie praying . . . What would she pray about? Sins? Tracy liked the thought of Dottie sinning. He laughed, lit his cigarette again, enjoyed smoking it. What would Dottie's sins be? In a life so neat, so orderly, like a folded handkerchief carried around all day and never crumpled—where would there be room for a life-size sin? Maybe she prayed for things she wanted, little itemized lists of things. Everything Dot wanted could be put on a list. Maybe she prayed for him. God-dammit, she probably did. Now why? Wanting for him what he wanted? Asking God to persuade him to keep the rules? Most likely. Yes, she knew them and wanted them kept. Simple to her as a recipe for making cake or peach pickle, and to be followed as carefully. That's—

*I'm pregnant, and I'm glad.*

Nonnie didn't keep the rules—or maybe even know them. He laughed, threw away his cigarette, ran his hand through his hair.

When he went out to Nonnie's he had no intention of going to the service or of seeing Dottie. And what did he do? After she talked to him, after he met that damned insolent brother of hers on the path, after that he went straight to the Pusey cottage, waited for Dot on the porch, went with her to church. Why? Who knows . . .

Dot seemed glad to see him, and glad that he had gone, with no protest, to church. But she had not enjoyed the evening. She kept looking at him inquiringly, watching his reactions to Preacher Dunwoodie's sermon, or trying to find some reaction on his face. Well, he had no reaction. It was the same old stuff he'd heard all his life—same cadences, same hell, same songs, same prayers, same people listening to the same old thing. Same people, never changing. All the prayers, songs, sermons, threats of hell couldn't change them! He had grown restless, wanted a cigarette, wanted to leave. But there was Dottie in her little summer frock sitting by him, looking up at him now and then, smiling tentatively.

Afterward they went to the drugstore. She had sat there drinking her coke, playing with the straw, thin fingers crumpling it, smoothing it, crumpling it, taking no part in the nervous talk and laughter still keyed to the pitch of emotion at which Brother Dunwoodie had left his congregation. . . . They were all there in Deen's Drug Store, drinking their Coca-Colas—the College Street crowd who had known each other from kindergarten, some young, still in college or just out of college, all casually intimate with each other.

No one was talking much except Harriet Harris, the redheaded daughter of Tom Harris, owner of Maxwell's big sawmills and turpentine stills. Harriet was talking to ease her feelings, not to change her mind or the minds of others. Just talking. "There's something immoral about a revival," she had just said, and had looked at Tracy, expecting him to laugh. She was the same pert-faced little girl who used to follow him and her brothers around, listening to their talk, always protesting, even as a kid, what other folks took for granted. He winked at her, turned back to Dottie, trying to think of something to say. After all, you take a girl somewhere, you ought to think of something to say to her that would give her pleasure.

Across from Tracy and Dottie, who were older than most of the others, sat Epp Rushton. Thin, small, sandy-haired, freckled-faced, elegantly dressed Epp—Maxwell's rich bachelor who lived in Maxwell's only stone house, alone with his books and nudist magazines and copies of great sculptures. Epp never had dates with the home girls. Only when a new schoolteacher came to town, or a visitor, would you see him driving his sport roadster with a girl in it. Most of the time Epp would be at the drugstore, alone, drinking a malted milk, in a never-ending marathon contest with his metabolism, grimly drinking malted milk, grimly weighing. It was the only interest he shared with his fellow-townsmen. Epp never went to church and no one expected him to attend the revival. No one had bothered Epp much about church since Mrs. Purviance ten years ago called on him to secure a pledge for the new church building and after sitting in his living room with his statuary had come out red-faced and breathy, saying, "There's nothing in that house but plumb nakedness, plumb nakedness! I'm going straight home and take a good hot bath." She was curiously evasive about the money and evil tongues said she had forgot to ask Epp for it, so busy was she examining the statues.

Epp sat at the table alone, watching Harriet, sipping her youth with his malted milk, now and then glancing at Tracy, at Dot, at the others, saying nothing.

"It's a debauch," Harriet was saying. And everyone laughed, shocked, relieved that none of their families was within hearing. But as they laughed, they knew she was fighting with her sharp tongue childhood memories of death and punishment and hell that were not hers only, but theirs also. Memories that went as far as feelings can go, groping around vague Rights and Wrongs. A revival meeting was a net that caught you and pulled you back into the deep waters of childhood, sifting out your knowledge, your grown-up critical faculties, leaving you only your fears and your guilt. It was as if the preacher said, Go back there . . . go back far enough . . . and dare tell me you have the strength to combat what you find . . . dare tell me you have no need of God.

"Why can't preachers talk quietly about Jesus? Why can't they talk a little about the way to live?"

Fatty Duncan said softly, "Hush . . . drink your coke." And Charlie said nothing, but pushed his glass around and around on the table, making little circles of dampness, his brow wrinkling above deep-set, intelligent eyes as he watched his keyed-up red-haired sister.

Prentiss Reid, editor of Maxwell's *Press,* stood at the cigar counter, listening, half smiling. His heavy gray pompadour gave him a dignity which cynical eyes and bitter smile robbed him of. Prentiss Reid was Maxwell's radical. Infidel, the churchwomen called him. Had he put in his paper the ideas he scattered around poolroom and printing office and drugstore he would have been called dangerous and something would have been done about him. But Prentiss Reid's *Maxwell Press* observed the publishing amenities of southern tradition, with proper space given to church news, to Society, to the Democratic party, to White Supremacy, to the protection of the freedom of big business, to farm interests, home hints, and obituaries. Only upon younger and less powerful ears than those of his advertisers and readers did his tongue drip its acid.

"You've got it wrong, haven't you?" he said now, clipping his cigar, looking at Tom Harris's daughter, and smiling. "What they want you to do, my dear, is sponsor religion, not practice it. Don't let your conscience mix you up. If you practiced the teachings of that man Jesus here in Maxwell, we'd think you were crazy—or communist. Don't make any mistake about it—be damned embarrassing—"

They began to laugh when he was half through. That was the pattern. Prentiss Reid said the tabooed, the terrible. Everybody laughed, making things all right, taking the meaning from words, leaving only their shells to rattle around in your memory.

"Hi, Editor!" Tracy waved his glass in greeting. "Shedding sweetness and light—"

"But, Mr. Reid," Dottie's puzzled voice cut across Tracy's words, "the Russians don't believe in religion, that's just it."

Prentiss bowed to his friend mockingly, turned to Dottie, "I beg your pardon, dear?"

"What I mean is," Dot groped for words to fit beliefs as defined as a row of little upright wires, "the difference in us and the Bolsheviks is that we are a Christian nation and Russia isn't."

Prentiss Reid happily lighted his cigar, came over to her table. "You are very pretty tonight, Dorothy, and that is the

46

simplest definition of two nations I ever heard." He patted her hair, smiled, put on his hat, tilted it to one side, walked jauntily to the back door. He stopped, turned around. "It almost satisfies me," he said, and disappeared into the alley.

Tracy turned to Epp, who was drinking his second malted milk. "What you say?"

Epp sipped the milk until the glass was empty. "Never say. Silly habit."

"You're right. Who wants to go swimming?" Everyone wanted to go swimming. All were up now, finding cars, pairing off, talking about anything on earth but religion and Russia.

Out at the Springs Harriet had sat down by Tracy, still talking. Seemed to feel that he knew the answers. "Saw you at the service tonight. Remember you said once you'd never go again?"

"No harm in going, is there?" He smiled at her, kept his voice teasing. *I am asking you as a favor, Tracy, to attend the service. Your father and I are supporting it. It seems strange for our own children not to be seen there.*

"Yes, I think there is harm." She'd hesitated, as if picking her way through thoughts with which she was not very familiar. "I wish I had more sense, enough to prove I'm right. I've only enough to know they're wrong."

Funny, the way she thought he could solve it. "I do the damndest things!" she turned restlessly. "Today I argued two hours with Mother about the virgin birth . . . and miracles."

He had laughed. It was pretty funny, and she laughed too. "Who won?"

"Mother. She believes in them. Anybody can win if they believe in something."

"May need a miracle sometime—better believe a little." Keep it light—don't let her get too serious, she's in a bad mood, won't help yours any.

47

"Don't worry. When I'm Mother's age I'll be believing everything she does, and maybe more. Everybody always seems to.

"That's not what's worrying me," she went on after a little. "It's that I don't have any more sense than to argue with her. It just hurts her, that's all. I don't want to hurt her. Only . . . sometimes, maybe . . . I think I do."

Funny crazy kid. Ideas stinging her mind like a swarm of hornets. She didn't seem to know how to protect herself from them . . .

Tracy lighted another cigarette. Used to think some too in the army. Months in the Ruhr Valley left you time to think. Cut off from everything that makes it hard to think at home, it was easier. Always a place here where you quit thinking. Quit or get out. You go so far, run into a sign: *Road Closed*. After that you start detouring . . . knowing you'll never get back on that road again.

Most of the men didn't talk much about ideas. It was women. And sometimes all they thought of were little things . . . like Ivory soap. One night a bunch of them got soap on their minds, went soap crazy. To hear them talk, you'd think a clean sweet cake of soap was all any one of them was living for. There was one fellow who'd sit there and cut out pictures of furniture and houses and paste them in his notebook while the others talked. He had a $2500.00 house, a $4000.00 house, a $10,000.00 house—all furnished with his pictures. Another talked of nothing but mowing his lawn . . . Sit there, tears rolling down his face, telling you about his lawn. He had a wife too but it was his lawn he talked about. It was green and smooth as velvet and six inches thick almost . . . knew it needed mowing. He was the one who cracked up. They took him away, sent him back home. Now in a veterans' hospital.

There was a guy from Newark, though, who talked ideas.

48

He thought the war was about democracy. Said he was fighting for that. Most thought he was nuts. Even after the armistice he kept talking. During the peace conference, when any fool could see what was happening, he said Wilson could still do it, if the people would stand by him. This guy was always saying things about a new world where everybody would have food, and a job, where one man would be as good as another, and there'd be no more wars. That sounds good, you said, but you don't know the South, you don't understand us. We'd never let the Negro into that world and I'm not so sure you up in Newark would either. We'd never let the Jews in, a Swede from Chicago said, not in my town. We'd never let the Japs and Chinks in, somebody from California yelled . . . And there was such an argument that nobody could remember heads or tails of it, everybody got mad, and one big fat slob kept pounding the table and cursing the Bolsheviks. And well, after a while the talk shifted back to women and things eased down a little.

But the guy from Newark kept talking, kept right on. Nice idea, Tracy used to tell him, nights, when they played poker together, but you'll never get folks to believe in it. Too much like heaven. Nobody but colored folks believe in heaven. White folks believe in hell. All time talking about heaven but it's hell they believe in.

When they talked about women Tracy would find something else to do. There was no woman he wanted to talk about or think about.

They sent him and his unit to Marseille. It began there, the thinking. He liked the place and used to walk for hours at night on the streets, feeling something about it—not easy to get at. It was as different from Maxwell as two places can be different, and yet it seemed familiar to him, as if a part of him that had never lived in Maxwell had found a home here.

One night—it's hard to know how a thing gets in your mind—he began to remember Nonnie. He was walking along

49

a street whose name he never knew. There was music somewhere and voices somewhere, and in the shadows a girl softly accosted him. He did not answer her, but a tone in her voice sounded in his mind after he passed her. There was a feeling in his mind, too, that he had been here before . . . the music, the easy soft laughter. He felt relaxed, relieved, as if a tight band were slowly loosening. He thought: I'd like to dance with Nonnie. He had never thought in his life of dancing with Nonnie, never had wanted to dance with her, but now he thought: We could dance here. That was all; but the words turned a key, suddenly opening his memories. She had never been something to think about until then. She had been something you tried not to think about—something you needed, took when you needed, hushed your mind from remembering. Now she was here. All the little things—filling his mind. Voice inflections . . . odd way she said the word *down* . . . brushed up hair above her temple . . . vein that throbbed there when she was tired . . . sudden quick way she would lean forward when excited, though her voice would stay low. She wasn't a Negro girl whom he had in a strange crazy way mixed his whole life up with. She was the woman he loved. And he saw her, tender and beautiful, holding in her eyes, her pliant spirit, in the movement of her body, her easy right words, low, deep voice, all that gave his life its meaning.

She was that; and he knew it. It was as if, walking along a road cluttered with people and things where all is confusion, made more confused by the rules the people move by, you almost step on something. You pick it up, knowing you've found the thing you've been looking for—covered with dirt, caked with it, yes, but you take it along, as you take a little image, knowing it has meaning for you. You take it along everywhere you go but you never seem able to get by yourself long enough to brush the dirt off.

He brushed the dirt off . . . those nights, walking up and

50

down the streets of Marseille . . . and saw for the first time what it was he had taken with him all his life nearly, but never had looked at. He knew this was Nonnie and he had to see her in Maxwell . . . like this . . . before the dirt and dust settled back on the image.

Once entering his mind, the idea never left him. He became absorbed in his memories, discovering countless little things about her—the way her eyes would shine sometimes in the twilight . . . the tremble of her lips when she talked of things that had meaning for her . . . her smile, always on the edge of laughter though rarely breaking into sound . . . the quick easy way she stooped to speak to a child . . . the bend of her body to his, the simple, the deep, profound giving of herself to him. He knew this now. And his mind ached for the completion of a reality that until now only his body had accepted.

When his boat docked in New York he saw Laura on the pier, and he was sorry. She was in school at Columbia. It was the natural thing for a sister to meet a brother who has been overseas for two years, but he was sorry, for he wanted to meet no one, see no one, hear no voice he had ever heard before until he saw Nonnie. Laura and he went to lunch together at one of the Schrafft places. They said what was expected. He said it was pretty swell to get back to some good American food, would be fine to take a swim in Sulphur Springs and go fishing. She said she was working hard at Columbia but liked it. And so on.

. She seemed older, more assured, still big-boned and awkward like a schoolgirl, and her sport clothes made her look more schoolgirlish. A quiet, pleasant girl, inclined to make too many decisions, perhaps, and too surely—no deferring, no bend of will to meet another's in the social trivia, everything moving in a straight line for Laura. That's somebody else, he'd thought quickly, somebody else moves always in a straight line—*Don't think, don't try to remember . . .*

51

Anyone glancing at them would have known they were brother and sister, though the resemblance was one in which each face emphasized what was minimized in the other. Laura's pale brown hair, gray eyes, were in sharp contrast with Tracy's black hair and deep blue eyes—her square face, her serenity and calm; his thinness and the tired lines around mouth and eyes—his quick, amused, half-mocking glance; her steady, kind, intelligent appraisal. And yet anyone would have known that they had the same mother and the same father also.

She went with him to Pennsylvania Station, and while he bought his ticket, she walked over to the newsstand, bought an *Atlantic Monthly,* was halfway back, hesitated, turned around, bought a *Saturday Evening Post* and *Life,* gave them to him instead. They both laughed, and he kissed her more warmly when he told her good-by than he had when he greeted her at the docks. She stood there waving as he went down the steps to the tracks, peering at him through her bifocal glasses, and smiling a little vaguely.

She had stood here on the porch tonight, waving, after he asked her to go with him and Dot for a coke. He had driven her and his mother home from the service. Suddenly he asked Laura to go with them to the drugstore. He did not know why he asked her. It seemed to him that she should be with the crowd, with Harriet, with the others her own age, not here with Mother. She'll be an old maid before she's twenty-five, he thought, and found himself angry. I have a book I want to finish, she'd said. I have a book. And Mother looked on, quietly triumphant.

*It seems to me, Tracy, Dorothy has been very patient.* That was all Mother said. Why did she say it?

Going from Marseille, from two years of war and army, from those talks with the Newark guy, down to Maxwell, was

52

something he never remembered. All he could remember about it was the knowing, the strange, urgent knowing that nothing must touch what he held in his mind.

He pushed the South from him as he went through it, pushed everything he had ever known or feared or hated or believed in, away from him on that trip down. It was in October that he returned, and the air was cooling. A thin blue haze was beginning to cling to the evenings. Leaves were falling . . . soon be time to go hunting. Gins were busy with the cotton. Trucks and wagons piled with bales jammed the roads. Hands still in the fields picking. He heard somebody say the rains had delayed the picking. He saw crowds of colored folks with lint in their hair and clothes, waiting to be paid off. A commissary. General merchandise stores with sheds piled with cotton. Somebody weighing bales. No feeling. The South was a picture full of things, people, smells, deeds, sounds. But no feeling. Things have changed, folks said. You won't know the place. Niggers all going North. Hard to get help. Everybody biggety. War's ruined em. Won't work. Cotton slumping. Boll weevil been terrible.

He listened. They were words as familiar to him as his own name, but words with which he now refused identification. It was as if he were the only thing real. The rest was made up.

His mother and father met him at the depot—Mother dressed in a new fall suit, tailored and smooth, driving her new Buick; and Dad sloppy and rumpled as ever, and a little tired-looking. There was a moment when Tracy looked at Alma and Tut and knew he was their son . . . One moment. And then he was once more the only real thing, all the rest was shut away from him.

Eenie was at the door, beaming. A good cook, but he had never liked her and she had never liked him. Now she was beaming. And Big Henry, his old childhood friend, who lived in the back yard and was now houseboy, was there waiting, grinning, and it was good to laugh with him and greet him, and yet there was nothing real about the laughter or the greeting. All day he did the expected. He drank cokes with the young pretty girls and with Miss Belle, who sold perfumes, and Miss Sadie the telephone operator, and Miss Eva who clerked in Adams Store, and all the other old maids who had drunk cokes with him at ten o'clock every morning in the old days. He shook hands with his father's friends, with Prentiss Reid, who was more his friend than his father's. He had to do these things, there was no avoiding it. He was a home-town boy come back from the wars, and people were glad to see him.

When evening came and he could leave, he borrowed his mother's car. Even as her face glazed, even as her eyes sharpened with the old unasked question, he did not let it reach him. It came toward him but glanced off of the wall he had closed himself in with. He drove through the back road slowly, enjoying the smooth shift of gears, the easy pull, after driving army trucks for two years. He stopped the car in the row of cedars near Miss Ada's and walked from there, knowing Non would be at the gate waiting, for he had written.

The old two-story ramshackly house in which the Andersons lived was just as it had been two years ago, ten years ago, maybe twenty years—paint peeling, roof needing repairs, two posts out of the upper balcony. But he did not look at it.

She turned, opened the gate. He saw her, cool and slim, dark hair brushed back from her temples, exactly as he had dreamed her, waiting. She was laughing softly, to keep the tears back, as he kissed her. Then she held him away from her and looked at him, his eyes, his face, hair, his eyes again—looked so long, so steadily, that he smiled finally and said, "Maybe you don't know me?" He began to guess then something of the emptiness his coming back had filled, and it surprised him, for never in all his thinking had he remembered that his coming back might mean something to her also.

"The old cabin?"

"Later—when Bess comes." She told him of her mother's long illness, how she could not be left alone for more than a few minutes. She was now sleeping. Bess would be home soon from the Stephensons'. After supper, after their mother and Jackie were settled for the night, she could leave.

He drove down Back Street, took the road toward Rushtons' farm, driving the hours away until she would be free to go with him. Swamp and pine and road grew dark, grew light again as a waning moon rose. The air was good to smell here, heavy with rotting roots and falling leaves and pond water, air he had breathed as a boy, good to breathe now. His eye moved over familiar flat country, moved with ease along slow-rising contour of fields and road, of sand hill and swamp, followed the road that stretched so flatly through pine trees . . . eye muscles resuming old movements learned long before he could remember. But no feeling returned with them.

In the car he had put his old portable phonograph and a record. Not a special record, just music he liked, a slow waltz. Everything he did now was as predetermined as the events of a dream.

When he drove back, closer to the gate, she was there. She did not ask why he carried the phonograph. She accepted it as she had always accepted him. Down the old path, beyond the grape arbor, through the field, to old Aunt Tyse's deserted cabin. The grass had grown high around it, as if no one had been there the years he had been away. He put the phonograph down, turned to her as she stood in the doorway. There was a shining in her eyes; he'd never forget it. "I've dreamed," he said and felt shy, as youngsters feel with each other, "of dancing with you. Seems a little crazy, doesn't it?" He laughed to make the words easy, for they seemed important and heavy with significance, and he did not want them to seem so. He put on a record, came to her. The room was dim, only a little light sifting through the broken roof.

55

He touched her, she was in his arms, and they danced together. In that old funny cabin with a floor that sagged at the left end and walls covered with cobwebs, they danced. Tracy and his image. And there was no dust, no dirt anywhere.

It was easy to stop, though the record played on until there was nothing but a scratching noise left, and finally she looked at the machine, half smiling, and he leaned across her and clicked it off . . .

Afterward they talked. He talked. They went out, sat on the steps of the cabin, and he talked more than he had ever talked in his life to anyone. Not of the important things, not much, not of the old worries with the family that he used to talk so much to her about, but of the little things. The trite, ordinary things that make one life so different from another. He told her about the men in his company, the guy from Newark and the boy who wanted to mow his grass, the way he'd think of Sulphur Springs when he was thirsty, though he had never liked sulphur water; time he picked up an officer in his truck who had known his grandmother in Macon, and they had talked of her. With shells bursting around them, truck bumping through holes and rain, they'd talked of the sharp-tongued vivacious preacher's wife who would never be forgotten by her husband's congregations. Then he talked of the future. Things he wanted to do. For the first time he wanted to do for Non. And he knew he could do it. Whatever he did she would like it, it would seem right, it would be enough, but she would believe he could do more if that was what he wanted, and he would want it. He talked of going into business. A chain of filling stations. Might make money at that. He laughed. Might be a good idea to make some money. Might go into politics also . . . things needed doing . . . never thought much about it until he talked with men in the army, but things had to be done in the

South—in the whole country—and nobody but the young men could do them.

"Or," he said suddenly, "we might go back to France—I made friends—I could work in a bank there—we—"

When he said the word something happened to Nonnie's face and he was startled—as if he had lighted ten thousand candles with one small half-thought-out word.

Then they stood to go, for it was late, and he kissed her. And there was between them that luminous moment caught and forever stamped on a memory, when every desire, every fantasy of one person meets and blends with those of another.

He left her at the gate, walked down to the car, sat for a while before he turned the switch, trying as he sat there to bend his whole life around that one moment. The old cedars behind him blackened out the moonlight, but between him and Miss Ada's house the path was as light as day, and the two rows of bottles that outlined the path glittered and winked in the brightness.

He drove home, put up the car, started upstairs. He wanted a smoke, had no cigarettes, decided to walk down to the drugstore for them. He wanted to walk, he was filled with energy, with a power he had never felt before, an absolute certainty. Whisky had never made him feel like this. He wasn't drunk. He was clearheaded, quiet, sane. For the first time that he could remember there was nothing pulling—no confusion, no two ways, no three ways. He knew what he wanted, knew what he needed, knew what he had. He knew for the first time who Tracy Deen was and what he was after —and he believed for the first time in his life in Tracy Deen's strength to get it.

College Street was dark. The homes where his neighbors lived were silent. As he walked opposite the Pusey cottage he did not even remember that Dottie lived there. It was still Tracy's new world and Nonnie stood in its doorway.

He heard voices. After the stillness they seemed loud,

57

noisy, although hardly above the usual conversational level. Under the street lamp near the drugstore he met the Reverend Livingston and Roseanna. The Reverend had on his preacher coat and Roseanna, his wife, was dressed in some kind of blue finery and a hat. Apparently they were coming from lodge meeting. They were laughing heartily, having the street to themselves at this late hour, and the Reverend's black face was crinkled with laughter as he walked along, spryly whirling the cane that usually he leaned on before white people. Roseanna was floating beside him, being one of those fat women so light on their feet that their weight seems to act as a sail filled with a stiff breeze. Her light-yellow face was merry now with her joking.

"If it isn't Mr. Tracy!" Roseanna's voice curved to the ground as she spoke his name, though he heard, too, the razor edge of mockery that cut a swath through her humility. He had caught Roseanna without her white-folks manner, and it was as if she were hastily buttoning it on as she spoke to him.

"Well, well, howdy, Mr. Tracy," said the Reverend, in the voice he reserved for pulpit and white folks. "Welcome home."

Although he had never liked him, Tracy decided he should shake hands with the Reverend. It was his family's custom to shake hands with a few of the colored folks on special occasions—their own house servants, certain ones, the Reverend, and the very aged. He shook hands with the Reverend, said, "Howdy, Roseanna, how are you?"

"Very well, Mr. Tracy, except for my blood pressure. Very well indeed," sighed Roseanna.

Roseanna knew her place and hushed after that, and let the men do the talking.

"When you git in, Mr. Tracy?"

"This morning."

"Just fresh home, then?"

58

"That's right."

"Mighty glad you're home. Mighty glad to have you back in Maxwell."

And that should have ended matters. In the old world that would have been all. They would have gone on to Negro Quarters, to be forgotten, and he would have stayed in White Town, forgetting.

But that was not all. As they stood there, between the speaking and the turning away, Tracy felt as if the blood were draining from his veins.

He went into the drugstore, lighted a counter lamp, took a package of cigarettes, sat down at one of the tables.

All the feeling he had was a physical sensation. He was tired as hell, that was all, and nothing was worth doing. There was not a word in his mind that explained his feeling. All he knew was that thirty minutes ago he had been with the woman he loved. Now there was a colored girl named Nonnie. That was all there was to it.

He did not sit there, piling facts here and facts there, weighing one pile against another. The anthropologists had proved there was no superior race. Sure, he knew that. Guys in the army had said the South wasted half its money and energy and time keeping the Negro in his place; if they'd stop doing it, things might not be so bad down here. He knew that too. Books were written showing this, telling it, proving it even. He didn't read books all the time, as Laura did, but he knew what the world was thinking. He knew what the facts were. They had no more to do with his feelings than knowing the facts about bone structure or the reproductive process has to do with your feeling about the mother who bore you.

There was a colored girl named Nonnie. That was all there was to it.

Why it was so, why the accidental meeting with the Reverend and Roseanna could have done this, he did not know.

59

All he knew was, as he stood there looking at them, a door slammed in his mind, shutting out the new world, shutting out Nonnie with it. He was just there on the sidewalk, where he had always been, feeling the feelings he had always felt. He had been somewhere . . . in a dream maybe; maybe crazy. Maybe it had been shell-shock. He laughed. Or plain amnesia. That's better! Maybe he'd lost, not his memory, but his white feelings. Ought to be thankful he hadn't lost his memory too. Well, he was sane now—the dream was over. Whatever he had forgot how to feel, Roseanna had made him remember. He had come back to Maxwell. Yes, the Reverend had said it, he had come back home.

He sat there in the drugstore, forgetting to go home. And after a time, he realized that someone was tapping on the window. Looking up, he saw Crazy Carl's face pressed against the glass. "Agh," the boy called, "let me in." Tracy opened the door. Crazy Carl clumsily pulled himself in. He was tall and big—heavier, taller than two years ago, when Tracy had last seen him.

"Acy," Crazy Carl's big hand stroked Tracy's shoulder, "Acy," he said, "Acy." And Tracy knew that Crazy Carl was welcoming him home also.

"Come in, boy." He spoke gently to the creature. "How about something to drink?" He went to the soda fountain, opened a bottle of Coca-Cola, handed it to Carl, who sucked and slobbered happily until the bottle was empty; then pulled himself to the candy counter and stared at its contents so quietly that Tracy forgot him.

The one dim light Tracy had turned on left most of the store in shadow. The soda fountain looked almost as new as when he had persuaded his father to install it six months before he left for the army. In the show window were the same powders and perfumes and toilet articles he had arranged there long ago. As long as he could remember before that, the window had been full of rows of Black Draught bottles.

60

Tut was too busy with his patients to give thought to such things as show windows, and it would not have been like him to change things much, anyway. But the powders and perfumes and cold creams seemed to be a relief to folks, after ten years of Black Draught, and Maxwell's girls had been quick to express their pleasure. Tracy had also organized a curb-service that made the drugstore the social center of the town. He'd used schoolboys who had not only quick legs but tongues quick enough to hand out a line of talk, edgy, yet never brash enough to annoy older women who liked manners with their sodas and Coca-Colas. The soda-fountain business increased, and with it, the drug business. Tracy had thought for a while that this was what he could do the rest of his life without too much displeasure. He did not mind the long hours—after all what can one do with hours? He had enjoyed the casual meeting with town and county friends, and it was as easy for him to be deferential to an old country woman who still thought the drugstore sold snuff as to his mother's College Street friends. People noticed it and said, "Well, Tut's boy seems to have got hold of himself. Doing all right. Drugstore's making good money."

Yes, he thought, as he sat there that first night after his return from the army, it's the same old drugstore. Same old world. It had to happen: like a time bomb, ticking off the minutes. Time comes—new world blows to pieces. Everything same as it used to be. Only it is never the same.

Tracy lighted another cigarette; looked at the Pusey home across the street. Dark. Yeah . . . everything dark.

The big old yellow house behind him was dark. And still. Upstairs, Mother sleeping. Dorothy, prayers said, sleeping. Preacher Dunwoodie, job done, sleeping.

Funny—how he used to feel about the drugstore. After coming home from college when he flunked out at mid-years, it hadn't been easy to settle down to anything. Helped around the store, loafed some, bought cotton for Adams Mercantile Company in the fall, played the cotton market, even made enough money to buy a car, wrecked it the next week one night when he was drinking. Loafed around and grew tired . . . studied law one winter. One day Tut had called him in and asked him to take over the drugstore. "Run it your own way," he said. "I've too many patients and the store needs a young mind. It's yours, Son, take it." Then one afternoon he had found his mother going through the books in the office. "Anything I can do for you, Mother?" he asked carefully, gently, as he watched his tall, grave mother adding up figures. "No, Son," she said without looking up, "I'm just running over the books." "Why, Mother?" She had looked at him calmly, her square jaws in high relief against the dim light of the room. "I've always audited your father's books for him—I've always managed his money. I'm sure that I can be of help to you too." And Tracy had stared at the wall, then turned, walked out of the office and out of the store. That night he stayed in the cabin with Henry, drinking the whisky Henry poured out for him from time to time. The next day he was drunk. He did not go back to the store. Never discussed it with his father, just didn't go. Told him he was tired, thought he'd sell cotton with Adams for a while. Yeah . . . he took the drugstore, and then Mother took it back, one afternoon. Long time ago.

Tonight seemed a long time ago to Tracy as he sat there on the steps. A long time since he had been with the crowd at the drugstore, out at Sulphur Springs talking to Harriet, telling Dorothy good night on her front porch. A long time since Mother had spoken to him today: *You owe it to Dorothy to make a decision.* A long time since he talked to Nonnie at the gate. A long time since he had come home from the army, going along without looking where he was going . . .

Now sign says: *Road Closed.* Better detour.

*I'm pregnant and I'm glad.*

*You owe it to Dorothy to make a decision.*

Behind him the house he was born in. Everyone sleeping. Everyone sleeping. Tracy stood, stretched, put out his cigarette. Lord . . .

# FIVE

WHEN TRACY walked in, the family were at breakfast, Dr. Deen finishing, Laura just beginning, Mrs. Deen pouring her first cup of coffee, having waited for Laura. It was the kind of dining room one associates, perhaps too glibly, with a Southern accent. Mrs. Deen poured coffee from her mother's old silver urn, which had been *her* mother's before her. It was clumsier than the electric percolator, but the family preferred drip coffee and Mrs. Deen preferred the silver urn. There was a bowl of figs at each place and a silver pitcher of heavy Jersey cream was near Dr. Deen's plate. Henry had just put a plate of Eenie's hot muffins in front of Mrs. Deen, and now stood, tray under arm, six feet two inches of cheerful, sweating servant, awaiting the family's wishes. Near the muffins was a small crystal dish containing butter balls that were rapidly softening in the heat of this August morning. There were lilies on the sideboard, a bowl of red roses on the table. The roses were crowded tightly into the blue crinkly bowl, as Tut had arranged them, after gathering them in the garden. Shortly, Mrs. Deen or Laura would rearrange them.

Tut was drinking his coffee and reading the *Atlanta Journal.* His seersucker coat looked mussed, and from the tentative glance Mrs. Deen gave it, anyone could have guessed

63

that in a minute or so Dad would be reminded to exchange it for a fresh Palm Beach coat before making his morning calls. Tut cheerfully read his paper, lifting his coffee cup with his left hand, not because he was left-handed but because he liked to do a few things in his own way.

Mrs. Deen looked fresh and cool in her thin blue dress and her hair, brushed high and smooth, was coolly gray against cool skin.

Tut chuckled. He was now reading the comic strips, and in a moment would look up and tell his family all about them.

Laura half smiled at her father, broke a muffin, buttered a small portion of it, looked at Tracy.

"Morning, Mother . . . Dad. . . . Finish your book?" This last addressed to Laura.

Someone had closed the east blinds, and the paneled wall opposite was striped by sun and shadow.

"Almost. Did you finish your—" Laura left her sentence uncompleted.

"Almost." He raised his eyebrows, laughed, turned to Henry, asked for two strips of bacon.

Dr. Deen folded the paper, passed it to his son, asked Henry to get his car. He was going to tell them now what was in the comics: "Maggie—"

"Tut," Alma Deen looked at her husband, touched her lips with her napkin. Tracy chuckled, Laura smiled, peered at her father through her bifocal glasses.

"Tut, your coat looks as if you've worked hours in the garden. Your fresh Palm Beach is hanging in your closet. Henry, get Dr. Deen's fresh coat for him."

Henry went for the coat, went for the car. The wheels slid on the gravel as he brought it to a quick stop in the driveway. Dr. Deen chuckled as he recounted some incident he had just read, and Henry's deep laugh came through the

64

window to the three who had not talked after Tut Deen left the room.

No one read the funnies. Each drank coffee, slowly, now and then glancing at one and another or out the window.

The telephone shrilled across the silence. "Hit's Miss Dorothy," Henry announced.

Mrs. Deen put down her cup, touched her lips slowly with her napkin, "Whom does she wish to speak to?" Words casual, quiet.

"She's atter Mr. Tracy, mam," and Henry grinned and cocked his eyes at Tracy, who would not receive the glance. Tracy tilted his cup against the edge of the saucer, looked in it, looked up. "May I have some coffee, Mother?"

Mrs. Deen poured the coffee from the silver urn, added cream.

"No sugar, please," Tracy said. "Tell her—I'll call later."

"Trace—you really can't do that!" Laura broke a piece of muffin as she looked at him, half smiling. "Or can you?"

Tracy laughed, drank his coffee.

"He ain't here now, Miss Dorothy." Henry's big voice floated back into the dining room from the hall. "Minute he gits in I'll sho tell him to call you. Yes'm, thanky mam." Henry laughed politely into the mouthpiece, softly hung up the receiver, came into the dining room, tray under arm.

Tracy picked up the *Atlanta Journal,* continued to drink his coffee.

"Mother—I'm going out for some tennis."

"It's ninety-three in the shade," Tracy said, "if that means anything to you."

"It's always ninety-three—best thing is to ignore it."

"You'll be back in time for a bath before the service?" her mother said.

"I don't know, Mother."

"But you plan to attend the morning service?"

65

"I don't know, Mother." A monotone of resistance crept into the voice.

Tracy laughed.

Mrs. Deen looked at him, with, she believed, no expression in her face, turned to Laura, "I feel that it's our duty to support the church in this revival."

"But why?" Laura spoke with sudden sharpness. "Why, Mother? It's all so—oh, I don't know . . . last night those mill people . . . wallowing in the sawdust—"

"Because," Mrs. Deen ignored Laura's description, "people need to be awakened. There has never been a time in our country when religion was at the low ebb it now is. Since the war young people have grown away from the church. Drinking . . . girls smoking . . . things happening in cars . . . and not only young people but their parents are—"

"But why such a crude method of winning us to God?"

"I am not pleased with that criticism."

"I'm sorry, Mummie. But in this day, to use frontier methods to save us does seem crude. Or worse."

"This isn't only a revival in our church. It's a community project. While some things may seem a little old-fashioned or unnecessary from our point of view, all of Maxwell has not had your opportunities. Brother Dunwoodie has a message people need, educated or uneducated. It is especially those poor mill people who do need God. And you must remember that none of us becomes so educated that we can do without religion."

Laura drank her coffee in silence.

Tracy looked at his sister, looked at his mother, smiled again.

It was after this second smile that Alma upset her cup. She began to tremble, her cup slipped, a brown stream ran slowly down the cloth, and on her dress. She could not remember ever having done such a thing. She felt deeply disturbed and, after her children left the house, went into

Laura's room. Seeking peace in old familiar routines, she tidied Laura's drawers, rearranged the books, looked over her dresses, and possessed once more the fringe of her life.

And then she found the clay torso. She found it in Laura's drawer, wrapped in a wet cloth. Uncovered, it lay in her hand, urgent, damp, like something in gestation. A lump of wet dirt. She was not able to take her eyes from it. And as she stood, unmoving, a bright red spot appeared in each cheek, her clamped jaws squared, shuttling her face into fresh planes, destroying the glaze which gave Alma Deen what her friends ardently called her "spiritual look."

She held the little figure, stared at each detail as if she saw nakedness for the first time. As if all she had feared had come to life in that lump of dirt. As if in it were hidden the key to Laura's secrets, and Laura's life, always as easily entered as Laura's room, now locked against her. In both she had once felt welcomed. She looked around the room. It was as inseparable a part of Laura as her gray eyes. Her bed, her books, her desk. In that desk Laura kept her writings; when little, her diaries; now older, her letters. And it was by means of these that Alma had maintained so intimate, so satisfying a knowledge of her child's thoughts and moods. For as Laura had grown older, and talked less—Laura seemed to talk less each time she returned from college—Alma had leaned more heavily on the written words in the desk. Laura's friends' letters, her journal kept during college days, meant so much to Alma. As did this room. When Laura was away, Alma often brought her mending in and sat in the old Morris chair. And occasionally, oh most rarely, she had slept in Laura's bed, escaping Tut's masculinity. Feeling at times a desperate need, she would slip into Laura's room. And on those nights her sleep would be dreamless and peaceful. Like a child, she had counted the weeks throughout winter until Laura's return. And now that Laura was here, the air was heavy with the slamming of doors, shutting her out of her

67

life. She was different. Withdrawn. Unco-operative. For instance, about the revival meeting. Anyone brought up in a religious home in Maxwell knows that revivals are necessary for the community. How else are people to be persuaded to live decent lives! And yet, at breakfast, right before Tracy too, when Laura knows that Tracy needs to be encouraged to go to church, she had criticized the revival. And he had enjoyed it.

She looked at the clay figure. If it had any beauty in it! But no, only nakedness. Why should Laura want to make naked things? A pelvis . . . what had she been thinking of that would make her want to make a pelvis! A man, a boy—you could understand men being dirty like that—men seemed made that way. But your own daughter . . . spending her time making naked things . . . What did she do it for! She'd call it art, and her lips would grow tight and thin as she said it. This was what she had been doing. Every day she had been going somewhere—like Tracy. It made Alma feel—

It made Alma remember a day long ago. She and three-year-old Laura had gone into the library where a breeze could be felt and she had sat watching the child play, watching the slow smile which came and went on her solemn little face. Alma had been happy that day. She remembered with startling clearness her feeling of peace, as if the baby Laura had for all time answered an old nagging doubt. She, who seldom was without some handwork, had sat with hands quiet as her heart, watching her baby. This child loved her. She loved it. Always they would understand each other. And then, as if something had crashed in the room, she turned quickly. What is it, she asked herself, her mind feeling around as one does for something run into in the dark. Tracy . . . so far away lunch seemed now, when last she had been with him. So remote had grown all the world save that small fragment which enclosed Laura and herself. With the thought of him, the old burden of motherhood fell upon

68

her. She hastily left the room to search for him, found him and his little black playmate Henry, behind the cook's house. Naked, unmindful of the broiling sun, they were crouched before an upturned washpot, beating upon it. Sweat poured from their grave faces, down their bodies.

"We're playing savages," Tracy declared stoutly, deserted by Henry, who upon her appearance had shot like greased lightning into his mama's cabin.

"Savages?"

"Yes'm. We're playing Africa." Six-year-old blue eyes looked into hers unwaveringly.

"Why did you take your clothes off, Tracy?"

"To play Africa."

"Couldn't you play Africa with your clothes on?"

"No mam."

"Why?"

"Cause Africa is nothing on."

"Who suggested such an idea to you? Did Henry?"

"No mam."

"Then why, Tracy, did you do it?"

"It's a game," doggedly.

"Have you been doing—anything else?"

He shook his head.

"Are you sure you're telling me the truth?"

Her young son did not answer.

"Tracy, you must answer me."

He looked at her, face flushed, blue eyes dark with feeling, lips together. Sweat poured down his body, streaked with smut from the pot.

"You must answer me, Tracy!"

He did not answer.

"You know that I must punish you for disobeying me?"

He continued to look at her, his lips pressed tightly together.

"You know that I should, Tracy?"

He stood there before her, blue eyes looking straight into hers.

She had been shaken with fury by her son's stubborn silence, his refusal to admit her rightness. And now, as she remembered it, she grew angry. So stiffly had he obeyed her, baring his thin thighs to the switching. Only a few light strokes of a peach-tree sprout had she given him. But when he put his pants on, breathing quickly though making no sound, and walked away from her, she queerly felt that she had lashed him brutally. Chilled by the thought, she had hurried into the room where Laura was playing and had pulled the child into her arms, seeking her lost self-esteem and the now lost peace. And Laura had snuggled close, patting her cheeks, pressing wet kisses on her face until she was suffused once more with the warmth of the child's love and the comforting knowledge that she was a good mother.

All these years Laura had given back to Alma what Tracy had taken away.

And now as she sat in Laura's room, holding the little clay torso, a hideous thought swept through her mind. *Tracy is destroying Laura.* Not directly, but by the subtle influence of his failures. Tracy's tight lips, his silence, his withdrawal from the family, his refusal to be someone worth while, the long hours spent . . . Wherever he spent his time it was wickedly spent—this she knew. And Laura must surely be aware of this, now that she was grown. Because of it, was she losing faith in her mother? Did she believe it *her* fault, that Tracy was no good, a failure? Could she be so unfair, she who had always been so close, so loving? Could she not see that all her life Alma had slaved to make something out of that boy? Was she going to take *his* side now—

She felt, for the first time in her life, that she might faint, and sat down. "It's the heat," she whispered. The room turned black, and for a moment she could see nothing.

70

Then, with the infallible weapon of her belief in herself, she fought back doubt. She was right. She could not be wrong. With infinite patience she had planned Laura's life. She had built it with care. Nothing—no one—could tear down what had been built with such thought and prayer. She began to breathe more quietly. Affirmations, soft to her bruised spirit, gathered about her:

Laura's *Yes, Mummie* trailing through the years, like a little song . . . the baby Laura's quick rush into her arms after being punished—the young Laura's *Mother dear, I have a good book, let's read it together—But what kind of dress would you wear, dearest?—I'd rather stay home with you . . ."* And then, fearing that the child was growing too dependent upon her, she had been firm about college and Laura had proved her right again, winning honors each year.

Alma breathed deeply, let her fingers relax, resting the figure on her lap. She had noticed lately that she was a bit nervous. *Change of life makes you like that.* She must not permit herself to go to pieces over something trivial. *After all, this is a little thing. After all, it is a matter of idle hands.* These months in Maxwell had made Laura restless. She quite likely copied this thing out of a book without realizing its—its—well, that it wasn't so *nice.* She remembered now a book around the house on Greek sculpture. Though this didn't look much like Greek sculpture. No Greek sculpture she had ever seen had looked so *naked.* Odd too, because of course it *was* naked, but there was a refined look about it, while this thing, with its great bulges, looked as naked as— once she had helped her old fat grandmother out of her chemise and she had looked—well this thing looked like that. And there was no art about Grandma.

She remembered that the young Laura had gone through a foolish period when she thought she wanted to be an artist. It had begun with the reading of a book. Laura rushed in to

71

her one day, eyes shining, "Oh, Mother, I'm going to be an artist." Mrs. Deen had taken care to smile sympathetically as she replied, "I am sure, dear, that your book must be interesting." "Oh yes, it *is*, Mother! It makes me want to try— it makes me believe I can *do* something— really *something!*" Mrs. Deen smiled into the eager face, "You *can* do something. Mother has a plan for you." And as Laura listened, Alma told her of college, of university, of teaching in some girls' college. "You are all I have to count on, darling," she'd whispered, and had smoothed back Laura's light brown hair from her wide forehead and told of her wish for her to work for a Ph.D. "You would like that, wouldn't you? And I should be so proud of you. It is what I have always wanted to do myself." No more was said about art. And later Alma quietly burned the book.

But this summer at home . . . it had been a mistake. They should have made the effort to keep Laura at the university for the summer. She should not have listened to Tut's talk of wanting his daughter at home. Laura said she didn't want any more degrees. But of course she did! Anyone who had as much sense as Laura would want a Ph.D. They would have a little talk about it. They would establish the old nightly exchange of confidences. It was foolish of her to let herself get so upset over a little lump of clay.

Mrs. Deen's eyes traced the curve of breasts, of rounded belly; moved inexorably downward, lingered, seeing the figure dimly now through the opaque film of confident motherhood. She had met every exigency of Laura's life. This, too, she could take care of.

She stood. Her face was calm, her jaws squared. Only the nostrils of her high nose quivered as she drew a deep quiet breath. Then, taking the figure more securely between her plump white hands, she kneaded and pressed and pounded it with slow deliberateness until it was reduced to a shapeless wad; and, walking swiftly through the hall, past Eenie in the kitchen, to the back porch, she dropped it in the garbage can. It lay there among corn shucks, okra stems, tomato skins—no more than the mud pies Laura used to make years ago; just another of the little messes Alma had cleaned up after her young daughter.

She lingered, looking out upon her back yard, blinded by the glare, feeling nothing, as if physical processes had stopped, blocked by some obstacle to which their pattern could not bend. Words moved through her mind, stripped of feeling. *Laura must go back . . . she hasn't enough to do . . . he can't do this to her . . . I won't permit it.*

"Miz Deen," Eenie called from the kitchen, modulating her voice to a bland mixture of subserviency and reproof, "hit's way atter 'leven by the clock and dey's singin deh heads off over at dat tabernacle."

Mrs. Deen turned to enter the kitchen. As she passed the garbage can, like a shadow come and gone Laura's face trembled before her eyes.

"I want you to make Miss Laura some fig ice cream," she said, her eyes focused now on nothing; "and get my hat, please, I'm late."

In the dim hall before the old pier glass that had belonged to her mother, Mrs. Deen carefully adjusted her broad-brimmed white hat, carefully powdered her nose, smoothed her heavy black eyebrows while gray eyes looked steadily back at her from the mirror, picked up her white pocketbook and linen handkerchief, took her hymnal from the console. At the front door she called to Eenie to tell Laura, should she come in, that she was at church.

The night was long, a weary stretch of time for Alma Deen as she lay beside her sleeping husband, thinking about her two children. Tut was snoring. She touched his shoulder. "Tut," she said, "you're snoring."

73

Tut turned toward her, hands fumbling sleepily, found her breast.

She pushed him away, moved to the edge of the bed. Tut turned on his back, breathed heavily.

"Turn over on your side, Tut!"

Tut mumbled, spread his legs wide, flung his foot across Alma's hip. It lay there like a log.

Alma pushed his leg away from her. Her smooth face twisted with distaste.

Sometimes all she could remember of hers and Tut's nights together was the lifting of his leg off her body. There was something almost *dissipated* about the way Tut slept, letting himself go, so, so uncontrolled, you might say. Alma had thought of twin beds but had never done anything about it, for she doubted in her heart that husbands and wives should sleep separately. It was all a little vague to her, but sleeping together, cold weather or hot, seemed a necessary thread in the fabric of marriage, which, once broken, might cause the whole thing to unravel.

Just how, she was not certain. She was convinced, however, that her own mother's custom of sleeping in a room separate from Father's had caused their family life to be not as successful as it should have been. "I can endure your sermons on Sunday," Mother used to say, throwing back her head and laughing gaily as she said it, "but to listen to you talk in your sleep is beyond my strength." And Father would laugh with her as if she had said something funny. He'd seemed to enjoy her in spite of her having done nothing to deserve it. Father would have been one of the big men in Southern Methodism, had it not been for Mother's frivolous ways. With her money and her family influence she could have helped Father but she had not seemed to care whether Father became a bishop or not! "Your father isn't bishop material, my dear. Don't make the poor man dissatisfied. He's a good man, God-loving and just right for the pastorate

74

of a small town like Maxwell. As for me, I'd loathe being a bishop's wife." And she had laughed.

Alma could see her now: dark, blue-eyed, with curly brown hair, tall and thin. She'd always worn little narrow collars and earrings and used violet toilet water, and always dropped her handkerchief, saying "Oh how careless of me!" whenever she grew interested in a conversation—which was frequent, as any conversation, no matter how foolish, interested Rosa.

"My daughter has never approved of me," Rosa Mathews used to say to her old Macon friends—and often before Alma. "No," she'd say, and pat Alma's smooth hair, "she doesn't quite approve of her mother. Oh dear," she'd laugh, throw back her head and her earrings would sparkle like two little giggles, "where did the child get her ideas, do you suppose?" Sometimes Alma, listening, would hate her mother, but later she learned to say, "Poor Mother," and to feel sorry for her, in a way, when she could forget how much sorrier she felt for Father. Mother had sent her to college for one year. After that, she insisted on her visiting relatives in Macon. "No intellectual for me! All I ask of you, my dear, is to be a normal girl and have a good time." And she'd pat Alma's ash-blonde hair. "I want you to know my friends' boys; something might come of it," she'd say, "although of course on the other hand . . . Remember, Alma, a little indiscretion is often very—successful!" And when Alma flushed, Mother would laugh gaily and fan herself briskly with her ridiculous Japanese fan.

So when young Tut Deen, just out of medical school, with the ink hardly dry on his state license, asked her to marry him, it was for Alma as if someone had opened a gate which led down a faraway road.

"I might as well let her marry him," Rosa told her Macon friends, but not before Alma this time. She had left Alma at Maxwell and had come up to the family house on Hardaman

Avenue for a few days just after Alma's engagement had been announced. "He's from a good south Georgia family and while he'll never set the world on fire he'll always have a comfortable practice. After all, Alma will never set the world on fire, either, with her plain face and her father's figure, bless him." She threw back her head and laughed cheerfully. "One has to take the children the Lord sends, I suppose. It's amazing, though, what He can send you sometimes." She turned brightly to her best friend, Ellen Williston, who was having the sewing circle over to see her. *"You know, Nell, Alma is an amazing child for me to have brought into this world. I can explain it only by conceding to the male a great potency . . . This chicken salad is delicious."*

The ladies giggled.

"Alma is much better than you deserve. She's a fine girl."

"She is, indeed! Every time I look at Alma I feel as if I've just read a chapter in the Bible and said my prayers."

"Rosa! I'm ashamed of you."

"But"—Rosa's deep blue eyes twinkled—"I want her to have a wonderful wedding. Something she'll always remember with pleasure." She set aside her plate. "Now let's get down to business and decide what kind of wedding dress would be becoming to my child." The ladies had planned the wedding, delighting in every detail; and young plain-faced heavy-set Alma Mathews had become the bride of Dr. Tutwiler Deen amidst white tulle and satin and lilies of the valley, wedding cake and reception, magnificent presents from Macon's old families and more modest ones from Maxwell parishioners, while her tall thin impresario of a mother alertly maneuvered each detail, vastly amused by all of it. And Alma, standing there at the altar with young red-haired, freckled-faced Tut Deen, had felt a lump come in her throat at the thought of leaving Father alone with Mother. And, making her marriage vows, she made another that she would be a *real* wife to Tut, helping him with his career, helping

76

him in every way in which he needed help; she would be everything to her children that Rosa had never been to her.

She had been a good wife to Tut, submitting to his embraces quietly, without protest—though that part of marriage seemed to Alma a little unclean and definitely uncomfortable; helping him with his practice; collecting the fees which Tut would never have collected; saving, investing; running a smooth home; carefully taking his calls; keeping Tut from going fishing too much and neglecting a practice that had grown large through the years. Always remembering Mother, Alma had urged Tut on.

But now as she lay beside her sleeping husband she was not thinking of him, but of their children. All day, she had been thinking about her two children. Strange . . . you do everything for them, you train them so carefully; they grow up and are people that you seem not to know.

She had been happy when her first baby came. At first the knowledge of her pregnancy filled her with a quick fear, which slowly changed into pride. She started the baby off carefully, fed him regularly, never picked him up when he cried, and even Tut noticed and complimented her on her efficient ways. Then Mother came.

Mother tripped in one day, eyes dancing. "All the way from Hawkinsville," where her husband had been transferred, "I've been reveling in being a grandma. Yes, my dear, I'm over my attack. Perfectly! Don't pamper me! I've never felt better in my life! Never! Now, let me see the little fellow." And proudly Alma had led her mother into her bedroom where young Tracy lay in his crib. "You've gained some, Alma. Don't give in to your appetite, my dear! Are you nursing him? You're not? Good. It's better for your figure and your disposition not to. I remember I nursed you for one long week. Terrible week! Then I called in Mammy and told her to work it out the best way she could, I was

77

through." Alma would remember all her life how Mother's skirts swished and the odor of crushed violets that filled the room with her every movement. Alma would always see her earrings gleaming. Mother sparkling.

Rosa took off her glasses, bent over the crib. "So this is the child." She stood there, looking down at the little creature. "He'll be full of spirit." Her bright, alert face softened. "He could be my very own," she whispered, and picked him up, and he smiled as she touched him. "Well," Rosa looked at her daughter brightly, "I must admit that you've done a much better job on your first-born than I did!"

And Alma, knowing that her mother always said whatever came into her mind, tried to laugh at the tactlessness, tried to laugh away the old hurt, but cried instead. She stood there, looking at the baby in her mother's arms, and cried. "I don't want it," she said in her bitterness, and turned away. "I don't want him," she cried, and knew that she meant her words.

"Of course not!" Mother said cheerfully. "A lot of people don't want their first baby. You'll get used to it, my dear."

Tracy never seemed quite hers, after that. He belonged to Mother. And Mother stayed for a visit that stretched from weeks into months, going back only occasionally to Hawkinsville. Mother stayed and played with the baby, telling her how to raise him, picking him up when he cried, feeding him whenever he whimpered, giving him a sugar tit, ruining his good habits, until you almost believed she was deliberately trying to keep you from being a good mother. Until sometimes it was difficult not to tell her to leave your house forever!

When Alma became pregnant again and her mother wanted to take the young Tracy back with her, it was easier to let her take him than to fight it out. But though Alma knew that in a test with her mother she seemed unable to win, deep within her she knew that she need never give in to anyone else. Never! And she had felt herself grow strong and firm and certain in the knowledge.

Mother never interfered with the training of Alma's second child. When Laura came, Mother said, "She looks like a fine healthy child, Alma," and showed no further interest.

Then one day, while telling one of her jokes, Mother had laughed so heartily that she dropped dead. She lay there, they say, crumpled up on the rug, still smiling. And after a moment, one of her ear pendants loosened and rolled slowly across the floor . . . the last little sound that Rosa Mathews ever made.

It had been a long, hot, weary day and night for Alma Deen. But, as she lay in the dark beside her sleeping husband she felt strength returning to her. As she faced her task she knew that she was equal to it. God had always given Alma strength for her duties to her family.

She had done the right thing to make that appointment for Tracy with Brother Dunwoodie. She knew he would not like it. She had dreaded to tell him. Yet she knew that unless she took matters into her own hands Tracy would never see the preacher. Tracy would evade him—as he evaded everyone who wanted to help him. Yes, he had his father's gift for evading an issue.

She listened to Tut's steady breathing. Sleeping like a child.

She had dreaded it, but she had done what seemed right to her. Brother Dunwoodie had a tremendous influence over young men. Everyone had heard of the hundreds of young men throughout the South whose lives had been miraculously changed after a talk with him. He understood them, knew how to get at them. She had expected Tracy's displeasure when she told him what she had done but she had not been prepared for the terrible rudeness he showed her. Never in his life had he spoken to her as he did today. And how it hurt—hurt like the old things Mother used to say. Standing there, facing her son, fighting to hold her composure, Alma had wanted suddenly to give up and cry.

A tear rolled down her face as she lay there in the dark, thinking over the day. It's so hard to give your life to your children and have them be ungrateful for everything you try to do.

Alma was crying quietly now in her pillow. Crying as she had not cried in years. It would be so easy to give up . . . so terribly easy when you aren't feeling well anyway, to use menopause as an excuse, and give up.

Tut moved restlessly, flung his legs wide.

"Move over, Tut."

Tut turned over, fumbled around, touched her back, touched her stomach. Sighed.

Alma quickly blew her nose. The sudden weakness had passed and once more she felt her strength returning. Change of life brings on strange spells. She must not let herself give in to her feelings.

Tut flung his leg across her.

Alma lifted Tut's leg off her hip, eased over to the far side of the bed.

# SIX

TRACY turned the switch, started the car. He had eaten breakfast late to avoid his mother. He had eaten just in time to keep his appointment with Brother Dunwoodie at nine o'clock. Even at nine it was hot. What a day it would be! He drove slowly up College Street toward the Harris home, past house after house, each set back in its small or large lawn. Here, there, a colored maid swept a porch or the walk in front of a home, moving slowly along, brushing away moss and sand and small crisp oak leaves, singing low, talking to herself. A child ran across the grass, stopped, pulled a sandspur from his foot, hobbled on, whimpering, suddenly forgot, began to run again. Across the wide street divided so exactly by the railroad was the honeysuckled Pusey home. Someone was in the swing. He would not look. He would not see who was in that swing, or in any swing, this morning.

He was on his way to talk to the preacher. If Gus or any of the boys had bet him, yesterday, that he would be seeing the preacher this morning, he would have laughed and told them he'd see them in hell first. Yet here he was, going to talk to the preacher, like a nice little boy, about his soul. If you thought you had a soul, or anybody had a soul, there'd be a little sense to it!

It'll be damned embarrassing. After all, you don't have to do it. Drive around the block, go on home. Like hell you would—there he is . . . waiting at the gate, lounging against it, a big hard-muscled man, at ease. You wonder why a man like that—how a man like that ever happened to be a preacher. Didn't seem to fit. A ball player . . . football, maybe, but not preaching. You think of a preacher as soft-fleshed, short-winded except in the pulpit. Grandfather was pudgy, irritable in his old age when he wasn't praying or preaching. You'd always remember him, pink face, blue eyes, heavy snow-white hair brushed back in a high pompadour, looking down at his cereal as if he were going to cry in it. A funny way to remember your grandfather, but that was your memory of him. But people said when Grandfather prayed men's hearts filled with the peace of God. Maybe it was Grandma. Grandma was pretty leathery. Maybe stropping against her day after day put an edge on Grandpa's nerves. You'd never felt that way about her, though every-

81

one else seemed to. With you she had been different. Gentle . . .

The preacher had seen you, was turning slowly. In a moment he'd say something. Lifting his arm now, vaulting the fence, easy, light. Good balance. What you reckon made him waste that body in a pulpit? What you reckon got hold of the man? Once you'd seen him, years ago when he was here, illustrate his text by climbing the pole of the big tent. Yes, he'd done that and you'd laughed at his fanatic craziness and all the other boys sitting on the back pew had laughed too, but you had sort of liked him for it—anybody think it easy to climb a thirty-foot pole had better try it sometime—and five of the boys sitting there with you laughing had joined the church before the meeting was over.

The preacher said, and shook his heavy black hair off his face as he spoke, "Well, you're on the dot."

Tracy smiled, stopped the car.

Brother Dunwoodie got in.

"Be cooler to ride around, don't you think?"

"Suits me all right."

"How about a coke first?"

"Be fine," said the preacher, shifting his wide shoulders to a more comfortable angle against the back of the seat.

Tracy stopped in front of Deen's Drug Store, ordered two Coca-Colas.

"Nothing like a Coca-Cola to cool you off. Old Asa Candler hit on a good thing when he fixed up a soft drink in—"

"In temperance territory?" Tracy grinned, looked at the preacher. Maybe he wouldn't think that funny.

The preacher laughed. "Well, come to think of it, if you take a man's corn away from him, reckon the Lord's right glad to give him some kind of sugar-tit to take the place of it. The Candlers have prospered, must have been God's will."

The preacher threw away the straw, lifted his glass.

*Tracy* . . . Mother's voice had faltered but her eyes had

82

looked steadily into his, *I've arranged for you to have a talk with Brother Dunwoodie at nine o'clock in the morning.* You kept thinking of it.

*You've—say that again, will you, Mother?*

*I think you heard me.*

*Sure . . . but I want to give you a chance to—take it back.* He'd kept his voice low. *Of all the goddam meddling—*

*Tracy!*

*I beg your pardon, Mother.* You'd never in your life spoken like that to her or to any woman. What made you lose your head, what made you— You'd stood there staring at your mother, shocked at what you had said—

"They make good cokes here."

"Pretty good."

She'd said, her voice as smooth and deliberate as the judgment of God, *In all your life I have never known you to speak like this before. It seems as if—as if you are deliberately ruining your life, as if you are doing this with a purpose.* Now what on earth could she have meant by that? She had stopped, begun again. *In spite of your—*her eyes traveled across his face slowly as if across his life—*weaknesses . . . I could at least hold to your courtesy to me. And now you've taken that from me.* Her lips suddenly trembled and it seemed as if she could not go on, but quickly her face composed itself, her voice steadied—

The preacher said, "Well, that's a good start for a hot morning. Much obliged."

They'd left the drugstore now and Tracy had turned down College Street toward the south side of town. Preacher talking about Grandfather Mathews. Of course. Everybody knew Grandpa, everybody who was a Methodist—and that meant half of Georgia. It gave the preacher a good opening.

"You remind me of him a little," the preacher was saying, "only you're leaner, harder. You're more like Sister Mathews, but quieter."

"Grandmother," Tracy laughed, "was energetic, all right."

"Energetic's hardly the word—if you remember her rightly. I'd say, more like a piece of shrapnel—if you've ever heard it singing straight at you."

"Were you over?"

"Yes. Y.M.C.A."

Tracy drove slowly through the heavy sand on College Street.

"You asked me, moment ago, how I happened to become a preacher."

Had he? He'd thought it. Didn't know he'd said it aloud.

"Well, it's pretty easy to answer that one. God convicted me of sin. Yeah. Simple as that. And convicting me, called me to preach the Gospel. Laid a burden on me that I couldn't shake off—"

*I've given my life to you and Laura—all of it—I've asked little of you in return and you've given me nothing—*

"Funny, way I tried. Joined the army—that didn't work. Went into ball playing—got in minor league, looked like I was headed for big league stuff—What? Oh, played shortstop —yeah. Nothing helped. Be on the train, be playing ball and I'd hear the Voice, nagging at me. 'What you going to do about it?' it'd say."

Tracy was driving toward the south of town, now through the glare of hot white sand, now in the cool of oak shade.

"This business of sin . . . strange thing—"

*I've asked little of you and you've given me nothing.* You couldn't get the words off your mind. *What have you given me? School? You stopped after that half year in college. Job —profession—you knew how I wanted you to be a doctor or a lawyer—*

"Each man has his own way of sinning. I'm not asking you yours. Some folks like to talk about theirs. Shake them out in the air, hoping a big wind will catch them, blow them away. Other folks trample theirs to pieces inside till there's

84

nothing left. Each man has his own way of getting shed of his."

*There's Dorothy. You know how I've wanted that. How we all want it. Yet you treat her like a little cheap thing—*

"And the way don't matter if you get rid of them to make room for God. I don't know what your way is. But I know a lot about sin. Some folks . . . it's money. Got to have it! You see little children stealing it before they know how to count. It gets folks that way. They just take it."

*What I ask now is such a small thing. It is difficult to think of a son making a scene over a small request like this—*

"Don't want it for nothing! Just take it. And there's others who want it for something. They go after it wanting it for something. And when they want it bad like that, nothing can stop them. Except Almighty God. And if He don't— death. But when they let Him, God can do it."

*When you can't ask a small favor of a son—there's not much left for a mother.* And he'd smiled, he remembered that, smiled as he looked straight at her and said, *You have Laura, you know.* By God, he wouldn't give in to her, he'd thought, not this time. He was man enough to hold out.

"I know you're saying, maybe, you don't believe in Him." The preacher looked at Tracy and smiled quickly. "Said it myself once. And what's more, listened to my own words. But I lied. You may not believe there's oxygen in the air. But you can't live more'n a minute or so without it."

And Mother had looked at him quickly. *Yes,* she'd almost whispered, *yes, I have Laura.* And as he had watched, something had happened to her face. Something had ripped the certainty from it, leaving it old and hurt, and unprotected. She who was never hurt—

"It's that way with God," the preacher's words went on. "You can't live in Maxwell without Him. Got to have Him to lean on. Man's a funny critter. Sometimes seems like the

85

minute he lets go his mother's hand, got to have something else to catch hold to."

Yes, something had hurt her. And standing there watching her last night, as she talked to him in the hall, he had felt that he had done something to her. Somehow she who had never needed help, never needed anything, had asked something of him, which had seemed to him a damned piece of meddling but to her was something she needed and he had refused to give it to her. *If it will make you feel any better* he'd heard himself say as he stood there watching her, wishing the hurt look would leave her face, *I'll go talk to Dunwoodie.* Her face had not changed at his words and he had wondered if she could have heard. *Mother,* he called softly.

*Yes.*

*I said I'll go talk to the preacher if it will make you—feel better.*

"There're other sins. All kinds. Gambling . . . you know folks who gamble don't want their winnings. Ever thought about it? They want something powerful bad but it's not the winning. When I hear a man's a gambler I know there's a lot of wrestlin with the Lord for somebody to do. Because he's after something else. Kind of like self-abuse. Now those are the ones! *Man, man!* Hard to get em to listen to you, and when they listen, even when they try—sweat with their trying—they turn back after a while to their own bodies. Worship themselves—like they were their own God. I'm going to preach a sermon on that. For men only. Next week. I'm telling you, there's sins most folks never dreamed of! You know, when you're preaching . . . going around from place to place on the Lord's business, you run into a sight of sin! Yes sir! All kinds. Some of em make you tremble to think of. It makes you wonder. Makes you wonder how God in His wisdom could've made a creature who would think up as many ways of doing wrong as man has studied up. You wonder why

86

He couldn't have done a little better while he was thinking up a creature—I say it in all reverence—but it makes you wonder."

Tracy had turned the car, was driving back over the road they had just driven down.

"But God gave us Jesus, His only begotten Son. And I can't forget that. And you can't forget that. To help poor stumbling creatures find the way."

*Thank you,* Mother had said, and turned, laid her hymnal on the table, for they had just come from the services, and he had come in only to get the car to take Dorothy to ride. And then she had turned back to him, and her face was again as smooth as glass. *I knew you would, dear. I could not believe you would embarrass me by not being a gentleman.* She had stood there, tall, a little heavy now, gray hair brushed up smooth and high above her forehead, heavy brows black against her smooth pale face. *Oh certainly not, he'd whisppered to himself, you always win, Mother. Always,* he'd suddenly said aloud, and laughed and walked to the front door.

*You're going out—again—tonight?*

*Yes, I'm going out,* he'd said and laughed again, and shut the door, knowing she thought he was going to Colored Town. And it gave him satisfaction to know this. It gave him satisfaction as he crossed the railroad and opened the picket gate which led to the Puseys' small front yard.

"Now there's another sin. Lot of men, when they're young, sneak off to Colored Town. Let their passions run clean away with them. Get to lusting—burning up! And they get to thinking . . . they'd rather have that kind of thing than marriage. A lot rather! Scared of white girls. Scared nice white girls can't satisfy them. And they're right! Of course no decent fine white woman can satisfy you when you let your mind out like you let out a team of wild mules racing straight to—"

Preacher Dunwoodie's voice had risen shrilly. Suddenly he

stopped. Spoke more quietly. "Well . . . that's youth," he said and wiped his face with his big handkerchief. "This world's full of young folks wanting—strange things. That's youth and the devil," he added softly, "and sooner or later you have to face it. Funny thing," he said, "once you make up your mind to leave colored women alone and stick to your own kind, you soon get weaned." He laughed shortly. "You don't think you can. But you do. I know . . ." he sighed. "As for the colored women, they manage all right. Always have, haven't they! Most of them sooner or later get a man their color, maybe marry him. Live a fairly decent, respectable life—that is, if a nigger woman can live a decent, respectable life." Voice suddenly bitter.

Someone's been talking to him. He's too smooth—knows too much.

"You see, Deen, you have to keep pushing them back across that nigger line. Keep pushing! That's right. Kind of like it is with a dog. You have a dog, seems right human. More sense than most men. And you a lot rather be around that dog than anybody you ever knew. But he's still a dog. You don't forget that. And you don't forget the other . . . it's the same. God made the white race for a great purpose. Sometimes I've wondered what that purpose is. Between you and I, I've wondered—with all reverence—when God is going to divulge that purpose, for up to now, seems like we been marking time most ways, or making a mess of things. Well," he suddenly smiled, drew his brows close, as quickly relaxed them, threw back his heavy black hair, "I've done all the talking."

"I appreciate your taking time with me. To tell you the truth," Tracy smiled quickly, "I'm—hardly worth it."

"There's people who think you are. The little Pusey girl . . . your own fine mother. A man's lucky to have two such women to love him."

Tracy speeded up the car, as quickly slowed it down.

88

"You know, Deen," the preacher went on soberly, "most men learn to love God because their women love Him. You know that? Same way they begin to love their own children. Ever thought of that? Or because they're scared . . . not to. You're not the easy scared kind."

"I don't know. Sometimes I think I am." Tracy spoke gravely. "Trouble with me," he said slowly, "I don't believe all that."

"Most men don't believe when they start. Most of us have to take some things on faith—like our children, for instance." Dunwoodie chuckled. "Yes sir, men have to take a lot on faith! Ever thought of it?"

Tracy suddenly laughed. The preacher wasn't so bad.

"You take things that *matter* on faith. There's no way of proving them! I don't say that in the pulpit, mind you, or to the ladies." He laughed deeply. "Reminds me of a story I heard once. A man had just got married and when he went to get in bed that night he suddenly looked at the girl and —well, never mind that," he frowned, stopped his words, picked them up again. "But I say it now. With all reverence, I say it."

Tracy looked quickly at the preacher. The old boy had almost forgot he was on the Lord's business.

"On this earth there's two worlds," the preacher continued, after a time, "man's and woman's. Now, the woman's has to do with the home and children and love. God's love and man's. The man's world is—different. It has to do with work. Women teach us to love the Lord, and our children, and then *we* build the churches, don't we, and *we* keep them going. Sure. Just as we make the living for those children, we do the farming, we create the cities. We do the work. Sure. That's right. Now, when a man gets over into a woman's world, he gets into bad trouble. He don't belong there. He belongs in a man's world. God wants your soul where it belongs, for then He'll be surer of getting it than if it was on the other side—where some woman'll get it all. May not sound like religion to you. And I'm not saying you can find verse and chapter exactly for it in the Bible. And, as I say, I don't preach it in the pulpit. But it's good preaching, just the same. Too much love makes you soft. No-count! Tying you to a woman's apron strings! That's what too much love'll do. Women wouldn't understand that—and, as I say, I don't preach it in the pulpit.

"Now, some men have a deep feeling for God. It comes to em easy. Others get it slow. The hard way. But a man makes a living and feeds those younguns his wife *says* are his, even if he ain't sure he loves them yet, don't he? And a man gets on the Lord's side and joins the church, supports it and his town's affairs, even when his heart's not in it much, at first.

"But this is what happens after a time. After a time God begins to seem like a real Man to you. Not something your mother loved and told you to love! But your own Kind. I mean that in a holy and sacred way. And what men are doing, their work, their interests, seems more important to you and satisfying than anything in a woman's world. So when I say, get on the Lord's side, I mean one thing when I talk to the ladies and another when I talk to men."

Tracy's teeth flashed again in a quick smile.

"As I say, I don't talk like this in the pulpit." Brother Dunwoodie drew his heavy brows together, and quickly relaxed them. "What you think?" he said softly, and his face eased into a warm smile.

Tracy half smiled. "I think maybe you're right."

"Well," said the preacher, "how about it? How about trying it on the Lord's side—and man's, for a while?"

"I'll think about it." Tracy spoke quickly and turned the car sharply through the deeper ruts in the sand road.

"God bless you," the preacher said and laid his big warm hand on the boy's shoulder. "God bless you," he said, and softly sighed.

Tracy turned the car toward Iron Bridge. You couldn't keep driving up and down through town all morning.

"I'd like for you to see the river," surprised at himself as he said it. "Maybe on the river it'll be cooler."

The preacher looked at his watch. "I'd like to go if we can make it back in an hour."

Tracy took Back Road and cut across the ball diamond.

"Four years ago I got as far as Sulphur Springs. A meeting don't leave much time for sight-seeing."

"We'll make it, all right," Tracy said and speeded up when once they were on the county's eight-mile stretch of pavement. "Most of us around here have been swimming and fishing in the river all our lives." He laughed. "Seems a good sort of place to us." Why did he keep trying to explain?

"Anybody likes a river." The preacher was looking now at the acres of yellowed palmetto brushing by the car like bands of copper in the sun. He half closed his eyes.

"Not much else to see around Maxwell—except sand and prickly pear."

Tracy crossed the Iron Bridge, slowed where the sweeping curve of brown water and white sand banks push sharp against overhanging live oaks, mammoth with age and their heavy burden of gray moss. Took the narrow road to the left, drove through deep sand, around hot-looking scrub-oak thicket and patches of grass and prickly pear, under low-hanging live oaks whose moss snagged at the car as it went under—on up the bluff. There, under a big oak, he stopped the car.

"Now that's fine," the preacher said, "fine! Does you good to see a thing pretty as that, don't it?"

It was cooler here, and the curve of the river was good on the eye, with its dark tree line above the cliffs.

Brother Dunwoodie eased down in the seat, stretched out his legs, sighed softly. "Pretty spot. Pretty as I've ever seen in Georgia." He closed his eyes.

Preaching must be hard on you, Tracy thought, looking at the sagged face. Must be a wearisome business struggling with other folks' sins. The preacher's mouth dropped comfortably open, his tie had pulled to one side, his heavy black hair had slipped down on his forehead. The crease in his neck was filling with sweat and he had begun to breathe deeply. A muscle in his relaxed hand jerked now and then. Might be any drunk sleeping it off.

Tracy turned away, let his eye follow the river, come back, follow the cool shade of the heavy oaks. It was here that they had come that night. Over there on the sand that they had lain, stretched out easy on its deepness. A piece of moss had fallen from the limb above them on her breast, and she had let it rest there. Any other girl would have jumped or exclaimed or thrown it off. But Nonnie let it rest there. Easy. And it had trembled as it lay there, rising and falling with her breathing. Easy and quiet. Everything about Nonnie . . . like that. It was a hot night—two months ago—two hundred years it seemed now! He had driven out to the old Anderson place in the car. She was at the gate waiting. Always there. And he had suddenly thought, It's so damned hot—why not take her in the car somewhere. And he suggested it and she went as casually as if every night of their life they had done the same.

He drove discreetly through the edge of Colored Town, took an old road that cut across to the highway, brought her here. She slipped out of the car, walked to the edge of the bank, stood there looking down at the dark river, at the cliffs white in moonlight. Then she had turned, slowly pushed her hair off her face, and smiled. And he had been profoundly moved. It was a little thing, a quick turn of her body, the slow pushing of hair from her face, her smile. But he knew that she had never seen a river in moonlight before . . . that somehow he had conferred a great favor. And he felt shamed and confused. She took his hand and rubbed it against her lips, then left him and walked a few steps away, and stood with her back to him, looking at the river. The wind was blowing enough to sweep her dress against her body, and to push her hair away from her forehead. And she seemed a sweet lovely thing to him there in the moonlight.

He moved to her quickly and pulled her to him, shamed and deeply touched. He had slipped his hand back of her head as he held her, now kissed her face again and again and again. After a time she turned away, took his hand; held it tightly, suddenly. And when he pulled her around he saw that her chin was shaking and there were tears on her face.

"It's a goddam mess!" he'd said and hushed abruptly.

She shook her head, smiled quickly, wiped her eyes. Then they had sat on the sand and neither had tried to talk. Neither liking to talk much. After a while he had drawn her to him and they were laughing together, for the sand was scratchy as the very devil. And everything seemed right and good, as it had always been.

But later, as they lay there, relaxed, looking up at the sky, she had pulled his hand to her breast. He felt her heart beating under it and suddenly, lying there, she seemed not the Nonnie whom he had a way of taking as for granted as you'd take a piece of cornbread, but a girl off somewhere by herself and sad about something. He drew her to him and ran his hand across her hair, not knowing what to say. Not knowing in this damned upside-down, devilish world what to say to a girl like this. He knew from the trembling through her body that she was crying, but there was no sound. Lying there, looking under the limb of that old tree sagged with moss, he thought about her. He remembered that when her mother died last winter, just after he'd come back from Europe, he'd hardly noticed. After that first night, he'd hardly noticed anything about her. For nothing in Nonnie's life seemed a part of him, except herself. He'd hardly noticed, and it must have meant a hell of a lot to Nonnie. It made

93

him a little sick to remember that now, as he lay on the sand holding the girl in his arms. And a day or two after the old woman had died and the funeral was over, he had gone out there—but to talk to Non about himself, having had another damned row at home. And she had sat under the arbor and listened to him talk, looking peaked and tired as she listened, making him feel good again and comforted by her listening. And the meeting with the Reverend and Roseanna had been almost forgotten as she listened to him.

"Would you like to talk to me, Non, about it?" It made him feel decent to say that to her. It made him feel almost as he had felt the night he danced with her. It was coming back, the feeling he had lost. He was finding it again. And his body and mind were quickening.

After a while she wiped her eyes, pushed back her dark hair. "I can't talk, much," she said low, "about things." She smiled at him, and he knew that, somehow, she was pushing that trouble back from wherever it had come. "I think it's like this—" she said quietly, "I've always known what I wanted. You; and Mummie, when I was little. I know people are supposed to want other things. I don't seem to. I suppose the way I've always felt about—Mother, goes back to those long days I spent by myself, playing around on the edge of the swamp and fields. All day long . . . saying to myself: when the sun goes down she'll be back . . . Sometimes I was afraid of the woods. I don't quite know how to say it, for I loved them too. But I'd be out playing, whispering to myself, and something would rattle and I'd begin to run . . . not knowing where to run . . ." She laughed and wiped her eyes again. "But when I heard her step at dusk, down on the path by Miss Ada's, things were—all right again. I suppose a lot of children are like that. Colored children," she said, and stopped.

*Negro.* She'd said it. Now everything would be spoiled. Ruined as it always was!

94

But it wasn't ruined. Out there on the lime cliff, brown water swirling below you, sky paled out by the moon above you, great oaks with sagging moss draping your nakedness, hiding you from the world, you could think that word without getting sick at your stomach. You could say it, say Nonnie's name after it, and still believe in her and yourself. The world's wrong, you could say. Dead wrong.

She'd turned then, as if she had read his thoughts. "Race is something—made up, to me. Not real. I don't—have to believe in it. Social position—ambition—seem made up too. Games for folks to—forget their troubles with. Bess says I'm crazy, that I live in a dream world." She'd smiled and looked up at the sky and both of them had watched a cloud drop behind the great oaks.

God! You could hear that damned word and not mind it. You didn't give a goddam what the world thought. She was yours, that's all! She's my girl. She's lovely and beautiful, and she's mine. He'd laughed, and pulled her to him again. Holding her there, he knew he loved her—as a man loves the woman who fits all his needs.

And he felt good. He watched a cloud pull across the moon and break in two afterward, he looked at the shadows under the oaks, and felt good inside. He felt he could help Nonnie through her trouble, whatever it now was, as she had helped him . . . all her life long.

She had her arm behind her head now, and the moss was there on her breast, rising and falling in the clear light. "The way things have to be . . . I don't—see much of you. It has to be that way," she said quickly, "I've accepted that. But tonight . . . maybe you shouldn't have brought me," she smiled at him, "it is so beautiful here and I—"

Yeah. The bluff belonged to white folks and every nigger in the county knew it.

"—I suddenly thought if we were—the same—color," she said the words very low, "this separation wouldn't have to

95

be. We could play together—this tonight—drive places in the car—play tennis, maybe . . . I know it sounds funny," she laughed and her breath caught sharply, "but I've never played except by myself. And it suddenly seemed as if it would be—nice—to play with you." She stopped for a moment and they both watched a bird fly slowly from one tree to another. "It's sleep walking," she'd whispered. She went on again, "This evening before you came, I'd been out weeding Mama's grave. It's been hot today too—and Boysie cried so much—maybe all of it together—"

"God . . . I can't let you put up with it!"

"It's all right, Tracy. I want you to know that," she spoke earnestly now. "I like having you come out to me . . . just as you do . . . I like being there—whenever you need me. Those things that mean so much to Eddie and Bess, and meant so much to Mummie, don't mean the same to me. I decided that, when I was a little thing—playing by myself. White boys, people, would try to—bother me . . . and I had to decide things. Maybe that doesn't make sense to you. But one day when I was a little girl, a boy tried to take off my clothes in a gallberry patch, and you stopped him. It sounds funny, saying it out loud, like this, but there you were, and I knew I was—all right. I've felt that way . . . ever since. All those things people think matter, don't matter."

She seemed like a little girl, talking so freely—like this; not the calm, quiet Nonnie who knew somehow always what to give you when you needed something, though she never said much. More the little tike in the gallberry patch. Yes, he remembered it, vaguely. Now Nat Ashley was mayor of some town up in North Carolina, he'd heard, getting ready to run for governor.

They'd gone back to town late. And he had taken her home and driven back to College Street. But the moment he opened the screen door of his house and entered that hall,

things changed as if he had found his sense of direction out in the swamp—and lost it again. He had done that when hunting. Many a time. You know you're going right, and suddenly you don't know where you're going. The moment he opened that door, tiptoed through that dark hall and up the steps, past Laura's door, he heard the whole town— *been out all night with a nigger gal . . . wasting your life . . . getting something you can't get here in White Town . . . Well, they've got plenty of that!*
Maxwell talking. All the world talking, maybe.

It's like an obsession. Seems true to you, but everybody else says it isn't. You can't love and respect a colored girl. No, you can't. But you do. If you do—then there must be something bad wrong with you. It's like playing with your body when you were a kid. You had to touch yourself. It felt good. It was good. But everyone told you it wasn't good. Said it would drive you crazy or kill you. Decent people didn't do it. Well . . . you did. You did it and liked it. And felt like hell, afterward. You'd outgrown that. Now the preacher said time to outgrow this other. Past time.

Sitting there under the big oak tree by the preacher, who breathed deep and steadily now, sweat rolling down his neck and forehead, legs spraddled out in comfort—Tracy tried to feel again what he had felt that night two months ago under the same oak tree, on the same old riverbank. But it wouldn't come. He remembered every word they had said, every moment they had been here—as if it had happened to someone else a hundred years ago. Nonnie was only a name today. A name and an obstacle. A colored girl blocking a white path.

*I've never asked much of you—you haven't given—anything. There's Dorothy . . . we've all wanted that—and you treat her like a cheap thing.*

There's Dorothy. Puseys lived across the street and you'd dated her all your life because she was near, and seemed to

97

like you all right. And now they blame you because she hasn't married—because she is twenty-five years old and has never married!

He touched the preacher's arm. "Reckon we better be going back," he said, and smiled at the startled face.

Reckon we better be going back to White Town. It hadn't worked. He'd come to the river to find her but she wasn't here.

Tracy drove quickly over the eight miles of pavement, slowed down as he once more entered the sand road. "I don't have much of a feeling for God," he said, "and all it seems to stand for in folks' minds. As for the church, it's not important to me. I don't know that I even believe in God."

"I know," the preacher said, and his heavy brows came together. "That's just what I was saying. That's the way it is with men like you. You're going cross-country—sort of cruising by yourself something you don't know what you're cruising . . . or won't do you any good to cruise, for there's no good timber there—climbing through palmettos, over fences and ditches, through the hammock. And along comes somebody and says, Son, you'll wear yourself out, plumb to death, fighting woods like that! Here, come round this thicket. There's the road, right before you. It's a lot easier on you to travel the road men have hewed out and made for themselves. It's a lot more satisfaction. And you might say, But I don't know where it leads. And I say, You don't know where this other leads either. But I know. And other white men know. It leads to death and worse than death. It leads to hell and damnation. And this road leads to life everlasting . . . and peace. And you can say back, Can you prove it? And I'll say No. I can't prove it. But I've tried it. It works. Thing to do is to git goin. When you once get going, faith comes. How it comes, I don't know. It's a mystery of God. But it comes. There're men all along the way that can tell you the same."

Tracy drove on. The preacher was silent now.

98

"If I didn't believe in God," he said after a time, "in a personal God, not just some theory—Deen, if I didn't believe in God the Father watching over me day and night, I'd be the meanest man in Georgia. I'd go on such a rampage . . ." The preacher suddenly sighed and rubbed his hands over his face. "You know, some men have the devil in them from the day they're born. And I'm one of them. Broke my poor mother's heart before I gave in. God help me, I put her in an early grave with my wild ways. Sometimes now when I get to thinking about it, I wonder how God has been so merciful to me, how He's been willing to reach down and save a good-for-nothing scoundrel like me."

Tracy was looking straight down the sand road.

"You haven't got that on your conscience. Don't get it there, boy, it's a hard thing to bear."

"I don't believe—anything," Tracy suddenly laughed, and his hand trembled as he lit a cigarette. "But if you did believe—how does a man get going?"

"For you, seems to me, would be like this: join the church, marry that fine little Pusey girl, set up housekeeping and make her a good living. That would be your way to begin. For other folks it might be different. Some I tell to get down on their knees and stay there until God lays His hand of mercy on their black hearts. Some I call to the altar, so they can prove to men that they mean what they say and in the proving give themselves strength to mean it. There's a way for every man. I've learned that."

Tracy turned the car into Oak Street, suddenly cut into Elm Street, headed toward the Harris home, where Brother Dunwoodie was staying.

"There's a colored girl—" he spoke abruptly, stopped.

Brother Dunwoodie let the car move a hundred yards before he answered. Let Deen drive slowly across the little wooden bridge that spanned the branch which ran through the Harrises' back field.

99

"Reckon when the merciful Lord listens to sinners down here, He hears that right often."

"She's going to have a baby."

"And what if she is? They all have em! Almost before they have their first sick-time!"

Tracy flushed. "I wouldn't want her to—have trouble."

"As far as I've been able to figure out—they don't." The preacher laughed shortly.

"I wouldn't want her to have trouble," Tracy said again low, and stopped the car at the Harrises' side gate.

"Then fix things! Find some good nigger you can count on to marry her. Give—"

God! If any nigger dared touch her, if any dared—

"—her some money. They all like money—all women like money, no matter what color! Give him some money too. To kindle a fire under him and get him moving fast. Get your Dorothy a ring. Go to her with your hands as clean as that fine little girl deserves, and ask her to marry you and marry you quick."

Tracy half smiled. "That the way you figure things out?"

"That's the way, Deen. And git goin." He said it a little roughly, but turned quickly and smiled and shook hands with the man who had forgotten to start the car. "There's a lot of important folks on your side," he called as he walked up the path under the big oaks in the Harrises' lawn, "and God's among them. Don't forget that."

"I'm much obliged to you, Brother Dunwoodie," Tracy said courteously and, starting the car, drove slowly around the corner to College Street and on to the yellow house where the Deens lived. He left the car in the driveway for his mother, skirted the house, quickly went to Henry's cabin.

100

# SEVEN

HENRY WAS SPRAWLED on the steps of the shed, sharpening pencils. He could no more than read his name and write it, but he liked pencils and kept one or two sharp ones on his bureau and on Tracy's desk no less than four or five.

Tracy did not stop but went inside. "Henry," he called, and sitting down near the window he opened his shirt. "Pour me a drink and be quick about it, for I reckon it's my last."

Henry laid his pencils on the step, eased through the door like a big black shadow.

"I'm joining the church," Tracy watched Henry's face.

Henry's mouth sagged until his bottom teeth showed. He reached for the jug, felt around with his big hand for the cup, never let his eyes leave the white man's face.

"We bof need plenty—ef dat what we doin. When us join up?"

Tracy drained the cup, threw back his head and laughed. He looked at big, black Henry a long time before he answered. "Boy, boy," he said softly, "whatever else . . ." He stared out of the back door, thin face sobered. Kept staring out the back door.

"Yassuh," Henry whispered.

"I don't reckon, you damned jackass, whatever else I did, I could do without you." He turned, smiled quickly at the Negro.

"Nossuh. I knowed dat since I kin remember."

Tracy lighted a cigarette.

Henry brought in the pencils. Laid them on the bureau. "When us join up?" Squatting now in front of the white man.

101

"Don't know."

"Why us got it to do?"

"God knows."

"But us is."

"Well, there's no hurry about it." He stared into Henry's wall, papered with a dozen years of funny papers.

Began to talk, still staring at the paper, "Things get you after a while. Everybody expecting you to— I've heard so damned many sermons—listened to so damned many revival songs all my life. It's not that you believe in all that— It's like ghosts and hants—you don't believe in them either."

Henry nodded a feeble negative.

"You know—your mind tells you they're impossible—they don't fit in with real life—in the sunlight it's easy but at night, if you were passing the graveyard and you saw a figure moving about among the graves you'd run your tail off, wouldn't you?"

"Gawd yes," Henry breathed.

Tracy laughed. "And like as not I would too."

"These things—hants—hell, they stand for something. I wish I knew what. There's an argument, a damned good argument against all this revival stuff, but trouble is, I don't know what it is. You'd think after we made fools of ourselves in the war, folks would be ashamed to hold revivals. And right now there's one going on in almost every town in the state. Henry, you ought to know the answer to all this."

Henry nodded slowly. "Yassuh, reckon so."

"You got out of the war. Must have had sense to do that."

Henry grinned. "Flat-footed. Born flat-footed, they said."

"Well, you see, I wasn't so smart. They got me."

"Told you, Mr. Tracy, to limp, told you dat, day you went to sign up."

"I'm not crippled." Tracy's voice was sharp.

"Course you ain't!" Henry said quickly, "but you is awful good at puttin on a limp, when you tries."

"Oh well, never mind all that." Tracy pu hed the cup away.

"Henry, what you think about God . . . that kind of thing?"

Henry shook his head, blinked a little.

"But everybody must have *some* idea about God. What's yours?"

"Mr. Tracy, you knows I don no mo know bout dat stuff—"

"Why you go to church? Why?"

Henry blinked at his white friend.

"You go to—worship?"

Henry stared hard at the cup near Tracy's foot. His mouth worked around in circles, he licked his lips, frowned. Then he giggled, figuring now that Tracy had chosen a new way to be funny. "Whooppee, boy! Dat a good one!" He slapped his thigh. "Sho is," he opened his mouth to give a loud guffaw that would compensate for his slowness in catching on.

"Cut out the funny business. I'm serious. Does God mean anything to you? You have any feeling about Him?"

Henry wiped his mouth on the back of his hand, then pulled at the crotch of his pants, one eye focused on Tracy's face while the other wavered helplessly in its periphery.

"Like for instance you have—for me?"

"Nossuh. Noth'n like dat—sho."

"Then why you go to church?"

Henry squinted. Big lips worked slowly as if he were reading a book in which all the words were new. He sighed, cut his eye around, chuckled, "Most time to git me a girl."

"I see. But there's—"

"Now ain't dat de Gawd's truf! Dis town plumb run dry of girls. Lemme tell you, I'm—"

103

"Oh for crap's sake cut it out! We're not talking women. We're talking—well . . ." Tracy laughed, picked up the cup, looked in it, put it down. "We're talking about getting converted and joining the church. What do they mean by it, you reckon?"

Henry knew now that Tracy was talking to himself.

"Dog ef I know."

"Henry—"

"Yassuh."

Tracy slowly pushed the cup along the floor crack. "Are you afraid of—" he laughed, let the cup be still, "hell . . . things like that?"

"Sweet Jesus," Henry's voice was low, "now you said it! What you reckon hell is like, sho 'nough? How it gon burn you forever—how it gon do dat, Mr. Tracy?"

"There's no such place, so why all the worry?"

"You mean—"

"You heard me."

"But da Bible, hit say it, don it—and sho yo ma and pa. How come you say dat? How come?"

"Because it's a goddam lie! Thought up by folks who want you to do their way. That's all. Want to control you. You know it's that and then when they give you the works—

"Makes me think of France. There we'd be—somewhere, hungry and cold and sleepy, itching like the devil—and I'd think suddenly, what the hell am I doing here? What's it all about? Then before you could finish thinking it, somebody would be ordering you to attack—you'd be attacking you didn't know what, running you didn't know where, shells bursting around you, men dying, and then quick as it started it would be over, you'd be back in the trenches—if you were lucky—scratching and cold and hungry—still wondering what it was all about. That's the way I feel now. Two weeks ago we were talking about fishing. Things like that. Now—"

104

"Let's go, Mr. Tracy! Hit'd do us a sight of good to go fishin a little. They bitin fine today." He went to the door, looked up at the sky.

"Now," Tracy went on softly, "we're talking about joining the church and God—"

You could hear Mrs. Deen start the car, go slowly out of the driveway, up College Street, to the meeting.

"If you could stop long enough to think, you'd know there's no sense to any of it." Tracy stared out of the window, laid his cigarette on the ledge, buried his face in his hands.

Henry studied the white man.

"How in hell you reckon us got mixed up wid all dem things?"

Tracy looked up, grinned. "I just don't know."

"How about disrememberin and goin fishin?"

"No. Reckon I'll go to the service. I don't know why I'm going, but I might as well go."

"Sho ain goin wid dat likker on yo bref. Hit'll fill a whole tent and ruin you wid yo ma."

Tracy paused.

"Here—you gon wash out yo mouf good." Henry put a teaspoonful of soda in a cup and added some water. "Rench yo mouf out an gargle."

"You big fool," Tracy laughed, took the cup, went to the back door.

"Ef you done wid dat—here," Henry was by Tracy's side now, "blow in ma face."

"Get out my way!"

"Blow in ma face like I tell you. Blow!

"Hit ain no good," Henry said. He frowned, went back in the cabin. "Here," he said, coming out again, "take a bite of dis gum."

"For crap's sake! Where you get the dirty stuff?"

"In my bureau."

105

"Put it back. Half-dozen roaches bedded a year on it. Where's your eyes? They'll have a nervous breakdown when they find it gone."

"Take it, Mr. Tracy."

Tracy threw it out of the door, walked back into the cabin, fastened his shirt collar. "Henry, why on earth don't you clean out this hole?"

"I been intendin one of dem cleanings since befo you come home from dat Europe war. But now you come, I ain had a minute to do nothin cept pick up atter you." Henry grinned widely and slapped his thigh in silent mirth.

"You mighty funny," Tracy said, "but if Mother stepped inside this cabin and saw this filth she'd burn it down over your head."

"Yassuh. But Miz Deen ain comin, I reckon. She keep so busy."

"Whether she comes or not, clean it up."

"Yassuh."

It was a well-built but old one-room cabin that Henry lived in, set in the Deens' back yard, close to the woodshed and the old abandoned privy. A brick fireplace on the north end, a window on the south, were the only variants to the walls lined with funny papers.

Above the mantel hung an oval frame containing two small photographs of Mamie and Ten McIntosh, Henry's parents. The picture of Ten had been taken before his leg was crushed by a log at the Harris sawmill—and subsequently amputated—and showed him to be a stalwart, iron-muscled, bulletheaded, long-armed, sober Negro of whom his son was an exact replica, save for his smaller eyes and big laughing mouth. Ten McIntosh was never known to laugh much at white folks' doings. Mamie's face, more placid, more patient, smiled from its frame at the world, white and colored alike. Mamie always got on with folks. She had cooked for the Deens from the time they married; her boy had been

106

born in their back yard six months before the Deens' son, and she had nursed them both, hardly knowing which was her own, as she used to say.

Tracy looked at Mamie's picture hanging there above the mantel. Mamie had one jagged tooth and a space where two had been knocked out by Ten in one of his gloom spells. And there was a scar on her hand where she had spilled scalding water when hurrying supper one night. Tracy remembered this even now, twenty years after. He remembered her faint clean body smell like a pile of fresh-ironed sheets and he remembered her rich sweet smell on Sundays, when dressed in black silk she left the yard to go to church-meeting. He remembered her deep full breasts. There had been a time when her lap was wide enough for him and her Henry both to crawl up in. She'd sit there, knees spread wide, jogging them from side to side, singing vague sounds, breaking off, taking up after a little where she had left off, sometimes reaching down for a corner of her big white petticoat to wipe one nose and the other. Knees jogging slowly, easing them back and forth, cradling them from time and its bitterness, glazing eyes with peace. Tune moving on, on, on, and body moving with it, and all the world no wider, no deeper than the space her knees enclosed—no wider than that, and no colder than the heat from her breast.

There had been a time when he was sick and no food would stay on his stomach, and Mamie had fixed little odd things, and sometimes had chewed them for him and slipped them into his mouth and he had felt better. He remembered his mother used to say after that, "The child won't eat for anybody but Mamie," or when he was hurt, "Nobody can quiet him but Mamie."

He remembered these things, as you look at clouds moving across a quiet sky, circling, coming close together, passing each other, moving in close again, almost making something of themselves, something that should have meaning

107

for you; breaking apart suddenly and meaning nothing at all.

But he did not remember, though it waited for a day to come back to him, the bad time when she whipped her Henry.

Henry was eight then and Tracy seven.

They were racing up and down the sidewalk. They'd chalked a line across it and were running, sliding to base. A little white girl on a bicycle was wheeling down the walk, arms up, face flying through space and cool air.

"Move, move, move!" she shrieked. And Henry, feeling the rush of air, the sting of flying, the thrilling power of speed, shrieked back, "Move, move, move, yourself!" and blocked the way, colliding with wheel and girl.

She had fallen, scratching her leg against the pedal.

"How dare you!" she said low, all the flying, the whistling air gone, only heaviness to breathe now. "How dare you do that!"

"Ha," Henry laughed, "ha ha ha ha!" he laughed, knowing nothing else to do, "ha ha ha—"

And Tracy laughed too, glad to see a girl fall, glad to see it happen, though he did not know why.

Mamie was sitting on the side steps, cooling off, resting a spell before starting her supper. Now she saw something she had to tend to. "You—Henry McIntosh, come here!" she called, standing, ease gone from her placid face. "Come here dis minute!"

Henry came and Tracy came with him, unused to the sound in Mamie's voice.

"I got to whip you," she said and hushed. And the two children stood there in the back yard and waited while Mamie went out to the garden and cut her a good heavy sprout from the pecan tree. They stood there and watched her strong wide back move resistlessly through space that enclosed all they knew of living, moving now sharply, drawing new lines they had not known before. They waited until

108

she came back with the switch, took Henry by the shirt, bent him over her knee and whipped him so hard that Tracy burst into sobs and covered his eyes from the sight though he could not make himself leave the sound of it.

Mamie whipped her boy. She whipped him, saying, "I got to learn it to you, you heah! I got to. You can't look at a white gal like dat, you can't tech one, you can't speak to one cep to say yes mam and thanky mam. Say it atter me. Say it!" And Henry, squalling and catching his breath in strangling gasps, said it after her, word for word, three times, as she urged him on, tapping his legs with the tip of the switch as he said it. Then black legs whitened by the lash of his lesson, snuffling and dazed, he ran into the cabin and like a shamed dog crawled under the bed.

Mamie's big brown hands took the switch and slowly broke it to pieces, and the sound of the breaking was something hard to listen to. Then she hurled them with sudden fury away from her. Her hands fell to her sides. She stood there staring across the roof of the big yellow house in front of her. Stared so long that the small white boy watching her thought she must not be able to find what she looked for. Slowly she sat down on the steps . . . wrapped her hands in her apron . . . lips pulled down with the weight of her thinking . . . slowly she laid her face in her lap.

"Mamie," Tracy had said the word with no idea behind it, "Mamie."

She looked up, brown face wet with her crying, and twisted. "Go!" she said, "go to your *own folks!*" she said. And he turned and ran quickly, cut to the bone by the new strange words.

But though he had run quickly he had not been able to get away from her words. They followed him into the house, drove him through the big rooms, made him wander, a lost thing, from side to side of a room, touching table, chair, wall, reaching down once to feel the floor though he didn't

109

know why he was feeling it, stretching, until he ached all over, to fill the empty dimensions of a life he had not chosen and did not know the size of and into which her words told him he must go and stay forever. . . .

He stopped at his mother's room—hearing her voice—opened the door, stood waiting. Alma was reading a big picture book to his baby sister, who solemnly listened. Seemed she was always reading picture books.

"Come in, Son," she said quietly and smiled as he stood there. He went to her, leaned on her chair, uncertain, anxious to do what would please her.

"You reading?"

"Yes, would you like to listen?"

"Yes mam," he said and stared at the picture, trying to find in its lines and planes and colors what he looked for.

Alma went on reading, answering little Laura's questions, laughing with her, showing her the pictures. Their words and voices and movements began to shut out the emptiness, shut out the bigness he had felt lost in; and he leaned closer, hungry now to push through this wall of softness and warmth and get in there with them.

"Don't lean so hard, Son," Alma said kindly, "you're so hot and sticky. And smelly—when have you had a bath?"

"This morning."

"I don't see how you and Henry can get so dirty. You must take another at bedtime." She went on with her reading.

Tracy moved away. Went to his mother's dressing table, lifted a mirror, put it down; moved the brush, moved it back; picked up the comb, put it in the brush; picked up a box of hairpins and dropped it, spilling the pins over table and chair and floor.

"Oh, Tracy! Now pick them up. If you don't want to listen, dear, why not go out and play?"

"He bad boy," said Laura, nodding her head in solemn

disapproval. And Alma laughed softly at the child's prattle and went on with the reading.

Tracy picked up the pins, moved quickly to where his mother was sitting, jerked the book from her, threw it on the floor. "I hate books!" he said, "I don't like her either," he said and gave Laura a hard push, then rushed from the room, through the hall, out on the side porch and stood there, breathing heavily, expecting his mother to follow and punish him, hoping she would follow and whip him, whip him hard as Mamie had whipped Henry. But she did not come.

After a time he heard Mamie's heavy clump-clump on the back steps. He heard the screen door open and close, heard her put down a load of wood in the box behind the stove, lift the stove lid, scratch a match, start her fire for supper. And unable longer to endure, he ran into the kitchen, stopped short inside the door, suddenly could not go farther.

Mamie turned. She held a piece of pine kindling in her hand, and her skirt had caught on the corner of the wood box. They stood there, a distance great between them, terrifying and strange and measureless between them. A floor that would not bear their weight to cross it.

Words formed in his mind and he opened his mouth to say them. "Mamie!" he whispered. He couldn't remember the others.

She laid down the wood, turned toward him, took a slow step. And now he was running. He buried his face against her, trying to keep the sound of his trouble in the apron. Through dress and petticoat he felt her leg and held on to it.

They didn't try words. She ran her fingers through his hair, over his head. He clung to the old leg until she almost lost her balance with the weight of him against her.

The small flame crackled, licked the air above the pot opening, pushing wisps of smoke through the room.

"Go git him and make him play," she said after a little. "Go git him," she said softly.

Tracy was glad to be told what to do. He ran to the backyard cabin, and into the room, crawled under the bed. "Come on," he said, "we going to play." And Henry obeyed the voice and crawled out, swollen-faced and bleary-eyed and stiff-jointed, and they went back to the lane and gravely played, and slowly the blood moved as blood ought to move in young veins, and after a while they laughed and yelled at each other. And the evening was like any other evening by the time Mamie rang the bell for supper.

When Ten came home from the mill he saw Henry's swollen face and asked questions that had to be answered. Henry said his lesson, for he had learned it well; and Ten listened, glum and tired as twelve hours in the sawmill can make you tired.

So it was easy—when supper was over and they had come back to the cabin—to let first quiet questions to Mamie turn quickly into all the words that hate and shame can form on a man's tongue.

"So you beats yo boy half to death cause you thinks white folks like dat."

"I learn him how to behave."

"You beats yo boy like he trash to please white folks."

"I learn him how to behave, Ten. He got to learn. You know dat!"

Tracy and Henry, playing in the dark yard outside, drew near the words like bits of steel to a magnet.

"You beat da sperrit outn him. He won't be a man fit fo nothin."

"Ten—our boy sassed a white gal."

"What ef he did! She sassed him first, I reckon. He's a good boy," Ten said, "good as any white gal in this goddam town. Say a word and folks beat you to death. Gawd help us, his own ma turns on him an—"

112

"Ten, I wants my boy to live till he's grown," Mamie's low voice did not rise against the high brittle sound of Ten's words. "I want him to *live!* He got to learn. He got to learn how to git along. He got to learn what he can't do. He got to learn there's white folks and colored folks and things you can't do ef you wants to live. Jesus help me, I'm goin to learn it to him."

"You goin to keep yo hands offn him! You hear! You tetch him again count of white folks an I'll beat you till you can't git offn da floor. He good as anybody, you hear! Good as anybody!" Words so heavy they seemed to fall back on his own chest as he said them.

"He ain good as white folks. I got to learn him dat. I gotta do it, Ten!"

"Gawd Jesus, I hate the sight of one! Hate livin in Deen's back yard. Told you a hundard time it'd be better in the quarters where we'd be free to do as we like. I don want ma boy brung up wid no white boy—don want none of it!"

"They's good to us, Ten."

"Good to us!"

"Good as they knows *how* to be."

"Tell you, I hate the sight of one!" And Ten walked quickly to the mantel and picked up the blue and white glass vase that once had been in the Deens' parlor and was now Mamie's one fine house ornament and hurled it to the floor, smashing it into a hundred fragments. You could hear the ring of the broken pieces, clashing as they rolled on the floor.

"Lawd, Lawd," she cried and hushed quickly, and now her hands sought her apron, twisting it in a tight knot as she stood looking at her husband.

And Ten satisfied a little, eased a little now, walked out on the shed and squatted there, staring into the dark yard.

Mamie found the broom, slowly swept the pieces into a paper and put them in her apron, followed him to the shed.

"Hit's easy to break things, Ten," she said, "mighty easy to break things. Ain't easy to mend em up again. Dat what I want my boy to learn early. Want him to learn early dat *no matter what,* white folks is always right! And you treats em *always respectful.*"

"It means I'm white," Tracy whispered, "and you're black," eyes never leaving the shed where the two stood talking, deep shadows against the lamplighted cabin. "It means," he went on and he felt a strange new swelling pride rising in him, "I'm always right, I reckon."

"How come?" asked Henry dully.

"Cause I'm white—you heard Mamie!"

"Do skin make the diffunce?"

"Reckon so," Tracy said, losing his new confidence a little, "yep, reckon it do."

Black boy and white boy stood there in the darkness, watching the grown folks' trouble, and slowly Henry turned and went to the cabin, and slowly Tracy went to the big yellow house.

After Ten lost his leg they moved to Baxley, for Mamie and Ten together could look after a little patch of cotton while Ten settin around in the Deens' back yard with nothin on his mind, as Mamie said, jes got black-sad bout things and made a grumblin world for everybody. They moved to Baxley when Henry was thirteen and left him living in the Deens' back yard. It was not easy to leave him there, for Ten was dead-set against it. Mamie made no argument, wanting only peace in her family, but she told Mrs. Deen she wished her boy could stay here where he could get a little schooling and be around folks who knows things. She made no argument with Ten, for all he would say is, "I ain leavin my boy in no white folks' yard." The day came for them to leave. Uncle Pete's wagon had been borrowed to cart their baskets and the old trunk and the boxes and Mamie's rocking-chair to the depot. Everything was piled high on it, Mamie was dressed in her good black dress, and Ten in his Sunday suit and Henry in his Sunday suit and his new shoes. Tracy was at the wagon, helping them put in the last box and suitcase. The two boys were strangely quiet as they ran back and forth, never looking at each other, lifting and loading and doing all the last things that a final leaving requires of folks. Suddenly Henry dropped the old suitcase he was lifting into the wagon, sat down on it and began to blubber; and Tracy began to cry too. Both of them like little children, with no attempt to hide their tears. Mamie was already on the wagon seat, sitting primly with her hat on, and her hands, in their black cotton gloves, folded in her lap. She looked at Ten, looked at the crying boys, looked at Ten, her placid face suddenly set in its rarely determined lines. She crawled down, pulled out the old box in which Henry's things had been packed, unfastened a basket, pulled out two quilts, handed them to Henry. She looked at Ten again, who looked away.

"You stayin here, Henry," she said firmly, "and you to mind Miz Deen. She to be the same as yo ma, you hear! She say somethin, you do it. You to tote in the wood, and do what she say and go to school when school takes in, come November. You to mind, you hear?" And firmly she kissed him and crawled back up to the seat of the wagon, eyed her husband sharply, turned back and waved at her son whom she had left to grow up in the Deens' back yard.

Henry had grown up there. He did what his mother told him to do. He toted wood, he went to school when school took in come November, he made the fires; and there was plenty of time for him and Tracy to play together. Sometimes they'd go fishing, and sometimes at nights, Tracy would go out and study his lessons in the little cabin by Henry's fireplace, to keep him company. But sometimes, if you happened to step out on the Deens' back porch, you'd see a boy lying on his stomach in a cabin all alone, staring into the fire, mouth a little open, eyes staring into the flames, as the light flickered across a face that looked as if it had never quite belonged to anybody.

Tracy turned from the picture of Mamie smiling down upon him from the mantelpiece, and looked now at her son.

"When have you heard from Aunt Mamie?"

"Hit's been a time."

"When have you written?"

Henry laughed.

"You scoundrel, you haven't written."

"I aims to. Seem like ain never no news to tell her. Fust time some'n happens, I aims to write."

Tracy laughed again, started toward the door. "Better be getting along."

"Wait a minute," Henry bounded over to a flower bed, gathered a handful of mint. "Fill yo mouf wid it. Hold it tight, den spit it out."

Tracy took a sprig, chewed a leaf or two, left the little cabin where he had spent so much of his life.

# EIGHT

OUT OF THE BACK DOORS went the cooks home to Colored Town. Some with bundles under their arms for the family they'd left there. Toting or not toting; no one paid much mind. Slow and heavy-footed, or sashaying along, tongues darting words at every black passer-by, or silent and

116

still—they went to the cabins rimming the town, a shadow behind Maxwell.

College Street children played under big oaks, running after lightning bugs as the dusk came on. And the few men who had lingered uptown now locked up, stopped by the post office, went south to their homes.

North of the depot, in Tom Harris's milltown, folks sat in chairs under chinaberry trees, shifted their snuff, spat into the road, chewed slow their tobacco. Smell of sawdust and tar in the air, and smoke from the dry-kiln black against the sky.

"Well," Mollie Echols said to the others, "who's going to the meeting?"

"Not me," her husband said, "not me. No goddam meeting for me. I don't aim to listen to Tom Harris thank the Lord another time for being so good to him. How about me? Why ain't God good to me? I say!"

"Well, I wouldn't go taking the Lord's name in vain just because you don't think Tom Harris treats you right!" Mollie eased her chafed breast up a little. "You know well as me hit's a sight worse to do that than what you's accusin him of."

"I don't aim to go," Willie said. "Shore don't aim to. All them College Street folks with their airs and their money! No goddurned revival for me. Not if the preacher was to climb the tent pole like he done before, I'd not go. Even if he was to set up there a week, I'd not go!" And Willie's thin angry face twisted into a grin as he spat into the road.

"I tell you, you goin to be punished for talking thataways, God will call you to account for it sure as the world!"

"He don't mean it, Mollie," Lewis said softly and eased the stump of his leg to the edge of the cart for a little air.

"Willie's all time talking crazy talk about wages!"

"Call it crazy! That's right. Call it crazy!"

"He pays you much as he pays the others, don't he?" And

117

Mollie shifted the weight of her two hundred pounds from one hip to the other.

"Shore he does. Exactly enough to starve on. And talking about shutting the mills down now because business is slackin a little. What we need is a union!"

"Listen at him! Ain't he wild! Talking like them Russia folks!"

"Sometimes I've thought we'd do the same as him if we was in his place," Lewis said, and lifted the other stub of leg to the edge of the cart for a cooling.

"I'd shore like to be in his place," Willie said. "That's right. I'd shore like to have the chance to be there." And Willie coughed and having begun, coughed on and on.

"Now see! What I tell you! Letting yourself get all upset over nothing's brung on your old coughing spell. Ever since I knowed Willie," Mollie sighed, "he's been wanting something he couldn't get. And J. L.'s goin to be just like him. Ain't satisfied with nothin!"

Cena eased the snuff from her lower lip, let it drop to the sand. "If they warn't so many niggers, might be folks would git more money."

"Way they streaking north now won't soon be no niggers."

The older man, Lewis, was watching the smoke from the dry-kiln, letting his eyes drift with the sparks in the darkening evening. He turned, looked at the two women. "Willie and me'll just set here and let you women folks go to the preaching. I'm sorter lazy, I reckon, don't seem like I want to walk that far." And Lewis smiled at his old joke as he sat there in the go-cart, legless for eight months, since he got caught in the saw belt.

"If Willie wasn't so no-count, he'd push you down to the tent and let you hear the preaching. Hit'd do you good to hear it. The man can shore preach, he can make you see hell and torment so plain, I declare, it gives you the shivers. Preacher Dunwoodie's got the power, if I ever heard it. He's

118

got the power of the Holy Ghost in him." And Mollie called J. L. and the other younguns from the spur track and with her friend Cena started toward the tent.

In the south of town on College Street and the side streets, men slowly rose from porch chairs, saying, "Well . . . it's about time for the meeting. Must be." And waited in their cars while the women powdered their faces and freshened up a little. Then they drove up College Street, stopping now and then to pick up a neighbor.

The town quivered, a great hollow bowl, struck by its guilty conscience. Whether you came to the tent or stayed at home you could not escape the meeting. A few hardened their hearts, and others smiled uneasily saying, "This kind of thing is for the ignorant." But only Editor Reid said boldly, "There is no God," and even Editor Reid did not add, "There is no sin." Men knew they had sinned and a dread of God's anger lay upon them. Only old Brother Graves who had had the Second Blessing could say tranquilly, "I am without guilt." And even his triumphant testimony to God's power to rid the human heart of temptation was marred by Sister Graves' twisting her shoulders noisily against the back of the pew as he testified.

The song had changed now to *What a Friend We Have in Jesus*. The pianist was jazzing the rhythm, urged on by the enthusiasm of Brother Trimble. Mill people were filling the left benches, people from College Street and the side streets hesitated, settled on the right. The two benches in the dark corner reserved for the colored folks were empty save for the Reverend Livingston. He had not been able to persuade Roseanna to come with him, though others would, when their work was done, join him and listen to the white folks' preacher talk about the white folks' God. And sitting there on their Jim Crow benches would sing the white folks' songs; would go and feel good in the going, for they knew their

119

place and humbly accepted a white God as they accepted His white children.

But some, like Bess, had not found it easy to mind their manners when the white folks invited them to gather up the crumbs from their Lord's feast. "Reckon I'm choosy," Bess said to Non, after Mrs. Stephenson had invited her to attend, "but when I pick a God, I'll pick a black one, black and kinky-headed! So black," she'd laughed but there were tears in the sound, "that He'll scare the wits out of white folks. Some day I'm afraid I'll blow up and say things Mama used to tell us she'd wear us out for saying. Sometimes," she whispered to Nonnie, "I'm afraid I'll—" she stopped, turned to her small son, who gaped at her in plaintive fascination, "Jackie, I've told you six times to go to bed!"

Non stood at the gate and listened. Across White Town came the singing. Yes, Bess was angry with the white folks.

Non thought now about her plump little sister. So plainly she could see her: honey-colored, worry lines around her gray eyes deepening these past months, a mouth that used to be wide open in laughter or talk, set now in tight lines . . . Bess had stopped singing, though she used to sing all the time and used to talk of some day singing maybe up North on the stage. But now she didn't talk any more about the stage and she didn't sing any more either. Bess was a cream-colored little luster jug, squat and pleasing, who longed to be a fancy crystal vase. If she could know the relief of letting things *be!* Non hadn't minded when Mrs. Brown spoke to her about the meeting. They don't mean any harm, these white folks, when they say things like this. No harm, really. You can forget them, so easily, if you've a mind to. You can forget everything except the one thing that matters to you. It'd always seemed strange that people like Bess could get upset over so many things. As if everything in the world you looked at was of the same height and size and shape and you

120

wanted it all instead of the one big thing you really wanted.

Nonnie heard her coming now down the path. The rapid thud of her feet through the dusk was as familiar as katydids and screech owls, as the rustle of palmettos.

Once she tried to tell Bess what the night meant to her but Bess said, "Listen. If it's good, don't waste it on me! Put it down and sell it. They'll buy anything a Negro writes these days, so surprised we can spell." All the nights of her life she had listened for Bess's quick steps on the path, and after her, their mother's slow, heavy ones. Sometimes in the old days, when they were late coming from work the house back of her would grow big and empty, its verandas would creak with ancient talk, and she would turn her back to it and look straight toward White Town. She would hold tight to the picket fence while the night sounds poured into her ears, and only when she separated from them that first quick thud of Bess's step would her hands loosen. Bess would say as she opened the gate, "Have you done your lessons, Nonnie? Where's Eddie?" And Mummie would say in her deep slow voice, "How's my baby? Give Mama a kiss, sugar lump."

She had feared the night and loved it. Like the swamp. All her life she had been afraid of it, afraid of the swamp and the night, of their loneliness. And yet they were a part of her, as was no living creature, except Tracy. Except Tracy. Except Tracy and his child. She put her hands where she knew the baby lay. She tried to imagine it as it would be when it came. Of course it would be like him. It must *be* him . . . She had forgotten the night. She was holding her baby, and Tracy was there, and somehow things had come clear in their life, defined, unmistakable. And he had reached out and touched it and whispered, "It's exactly like you, only my eyes of course." And they both were laughing. It was like her— creamy skin, dark curls, but plump and soft against her hands. And it turned and solemnly looked at them both and

121

its eyes were blue, like Tracy's—happy, not troubled like his. Always they'd be happy eyes—she'd see to that—never—

The dream ended. Tracy . . . so far away tonight. It was as if she could never again bridge the distance. Thinking of him now made the distance greater, as if something were pulling him away and she could only stand and watch his going. She was cold and afraid. The swamp behind her, the night, were ugly and threatening. The rattle of palmettos near the fence, an evil sound. Maybe she was wrong. Maybe she had made it all up. Maybe it wasn't any of it real—hers and Tracy's life together. Maybe Bess was right when she said as she said so often, "Non, you don't know what real life is!" When she had thought she knew the only real thing there was in life for her . . .

Bess's steps grew near, and the sound of them quickly steadied her. Tracy needed her. She had to hold to that. Needed her, and cared. Nothing could change that. Nothing anyone could do or say could change that. She must not worry about foolish, imaginary things, making up dangers, like Bess, to scare herself with.

Bess said as she reached the gate, "Where's Jackie?"

"At Miss Ada's. I'll run over for him. You're late."

"Supper was late. Everything wrong today. Even my dinner didn't please, though God knows the preacher ate enough. Lord, I'm hot! I—Nonnie, you look half sick!"

Nonnie smiled at her sister's searching glance. Ed would say, "Old Bess, drumming up trouble."

"I'm well and happy and hope you're the same," she laughed and suddenly felt that she was.

"Well, they're not! The Stephensons. Mighty upset over something. Tried all day to figure it out. Know I sound dirty-minded, but I believe Grace is going to have a baby."

"Oh, Bess—she's a child!"

"Mrs. Stephenson found out today she'd missed her period two months. Took her to Dr. Deen. They came back like ghosts." She shifted the bundle in her hand and slapped at a mosquito. "Lord, think of it! Raised three daughters, got them safely married off. Now this."

Nonnie was silent.

"Always nuzzling around her folks. You wouldn't think she'd be up to tricks like that, would you?" Bess shifted the package under her arm.

Nonnie said, "I'm pregnant too."

Bess stared at her. "I don't believe you."

"Yes."

It was a long time before Bess spoke again. "Tracy?"

"Yes."

"I knew . . . I've always known he'd ruin you."

"I'm not ruined. I'm happy. Very happy," she added softly.

Bess stared at her. "I believe you think he loves you," she whispered.

"Yes."

"But, Nonnie—" she stopped. Began again, "You're such a fool! How *could* you be such a fool? Going to college and everything! You'd think you were some little country nigger like Dessie who'd never had a chance— You *know* no white man—you know, Nonnie, no white man loves a— And I've tried so hard to look after you—" Bess's voice broke.

"You have looked after me, honey."

"A fine mess I've made of it! Oh, Nonnie, how *could* you! After all Mama— Even if he loved you and respected you what good'd it do, with you colored! What *good*, tell me that!"

"Let me talk a minute. I know Tracy lives in a white world. I know what that means for him and I've accepted it. It was hard—" her voice faltered, grew more certain, "at first . . . but . . . I know he will have to live in that life. I—" she paused, went on, "understand that. It won't change things for us. It can't." Suddenly she began to tremble.

"It can't! God Jesus, you say it can't! What do you think love is—a charm you wear around your neck? You don't know

**123**

what's ahead of you. You haven't any idea! And a baby! Lord God, what chance would a child have—how could you want to bring one into this world and subject it to— Trouble is, Non, you won't admit this world! But it'll make you admit it sooner or later. It'll pound you and beat you over the head until it gets you down on your knees, begging it to—"

"I know what's ahead, Bess."

"You'd make me laugh, if I weren't so sick.

"You won't have the courage to see it through," there seemed no end to Bess's words, tumbling out as if freed from a too-long restraint, "and don't you dare tell me others have! Just look at our skin! What does it mean to you, that color— just a pretty shade? You know what it meant to the women back of us—you've got to know, Non! Shame and degradation and heartbreak. Now here you are—as well educated as any girl in this town—as Laura Deen, his own sister, Non! Mama saw to that with her hard labor. You can't be satisfied with a concubine's life—that's what you'll be, that's the Bible name. There're worse—God knows—and you'll hear them all before you're through."

"There're back ways to happiness," Nonnie said softly, "and the Negro knows them all."

"You make me sick!"

"Please, Bess."

"I mean it. I could vomit. In slavery maybe, in those bad years afterward, folks had to find back ways. Had to! Not now. We've got to follow American ways. We've got to be respectable. We *are* respectable, Non. Our folks were decent people—fine good people. Biddy, don't you see! We're on Main Street now even if white folks do push us off the sidewalk. We're there! We've got to stay there."

Nonnie's unyielding silence whipped Bess on to more words. "Better do like me, marry a porter—a plain ordinary— Guess that's why—" She paused as a great wave of song from the big tent swept over the town, backwashing against the

124

swamp edge. "Guess that's why you're looking for something you think's better. Well, it isn't better!" She turned fiercely on her sister. "Always, Nonnie, you've wanted things better than you could have—"

Nonnie touched Bess's arm. "I don't think anyone could be better than Jack, Bess. Grinding ahead, the way he does, waiting on people, emptying spittoons—"

"Yes, but you don't want *your* man emptying spittoons, that's it, isn't it? Well, let me tell you, I don't want mine doing it either, but he's Negro and that's all he can find to do. You hear that! There's nothing else!" She paused, went on, "God knows it's better than being a white do-nothing like—"

"Don't let's fuss, honey. You know what I think of Jack. I've always thought him the finest—"

"Oh God, I wish I did," Bess groaned. She said very quietly after a moment, "When he's away I see it. When he comes home I don't do a thing but give him the devil. He wants to have a big time. I want to settle everything that's come up while he's been away. We end by telling each other to go to hell." She laughed tremulously.

"But he understands you," Non whispered.

Across town the music had grown mournful.

"They're having the propositions," Bess whispered.

*Just as I am, without one plea*
*But that Thy blood was shed for me*
*And that Thou bidd'st me come to Thee*
*Oh Lamb of God, I come, I come.*

You could fill in the words you couldn't hear. Anybody born in Georgia could fill in the words.

Tracy was there, sitting on the back seat with Gus Rainey and the boys, listening to the music, listening as that preacher talked about hell and its torment, listening as he begged sin-

125

ners to take this last chance to make themselves right with God. But he wouldn't be moved by it. No. He'd told her too many times no preacher could ever get him worked up again. He'd sit there, rubbing his fingers up and down the wood of the pew, a half smile on his lips. He wouldn't be moved by it—

And then Nonnie's mind filled with Tracy's white world. Tall lady with the square jaws . . . little thin Dorothy Pusey he had gone with since high-school days . . . Laura so aloof, so hurting to his pride . . . burning-eyed evangelist raising ghosts with black-magic words. She saw Tracy, young sixteen-year-old Tracy as he told her once how he felt when he got converted and in the telling of it had grown restless and troubled . . . telling her how when he was twelve, he had not been able to sleep at night during a revival because of a dread of dying. And then she saw him as he had come to her six months ago, drunk after a fuss with his mother. . . . And suddenly it seemed to her that she had already lost him— that between her and him great white waves were growing higher, pressing him back, farther and farther—

*Just as I am, without one plea . . .*

—farther and farther—

They were singing it again. That meant the preacher was calling them again to the altar, that—

Bess said, "They've learned to do it better than we do. More efficient—more gloom to scare you with."

"Oh Lamb of God," how easily the words wove themselves into her aching mind, "don't let them do it—don't let them do it—"

"Well, let's leave them to their sins and go inside."

They turned toward the dark house.

"Lord, how my corn hurts! Here," Bess caught hold of Non's arm, "hold this." She gave Non the bag, stooped, took off her shoes and stockings, wriggled her toes in the sand, sighed. "They didn't touch supper. She told me to take what

126

I wanted. Thought we might as well enjoy the funeral food. Didn't know I had one on my hands here."

"You haven't. Tracy and I'll work it out."

"Tracy!"

Bess reached the steps, sat down. "Before you go for Jackie, sit here a minute and listen to me. Now how long since?"

"Nine weeks."

"We'll have an abortion. Sam—if he'll do it. If not, Aunt Mag. Whoever does it, I'll be there to see everything's clean. We'll manage it, Biddy, right away."

Nonnie saw Bess press the back of her neck in the old gesture of strain. The house was terribly still as she searched for an answer, as if her unsaid words had cut it off from the night sounds. She wanted to give Bess peace, to accept her sacrificial offering; but she had no words to explain why she could not, so she said simply "I've got to have my baby, Bess."

Bess did not answer, and Non knew she had turned her face toward the clump of cannas because she couldn't keep her chin still. She watched the fingers move in the old rubbing gesture against her neck.

Bess felt around for her shoes, picked up the package, started into the house.

Non whispered, "I'll go for Jackie."

It was almost dark on the back path and she walked quickly, running from this talk with Bess, from these doubts released by their words.

Jackie was asleep. Miss Ada had put him on her bed and spread a piece of mosquito netting over him and sat now at the open door. Across the pauper lot, edging the back side of the cemetery, in the pale afterglow, the Massey tombs held three thin white shafts against the sky, and at these, or beyond them, Miss Ada stared as she bit her nails and rocked her straight chair with a tap-tap-tap against the wall. Her gray hair was hanging loose about her shoulders and she wore her old pink Mother Hubbard. In haste she gnawed her nails

127

as if it were a task to be done so other tasks could begin, but her gaze across the graveyard was slow and fixed as the passing of time. So she had looked for years; so she would continue to look and no one would know, no one would ever want to know the dull adumbrations of thought that stirred like heavy moths behind that old face.

Nonnie leaned against the boxwood, feeling its rough sturdiness, its age, feeling within herself an awakening as if eyelids long closed had opened. She knew now that Miss Ada, the old dope fiend who had frightened her as a little girl, who even yesterday had been someone to pity smilingly and to be gentle with, was herself. Herself projected into a past, and an inexorable future. She had often wondered in idleness what manner of man Miss Ada had loved. She had heard white folks say they'd never understand Miss Ada, grieving her heart out for Syd Rogers. As pretty a girl as she had been could've picked a half dozen that would have averaged up a sight better and could've had them for a glance. But they did not know what Nonnie knew in sudden divination of the truth, that there could have been no one else for Miss Ada, no picking of the "best," for there was no one else in her world. No fibers twisting about in rich soil, sucking up nourishment where it could be found, no taproot reaching downward into the deep earth of old biological satisfactions. They were parasites, she and Miss Ada—Nonnie tried to smile but instead began to tremble—like the Spanish moss, like the tree ferns in the swamp, living off their one love, nourished by it, until it died; living off it still, slowly dying as it rotted and shriveled, becoming ash with its ash.

"Miss Ada," she whispered, and repeated it aloud, "Miss Ada."

The paper-yellow face was a blur in the dusk, and only the tap-tap of the chair gave life to the old house, set in a greenness that age and decay bring, now turned black in the night.

"Miss Ada," Nonnie said and touched the thin old shoulder.

"Yes, dear," a soft voice answered, soft and as young as Nonnie's own.

"I've come for little Jackie, Miss Ada."

The chair grew still. Miss Ada slowly traveled the distance from the graveyard to her porch. "Yes, dear. Let me see, where can he—where—yes, yes, I know. Come in here, he's in here." She turned, lowered her voice. "He's asleep."

Through the dark room they felt their way until Miss Ada found the lamp on the bureau and struck a light. She shaded it with her hand as she lighted it and turned the wick low. "He's a sweet child," she whispered. "Come and look." And taking Nonnie's hand she tiptoed to the bed.

Jackie lay sprawled on Miss Ada's counterpane, a little brown smudge against the whiteness. Nonnie remembered as she looked at him, lying there, red lips pouting in sleep, brown hair curled tight against damp forehead, what Bess had once said of Miss Ada. "She's a sleepwalker," Bess had said, "but some day she may wake up and remember that we are Negroes. She'll some day remember about race, and then what will happen to Jackie? Suppose," she had gone on with sudden animation, and her voice was serene, but Non knew she was scaring herself in spite of her lightness as they had done as children when they ran through the graveyard, "suppose she remembers and in her hate and shame she kills him or hurts him in some awful way, or makes up a wild story and sicks the Ku Klux on us. Suppose—" But Jack, home from his run, had interrupted her with mingled impatience and commonsense. "Good Godamighty, Bess, hush! You're working yourself up and having a big time, but you'll keep me awake all night with your worrying, and tomorrow you'll go to work with a headache. Sure she's cracked! That's what makes her safe. C'mon," he had added suddenly, "let's go to Sam's. We need to be around somebody who talks sense. I do wish to God," Jack had added as they went down the steps, "that the boy had somebody else besides that old woman to play with. Fine start for a boy!"

"Better than these wild little tikes who spend their days in the ditches doing—well, you know—"

"No I don't," Jack said belligerently. "What are they doing that they shouldn't be doing or that white kids don't do?"

"What you did at their age, I reckon—and you know what that was."

A glance like heat lightning between them, then Jack had laughed, muttered something about Bess' being the biggest goddam idiot, and suddenly all of them were laughing, and they had walked down the path toward Dr. Perry's. But later, after Jack had gone back on his run, Bess mentioned it again and again to Nonnie. "I wish I hadn't thought it," she would say, and rub the back of her neck.

Nonnie was conscious now of Miss Ada's hand against hers, of the dry hot flesh, as she whispered in reply, "Yes, he is sweet and getting so big." But she knew that Miss Ada was as harmless as she—that no injury would ever come to them through her, for this world with its racial hate, its bitterness and struggle for bread, would never exist for Miss Ada again.

Nonnie picked up Jackie, turned to whisper her thanks, and paused. In the sputtering lamplight a thousand lacy valentines shimmered fantastically from ceiling to floor—the gifts of Maxwell children who had discovered long ago Miss Ada's pleasure in them and each year, giggling and whispering in derisive sympathy, brought to her their pretties when they were done with them, in annual payment of tribute to her who had added so much to the mystery of their young lives, becoming for them, as the years went by, their Valentine Witch . . .

Miss Ada stood in the middle of the room, clutching her wrapper close to her thin body, strings of hair about her face, eyes fixed on a faraway point, unmindful now of the girl and the sleeping child. From the far side of the old house came the hollow tap-tap of Mrs. Wood's cane as she crossed the runway, coming to bring supper to her daughter. Ninety years old she was, a little gray rag of a human, grimly holding on to the last thread of life, so as not to leave poor Ada alone.

Quietly Non went out and down the steps. As the path turned she looked back. Miss Ada had not moved, although now her mother stood before her and was holding out a bowl to her.

Non stood at the gate waiting, as she had done so many evenings of her life, and would do again. The last song in the big tent had ended, and white folks grown silent had gone to their homes, and some were asleep, worn out with penitence.

For tonight Brother Dunwoodie had been filled with the power of the Holy Ghost and had preached as he had never preached before his sermon on Mother Love. Some had heard it before, for Brother Dunwoodie had held a revival in Maxwell four years ago, but no one had ever heard him preach with the power that was his tonight. And when he had done, Brother Trimble sang in his clear tenor voice *Where Is My Wandering Boy*. Out there under that tent covering, where great shadows wavered, splotched here and there by dim lights, the people sat hushed and unmoving, waiting for the next words of that tired-faced, burning-eyed, black-haired man of God. When he spoke, his words were so low that you had to lean forward to hear. "I've done my talking now," he said, "I'm through. There's someone else talking now. I want you to listen. I want you to bend down and listen, for it's mother love whispering. Whispering to you to come home to God. *Come home.* Whispering to you to come back, not to her arms, but to Jesus' arms, where she knows you'll be safe. Maybe she's already taken her place up there with God, but she's lonely there without you . . . she can't be happy even in heaven without you. Listen . . ." The pianist was playing softly now *Almost persuaded now to believe.* "Listen . . . to her soft sweet words . . . whispering to you to give up sin and be her little boy again, pleading with you to promise that some day you will meet her there . . ."

The town was quiet now. White Town. Colored Town. And Nonnie standing there at the gate had not heard the preacher's words. But her mind was full of revival sounds as after a fire bits of ash float for a long time through the air.

A crunch of sand underfoot made her turn and open the gate, as quickly stop as she recognized the impatient rhythm of Eddie's footsteps.

He said, " 'Lo, Biddy," and held the gate ajar.

"Hello, Eddie."

"Feel like walking a bit?"

"Let's just stay here."

"O.K."

They stood looking out over the palmettos.

"You know," he said after a long silence, and laughed, "sometime I'd kind of like to get acquainted with you again."

She smiled, said quickly, "What have you done today?"

"Nothing, as usual. Salamander's for a coke and sandwich. Out with Sam on a call. Hung around the tent tonight and watched that white man save souls. He's damned good at it."

She tried to keep her voice casual and light. "Save many?"

"Did a pretty good job."

"Is it—fun, Eddie, to watch?"

"Depends on your idea of fun. Sort of, I reckon. Kind of like watching folks strip in public. Tickles me to see these white folks—"

He seemed to have forgotten to finish his sentence. "See them—what, Eddie?"

"See them crying and praying out loud, telling the world things they'll be sorry as hell they told after that preacher leaves town."

132

"Why do they do it?"

"Search me. Why do we do anything we do?"

Above the ditch on the far side of the road lightning bugs kept up a steady movement of light as if someone with a big incandescent pencil were making quick sharp marks on the night.

"But he gets you worried too, kind of." Ed laughed.

"You mean—"

"Oh, he didn't make me run to the altar—what you reckon they'd do if a Negro did that?—but all that talk of hell and death and sin and God's anger and—I don't know—"

"Tell me, Ed, how it made you feel." Nonnie's voice was urgent.

"Why the curiosity? Lord knows you've seen plenty all your life."

"Tell me, Eddie, how it makes you feel, please."

"Non, I'm no good at saying things." He paused, began again, "Just tears you up, like a bad fuss with somebody you like a lot, or like liquor does you, sometimes. Oh, I used to feel kind of like that when Mama got after me bad about something I'd done, when she made me feel I'd lost out with her." He laughed, grew silent, said softly, "Hell would never get a chance at her, would it, kid?"

Non shook her head.

"She worshiped you, Non," Ed said slowly.

"She worshiped us all."

"But you especially. Bess and me—we filled out the empty spots you left."

"Don't say that, Eddie."

"I wish she could have lived."

"We all wish it," Nonnie whispered.

"Because you've changed since she died." Ed spoke harshly. "You're not the same person! Sometimes it seems to me you're acting out something that's not real, you're—"

"What do you mean, Bubba?"

133

He smiled quickly at the old nickname, but his voice grew angry again as he continued. "Here you are, educated, intelligent—you made good grades at college, you can't deny it—" his voice grew more belligerent. "And yet you seem unwilling to *use* your brains. To *be* anything."

"I'm happy as I am," she smiled.

"But how can you be, living like this? Country slums, that's what it is, taking orders all day long from crackers—dirt—"

Nonnie smiled into his angry face. "I've always been happy, Ed, all my life. You never were—or not often—you and Bess. You're ambitious. I'm not. Sometimes I don't think contented people ever are."

"That's a damned lot of rot, and you know it. Anybody with brains wants to *be* somebody—to get somewhere. We've got to get somewhere! We're colored people, Nonnie! Sometimes seems to me," he grew silent for a moment while his fingers picked at the old fence, "you pretend—you're not."

She turned quickly and touched his arm. "Don't scold me any more tonight, Eddie," she whispered, and bit her lips to keep them from shaking.

"Sorry, kid." He started toward the house. "Don't suppose you're coming in—now?"

"Not just now," she answered.

She listened as he went in, heard him run up on the porch, slam the screen door. And then she forgot him, for now down the path toward Miss Ada's she heard the first faint slur of Tracy's steps—limp, swagger . . . Through the dark she hurried toward him, running a little. They met around the curve under the last of the cedar trees. There was no one but Tracy to see her as he drew her quickly to him, and not even Tracy heard the sob which she smothered against his shoulder.

# NINE

TRACY LOOKED DOWN at Nonnie.

"Arbor?"

"No, the old place."

"In the dark?" Laughing suddenly. Feeling glad to be back in a world where nothing was ordered as in white Maxwell.

"Time we cross . . . the patch . . . it'll be good and light," whispering, voice like leaves scuttling down a path.

"Nonnie, you're scared of something."

"No."

"Hands cold and you're— What's happened?"

"Nothing. Let's go."

He followed her white dress through the dark as she went quickly along the path, circled the old house, slowed to push through canebrakes. He followed her, easily keeping close to her white skirt.

She looked so little, walking in front of him there, as if the light of the moon had cut off height, slivered off years.

Just so she had run ahead of him when they were on their way to the swamp or to the high place in the hammock on fall days. Or in the wintertime when he would have his gun and would be hunting a few birds, she'd tag along, only always scampering ahead of him like a brown leaf just turned by frost. He thought that now, but then he'd thought she was thin as a rail, nothing but a sack of bones, and he used to scold her for not eating, until one day he remembered that her sister was off at college and her mother worked all day at the Purviances', and maybe the kid didn't have anything much to eat and nobody much to look after her. So he had begun asking Eenie for an afternoon snack, saying school made you hungry. He would find excuses to go by the old

Anderson place, and there he would urge Nonnie to eat. Watching her eat a cold sweet potato and sausage or some of Eenie's tea cakes, or a slice of bread and butter and sugar, he would feel good inside. Satisfied. Better than he had ever felt. Only time he ever had the same feeling was when an old starved dog took up with him and he had fed him until he was fat and sleek. Funny, how that made you feel so good, feeding a dog. A little colored girl and a dog, he thought now suddenly and felt quick displeasure.

Nonnie had paused. "Mind," she called, "I've seen a cotton-mouth here, lately."

"Fine news for a night."

She laughed, went on, and her laugh made him feel good.

He had fed her all that winter. And he had liked it. Before, she'd been a funny little nuisance tagging him whenever he was out beyond the graveyard, solemnly following him. He had been shamed a lot of times by her tagging, and sometimes had run her off, like you'd shoo a chicken back. He had tried to keep the other boys from knowing it . . . they'd never believe she was just a fool nigger kid following him around. They'd think, well, what you'd expect them to think, and there'd be no use to tell them better.

He had begun to ask her things about the family. Her sister Bess was at Spelman, and Ed was to go to Atlanta University next year—now he worked early mornings and evenings at the Supply Store. And later, when she was older, she was to go. College . . . It had seemed funny to think of colored folks wanting to go to college when not many white folks from Maxwell went, or wanted to.

"You stay out here by yourself?"

She nodded.

"Even when Til—when your mama doesn't get back until after dark?"

"Uh-hunh."

"What you do?"

136

"I set and think."

"You mean *sit*."

"I sit and—"

"What you think about?"

"A lot of things—you, I reckon, mostly."

"Me? That's funny. What about me?"

"How I first met you—that time a boy knocked me down."

"When was that?"

"Long time ago. He knocked me down and you picked me up. Ever since then."

"That all?"

"How smart you are. How you've always answered questions—rithmetic—" she smiled.

"That's nothing—"

"Rithmetic," she went on, "and other things. Always when I don't know something I think, 'Tracy'll tell me.' "

"What have I ever told you?" He liked it, but—

"You told me about the other side of the world—geography —I didn't know a thing about that," her eyes were serious and he noticed little black specks in the iris and was surprised that he had not noticed before. "You told me all I know about stars. You told me how bugs are put together—and," she quickly smiled, "how automobiles are put together, but I can't remember."

"Dumb, huh?" He reached over, pulled her hair.

"Uh-hunh, about that."

"You—mind being dumb about things, some things?"

She shook her head.

"Not ever?"

She shook her head.

"Even if your own sister knows it and lot more?"

"Bess? She knows so much I don't know. Reads a book quick, remembers all about it."

"And you don't?"

"I remember it if I like it."

"I wasn't thinking about Bess," he said slowly. "It was Laura."

She reached across him and picked a thistle bloom. He could not take his eyes off the brown fingers as they played with the soft oval, moving it gently, brushing it against her palm, brushing it in slow circles, as her lips opened and closed without words, her eyelids dropped. Suddenly she gave it a flick. "Laura," she laughed softly, and brushed her out of their lives as easily as the flecks of down had fallen to the ground.

"It's how wonderful you are that I think about."

"How?" He grinned, embarrassed but sort of liking it.

"Of all the men I know you are the finest—"

He laughed. She was a crazy little thing. "But you don't know anybody, Non."

"I know them!" Her cheek quivered.

"Why, Nonnie!"

"White and black! Only—" now her face was as calm as the little brown pool below the cypress, "I don't think about them." She smiled and ran the stem of the shattered thistle back of his ear.

He caught her hand. "Do they—bother you, Non?"

"They try. Sometimes. As they do every colored girl. But they've learned it's no use."

"How old are you?"

"Most thirteen."

Thirteen, and knowing this. "Nonnie," he took the stick from her, threw it away, laid her hand gently on a pile of leaves. "Nonnie," he was feeling strange responsibilities, "it would never be any use for them to try, would it? Not ever?"

She shook her head gravely.

"That's fine," he said, and wondered what the devil to talk about now.

"Because, you see," she went on, "I belong to you."

Her thin face was so earnest that he found it not easy to

take his eyes from it. "Ever since," she went on, "you brought me books to read about those knights of the Round Table, ever since then, you've been my knight." She said the words proudly, seriously. "For me there is no one else."

He felt his face redden. Her words were crazy in his ears. The fool kid didn't know any better—he shouldn't let himself get so damned uncomfortable—over a colored kid—but—

"Good," he said awkwardly. "Of course, when you grow up you'll naturally meet somebody."

She was looking at the sun, low in the trees, and did not answer. Her fingers lay curled against her blue dress, he remembered it to this day, pale, pink, coppery, with the sun shining on them, and the sole of her sandal had a hole in it, he remembered that too. She had turned then and stretched out on the grass, raising her arms high above her head, and her hipbones had pushed against the tight dress like two little knobs—

"It's late," he had said. "Better be going."

She turned, reached in her pocket for a scrap of paper, unfolded it. "It's in partial payments and I don't know why, but my answer comes out wrong every time."

He took the scrap, read her figures quickly. "Dumbbell, look what you've done here."

She pushed back her hair. "I knew you'd fix it for me," she said.

And he had fixed it for her. And then he had gone home, a seventeen-year-old white boy, cutting through the gallberry patch, for it was late; feeling like all medievalism with the sun on his shield. Feeling like a damned fool.

She had turned, he saw now, away from the hammock and was following the path to the top of Sandy Ridge, where the moon, directly above them, sharply defined palmetto clumps and pine and oak, and as plainly, clusters of prickly-pear sprawled on the sand like big crabs. The midnight freight,

139

crossing the cypress swamps before beginning its pull up the side of the ridge, sighed like some great heaving creature.

They found an open space, free of prickly-pears, and sat down. To the left and below them lay Maxwell, dark, unseen, inescapably there. There was no wind, only light; and the left-over heat from the day.

The freight was climbing the ridge now across fields. The sigh grew into a chuff, grew loud and importunate—in it the creak and whine of steel and wood. The whistle sounded and the line of cars pulled into view below them. Watermelons . . . a hundred cars maybe, or more—

They did not try to talk until the last shriek of wheel against rail had died.

She laid her hand on his knee.

He said, "Dorothy tried for two hours to save my soul tonight."

Only a pressure of hand.

"Mother's tried, Dunwoodie, now Dorothy. They evidently believe I've got a soul," he laughed harshly.

"What do you think?" He turned to the silent girl.

"You know what I think," she whispered.

He looked down at her hand, a smudge against his white trousers. And then he slowly looked into eyes shining like lights across a swamp.

He said suddenly, "I'm so damned tired!"

She drew his head down to her lap; he settled against her body, and closed his eyes. Softly her fingers pressed temples, moved along the nerve back of his ears, down into his neck. Again, again, again.

He muttered, "Soft and cool . . . like the ivory keys on Grandma's piano in Macon . . . cool and dim it'd be in there . . . and I'd go . . . lay my face against them . . . when I was a little fellow . . . and they'd make me feel . . . like this . . ."

Again, again, again, fingers pressed gently. No words.

140

"It was always when Mother had got me for something, and I'd be crazy as hell—mad—wanting to bawl . . . and I'd go and it'd be dim in there . . . and the keys cool to my face . . . like this . . . Have I ever told you that before? Guess I have."

She leaned over and kissed him, and as she moved her breast touched his throat and it was as if he had cupped it with his hands, so easily he knew its size and shape and texture.

"Yes," she whispered, "many times."

"Yeah . . . reckon so."

"Do you remember the first time?" Her low voice faltered suddenly.

"First? No, reckon not."

"Try," she whispered.

He could not remember.

"It was at Christmas time," she reminded him, "and you had come home from college and—didn't want to go back—"

"Sure. I'd flunked my exams. Every goddam one."

She went on swiftly, "And we were in the little hollow back of the big cypress, and the sun was warm, not a bit like Christmas weather. You remember?"

He did not answer her.

"And you talked a while—and then you said suddenly, 'Nonnie, you've grown up. You're not a kid any longer.' And that made me very proud—for I was only fourteen."

"Did it? You were a funny little thing," he interrupted.

"And then I got tongue-tied and shy—as if I'd never seen you before. You seemed so grown up yourself. And you stretched out on the grass and put your head in my lap and I rubbed your head—and that is when you told me about the piano keys . . ."

"Then what?"

She kissed him again. "I think maybe you remember 'what.' "

141

"First time too?"

"Yes," she whispered.

"You were scared."

"Not much."

"But a little."

"Yes." The fingers followed the path of pain along his temples.

He laughed softly—at ease—

"Happy though," she added, "happy every time since—"

Every time since. There hadn't been so many "times," he thought now in surprise. Then—but no more until she was sixteen, for she seemed such a kid and was peaked-looking afterward and he was afraid maybe she was too much a child, though she seemed so old—and then he had been away in the war—and she at college—and this past year—

Funny record for a white man with a colored girl. *Colored girl. Negro.* Spoiling every good moment, like a hair that's got into your food. Why under God's heaven did he keep on thinking those damned words! Why couldn't he— Jesus!

He sat up, ran his fingers through his hair. "Gotta be going," he said. "It's late."

He left her at the arbor and took the path through the field to the railroad track. God knows he knew plenty paths to take. All his life he had been coming out to the old Anderson place. All his life he had been making new ways so as not to flaunt in the town's face what he was doing. But lately he had used the graveyard path as if he had forgot the others, had given up caring what folks thought. Tonight he chose the field because it was a longer way home and he had a lot to think about.

Lot to decide. He had come to a place where you had to—

Dad had pushed him today. About the farm. Shortly after he came home from the war, they had talked about the farm, and he had kind of liked the idea. Better than staying at home in the same house with Mother and Laura. Better than hanging around all time with same damned crowd. Maybe he'd like dirt. Seemed to. Maybe that's where he belonged. Out on a farm with the niggers and plenty dirt. But it'd been too much trouble to decide. Dad pushing now. Mother behind that. Sure. If he didn't want the farm, decide what he did want—store, filling station—and they'd see that he got it. Oh sure they would—sure, they'd make him respectable, that's what Mother—

"You're twenty-six. That right, Son?"

"Right, Dad." You grinned, feeling sorry for Doc in this new advisory role.

"Twenty-six, time to settle down. Don't you think?"

"Yes sir. Reckon so." With him so damned uneasy you couldn't—

"I'm fifty-five. If anything were to happen to me, I'd feel a lot better if I knew you were married and settled and in a position to see after your mother."

*See after Mother.* Funny . . . to think of Mother ever needing you to see after her. Made you laugh. Crazy to think of her needing anybody. Made you want something to— Wonder if she'd—how she'd be—if she got in a tight spot and had to call for help. Had to lean on Son—

"She's going through a hard time now. Women go through a hard time at menopause. If you could just get things sort of settled in your life, you'd make it easier on her now. There's the drugstore," Dad went on, "it's a paying proposition and you could take my share of it over, if you really want it"—as if you'd have it now!—"but I've been saving it for your mother. But the farm now. If we could buy back the old place . . ." Tracy watched the farm-look come on his father's face. "If we could get it back, you be willing to take it over? Or if we couldn't get it," and Tut's face resumed its everyday acceptance of what life had turned out to be, "if we couldn't get it, there's plenty to be had. Boll

143

weevil makes that easy." He laughed. "But a farm . . . tell you . . . there's nothing better . . . take it from me. Hard times . . . sure . . . there'll always be hard times, and right now is one of the worst, but it'll get better, and the farm's better than most business, even with hard times. Good thing to live on . . . What say, Son?"

"Let me think it over, Dad."

"But not a year this time?"

Tracy laughed. "Not quite."

"Now if I were running a farm again," Tut's eyes lighting up with the old dream, "tell you what I'd do. I'd put in peanuts and some hogs, as well as cotton; and I'd do a little trucking on the side—cantaloupes, say, or beans. And if we could get the old Deen place, I'd take that hillside stretch back of the old barn where there's a big gully now and I'd put it in grass and get me some good stock—"

"Dad, I don't know a darned thing about that kind of farming. If I took it, it'd have to be cotton—"

"Well," Dad interrupted swiftly, "the easiest thing's cotton, of course. Reckon the old way is maybe the surest, as well as the easiest." Dad had half sighed, suddenly.

Tracy did not answer his father. All he saw was his mother's face, watching him, waiting for him to turn respectable, waiting . . . And if he did . . . suppose he did —would she like it? Would she . . . or would she find something else? Sometimes he had a crazy feeling that she wouldn't be satisfied if he wasn't a failure. Needed to be disappointed. Sometimes he wondered if he'd lost his mind when he thought things like this . . . if anyone else ever did . . .

His father was talking again. ". . . as to getting married . . . Time comes when a man needs to get married. Sometimes it's the only thing that'll keep you going. You've got to have a goal, somebody to work for . . . or else there's no sense—" Dad paused, picked up his words a little wearily, as if he had made a long journey somewhere in those seconds—

"plugging at it. I know some boys have to put it off a long time, try a lot of other things first. But . . . time comes. And on the farm you'd need a wife. Somebody smart and willing to make a nice home. Who it's to be is up to you. Though your mother and I would like to see you stick to Dorothy."

That was a long and intimate speech for Tut. And they stood facing each other in a silence hard to break. "Well," Dad said, finally, "got some calls to make. Think it over, Tracy."

"O.K., Dad."

*O.K., Dad.* Well, it wasn't O.K. But what was wrong with it now? You had to settle down sometime—couldn't keep on living off the family, though the farm would be living off them in a way. And maybe a more expensive way. Still, it'd do as well as anything else. About as good a way of half starving in Georgia as any other. As for Dorothy—Dorothy . . . Dorothy . . . thrown at you everywhere you turned! Mother, now Dad, Dorothy herself. In a nice way of course —it'd be nice if it was Dorothy! All of Maxwell deciding it was time he did something about Dorothy. They didn't say anything—didn't have to when it was plastered on their faces big as road signs. Just because he had started taking Dorothy to parties when they were in high school together. And starting, didn't know how to quit. Trouble with him . . . he never knew how to quit anything—didn't know how to quit any— Get started, keep on, like a fool—like a damfool. Everybody pulling at him—Mother, Dorothy, Dad . . . that ass of a Henry'd be doing it next. And because he didn't come up to something they expected of him, he was a failure. Sure . . . when all he wanted was to be let alone. Yes, by God, *to be let alone!* No-count . . . sure . . . while everything Laura, with her degrees decorating her like a slimy French general, did was just right. "And what honors did you bring

145

home this time . . ." Cackling geese, the whole town. After him now . . . evangelist hot on his heels . . .

Tracy sat down on the railroad track.

God, he breathed, how easy . . . how damned easy . . . it'd be to let a freight flatten you out. Nothing left . . . to be pulled at . . . disappointed over. If you could decide to do it. . . .

And then it was as if Nonnie sat there beside him. Cool, quiet . . . waiting. Not saying a word. Waiting.

So strong was the feeling that he turned to see.

He laughed. Hell of a good time you can have feeling so godawful sorry for yourself . . .

He was suddenly at peace, as a lull comes in heavy winds.

Nonnie . . . yes, she pulled too. She wanted something too. But it was not something he could not understand. Something he could not be. Crazy. Sounded crazy in his own mind even, but she wanted him just as he was.

He laughed aloud.

Yes, Nonnie and the hound dog long dead and Big Henry were the only ones satisfied with him. A hound dog and two niggers. High-falutin list of friends. Fine honors to please the family with. Well, he could add Dorothy to the list. Maybe that'd help.

He laughed again, hurting now, pressing the thought in as if this hurt eased another.

Dorothy . . . He could see her as she had been tonight in the porch swing. Wearing a green voile dress which she had made herself. She'd told him that. Crisp black hair, gray-yellow eyes. Face thin, as was she, and sometimes with a way of looking very pretty and petite in a small-town way. Most of the time vivacious and cute. She'd be cute at fifty and not so petite either—probably skinny. Well, that was Dorothy. Clean, herself, and kept the Pusey house clean. Made good cucumber pickle and excellent fudge and was pleased over doing both. Sang in the choir. Nothing really

146

wrong about Dorothy, Always cheerful and bright . . . full of
energy . . . talked enough so that he didn't have to bother to
talk much. Liked him. Yes, she liked him. If it was just to
change him. As she was always doing to the Pusey rooms.
She liked them too. Satisfied with them in a way. Fine house
for changing. Always changing the furniture around and
painting something a different color. Be what she'd do to
him too. Have a brush out after him . . .

God . . . he didn't have to marry the girl! No Papa Pusey
with a shotgun after him— The idea of little Pug Pusey clucking along with a shotgun was funny enough to make Tracy
smile and shake the hair out of his face.

But he might as well, he sighed. Might as well give in.
Never been able in his life to have a run-in with Mother
and win. Whole life spotted with times he'd kept his mouth
shut and taken his beating. Could take his beating now.
There'd always be Nonnie. Yes, there'd be Nonnie. When
Dot got behind him too much with her paintbrush he'd go
to Nonnie and she would peel the new paint off down to the
old Tracy. And she'd let him get everything out of his sys-
tem and would sit there, not talking but there. And whatever
he wanted she would give him. That was Non. Her body—
or a drink of water. It'd all be the same. And she'd give it
like a swamp bay lets you smell its sweetness. Just as simply.

Not Dorothy. He'd have a time with that girl. He thought
now of her sallow-faced mother. Dorothy'd think it wrong or
the way wrong, or too much of it wrong, or something. It
didn't make much difference. As long as he had Non.

Non . . . Once he had been down at the depot when she
came home from Washington. Non got off the day coach,
walked across the cinder square, a queen in her gray tailored
suit and plain blouse, her head held effortlessly high, dignity
as much hers as her eyes. She did not see him, nor did he give
sign of recognizing her. But his eyes followed her swift sure
movement. She had not yet assumed her "Mrs. Brown's

147

maid" demeanor. It was as if she was not yet aware that she was back in Maxwell. And it gave him a thrill to see her like that, until he remembered her race, and then it made him sick at his stomach and confused. He'd tried to laugh it off. Who wouldn't! He'd—

Once he had dropped in to see her. Late. Nonnie came out to the arbor in a yellow chiffon evening dress. She and Bess had given a party and had dressed up in honor of some out-of-town friends. He could not keep his eyes off of her. Bewitched at the girl's beauty and poise. Bewitched. And angered. You'd think God wanted to play a fine joke and had made Nonnie. Here, He said, is a woman any man would love and be proud of. She has everything you could desire. But you can't have her. No. You can have sips and tastes, but you can't have her. And you'll be ashamed and sneak around and feel nasty. . . . That's the price you have to pay—for the sips.

Well . . . white men had paid it before. And thought it cheap. Guess he could too.

Nonnie . . . going to have a baby. He hadn't thought of it once when he was with her tonight. And Nonnie hadn't mentioned it. Nonnie never bothered you with . . . things . . . You'd think having gone to college and everything . . . she'd know how not to get herself in this kind of trouble. You'd . . . well, lucky she's colored. Or else! Said she didn't mind. Said she didn't. Now damn it, isn't it the strangest thing how nigger will out! Here's Nonnie, college-educated, smooth as any Atlanta debutante could hope to be, making most Maxwell white girls seem mighty small-town. Yet when it comes to a thing like this, she doesn't mind any more than a turpentine nigger gal. Said she wanted it. Said— Funny. Yes . . . Non's funny . . . queer . . . Wonder—

Oh, he'd fix it up some way. Make it as easy for her as he could. Long way off . . . no use to worry now . . . put her out on the farm . . . fix it some way . . .

All settled as far as he was concerned. Ready for the wedding bells. With this ring I make thee respectable . . . your mother's son. Ready for Dorothy. If she could put up with him, he could with her. And maybe things would be better . . . away . . . in their own house. Maybe . . . Lord God . . .

He stood up. The moon was dropping below the line of pines west of the hammock. There was a cool stir of air, as if dawn were about to break.

Better be going. He started up the track toward home. Started walking up the track. Stopped. He'd left something. Nonnie sitting there on a crosstie. A huddled-up Nonnie in the moonlight. Looked back, kept looking back at the empty track. Kept looking back, cursing his craziness. Kept looking back, cursing the emptiness, cursing the craziness. Kept looking back as a hand pulled at his coat, a life at his memory.

Lightheaded. Drunk. Weak. He closed his hand, tried to tense muscles, couldn't get a grip. You feel like this with a spell of fever. You feel like this . . .

At the Deen gate he stopped. Looked across the street. Pusey house stood as it had stood forever, curlicue porch and banisters, honeysuckle sticking to everything, gluing everything together, swing, rockers, Mrs. Pusey, Dorothy, himself. Half a mind to go over now and get it settled. Half a mind to do it now so it couldn't be changed. Go over and wake up blue-faced Mrs. Pusey. Sick mother of Dottie—all the rest of her children dead in the graveyard. Everybody better dead in the graveyard . . . go to graveyard and wake them up . . . tell them . . .

A neighbor's cat ran between his legs and disappeared in the oak gloom. He listened to its pad, pad, pad, pad, pad, pad, pad . . . listened long after it had left the street, filling in the silence . . . listened, making the sounds come back in the silence.

A driblet of moss loosened from the oak limb above him, fell on his shoulder. He jumped. Laughed. Oh well, noth-

149

ing like a little sleep. You need a little sleep, you know . . .
better sleep some . . . better die some . . . better—

He walked with no sound through the living room, felt
around in the dark for the turn in the hall, feeling his way
now up the stairs. A sound from the library. He paused.
Sobbing. Somebody crying. You're not crying . . . you . . .
No light in the library. Just sounds. Young girl sounds.
Laura. Never'd seen Laura cry. Everybody crying . . . crazy
. . . everybody . . . better . . .

Slowly he went up the stairs, stopped on each step, feeling
for the next with his foot. Slow and dull, as if he had heard
strange bad news from a far country.

# TEN

TUT DROVE slowly home. Already late for dinner and
with calls to make, he let the car move as slowly as it would
through sand ruts; his mind moving with it along the ruts of
right and wrong.

You can't change right and wrong because somebody you
love stands in the middle of the road—

*Then what you do, run over her?*

But if something's wrong and you do it to save Grace, then
where are you—where's your ethics—where's your medical—

*Where's little Grace?*

Let somebody else—

*Sure, let Aunt Mag with her dirt—let some crooked abor-
tionist in Atlanta—let anybody do the sinning but—*

Tut straightened the car in the road.

150

If a nigger had raped her it'd be different—it'd be different, but—

*What's going to happen to Grace?*

—but this was—she did it for fun—for fun with a boy she liked—

"She's a baby, Tut! Not fifteen." L.D. talking, his best friend talking, in the office this morning. "She's not a bad girl, you know—you know that—"

"Yes, I know that."

"You love her, Tut—"

"Next to Laura."

"Then why the devil—"

Tut had dried his freckled hands, eyes staring into the towel, trying to think of an answer. Turning the roller-towel to a fresh place, drying again the red hairs on hands already dry, as his slow tongue hunted words.

"How long, Tut—since—"

"Two months, or more."

"You're sure—you're sure it couldn't be somethi—"

"No doubt about it." Tut sat at his desk now, fingering a prescription pad, picking at his mustache.

"It's that damned Mart Paine . . ."

Tut picked up the pad, put it down.

"I could shoot him of course. What good would it do?"

"There's marriage."

"Not to that white trash. He'll never amount to a hill of beans."

You could hear Mrs. Stephenson talking to Grace in the adjoining room. They'd be out soon—they'd—

"And I'll not let Maxwell talk."

"There'll be talk."

"Not as long as I live."

The unasked question made more words between the two men hard. Tut played with the pad, laid it down, picked at his mustache. L.D. Stephenson's strong brown hand rubbed

151

the side of the old leather chair, rubbed, paused, rubbed again. Finally:

"You'll do it, Tut?"

Dr. Deen shook his head.

"If it's money—"

"You know better than that."

"Friendship?" On Stephenson's dark face a sneer, as quickly gone.

But he didn't mean it. "You've never failed me as a friend," Tut said. "I'd do almost anything, God knows, but murder."

"Don't reckon you've ever killed a patient?" Bitter now.

"Not on purpose," Tut half smiled.

L.D.'s eyes were hard. "So you'll drive me to Aunt Mag instead—with her damned filthiness—I suppose you know what killed Katie Dillon?"

"I know."

"Drop your medical rot and use your brain. What's the difference? Suppose she dies at Aunt Mag's? Won't you be as responsible for that death as for the—other?"

"I don't see it that way."

"No . . . you doctors, all fools and hypocrites. Damn the whole lot of you! I thought you loved the kid—"

"Almost as much as Laura."

"Then why the hell—"

Tut started again. "If a nigger had assaulted her, or if she would lose her life in childbirth I'd—"

"Oh sure! Sure . . . I know all that talk." L.D. now reverted to the familiar role of a bargaining politician. "Tut . . . there's the old Deen place. You've been wanting it a long time . . ."

Tut waited. L.D.'s eyes lighted and his words came fast. "Tut, you could put Tracy out there. You've wanted it back ever since you lost it. I know. It'd solve a lot of problems. We'd do things for Tracy. Put him in the legislature. Give the boy something to do, to think about. Get him out of this town . . . away . . . I'll—" L.D. paused, studied Deen's face, suddenly changed his words. "You've got me. All my life I've put things over on you. I've ridden friendship to the limit. You've got me now. Anything you say, Tut. It goes."

Tut did not hear the melodrama of L.D.'s words, nor feel the thinly concealed scorn which was so habitual to L.D. that even now when he was asking of his friend the biggest favor he had ever asked of any man, it slipped over his words like a bland film of oil. Tut was remembering Little Ma. Remembering her words: "There's right and there's wrong. You'll do right as a doctor, Son, or wrong. There's no middle road."

He shook his head. "I can't do it."

L. D. knew when he was beaten.

"Well . . . if you can't you— Is it Aunt Mag then?"

"I . . . don't know."

"With all my friends, after twenty years in the legislature, I don't know a damned soul I'd ask the name of an abortionist of. There must be a decent one in Atlanta. Who is it?"

Steps in the other room moving toward the door. "For Christ sake, don't be so squeamish!"

"Try—" Doc turned, wrote a name on a prescription slip. "You'd trust him?"

"He knows his business. And if you're going to do it, better hurry."

Mrs. Stephenson and Grace quietly entered the room.

"All right, sugar," Dr. Deen smiled at the pretty little blonde Grace, rumpled her hair, "run on to church," pulled her hair again, evaded Mrs. Stephenson's eyes.

"Now, Helen," Stephenson spoke briskly, "I want you and Grace to go on to church as if nothing had happened."

"Brother Dunwoodie is having dinner with us," Mrs. Stephenson said in a level, colorless voice.

153

"Good. I'll get back. Gotta run out to the farm now. All right." He smiled, evading Mrs. Stephenson's eyes. "See you later."

*There's right and there's wrong.* There's got to be right and wrong. You couldn't, you wouldn't, know where to turn—

Tut straightened the wheels of the car.

Yesterday—today—yesterday—you couldn't get it out of your mind. You couldn't get little Grace out of your mind. *She did it for fun because she liked him* . . . Grace . . . no more than a baby, it seemed to them, but with a body full-grown and lovely, went out to the woods, or in a car, somewhere, with that seventeen-year-old Paine boy, and let him have her . . . in sweet giving she let . . .

Lord . . . suppose Alma had done that. Suppose, that first year when her father had come as the new Methodist preacher to Maxwell, suppose young Alma had done that. Suppose he had had the nerve to take her some time when they were out walking on Sunday, behind a clump of bushes somewhere, had drawn her down by him in the warm sand. Would she . . . would she have laughed and let him . . . let him . . . laughing softly . . . drawing nearer . . . and he in sudden strength, feeling good, feeling good and strong, would have pressed her body down . . .

A horn blew long and angrily at him. Tut put on the brakes, wheeled sharply to the right. A Ford slowed as it passed him, a head leaned out the window. "You were sound asleep, Doc! Better ease up and get some rest."

Doc drove carefully into his driveway, softly stopped the car.

Alma was sitting in the library. Waiting dinner for him. He'd go in and talk to her about Grace. Should have told her last night. Alma would agree that he'd done the only thing he could do.

154

He went in, quietly sat down. Alma did not ask about his morning calls. She sat calm, unmoving, on her face the abstracted expression which Tut had long ago learned to recognize as Alma-with-a-plan. Alma was planning something for them—for the good of them all. He looked at her guiltily. He was glad that she did not look at him, for he had the feeling that Alma would know what he had been thinking about —that she would see him in all his dirty-mindedness. My Lord, he thought, getting as nasty in my old age as Old Culpepper.

He surreptitiously looked at his watch. Two o'clock. Old Mrs. Reid had called twice before he left the office. He softly rattled his Jacksonville *Times-Union* and moved the ash tray a half inch, hoping Alma would suggest dinner. She gave no indication of having heard him. He began to dread Mrs. Reid's third call. "I'm sorry, Alma," voice tentative now. "Shall I call Henry?"

"If you will, Tut." She quietly followed him into the dining room.

They sat facing each other as they had done for twenty-seven years, the two places between them now vacant.

Tut unfolded his napkin and waited for Henry to serve the vegetables.

Mrs. Deen picked up a slice of lemon.

"Couldn't make it this morning," said Tut. "How's the meeting?"

"Brother Dunwoodie preached well. But little real response."

"Oh, it takes time," Tut said cheerily, "to work up feeling in a revival."

She squeezed the lemon against the rim of her glass. "Neither of our children was there." She dropped it into the tea, wiped her plump white fingers on her napkin.

"I'm sorry, dear." Doc's brown eyes scanned his wife's face for embellishment of a subject too painful for words. He

155

felt that he must make up to Alma for the shocking thoughts he had had about her, and searched now for a way to express his sympathy. "I'm surprised, really surprised at Laura," he finally contributed. "Of course," he hastened to add, as Alma's face did not respond to this effort, "Laura has always been a great comfort to you."

Mrs. Deen did not reply.

Tut looked up, surprised at her silence. "We're fortunate," Tut said, and stressed his words as if to rub out the interlinear doubts which her silence had now made legible, "we're fortunate, both of us, Alma, to have such a daughter as Laura." If she knew about Grace Stephenson she'd understand just how much they *did* have to be thankful for. "I tell you, parents sometimes don't know how thankful they should be—"

Mrs. Deen put down her napkin and moved her foot on the rug in search of the butler's bell. "Of course, Tut," she spoke as if to a reiterative and trying child, "I *fully* appreciate Laura."

As she lifted her hand he noticed the zigzag sparkle of diamonds and saw that her fingers were trembling. He felt in his wife a new quality of uncertainty. He had not realized before how old she was—how old we both are, he amended, for Tut's thoughts were ordinarily as well sifted as his words. Past middle age—and showing it. And he looked at Alma's breasts; he followed them, compressed flatly by her form-fitting girdle to her thickened waist; his mind continued the scrutiny beyond his eye's line of vision. Well, well, well, he thought, age sure creeps up on you. Yes sir, age. . . . He felt his thoughts straying back to his day-dream and jerked them away quickly, and then he saw in his mind the white cow. Sometimes that white cow would appear in his mind while he was reading up on a case, or driving along country roads, and sometimes he dreamed about her, and always when he envisioned that cow he thought of Alma. It had begun to

156

give him actual worry, for it came into his mind so often and there was no sense to the thing. It had started, he remembered that clearly, one day when he had been driving out to the Rushton plantation, past lonely stretches of palmetto and pine. A big white cow had clambered up in the middle of the road and had stood gazing at him unwaveringly, and he had thought: "Now if that ain't Alma all over," and had laughed aloud, and as quickly hushed in shocked surprise when he realized what he had thought. And ever since, the thing had dogged his tracks.

Henry brought in the ice cream.

The telephone rang.

"Yas'm . . . yas'm . . . I sho will . . . Yas'm . . . No'm, she ain't worried a-tall . . . *No'm* . . . Sho . . . Sho, Miss Laura. Thank you, mam . . ."

Tut smiled reassuringly at Alma.

"Miss Laura say don wait dinner on her—she stayin again wid de Harrises and Miss Jane." Henry waited until Mrs. Deen thanked him, then with big strides made off to the kitchen as if he had a cotton field or two to cross. At the kitchen door he automatically stooped, but in his haste to relay the message to Eenie he forgot to use caution and struck his shoulder a hard blow against the door jamb, righted himself, eased through, closed the door behind him, lost his balance and dropped the tray.

Tut chuckled. "That boy belongs in a house about as much as a turpentine mule."

"I've always told you that. Hasn't enough sense to set a table. Look at this!"

"I know. But we'd hate to run him off after he's been raised in our back yard." Tut considered the subject closed. He finished his ice cream. "Good ice cream."

"Tut—I want to arrange for Laura to go back to the university in September."

157

Dr. Deen searched his wife's face, but his glance ran as easily off that composed countenance as water down glass.

"Dr. Snell promised the place at Wesleyan to her when she gets her doctorate. She's wasting her time in Maxwell."

"But she's just home from college. We've hardly seen the child. Let's keep her with us awhile."

"Maxwell is no place for her, Tut. I want to get her away. I want her to get her degree."

The telephone was ringing. "Did you remember to speak to Tracy about the farm?"

"Yes, Alma."

Tut answered the phone. It was Miss Sadie, the operator, saying that old Mrs. Reid had telephoned for Dr. Deen the third time, but she had told her that he was out on a call, that she would find him and he would come there in about half an hour. "Thought you might work in a little nap," Miss Sadie chirped.

"Thanks, Miss Sadie. Don't know what I'd do without you."

Yes—a half hour later, as he drove toward old Mrs. Reid's —yes, he'd spoken to Tracy about the farm. But he wondered how much good it had done. Talking about it only made him want to go back there himself. Like to live the rest of his life there . . . like to die there. It'd be a good thing to try to buy it back. Take about all they had except the drugstore to do it, but it would be worth it. Like to live out his old days there . . . Wonder if the kitchen rotted down . . . a good place to sit when you were a little fellow, up in the fireplace, watching Little Ma and old Poggy cook supper on the big stove. Sometimes hiding in its corner when Pa came in grumpy and blue. Back of the kitchen, beyond the first field was the family burying ground, closed in by old cedars . . . a place still waiting there for him and Elmer. Reckon Elmer would never get back . . . Ran away after a row once with Pa—alike as two peas Little Ma used to say—Elmer ran

158

away to Texas. Quick-tempered and easy hurt and bold. Sometimes so bold it took your breath when you were little, and younger than him too. Little Ma used to say Elmer by time he was three months old was slapping her breast and biting her. And she'd laugh as she said it, and somehow her laughing would hurt Tut as if *she* had slapped *him*.

Yes . . . boys used to run away . . . to Texas . . . or farther west . . . some prospered . . . some you never heard from again. But nowadays, nowhere for boys to run, except to poolroom and Colored Town . . . Tracy a lot like Elmer. Must have inherited a lot of Elmer's wildness. Must have. Never heard of any wildness in Alma's family.

Maybe if he bought the farm, the boy would settle down, marry that nice little Dorothy Pusey, and leave colored women— Well, Tut suddenly justified his son, he's no worse than plenty of boys! Plenty!

# ELEVEN

ED OFFERED a cigarette.

"No," said Sam, "chewing's easier on these roads."

"Trouble is, Eddie," returning to their talk, "this thing you feel is shame, not pride. If it's pride, it's—" He slowed the car. A cow walked down the middle of the road in front of them, stopped, turned, gazed emptily at them.

Ed moved uneasily. Why doesn't he blow at her?

"—a kind of coat you're wearing to hide a dirty shirt under," voice even, not worrying about the cow.

159

Cow sidled up to the fender, turned around, took her stance across the ruts—

Godamighty!

—relieved herself in massive deliberation, crossed to a patch of grass.

"South's full of that kind of pride—that kind of shirt."

Ed watched Sam's hands as they lay easily on the wheel. Sunlight catching black hairs, lifting them off of brown flesh, outlining the scar across thick thumb made by a fishhook when they were kids. It had gone in deep. So deep Sam had made him take his knife and cut the flesh away, encouraging him, urging him on, while Ed cut and cried as he cut. "Now cut deeper," he'd said, "cut around the hook."

Ed had shaken his head dumbly.

"Sure you can! Anybody can cut a little flesh. Here, cut straight through."

Ed had cut straight through, but he'd grown so sick at the pressure of flesh against the dull blade that he reeled dizzily and only Sam's pulling him to the ground saved him from fainting. They'd sat there. Fishing poles laid up against a mayhaw bush, cans of bait on the grass, fish flopping against the palmetto stem on which they'd strung them . . . blood from Sam's hand making a little wet spot on the sand. It shamed him to this day to think of it—Sam letting blood roll easily over his hand while he waited for Ed to get over his sickness.

Sam was talking now, slow words pushing through something deep as sand. Talking about Negroes, the South—Negroes, the North—Negroes—white folks—Negroes—jobs, when all in the world you want is to forget you're Negro, that anybody is Negro— It was as if he had to get Ed straightened out about something, though God knows what. Well, you don't have to listen.

Yeah . . . to think about that fainting spell shamed him. But all his life he'd been glad it was Sam and not Jack—if it

160

had to be. Whatever Sam wanted, it wasn't to take something away from his friends, while Jack was always measuring himself by other folks' failures. They'd be swimming in the old days in Cow Pond. Sam would pick him out a cypress half across the pond and swim easily to it, and sit there watching the others. But Jack—it was always, "C'mon, Eddie, race me to the old log across there . . . race me to that stump . . . race me across the pond." And if he won, his face would ease a little and he'd be mighty nice about your failing. But he'd make you think that anybody should've been able to do it. But if he failed, he'd suck his lips in and wrinkle his forehead, still pleasant, but you'd know he was beating himself half to death inside, over his failure. Leave you feeling mighty bad either way. Yeah, Jack had swum ponds until he was sure he could outswim everybody in Maxwell, and now he was doing the same way with other things. You had the feeling every book he read, he read it just to catch up with the author—to know as much—then to know more—

Sam's words moved on as the old Ford pulled the road out toward Shaky Pond, slowed to cross the branch, churned in the thick sand on the other side, stalled, picked up a smoother stretch of speed. "I always say, get through college and then you've got a chance."

"All I see it did for Non and Bess was ruin them," Ed said, moving his hand up and down the back of the car seat. "We used to have fun. You remember we did. Now look at them! No life! I say it's better to be like that little nigger round town, that Dessie somebody, better be like her and her rump-twisting little friends than like my sisters. Those others at least have a laugh left in them."

"You're as bad," he added when Sam had nothing to say.

Sam chuckled. "So damned much sickness. Got me hog-tied, I reckon."

"What you get out of it! Don't get money. If you do—you bury it. See you haven't been to the store."

161

"I'll get around to the shoes one of these days." Sam drove a mile before he said more. "As for the other, Aunt Easter would say, enough to bread us."

"Sure! Say they're all sick—and you make them well! Then what you got? Make them well for what?"

Sam made no answer.

"So they can do their work for white folks better, I reckon," voice quick now, running into Sam's silence, trying to hurt himself on it. *Pleasing Tom Harris and other white men.* Ed wanted to believe that—

"It's what I can do for folks."

They were moving through the last stretch of hammock before getting to the Talley farm. There was a fine shade here, a good thing to pass through, but neither noticed.

"Don't get it. You'd think it was a debt you had to spend your whole life paying off!"

"Maybe just the interest on it, boy."

"Nobody's done anything for you. Or me either! Why you got to put yourself out like you do? You're killing yourself. What for? What's anybody done for us?"

"You're forgetting your mother."

"She didn't send me to college to do for other people. Mama sent us to college to better ourselves. Look at us! Look at Bess and Non! Servant girls! Sometimes I think they like groveling to crackers . . . sometimes—"

"Bess is trying to help Jack get ahead. You're not fair to them, are you?"

"That doesn't explain Non."

"She has a right to her own way of life."

"She has no right—" Oh well, what's the use to keep on! "Sorry, Sam, forget it."

There was no sound now save the puff and pant of the hot engine.

What makes you say things like that! Hurting him. What's he done to you! Ed looked at Sam. He didn't look mad. No,

162

just hot and a little tired, as he stared stodgily ahead at the white glaring road.

Sam was slowing down now at the branch. "Reckon a little water might help her feelings." Ed was glad to hear the easy voice, to hear nothing in it that was not of the casual words. He picked up the old tomato can, filled the radiator, poured a little over his hot hands, got back in the car.

They plugged on down the road.

"Sam—" Ed laughed a little to make the words come easy. "You know a lot about—things. Way people are. Ever know of anybody, except crazy people, getting a notion in their head they couldn't get out?"

"Like what, for instance?" Sam said after a half mile of silence.

Ed did not try to say.

Sam looked at him, half smiled. "Like—say, a tune you get in your head that you can't get out?"

"Something like that, I reckon." What made you start it? He'll think you're nuts.

"Had a few myself. Maybe doctoring's one," Sam smiled quickly at his friend.

"No—I tell you," Ed drew in his breath, hesitated, went on, "I was walking along in the park one day, two or three months ago." Make a joke of it. He's likely to think you need a strait-jacket. "There were some ants on a stone. Just plain damn ants, you know. I stopped, and stepped on one, mashed it flat. Just not thinking, see, one way or another particularly. Minute I did it, something flashed through my mind: 'You killed Nonnie.' Had no sense to it, see? But it kept coming back in my mind. At first, the thing was so crazy, it didn't bother me. But it kept coming back . . . sort of . . . gets . . . on your . . . nerves after a while . . ."

"People are funny," Sam said slowly, "way they think their mind is something different from their body. You don't get nervous when you have a sharp pain in your belly for a

163

second. Goes away. That's the end of it. Let a little gas pain come in your mind, you keep worrying."

Yeah . . . sounds fine. He doesn't understand it any more than I do.

"Of course it's damned silly. As I said, at first it didn't bother; then it began to come back. At night, at work. I'd be in the midst of something. I'd hear it. It's got so it keeps on —" Ed broke off his words, wiped his face.

"You run into a lot of things with sick folks," Sam went on. "For instance, folks who make you operate on them."

"Sure, want a little attention, I reckon."

That's different.

"Maybe more than that. Seems sometimes they want you to hurt them. As if they had to suffer. Something they had to do."

Nobody wants a thing like that. He's trying to get my mind off of this—

"Better stop here, I reckon," Sam said. "Old Talley don't like to see us riding in automobiles. Might as well walk the rest of the way."

Sweat was running off their faces by the time they had walked a hundred yards up the road edging cotton fields. They turned in at the lane.

On the piazza of the old two-story frame house sat Bill Talley, flesh moving under loose seersucker pants as he moved, mounds of soft jelly; wide straw hat pushed back on head. Shoes by the chair; feet on banisters. In a hammock lay his friend, Dee. Wherever you saw Bill, you'd likely see Dee. Going to town in Bill's buggy or hanging round Rushtons' Mule Lot. Dee would stand on the street corner, smiling vaguely, whistling under his breath, or scratching himself, while Bill tended to their business. Or here on the farm, he'd be on the piazza, his long thin legs folded up in the hammock; or he'd be following Bill through the fields— like a stretched-out, grotesque shadow.

164

"Reckon I'd better go over," Sam said. "You don't have to."

"Well, Sam," black eyes polished as chinquapins staring out beyond Sam into the boxwood hedge, "out here again, huh?" Chewing on straw between words.

"Yes sir."

"Whassa matter now? Believe you make my niggers sick a purpose so you can git their money."

"Well, sir," Sam laughed at the white man's joke, "this time it's old Aunt Cyn. Rheumatism's got her in a bad fix."

"You know well as me," eyes not bothering to look at the man he was addressing, "you can't do nothin for rheumatiz. If you could I'd a had you tryin your tricks on me."

"Maybe not much, sir. That's right. But I can give a little something and make like I'm helping." Voice soft, pleasant, respectful.

"Who that with you?" Dee Cassidy creaked and swallowed his Adam's apple.

"Aunt Dezie Turnbull's great-nephew, sir."

"Looks like a city nigger to me."

"No sir, just got on his Sunday clothes. It's his old aunt's birthday."

Dee folded his legs in the hammock, put a handkerchief over his face. Bill continued to stare beyond Sam into the hedge.

The amenities seemed over.

"Thank you, sir." Sam went back to Ed. Wiped his face. "Let's get a move on."

The lane turned sharply to the right, thrust a road through fields, dwindled to a footpath wide enough to let a man and a mule through. They stopped at the Quarters—cabins strung out in a row, near enough to share smells and flies, dirt, heat, voices. A girl rocked back and forth on a shed, chewed her dip stick, eyes shut against the glare. She stood when she

165

heard them, came slowly toward them, bare feet moving easily on hot sand, coughing a little with the walking.

She led Sam into a cabin as if she had done it before.

Ed turned away. Never could be around sick folks. How Sam went through it day after day—

Beyond the cabin a sunflower leaned against rotted planks of a privy, its heavy head swinging crazily as a breeze flapped the crokersack in the doorway against it. Ed turned away. Cotton looked fine, weevil must have skipped it. He stepped over, picked a boll, tore it to soft shreds. Funny, way you like to pick a thing like cotton.

Sam stepped out on the shed. "Mind coming here a minute, Ed, and helping me?"

Ed followed Sam into the dark cabin. Huddled in a chair before a small fire was what must be Granny, though after the sunlight he could see only moaning rags, and not until he was up to her could he find the old snuff-colored face.

"Her say her cold. Make me wrop kivers on. Reckon her mixed up." The young girl giggled.

"Yeah. Reckon she's a little mixed up." Sam went up to the old woman. "Come on, Ed, help me here. Got to get her out in the sunshine." They picked up chair, quilts, rags and Granny, started to the door, while the girl ran around their feet, like a puppy, beating her hands together. "Hit'll kill her . . . Lawd Jesus, hit'll . . ."

And then Granny, dimly perceiving some great change occurring in her life, joined in the girl's protest, "Holp . . . holp . . ." Cries dry and screechy as an old bird's. "Jeeeee . . . sus . . . Jeeeee . . . sus . . ."

You could see clear down the old woman's blue mouth. Sweat poured off Ed's face, down his legs. What the devil was Sam up to!

"All right, here will do," Sam said. "This is a fine place. Half in the sun, half in the shade. When it gets too bright, get somebody to help you move her in." He took a bottle out of his pocket. "Get me a cup." Pushed it against the old woman's lips, nuzzling it against gums until muscles swallowed. The girl stopped beating her hands, began to cough. "Here you—take some too." Poured another drink. "Keep taking it twice a day."

He pulled off a quilt, let the sun find the old body. "Look after her." Started down the path.

"Yassuh," the girl sobbed softly after the coughing, kept on sobbing as if it made her feel good.

"You sit out in the sun too. Do you good," he called back, turned, smiled at the girl, waited until he had her smiling. "Do you both good," he smiled, walked away.

He wiped his face. "It's hot. Damned hot," he whispered.

They walked on past cabins, stepped aside to avoid a child asleep with its head in a bucket for shade. On down the hot lane to the road. As they passed the old house, Bill Talley was talking to Lias, his foreman.

"How come you can't git hands?"

"Boss, dey's gone no'th."

"Well, they ain't all gone, can't tell me that."

"Nossuh, dey ain't all gone, but they alightin out fast-ern—"

"Pretty come-off."

"How come they go?" creaked Dee. "You know?"

"Nossuh, Boss. Don know how come. Nossuh."

"Flyin off like a bunch of buzzards." Dee's laugh shrilled across the hot still morning.

"Git um some'ers," Bill said. "Don't matter where. Git um!" He threw away the straw, pulled his hat over his face, slid down into the rocking chair for a nap.

"Yassuh, Boss. Yassuh." Lias went around the house, hat in hand.

Sam and Ed walked on down the road to the car.

"This keep up all day?" Ed grinned, enjoyed having Sam a little on the defensive.

167

Sam laughed. "Bout like this, I reckon. There's fever at the Rushton place. It's a hot trip, wish we didn't have to go."

"It's O.K. Be glad to see the old place again."

Driving to the turpentine farm was a journey to Ed through a lifetime. No chronology smoothing event into event, but a collision of memories, pounding him without relevancy or ease.

There was Mama . . . coming back for the first time after her death . . . she seemed here. Nearer than at her funeral, for then her dead body blocked him from her living reality. But now . . . she was alive . . . everywhere . . . He'd hear her voice, some tone in Bess's voice that sounded like her, a sudden turn of Non's head . . . there was Mama. He'd start eating—something about the dish would be familiar and he'd see her brown knubby hand setting it down on the table, full of something he'd liked when a kid . . .

You keep thinking. Time you ran way. You'd got as far as Ellatown, before Pap came after you. He had borrowed a mule and come after you, and you ran behind a privy back of the whitewashed commissary. You stood there, knowing they'd come in a minute, eyes full of yellow snuff picture plastered on the boards, you couldn't stop looking at it; and as voices drew near you crouched down, smelling the stink of privy, feeling a sandspur in your foot, letting it hurt to stop the hurt inside you which you didn't understand, and never had. Pap came, walking slow, hat in hand, following the storekeeper, sallow white man, cheek bulged with tobacco. "Give it to him," the storekeeper said, laughed, scratched himself between the legs. And the other white men laughed. Seemed the road was full of white men laughing! But maybe only three or four, thinking back upon it. Pap said, "Git on the mule." You got on and he took you home. All the way you kept reading the word on the buckle of his overall strap, as you jiggled down the road behind Pap's silence. When you got there he took you out to the arbor and

168

tanned the life out of you, almost. But you didn't mind
much, though he beat you as if he hated you . . . or something. But when you went inside, sniffling and shamed, and
Mama said, "You don git nowheres by runnin, Eddie.
Member dat. Nowheres by runnin! You has to walk. Everybody has to walk. But *folks our color walks slow.* You hear?"
you'd cried yourself to sleep afterward, hurting all over, for
with those words she had branded you and your family and
everybody you knew this side White Town, and set you apart
forever. Those words and the white children's *chocolate drop*
hurled at you on your way to school, which was their back
way to school and the way they used most, you'd never forget.
You'd picked up cow dung and thrown it and *yan yan yan*
back at them. It didn't help much. They could wash off cow
dung, forget a yell that had no meaning. You could never
forget *chocolate drop* long as you lived. It was smeared on
you to the bone.

Funny . . . riding along like this over deep slow sand . . .
feeling heat . . . hearing creak of springs . . . loose body of
car . . . watching the light glisten palmettos like water . . .
watching your friend's face . . . wondering what lay behind—
everybody's face . . . Things used not worry you. Sometimes.
Not much. And now you keep thinking. Maybe you oughtn't
to come back to a place after your mother dies. Maybe you're
a fool to do it! You keep following her around. Not to her
grave in the hammock—no, never once there. Not to the
end of her life. But to its beginning. Your beginning. There's
nothing to hold you from going back . . . to keep you safe
from going. When she was alive, it was different. Her being
there in front of you made the present the only time. Shut
off the way back. You couldn't get beyond it. She stood there,
smiling at you, holding you safe to everyday ways, handing
you a hot fluffy buttered biscuit . . . making you think *that*
was life . . . all of it, sometimes. And sometimes you'd believed her—almost.

169

You keep thinking . . . time Bess told the kinfolks about you crawling up in your mama's lap, nudging the baby Nonnie out of the way, grabbing the teat for yourself, patting the breast, patting, patting, she'd said. And she said you'd laughed and chuckled as you patted it. And everybody hearing her silly talk had hollered in their amusement at what Bess told them, until you wanted to cry, until instead you wet your pants in helpless four-year-old despair and went stiff-legged around the house, as far away as you could get from the voices. But not far enough to avoid hearing, "Reckon that youngun's plumb jealous of the baby. Reckon he's jealous of such a bright baby." He hadn't been jealous of Non—not that he could remember. But he'd hated Bess. Sometimes now he hated her to the pit of his stomach. Yet— sometimes you could die laughing with Bess over things. Funny, how Non never cut the fool, didn't seem to know how. Always played by herself, never cut monkeyshines with other kids. Sometimes, when she was little, on blowy days in the spring, when everything was blowing, trees, grass, leaves, palmettos slashing together, sand flying, whole world bending and whirling—making you feel daft and wild and shouting—Nonnie would whirl too, around and around, gravely, all by herself, around and around and around—not like play, never quite like play, though her eyes would be shining bright. But Bess . . . get her started. My Lord, what a time everybody had when Bess got started! Switching her hips, waving those hands, opening that mouth, laying her tongue flat, and letting the music out. Then suddenly she'd be prim as Mrs. Stephenson, and bossy as God.

Sam stopped the car. Air heavy here with the smell of rosin. Across the road the turpentine still. Old barrels grayed with the residue of pitch, shacks grayed with years, stretched out in two long rows.

Ed sat in the car. Sam could do his doctoring by himself. Across the road, on the shed nearest him, a big wench lay

170

asleep. A fly played on feet stretched out in the noon sun. Ed looked at the big brown feet, at the darting fly. Found himself getting involved in the struggle. Fly swung about in the air a little foolishly, swooped down, crawled on the brown skin . . . on nail, on tough muscle, until a tender spot of nerve endings was reached. Big brown foot slowly moved. Fly held on. With ponderous patience the other big foot lifted itself, brushed the little fly away. Battle began again. Fly would grow dizzy with its whirling in the bright air, fall on the foot, start its slow inexorable exploration. And Ed would count the seconds until the nerve spot would be reached, the big brown foot move to its defense. Bored with the silly, endless struggle, he would raise his eyes, stare across acres of palmetto, thinned trees, follow heat shimmers above the sand road, idly count yellowed gashes in row upon row of pines, come back to the fly and its big brown opponent. Somebody ought to finish the damned thing.

He must have dozed. Sam was saying, "Got to go up to Cap'n Rushton's office. A chinaberry's there. Might find it cooler."

Cap'n Rushton sat on the shed of the unpainted office shack, eyes closed against the noon weariness. Old man looked petered out, slumped down in his chair. Not as he used to be, riding his white mare across fields, jacking up the choppers, throwing words around like a hailstorm, though most took them with a laugh, liking the boss.

"Howdy, Cap'n Rushton."

Old man opened eyes, reluctantly. "Howdy, Trouble. What's the matter this time?"

"The fever. Three down."

"Could be worse, couldn't it?"

"Yes sir. It will be."

"Always calamity! 'It will be.' How under heaven you know it will be? You ain't God, are you? Or *are* you?" The Cap'n cut off a sliver of tobacco, nudged it into his mouth.

Same old voice. You'd never forget that summer you'd spent here when Mama sent you, almost ready for college, out with colored boys who couldn't read or write—for you to be taught something she'd been teaching you since you could remember. Old Cap had taught you plenty before the summer was over—about work. Golly . . . how long the rows used to be. But you'd liked it.

Sam was laughing now. You'd missed what the old man had been saying. "All these folks tote water from the well down near the branch. There're a hundred palmetto bushes and every one a privy, draining into it, straight as my old man used to go for likker on Saturday night. Flies everywhere. Same old story."

"Yeah. Same old— You can't teach em anything! Built privies once down at the branch. Nobody'd used em. Too far to walk! What you want this time, Sam? Got a fool notion, can tell from just seeing you git out of that rattle-bang Model T—" The old man stopped his words.

"Well sir, we ought to nail up the well—"

"Nail up the well! And it a hundred in the shade. Sure! Nail it up! Go right ahead! Let everybody die quick of thirst and be done with it." He sighed and spat. "Might be the best way out, at that. Sam, you can't convince me you're the fool you make out to be." Cap'n chewed in slow disgust. Across the road from the little office the low song broke off, started again as hands rolled another load of barrels off the shed into a freight car.

"Thing now, seems to me, is to get them all inoculated." Sam wiped the sweat off his bared head.

"Inoc—"

"Give them the typhoid serum. Only way to avoid a first-class graveyard. They've all got the germs."

"Don't believe in it. Nobody's going to stick a durn needle in me. Black magic. Things so bad doctors falling back on

172

black magic. I'd as soon let Old Suke work on me. At least she'd say words."

Ed found himself laughing with Sam. Sounded like old times.

"I've stood by you— Sam—I've stood by you when I was shamed to look my face in the glass, falling for your damn schemes. This is too much. Too durn hot to act the fool— Ain't it?"

"Yes sir. Maybe, if you wouldn't mind talking it over with Dr. Deen—he'd advise us."

"A lot of good it'd do. Deen backs you up in your craziness and you know it." He laughed, looked beyond Sam, stopped his look at Ed. "Who is that?"

Sam hesitated, decided upon the truth, "Tillie Anderson's son, Ed."

"Tillie Anderson's son . . . Well . . . well . . . Tillie," staring across the palmettos, a slow juice easing from the corner of his mouth. "Best cook Maxwell ever had. Best in the county—and you know what? My wife let them dadblamed Purviances steal her, right under our noses, and they—" he broke off, looked at Ed again. "Come here, boy, let's see what kind of credit you are to your old mother."

Ed took off his hat, hurried over. "Howdy, Cap'n Rushton."

"Howdy, Ed. What you doing in them clothes this time of day? Where your work clothes?"

Ed laughed, showed white strong teeth. Washington had not rubbed out manners his mother had pressed in so deeply.

"Ed's working in Washington, for the government," Sam interposed smoothly. "Home for a day or two to see his sisters."

"Government, huh? Working for the damyankees. Reckon you've found out they're not so much."

Ed grinned disarmingly. "Can't touch Georgia, Cap'n Rushton."

"Find me a place that can! You better come on back here where you belong, where folks treat you right and understand you."

"Yes sir. Guess I'll be back before long."

The Cap'n turned to Sam. Ed dropped back to the chinaberry.

Only the murmur of voices reached him. The Cap'n looked sick, as if he might be dying of something. Yellow where his face was once fiery red. Queer how folks change when you've been away a few years. As you get older how things change . . . things you once took for granted—

She'd hardly sent you there for sassing Mr. Pusey. She'd lashed you with her tongue maybe, but no more. Must have read your mind when it was full of crazy thoughts about girls —white girls—all kinds of girls—

It started one day when they'd been talking. Sam and Jack and Ed. They'd been in the bowling alley watching the white boys. Had come out and were going over to Salamander's for a sarsaparilla. Funny how you remember a thing like that, so exactly. As sometimes you remember a dream. Everything. Jack had on a pair of new white shoes. Ed had never owned any.

Ed was sixteen. The other two were home from their first year at A. & M. They'd been talking about things Ed had never heard of, people he had never known, places he'd never been to, until he was half crazy with the feel of his ignorance.

Two white girls walked past the boys—one the Pusey girl, the other a new girl who had not been in town long. They walked past the boys, eyes straight ahead as if they had the whole sidewalk. "Girl with Pusey's daughter got half the white boys in town tailing her," you'd said, trying to get the others' mind off the college talk. "Wonder what she'd do if we whistled at her. They say she's easy," looking at your friends, knowingly.

174

Jack laughed carelessly. "You might try and see."

"What you mean, saying that to Eddie?" Sam's voice hadn't sounded like Sam.

"Why not?"

"You know why not!"

"What's the dif? He's got better sense than to try it."

"How you know he has!"

They seemed to have forgot he could hear. Jack was angry, you knew from the way he sucked his lips in, not liking to be put in the wrong before the younger boy.

"Anybody who wants to live the night through would know better. Anybody who's not a fool. Didn't know you rated Ed a fool."

"Sure I don't. But he's younger—"

"Maybe not so young as you think," Ed said, hurt to the quick. "I know a few things—know white girls maybe a sight better than you do." And in his anger he'd raised his voice.

"Shut your damned mouth," Jack hissed and pushed Ed into Salamander's. "Now listen, Ed—don't you be a fool just because I joked with you!" Jack's thin face—anybody could see now how much little Jackie was going to look like him—was turned on Ed worriedly.

"Boy," Sam laid his hand on Ed's shoulder in his slow way, "leave white girls out of your mouth. And your mind." He added, "Might as well pick up a rattler, Ed."

Ed was half crazy with his shame. "I could tell you things," he bragged, almost in his crazy shame believing the lies he was desperately trying to invent, "I could tell you about white girls—in this town I know white girls who'll let me—"

Jack laughed in bitter distress. "He's a fool and a damned liar. Come on, Sam, let's find something else to do." You'd never hurt so much. If he'd stomped you hard in the belly it could never have hurt so much. And to finish it off, you were near to tears—

175

"Ed's all right," Sam said. "Wherever we go, Ed's going with us. He always has. Always will. Let's cut out this talk!"

No more was said. Sarsaparillas were drunk in silence. Bottles laid down. Nickels handed over to Salamander. Three boys walked out of the café, turned into Back Street, past the water tank, on toward Colored Town.

Sam wiping his bared head. Cap'n wouldn't think to ask Sam in. Not that he'd mind Sam stepping up on the shed while he talked to him—he'd just not think.

Ed spat, pulled a chinaberry leaf, pulled a handful of them.

The Cap'n was laughing. "All right, have it your way. If it don't cost me anything—not a red cent, mind you—you can stick that fool needle in every son of a gun. You'll need a dozen to hold one down."

Sam laughed. A laugh seems easy to Sam. Turn it on, turn it off. "There'll be plenty hollering. Thank you, Cap'n Rushton. I'll be back in the morning. Is Mrs. Rushton well?"

"Yes, she's all right. I reckon she is—haven't been in town in a week. Hold on! I've had a passel of figs for her all day, wondering who I could send them in by. Been smelling up the office until— Drop em by the house when you go in, will you? Be much obliged."

"Glad to, Cap'n Rushton. Anything else I can do?"

"That's all, Sam."

"Thank you, Cap'n."

"All right, Sam."

"Lord God," as they walked away, "and you go on like that day after day after day."

"It's my life," Sam said.

"It's a hell of a life, if you're asking me!"

"I see it different. I've got my work. Got to do it the way white folks will work with me. If it takes a little lying and hand-licking, what difference?"

176

"What difference?" Ed whispered softly.

They ate the lunch Aunt Easter had put up for them, squatting there under the chinaberry tree.

"Difference is," Ed was standing now, crumpling up the lunch papers, "I'd rather die first."

Sam smiled, laid his hand on the younger man's shoulder. "Ed," he said quietly, "you're butting your brains out on that stone wall. It'd be easier to climb over."

"What you mean?"

"I mean, clear out! You don't belong any more in Georgia. Not even for two weeks. Stay out! Things worrying you may settle themselves. Things do sometimes. If they don't, you can't help them any, God knows! How about forgetting our troubles and going fishing tomorrow?"

"Sure," Ed said quickly.

Sam drove along the narrow road. It was hardly more than a path browned with pine needles, which wound resistlessly through acres of fine long-leaf pine timber. Bands of shadow streaked the ground, bands of sunlight streaked trunks of trees, tops of palmetto clumps, building peace and order in the forest, until a breeze would sweep through, mingling them in a bright confusion which hurt eye and mind, and as quickly would subside.

"You see, seems like this." It was as if Sam were carrying on their conversation in his mind. "We gotta remember there are a few decent white people. Helps to remember that. They're not all Bill Talleys, nor W. Y. Rushtons, though he has his good points."

Ed laughed. Sam didn't seem to know when the preaching hour was over. "Name em, Sam."

"Well," Sam's brown serious face eased into a smile, "you think you've put me on a spot, but there're a few. Even here in Maxwell."

"Go ahead."

"There's Tom Harris," Sam said slowly, "he's all right.

177

Drives hard. White and black. Drives himself the same. Treats you fair, white or black. Don't seem to matter. When you think of what he's done for Maxwell! Every good thing this town has, Tom Harris brought it here—"

Sometimes Ed thought Sam liked Tom Harris better than any man alive, though he'd never admit it. When they were kids working on the slab pile, Harris's jokes had seemed a white man's funny business to Jack, making his forehead wrinkle, making him suck his lips in; had seemed to Ed, younger than the others, the signal to act like you working mighty hard; but to Sam had seemed something good to laugh at. Sam laughing at Tom Harris's jokes, finding quick answers in a soft voice that Harris laughed at as heartily, had been the beginning of Sam's getting on in the world. The two of them were one man saying something funny to another man he likes. And Sam, ten years younger than Harris, had begun to stick around the white man, as if he was learning a lot he wanted to know.

"I couldn't have seen it through, up there, without his help," Sam was saying. "Mighty good to me those years in school."

"Course that's what you might call personal," Ed said. "There's always plenty of that kind of giving done by white folks."

"Just the same, he's been a good friend to me and to others like me. And there was Dr. Munson, when he lived—"

Ed watched the slow drip of gum into the tin cups fastened on the near pines, watched the drip, drip, drip, big slow drops, tears, tears slowly falling . . . She was near crying last night . . . near crying when he talked to her . . . not many times had anybody seen Nonnie cry. As a kid when she cried, she'd never make a noise, just let tears roll down her face. Wonder what it was . . . what made her last night . . . stand there . . . lips shaking . . . tears running slow—

"—there's Tut Deen. He'd do no colored person harm,

178

intentionally. Tends a lot of sick folks free, black and white. And there's Pug Pusey—"

Wonder what it could have been—

"Yeah," Ed nodded, "Pusey was good to us boys."

"I can keep on a good while longer," Sam smiled, stopped the car. "There's a lot more."

They went behind a palmetto clump.

"I'll take your word for them. You win, in a way. Not any of them would call you 'mister' though."

"No. Not any of them would call me 'mister.'" He sighed. "Maybe if we were white and in their place we wouldn't call Negroes 'mister' either. I say maybe. Don't know. Not so easy. Things . . . when things get into such a mess and long before anybody living was born . . . mind you, I'm not excusing. Just trying not to waste my time hating white folks when there's so damned much to be done for the Negro."

They stood there. Sam, big, heavy-muscled, a streak of light bringing out red under brown pigment, coloring him to the rich tone of swamp water with the sun in it. His forehead ran up high, for he was getting bald, his black hair clung close to his head, abruptly outlining edge of forehead and temple and shape of skull. He was growing heavy in spite of busy days, from too much sitting in a car when early years had been spent driving a double mule team at the logging camp, and heaving big timbers. Ed, shorter, thin, quick in his movements, hands pale as fresh pine, heavy black hair brushed slick to his head, looked ten years younger as they stood there side by side.

Standing there listening to spatter of urine against hard fan-spread leaves of palmetto, Ed heard Sam's words. "Maybe you're right, Sam. God knows I wouldn't know how to straighten anything out." Five years in Washington and now back again. Things like this ripped the years off—smell of pine—smell of hot dirt— Once when he was little, he had gone behind a bush, as now, and three little white girls had

179

come along the back way from school and had seen him, and giggling mightily had looked at his bared genitals, then run dizzily away as if he were pursuing them. He had felt shamed somehow and had stood a long time gazing at his naked brown flesh . . . wondering . . . shamed and confused. For a long time he avoided white girls. When he grew bold, learned once more to look, they looked through him as if he were a hole—

"Sam . . . Ever think much of time we were kids? Coming back like this . . . I—keep thinking things—all the crazy unimportant things that ever happened to us."

"Guess you would. When you live here, like me, keeps you so busy holding onto the coattail of all you got to do in a day—don't have time to think much."

They went back to the car.

"We had a darned sight of fun, anyway," Ed said and grinned. He touched Sam's shoulder, left his hand there. Such a damned old solid rock, he thought, and eased with the thinking.

"You mighty right!

"Thing I remember most," Sam went on after a little, "was way your mama used to come home in the evenings and fix things for us. I'd always manage to be there that time of day. Best eating I ever had. Way your mother and Jack's took me in when my mother died is something a man'd never forget."

Always hard to remember Sam had been an orphan since he was twelve years old. Sam seemed to you to have more family than anybody you knew.

It was a long way home, a long afternoon. Sam had begun to talk now and talked on, on, on. Bringing up all the good things a memory can be filled with. Just dipping down, straining out all but the funny, the good—trying to entertain you. Bess planning a party—Sam talking his head off—

Now it was the old Hinton place he was talking about.

180

Once a fine big farm—later on, Negro tenants lived there—
child fell into a washpot and boiled before the rest of the
children playing around could get him out or call their
parents from the field. A white tenant lived in it—his wife
hanged herself with the plow lines in the barn—about that
time folks began seeing lights in the empty house at night
and hearing cries in the daytime—

Every county has a place like that, some have two or three.
Sam talked as if you hadn't been born here—

"So the Rushton boys got it dirt cheap at the time they
bought up the timber rights on the fifty-thousand-acre tract
south of the place."

"What's happened to them?" Keep on talking. Maybe it's
helping Sam. God knows it's not doing me much good.

"Nothing, except they're making more money than anybody else in the county. They painted and papered the house
until it's all right to look at inside, and Epp and Sug use it
for parties."

"Cap'n in on them?" Got to say something.

"Too sober. Sug comes out, folks say, to get away from
his wife. Epp—" Sam tried to laugh big now—"Epp brings
nice young school teachers out and deflowers them. Hasn't
got any use for a woman unless she's a virgin. They say.
Afraid of syphilis. That's why he's called Epp. You've heard
that story?"

"No," Ed said, though he had. Sam pretty desperate telling
all the county's dirty stories to make me laugh.

"Seems when he was about fourteen or fifteen some
pimples—"

They were driving now on the edge of Cow Pond, getting
near home. Strands of moss hung almost to the ground from
oaks encircling the water. The late light was soft to eyes after
a day's glare.

"Member, Ed," Sam broke from his uneasy anecdotage,
"member the fish we used to take out of that hole?"

181

"Yeah."

"Down here two weeks ago. When Jack was off his run. We caught the finest cat I ever—"

"Sam," Ed said slowly, "it's not all that race business I'm worrying about. It's Non."

Sam drove on, a little faster now, eyes straight ahead, and did not answer. Ed could see a tightening of muscle around mouth and jaw. Suddenly he did not want to talk to Sam about Nonnie. He didn't want to mention his sister to him. He didn't want to mention his sister to anybody on earth! He had to go on now and say something.

"It's her being willing to—stick in this hole. She could go up North—" stopped. What's the use!

"And what would she do up North?"

"She could get work that wouldn't shame her! She wouldn't have to be a servant to a cracker family like the Browns. Maybe meet someone and marry and live decent—"

"Nothing Non does can—lower her. She lives above her job, it doesn't touch her spirit. See what I mean? She can go through all—kinds of things—all kinds of things," Sam was looking stolidly at the road, "and come out of them, the same Non."

What he mean by that? Now what did he— God! Stop it!

"If you could help me persuade her to go back," Ed tried to laugh it all off now, "maybe I'd stop hating white folks so much. She's a sister a man'd be proud to take to Washington with him."

"Yes," Sam slowed the car to make the last turn at the bend of the old cedar trees past Miss Ada's, "yes, she's a sister a man'd be proud—"

"There she is!" Ed hushed. Non was going around the house and to his straining eyes there was someone in front of her—there was a tall blurred something moving in front of her white dress. He was seeing it now again. Every time he thought of her he saw it—

182

"Sam," he said and wiped his hands on his knees in quick jerks, "this old place gets on my nerves like the devil! How about dropping me off in town?"

"Sure," Sam said smoothly, changed gears, turned the car, "anything you say, old man."

They drove back through the old cedar lane, past the graveyard, on past the A.M.E. Church, neither speaking.

The Reverend Livingston and Roseanna were walking toward the church. Somebody was ringing the bell for prayer meeting, and a group had gathered in front of the steps. Some young boys and girls were making passes at each other, shrilly laughing. You saw them as you'd see the world again after you'd left it. It's there, but not yours any more. Or sometimes after you've been in a heavy sleep, you'll awaken, see your room, chair, table, bed, only they aren't yours any more.

Roseanna was walking ahead, which put the Reverend very much in the rear. He was scowling and hot and wiping his hands, while Roseanna in a big picture hat and a blue organdy dress plowed on like a schooner over the ripples of his injured prestige. You knew they'd had a quarrel.

Sam chuckled. "Never could see how Roseanna could stand the idea of God being her superior."

Ed laughed, wiped his face. "Sometimes, Sam," he said, "I believe I need glasses. Things get blurred, bother me, sort of. Ever have any trouble like that? Seeing things you—don't know whether you see or don't see?"

"Doing the close work you do in the office, you ought to need them whether you do or not. Better have your eyes tested when you get back."

"Yeah," Ed said and drew in a deep breath, "yeah, I'll do that."

# TWELVE

M A X W E L L   W A S on his side. After Brother Dunwoodie announced Tracy's decision to join the church Sunday, men stopped and shook hands, as if he had been away a long time and had come back laden with honors. Yes, down on the street, men stopped and shook hands and said vaguely, "It's fine, Tracy, fine." Or after the service gripped his hand and muttered awkwardly, "God bless you." And women touched his arm, with maternal affection, letting their hands linger as if loath to give up what had been so long in returning to them. And always there was Dorothy by his side, smiling and crisp and neat and devoted. Enjoying her small triumph. For they were saying that Dorothy had done this. It's that little Pusey girl whose influence has done this. She's all right, men said. She'll make Deen a fine little wife, better than he deserves, they said.

Sitting in the swing on the Pusey porch tonight, Dot had drawn close to him. In the dark the swing had moved back and forth, creaking with its movement, and Dot had drawn near. She had placed her body close to his, in brittle proximity. Not a soft fluid unmeasured giving to him, or taking from him, but in precise definition of their relationship. *We can go this far now,* her body said, as it edged up to his, *this far. After we are married, a little farther.*

He had grown restless and impatient and had stopped the slow movement of the swing with his foot, as if to stop . . . everything.

Dot was talking. "We'll make the old farm over, if you decide on it. I know where we can get a loveseat for the fireplace, and your mother is giving us that beautiful old mahogany card table. She's been so sweet and generous, Tracy, about everything. I feel guilty taking it, but she wants us to have it—your grandmother wanted you to have it. She says there's a spool bed in Macon that belongs to you. Your grandmother wanted you to have it too, and maybe other things—"

The old piano in the parlor—wonder where it went to—whatever became of it— You'd go in and lay your head on the keys—you'd hide yourself there—and Mamie would find you and hold you against her, saying half words through her crooked teeth— Old Mamie—you hadn't seen her in years—you must have been a funny little fool—a crazy kid—

"And I know you want it. We'll have a beautiful old country place. You'll like that—"

He stopped the swing.

"You'll like that, won't you? It will be fun to have our own place, our own things. I've always loved collecting antiques—"

God yes! Have your own things—have what belongs to you—

"Tracy . . . What's the matter? You aren't listening."

"Sorry, honey. I'm listening." He turned, looked at the girl by his side in the swing, touched her hair, took her hand. "We must get your ring tomorrow. Or shall we send to Atlanta or New York for a nicer one? Perhaps we should." He had found her third finger now and was softly rubbing the nail. "After all . . . it won't be easy to find one good enough."

"But I've already found one that suits me. At Ferguson's."

Tracy laughed.

"Why are you laughing?"

Yes, why do you laugh! "Oh, I don't know. The old fox probably had it there ready for us."

Dot smiled. "Maybe so. Anyway it's there. I've often looked at it. It's simple, not expensive. I like it."

"Good! We'll go first thing in the morning and get it. That suit you?"

185

"Of course."

Tracy stood up. "Better be going. The neighbors will be talking if I spend the night on your porch." He laughed again. "Good night, Dot. You're a nice kid."

"Good night, darling."

He stooped, kissed her lightly, suddenly rumpled her hair, as he used to do when they were in grammar school together, turned quickly, ran down the steps.

It wouldn't be so bad. She was a nice decent girl who would make a comfortable pleasant home for him. After all, what more should you expect! They'd be by themselves in the country, he'd hunt in the fall—take her with him sometimes, pretty good shot, Dot . . . and all right in the woods. Kill hogs in the winter, put up meat, hams, shoulders, make sausage, put up some syrup in the fall. There'd be the planting in the spring. Most anybody likes to see about planting in the spring. He'd manage.

He crossed the railroad to his side of College Street, pulled a piece of moss from an oak limb, walked on. The moon was coming up now, though lawns were still dark. Front porches silent. A low hum here and there from unseen voices. A swing creaked on the Harris porch. Harriet and Bill Adams. She'd fool Bill. He might as well stop wasting his time and money on her. She'd never marry a Maxwell boy. Too ambitious, too restless to stop at Maxwell. He turned again, started toward his own home, tearing the moss, dropping the shreds on the sidewalk.

He'd manage. There'd be children. Maybe. Maybe he would like that. Hate it or like it. You couldn't be sure. Be funny to have them. How the devil would you go about raising one! Dot would know. Yeah . . . she'd know . . . like every woman knows. They always know exactly how it's done. Think they're born knowing. Or learn it during coition, maybe. And the less orgasm, the more they learn about child-raising. Seems to work that way. Well, by God he

186

wouldn't let her bully his kid. He'd see to that. Leave him alone, let the kid raise himself—

He laughed. Sort of getting ahead of schedule. Well . . . it wasn't so bad. There'd be no more rows with Mother. Things ought to be peaceful. Things ought to be . . . Now . . . maybe she'd feel a little pride . . . maybe she'd like a grandson. Things hadn't been too easy for her . . . he'd trampled pretty hard on her hopes and plans all his life. Maybe a grandson . . . would sort of make up for everything . . . take him in on Sundays, let her play with him . . . do her good . . . After all, things hadn't been smooth for her. Dad—Dad's all right but none too easy to live with, maybe. Lets things slide so. Always Mother who looked after the money—turned it into more. Shrewd, as Dad was easy. Bought a block of nigger shanties in Macon, against Dad's advice, and made money on them. Cleaned up on them. Always niggers needing houses and Mother smart enough to know it. Mother pretty shrewd. Sends out Dad's bills and, what's more, collects them. Manages everything. Now she's going through a bad time, Dad said, on a strain, change of life. Some women lost their minds at menopause, he'd heard of it. Gus Rainey's mother lost hers—in Milledgeville now. Gus said all she did was stand in a corner, walk four steps out, turn, walk back again. The livelong day! All she did. Every time Gus went to see her, it tore him up like a baby. You could tell when Gus had been up there. Ordinarily he'd shortweight the fussy women who were so particular about their meat cuts, smiling and talking soft to them as he slipped his hand on the scales. But after a Sunday at Milledgeville, he threw in a little extra on every order. Red-eyed, wiping his nose across his bloodied white coat sleeve, he'd humble himself even to cranky old Mrs. Reid when on other days he'd be muttering some obscenity about kicking the goddam old bitch in the—

And then Monday night Gus would get drunk. Hog drunk.

187

Four steps out . . . four steps back . . . God . . . if Mother were to do anything like that—you couldn't go through it.

Tracy had come now to the yellow house on the corner. He walked through the lawn, sat down on the porch steps. A light was in Mother's room upstairs. He wouldn't go in—yet. Hot. Terrible night. Mosquitoes better than the heat inside.

Everything settled now—but Nonnie. Nonnie . . . a piece of unfinished business . . . Maybe she'd want to go North. She'd get along better there—it would be better for everybody. End the whole thing. Finish it! Mother . . . Dot . . . they'd been damned nice, come to think about it. You ought to play straight with them—if you're going into this at all. If you're joining the church, at least make a try at being decent. After all, you've never been much of a son to Mother. Maybe now you can show her you've got a little something she can be proud of—

*You'll begin a new life,* Preacher Dunwoodie said today, *a new life, Deen, with the pages bare.* And for a second the words had snapped a chain in two. There'd be no more pulling . . .

Whatever you do, finish it!

Tracy lit a cigarette.

No more feeling. Strange. Done with. Through. Funny—not to feel anything. Relief. You make a decision. Things stop. Like cutting off your circulation. Numb. Relief.

Thing to do now, get it fixed up. It'd take money. A lot of money—to help Nonnie through the months she couldn't work and her doctor's bills. Later, he could give her more if she needed it. Dad offered to pay for Dot's ring. Darned nice of him. You couldn't ask him to do this too. After all, it was Mother who— Well, she had it, and it wouldn't be a hardship on her to lend it to him! Borrow it from her, pay it back some day . . . She'd started this . . . might as well see it through.

188

Tracy laughed, rubbed his hands over his face, sighed. Might as well go in . . . have it over.

He threw away his cigarette.

One . . . two . . . three . . . four . . . turn. One . . . two . . . three . . . four . . . turn. One . . .

Good Lord! What had got *that* on his mind now! After all, he hadn't done anything criminal—never been in jail—never killed a man—never robbed a bank. Why all the to-do? Just what had he done now that would put Mother under a strain? Dad talking other day, looking at him, as if it was all his fault. Mother—going through so much. You'd think to hear them talk that he'd spent his whole life so things would be hard for her at menopause. Why the devil do people hint things? Why don't they come out and say what they mean?

God . . . you let yourself get shot up over nothing. Dad in his funny way probably didn't mean a thing.

He had better go in now and speak to Mother before she turned off her light. Get everything settled tomorrow. Off your mind. He threw down the cigarette, stepped on it, went inside the house.

Tracy tapped on the door, opened it slowly.

His mother was brushing her hair.

"May I come in?"

Her plump white arm moved up and down in the shadows, the smoky blue crepe of her dressing gown falling away at the elbow. Mother wore the right clothes. Plain. Right. Wonder what kind of things Dot would wear. Lots of lace. Yeah, she'd wear lots of lace.

"Dad out?"

"At old Mrs. Reid's."

That's good. Easier to talk here than downstairs. "You'd think he'd give her a little extra in that hypo one of these nights, wouldn't you?" She won't think that funny.

She smiled, continued brushing her hair. It used to be

189

heavy and blonde; now gray and thinning, and shorter. Watching her, he had the feeling that he used to brush it for her when he was little. He still remembered the feel of it. But he must have made it up. A pair of tweezers lay near the comb. She'd been pulling the hairs from that mole near her lip. Glad she wasn't doing that now. It made him uneasy to watch her jerk at herself like that. Dangerous. Heard Dad tell her time and again it was dangerous. She'd put cream on her neck, and as her arm moved it glistened in the creases of flesh, catching the light. Every night she went through this ritual of cleansing and smoothing her body and making it as attractive as she knew how. Funny thing. Once he'd heard Harriet Harris say her mother spent an hour getting ready for bed. What did they do it for! What did they expect after they went to bed? Not a thing. "You see," Harriet had explained, sounding a little drunk, though she wasn't, "after a time, down South, there was a migration. Sex left its old habitat and moved to woman's face." They laughed—all these youngsters seemed to know so much, he'd thought, when he got home from France, and talked so glibly about what they knew or didn't know. Dottie, older than this young crowd, had said on the walk home, "You mustn't misjudge Harriet. She's just indiscreet—doesn't mean things the way they sound." "Oh, she's O.K.," he'd said and laughed. "Nothing wrong with Harriet except she notices too much."

"Why are you laughing?" his mother said, and smiled.

He smiled at her. "Oh, I think maybe I'm feeling pretty good." He sat now on the arm of his father's chair.

She was pulling the hairs from her brush, dropping them in the wastebasket. A wad of yellowish-gray hair. Old. She's getting old. After all, her life hasn't been so happy—it's the least you can do—maybe she'd enjoy a grandson—maybe she'd enjoy coming out to your place—

Wonder how she's feeling about me. What she's thinking as she sits there brushing her hair. You . . . you have a picture

190

of her in your mind . . . Wonder what kind of picture of you she has . . . Wonder what she thinks is her son . . . if she knows what her son is . . . what . . . All day you had expected her to say something. About Dot. About joining the church. Though it would have been embarrassing. It was better like this. No talk about it. No strain. You have given her what she wants; you know how she feels.

Her hand moved toward the tweezers. Good Lord, she's going to do it right now. Women don't have a bit of shyness.

"Don't!" He hadn't meant to say it. Now you feel like a fool.

His mother smiled, picked up a small bottle of alcohol, wet a piece of cotton, wiped off the tweezers. She's going to do it, anyway.

"Mother," he said, "Dot was telling me about the furniture. That's nice of you to give it to us."

"Your grandmother wanted you to have it."

Grandmother . . . you'd always think of her . . . as real now as she was when alive . . . tall, thin, sharp-eyed, earrings sparkling and tinkling, brandishing her will all over the state, wherever Grandfather was sent to preach. "Leave the child alone," the old lady used to say. "Alma, you drive him too hard!" "Mother, you must let me train my son in my own way. I insist!" "When you're old as I am you'll know a child wetting his pants isn't the most critical moment in either his life or your own. After all, privies had their blessings. They did indeed! A water closet a hundred yards from the house made a little pants-wetting seem quite understandable." "Mother! You forget children have ears!" "Tsssch-tssssch—I never forget anything!" And she had bent over and picked a pin off the floor without flexing her knees, straightened up, face mottled. "Son," she said, "never marry a woman who has to bend her knees to pick up a pin. She'll be a lump of wet flour on you in ten years." Gave her daughter a triumphant look, for Alma was heavy and slow-moving, and left

191

the room. He'd spent his summers in Macon after Grand-father died and Grandma went back to her old home on Hardaman Avenue. "Your grandfather was a deeply religious man, and the Lord's good shepherd," she'd said to him often, "but I must confess these parsonages are more like that place the good God consigns lost souls to than anything I can now think of. I'm glad to be home again, with no Missionary Circle hovering over me—even if I do have to pay taxes."

"Wish we could have kept the old place," he said now.

"The section's changing. Better to have sold it when we did."

"I suppose so. Mother—" the delay wasn't making it easier —"could you let me have—some money?"

Alma laid the tweezers down, turned to her son, searched his face. Something had snapped tight in her eyes. "How much, Tracy?"

"Three hundred."

"That is quite a lot of money."

"I know. I hate to ask you. Maybe I can pay it back—when I get the farm going." She hadn't said a word about his going out on the farm.

"Why do you need it?"

"I'd rather not say."

"For Dot's ring?"

"Dad gave me money for that."

"Then why do you need it?"

"I'd rather not say."

"Have you asked your father for it?"

"No."

"Why don't you take it up with him?"

Tracy was counting things on the dresser—powder puff, comb, brush, mirror, scissors, cold cream—*keep on counting —don't have any feeling—*

"Why, Tracy?"

192

"I'd rather not bother Dad."

"You've been—gambling?"

Tracy looked at his mother. She had picked up the tweezers, laid them down again, now let her hands lie in her lap. *Sure he's been gambling!* "You can call it that." He lit a cigarette, tossed the match to the water-pitcher tray.

"Have you—told Dorothy?"

"It's none of her business."

"Everything that concerns you is Dorothy's business now."

"If you can't let me have it, just say so, Mother. Let's don't argue about it."

"I can let you have it, Tracy, but it displeases me for you to be stubborn. So secretive."

She had picked up the tweezers again now and was sliding them between her fingers. "I have wanted to say this to you for a long time, but somehow—we don't seem to have time for talks. It is very nice that you are going to marry Dorothy. It makes me very happy. She's a fine girl, a fine good girl, and will make you a fine wife. But you will make her life miserable if you continue with her the kind of relationship which you have had here in the home with your family. You have never given us your confidence, Tracy." She smiled to soften her words. "You know that. And it has made it hard —for all of us."

Tracy felt unable to move. He was simply there. Staring at his mother. Like a fool. He had somehow thought she would be glad that he was marrying Dorothy, really glad, glad about the farm, glad about the church. And here she was, finding new faults to pick on. Always finding—

She was talking again and wiping the cold cream from her neck as she talked. "I'll give you the check in the morning," she said, "and then I want you to go straight to Dorothy and talk this whole thing over. Whatever the—escapade was, she'll forgive you, and you'll be starting out together as real partners. Dorothy can be a great help to you, Tracy, if you will

193

let her. And you'll find her a person who can—forgive things."

Forgive things!

Tracy wheeled, walked out of the room. Turned toward a path so worn, so familiar, so effortlessly followed that he seemed to stand still while traveling it.

The moon was high, but if it had been pitch-dark he could not have seen less of blobs of houses, late pedestrians, of trees and sand. Blind to Maxwell and its connotations, he stumbled on, seeing one thing now, seeing only what awaited him at the end of his path. She'd be there. She'd be there waiting. Things would somehow right themselves in swift orientation as if you'd roused from a nightmare, and waiting a moment in the dark had found yourself and one by one the pieces of furniture in the room. Being within sound of Non's voice would do that. It had always done that. It would do that now. Funny . . . how a thing like that could be. How you could go to her time and again, just to talk things over, and in the talking things would ease down for you. Never think sometimes of taking her body . . . Never cross your mind. Come to think of it, it's queer. Maybe another damned queer thing about you—not like other white—

He stopped as if he had lost his way. White laughter rang in his ears.

He saw now that he was on the short cut through the gallberry bushes, knew he was listening to voices too far away for their words to be clear. Gus and the boys. Coming from the shanties behind the A.M.E. Church. Used to try to get him and the Harris boys and Clem Massey to go. They'd never gone. Never talked it over, never thought much. Hadn't wanted to go. On the short cut that stretched like a thread between White Town and Black Town, he stood, halfway across the green. They must be in front of the old church. They'd meet beside the minnow pond. The glutted and the hungry. *While these retire, let others come.*

He laughed aloud. Back of him White Town. Back of him

194

white women. All the white women in the world. Yeah . . . they tie their love around you like a little thin wire and pull, keep pulling until they cut you in two. That's what they do. Back there, they're asleep now, stretched out on their beds asleep, ruling the town. White goddesses. Pure as snow—dole out a little of their body to you—just a little—see—it's poison—you can't take but a few drops—don't be greedy—do as I tell you—do as I tell you now—be good boy—do as I tell you—just a little now—Tracy!—that's not nice—that's not nice—

Hear Gus laughing. Gus went to the altar tonight. Didn't get saved. No. Getting harder every year for the preacher to convert Gus. Get saved in Colored Town—get you a nigger—she'll save you—make you feel good—make—O.K. by him. If that's the way men work things out—O.K. by him. He'd marry Dorothy, join the church. Sure! What's the harm in joining the church. Sure! He'd live a respectable life from now on—but by God he'd have his nigger. If that's the way they did it. All right by him. He'd fix things. But he'd still have her.

He stopped. Some whisky somewhere around here. At Snooks' Place. Do him good to have a little whisky—that's why women hate it so—do you good— *Give it up for my sake.* Sure. *For my sake—do this for me. You'll hurt your mother. Do this for me—do that for me.* Sure—sure. *She worries so—you're making her nervous. It's her bad time—change of life. Try to be easy on her now—try to—*

He cut across to avoid the boys. Went back of the A.M.E. Church to Snooks' cabin. Snooks waddled to the door, gleaming like a sunset, her yellow vastness encased in pink silk.

"En will you be comin in, Mr. Deen?"

"Just give me a pint, Snooks, and make it snappy, will you?"

Snooks waddled back with the pint, decorously closed the

door behind her. You could hear the girls laughing inside. Gus's girls—and the other boys' girls.

"Hit's a purty evenin, ain't it?" crooned Snooks.

"It's all right, I reckon." Tracy turned quickly away.

He sat down on the steps of the A.M.E. Church, and drank the whisky. Back of him in there they worshiped God too. The blacks. Yeah—they had their razor fights and their women—went on their drunks and stole and worshiped God. Scared of something—like white folks. Everybody scared. All but the women—they're not scared. No, God! All they want is to keep *you* scared—keep you from having—

Tracy took another drink. So still back there . . . everything dark. Nobody there . . . not even God. Empty. Empty —everything—so—

He drank from the bottle slowly now, held it afterward, rubbing his finger down the smooth surface . . . up . . . down.

—so goddam lonely—church so lonely—things so—

He laid the bottle on the step. Stood up. Time to go. Yeah. Go to his nigger— *Go to your own folks!*

He stopped. He could not remember where he was or what he had to do.

The path was dark here and still. Ahead of him was the row of tall cedars, edging the graveyard and Miss Ada's place. He walked on slowly. Stopped again, feeling confused, sick. As if he'd lost something. He felt that he must remember what it was—he had to remember—it was absolutely necessary for him to remember—

Yeah. That's right. He was on his way to Nonnie.

At the arbor he called, stood by the old wicker chair and called. "Nonnie!" He listened. Yeah—that's her name. That's right. "Oh . . . Nonnie!" That's right. That's her name. Sure to be her name. "Oh . . . Nonnie!"

She came quickly out of the back door. "Tracy! I'm glad you've come," she whispered.

"Come on," he said.

"Sssh," she whispered, and led the way quickly down the path toward Aunt Tyse's cabin.

"Sssh yourself," he said, but she was hurrying on down the path. "Got a surprise for you," he laughed.

"Surprise?"

They walked on, Nonnie ahead of him. Now at the cabin door. Nonnie looking at him as if she didn't know him.

"Surprise, Tracy?"

"Sure. Caught you, see? Caught you. Caught on. See?"

She looked at him a moment, said very quietly, "Let's sit here on the steps and talk. It's so warm."

"Stop talking like that. Think you can act like a white girl, huh? Well, won't let you. Been playing that trick on me all my life, haven't you? Mighty smart—yeah—making everybody laugh at me—making everybody laugh, you hear? Making the whole goddamed town laugh its head off—you—"

"Tracy—"

"I've caught on. You're nigger . . . yesh . . . nigger. Thass all. Thass all I wanted—all I ever wanted—anybody say I wanted more goddam lie."

Girl staring at him. Face white. Eyes staring black. "Let's go back. You're not yourself. Let's go. Let's go back—" saying it as if she knew no other words.

"Not myself? Maybe you don't know myself—what nigger girl knows myself?"

"I'm going back. When you feel better—"

"Oh no. Since when? Since when? Get this. I've come for something—not going till I get it. You know! Not going till I— Come on—show me—you know—show me quick!" He had pulled her inside the cabin now, and they stood just inside the door facing each other. Nonnie did not move toward him.

"Goddam you—when I speak—I—I— Come here!"

Non had not moved. Now she walked up to him, laid her

**197**

hand on his shoulder, looked in his face. "Tracy . . . they
. . . they're wrong—you don't have to listen to them when
they say things—you don't have to believe it— Let's go outside—let's go and talk—"

"Talk—like hell talk. Goddam you— Didn't come here to
talk."

"You're tired. They've done so much—"

"Tired! Take your hand off my shoulder. What you—"
Suddenly he shoved her from him, and she fell against the
wall, struck her breast against a stud, lost her balance, fell
to the floor. For a moment she could not get to her feet.

"Non! You're hurt!" He had quickly come up to her.
Stopped. "Well, I'm glad. Yesh, I'm glad. Why should I do
all the hurting? I'm glad—you hear—" Now he was down by
her. "You're mine—even if you're just a little nigger, you're
mine and I love every inch of you. How about that coming
from a white man, huh? How about . . . I love every inch
of you. . . . goddam em, I love every inch of you—every
inch of you—they can't keep me from loving every inch of
you—they can't keep me—they can't keep me—give you the
works, that's what they do—every inch of you—that's what
they do—that's—"

"Tracy—please—you're drunk—you don't know what you're
doing—you don't know—you—" She was crying now but she
made no effort to stop his hand.

He saw somebody pulling at her dress, fumbling with but-
tons, tearing it from her shoulders. Saw somebody tearing
her blouse off, tearing her skirt off, pulling at cloth until
there was nothing between his hands and her body. He saw
a man—couldn't see much, couldn't see much—a man above
her, saw him press her down against the floor—don't do that!
—saw him press her body hard—saw him try and fail, try and
fail, try and fail . . . heard a low sobbing . . . a deep harsh
cry—she's crying—no, it's you crying—it's you—you couldn't

—you—couldn't—couldn't . . . you couldn't—you couldn't—
you couldn't—

She was gone. The moonlight sprayed across Aunt Tyse's
cabin, lighting the floor, opening boards on the wall, cracking old shutters, making a big empty space between dark
corners. She wasn't there. "Nonnie! Where are you? Oh,
Nonnie!" And then he heard someone calling somebody.

He sat on the broken-down steps of Aunt Tyse's cabin.
His head ached and his muscles were sore. Morning was
breaking over the pine trees. Back of him the palmettos
cracked and snapped with the wind that blew close to the
hot ground, cooling the early day.

Non was gone. He could not remember when she had left
or what had made her go. She was gone from the cabin and
out of his life. All the women that had ever bothered him
were gone. Yeah . . . something swept through his life,
cleaned the women out.

He tried to laugh. Thinking a thought like that ought to
be funny. You ought to laugh at anything that's funny. You
ought to die laughing at a thing that's funny—what's funny—
what—ought to die—laughing—funny—die—

A board creaked in the house and he was standing. Why
he'd moved so quickly he didn't know. He knew he'd better
get going. Better get going and keep going from this old
cabin. From this old path that led to the swamp. How come
he ever got on it, he'd never know. All he knew now, he was
leaving it. Walk out of a house, slam the door, lock it, never
return to it. Maybe that's what conversion is. Shutting a
door, locking it. Funny thing . . . how it had always worried him. Always worried him. That, and hell. Didn't believe in hell but you let it worry you. Yeah—you let things
worry you. Well, nothing'd worry you now any more. Now
any more—

He was on the path leading to White Town. On the right

199

path. He stopped by a palmetto and relieved himself. Watched the urine sink quickly into the sand. Be fine if you could get rid of your troubles easy as that. Pour them into the earth. Easy as that. Easy as—

From the path you could see the roof of the old Anderson house if you looked. But you didn't have to look. And between you and its back shed and grape arbor was the cane patch. You didn't have to look.

He cut across by Miss Ada's, across back fields.

Better not try the house. Dad up pottering around on the side lawn with his flowers. Dad goes to bed late, gets up early. As if there's nothing much to stay in' bed for. Take the lane. Go to Henry's cabin. Better get a little sleep—see Dot. Get her ring. Poor little girl waiting for her ring.

When Tracy walked in, Henry jumped out of bed, expressing no surprise. He dressed, made up the bed with clean sheets, clean counterpane. Tracy fell across it, did not remember anything more until Henry was shaking him.

There was a pot of coffee and some breakfast on the table. You didn't want it.

"Your ma asked me if I seen you dis mawning. I say I seed you out walkin wid Miss Dorothy."

"How about a drink?"

"Better take yo breakfast, Mr. Tracy."

"How about a drink?"

Henry poured a little whisky into the old crockery cup.

"She say give you dis envelope."

Tracy laid it aside.

"Henry—" Tracy poured himself another drink.

"Now eat yo breakfast, Mr. Tracy."

Tracy picked up the envelope, laid it aside.

"Drink yo coffee, Mr. Tracy."

Tracy drank the coffee.

Henry put the plate before him. "Eat yo breakfast."

Tracy pushed the plate away. "What time is it?"

200

"Goin on leven."

"Lord! Had a date with Miss Dorothy at ten." He laughed. "Pour me a drink." Henry poured a very little in the cup.

"Henry . . . ever thought of getting married?"

"Gawd no!"

Tracy stared out the back door. Picked up the cup, drained it, pushed it slowly along the window sill.

"Henry—I'm marrying Miss Dorothy."

"Gawd Jesus—you jokin!"

Tracy did not seem to hear Henry's words, continued to push the cup slowly up and down the window sill. Up it would move, a white object, towards the window frame, back again. Up and back—a heavy white cup on a splintery window ledge.

It was a long silence. Black Henry scratched his head, studied the face of this white man he had known and played with all his life. Then like a shadow that disappears as one changes direction in the sun, his black sycophancy dropped from him. "Tracy," he said softly, "whassa matter, boy? Tell a man whassa matter."

Tracy turned and looked at his friend. White face twisted, despairing. Black face bulged with sympathy, lips pouting with affection, eyes batting dismay.

"I wish to God I knew," he whispered and covered his face with his hands.

Henry squatted down by him. Once when Tracy was fourteen he had cried. The day the two of them found his dog after the Five O'clock had run over it. A look at the creature and Tracy had flung himself beside it in the sandspurs. Appalled by the spectacle of so desperate a grief, Henry had watched him, with tongue too thick for words. But after a time his hands had found their work and slowly he had picked up the fragments of the little animal and laid them on a board in careful semblance of what had been destroyed.

But now his big hands hung idle. He listened to the tearing sound of Tracy's sobs and made futile movements with his tongue while sweat poured from his armpits. And then in a frantic gush of sympathy, half falling over his own big feet, he knelt beside his friend and put his arms around him, grunting out inarticulate comfort.

On Back Street a Ford chugged through deep sand ruts, past the Stephensons', turned toward Colored Town. From the kitchen Henry could hear Eenie banging pans in ill temper because he had not come to help her, and he knew it would not be long before she would whirl like a black cyclone down the path and into the cabin to see with her own eyes what was keeping him, and to see with her own eyes whatever else she could see . . . The damned old bitch-louse, he thought lucidly, and to his surprise, aloud.

Tracy raised his head, stared at Henry, "Well, I be durned. What're we doing, having a love feast?" Laughed, pushed the Negro away from him.

"Henry, for Christ's sake you stink like a polecat. Don't you ever wash?"

"Yassuh. I washes. I sho does. Mebbe not so sufficient."

"I say not so sufficient! Pour me a drink and get a move on you to the house. It must be late."

Henry poured a drink. "Hit's yo fourth one, Mr. Tracy," he said quietly.

"What the hell if it is?"

"Yo ma will smell it sho."

"Tell her I won't be in for dinner. And use a little bar soap before you go in or you'll turn her stomach. Hear?"

"Yassuh."

"Go over and tell Miss Dorothy that I'll see her this afternoon. Tell her I was called out on business this morning."

"Yassuh."

"Get on with you. I'm tired of seeing you around."

"Yassuh," whispered Big Henry McIntosh, and walked

202

softly out the front door of the cabin toward the kitchen. He paused, took the path to the servants' lavatory underneath the pantry. He walked slowly in, picked up a piece of yellow laundry soap, turned on the faucet. He watched the water dribble into the sink, swirl around the rusted bottom, disappear into the drain. He wet the soap and rubbed it on his armpits, sloshed water until heavy suds foamed on his black flesh and rolled down his muscled forearm. With a finger he raked the suds down his arm to his hand. "Hit's da meetin—dey got im plumb crazy," he sobbed, and swallowed the sound against the towel. He washed his face and neck and dried thoroughly and took out a fine-tooth comb and ran it carefully through the front of his hair. He looked at the dark brown reflection in the blurred mirror over the sink, and once more he washed his face.

And then he went up to the kitchen.

"So hit's you, sashayin roun like you was in Noo Yawk—one hour late, dat all, dat—"

"I stopped to rench off a liddle—"

"Hit'd take mo'n a cold water rench," Eenie interrupted, "to wash dat likker off'n yo breaf, ef dat how come you a-renchin—"

"Listen, big gal—spose you could shut yo mouf?"

"Big gal . . . Big gal . . . Is you crazy! I done tuck all I gwine take fum sech as you. Me and Miz Deen done put up with a Gawd-sight of fool triflin on count of yo po ma and pa. And we thoo . . . Thoo!"

"You an Miz Deen, huh?" Henry shook his hips at her in disgust. "A lot you got to do wid it! Mr. Tracy is my boss—hear tell of im befoh?"

"Dat white boy . . . he done spiled you, en you is pizened him. An him makin tracks fo de bad place fas as de devil can pint em out, a po los soul— I asses you," Eenie swelled out like a pompous toad, "who to blame—"

"Shut yo mouf, you blabbin old black bitch," Henry was

203

suddenly beside himself. "You asses *me*, does you? Well, I'll ass you ef you lets out anudder soun—en hit won't be wid ma mouf." Henry pranced over to the wall and picked up an iron skillet and, on his toes now, edged nearer the object of his anger. "Jes one soun, en I'll lay dis iron on yo old black tail and beat it to jelly! I plum sick of you and yo Miz Deen," his voice squeezed out slow words, "you—an—yo Jeeee-sus—"

Eenie blinked and showed the whites of her eyes in one mighty convulsion of shock, then grabbed her butcher knife. "One step, nigger, en foh Gawd I'll slit you fum yere to yere." Her knife cut beautiful, precise half circles out of the air as she moved closer to him. "I calls on my Saviour to witness dat enough enough."

In answer Big Henry flourished the heavy skillet close to her face and suggestively down toward her buttocks, as if it had been a palm leaf fan.

Sweat poured from both faces. The day was as hot as any that a hot August could bring forth. Eenie in her exasperation at Henry's slothfulness had piled on more and more wood until her big iron range was red hot. Steam coiled from her vegetable pots, the lids jiggled up and down in staccato urgency. Spurts of steam gushed from the hot water faucet, the tank behind the stove groaned and crackled with the pressure of increased heat, and now a smell of burning bread thickened the air. Unmindful, the two enemies glared and pranced at each other.

The door from the dining room swung silently open. Mrs. Deen, immaculate in white linen, her cool composed face half shadowed by the large white hat, stood unobserved, and watched her servants. Like raging beasts they stalked each other around the room, big mouths half open, breathing hard, eyes reddened by heat and hate.

"Eenie," quiet and cold the voice, "your bread is burning."

Slowly the knife and skillet descended. Slowly the ene-

204

mies assumed a decorous position of limb. The voice went on. "Turn the damper, the stove is too hot. You'll burn the place up. Your kitchen is sweltering. Henry, your table isn't set. It is late."

"Yas'm," Eenie murmured and waddled to her stove.

"Yas'm," Henry murmured, "hit won't take me mo'n a minute." He grabbed the silver tray.

Mrs. Deen closed the door behind her.

When Henry entered the dining room she was standing by the double windows looking out on the lawn. "The grass is brown and dead," she said in a voice emptied of all feeling.

"Yas'm, hit is sho. I'll water it ter seevnin." He laid the silver with meticulous care, cutting his eyes toward the motionless back. He brought in the plates and goblets. She had not turned. "Anything else, mam?" voice curved in deep obeisance.

Mrs. Deen turned around. "Henry," she said, "where is Mr. Tracy?"

She searched the Negro's face.

"He was not at the service," she said quietly.

"He weren't? He meant to be there sho. Mebbe," Henry said deprecatingly, "he was settin to the back where he were not in sight."

She did not take her eyes from his face.

"He did say for me to be sho to tell you not to wait dinner on him, mam. En I clean forgot to tell you ontil now." He smiled at his mistress with ingratiating candor.

"Don't serve dinner, Henry, until you hear Dr. Deen's car," she said evenly and left the room.

Tracy pushed the cup to the end of the window ledge.

He picked up the envelope, slowly opened it. $300.00. He held the pink slip of paper and looked at it. First National Bank of Maxwell Georgia . . . Pay to the order of

205

Tracy Deen . . . $300.00 . . . Three Hundred Dollars and no cents . . . Alma Mathews Deen.

Out in the lane a hen was cackling. The lily-lined path leading to the kitchen door was hot and bright in the noon glare. Dr. Deen's car pulled to a stop on the graveled path. A screen door slammed. There was a rattle of dishes in the kitchen. A faint ring of telephone. Dr. Deen's car pulled away from the driveway, turned into Oak Street.

Henry came to the door of the little cabin; stood and watched the man holding the pink slip of paper, looked at the tired thin face, looked at the hand, white with black hairs across it, holding the pink paper; tiptoed away.

$300.00. Pay to the order of Tracy Deen . . . Three Hundred Dollars— Pay to the order— Alma Mathews Deen— Pay to the order— *Find some good nigger you can count on to marry her— Give her some money— Give him some money —And get going! Deen, get going—*

Tracy stood, put the slip of paper in his pocket, went out of the cabin to the big yellow house. His face was quiet and composed, his step was steady as he started on a road whose map had been drawn long ago, so long ago he could never remember.

# THIRTEEN

DESSIE SAT on the back porch of the Anderson home. Inside, one of the Livingston twins was playing the piano. Folks were still dancing, or walking in the yard to cool off. Dr. Perry had been there all evening and was helping Miss Nonnie and Miss Bess with the drinks. They'd tried out some new records Mr. Eddie had brought home, and everybody had had a good time. Even the Reverend Livingston and Mrs. Livingston had dropped in for a little while to watch the fun. And the freckled gentleman who sold insurance was there—he'd sold her some too, twenty-five cents' worth a week—and the schoolteacher, and a man whose name she didn't catch, a friend of Dr. Perry's, from Valdosta. It was a fine party. They had little cakes iced in colors, and punch and Coca-Cola, and there were some bottles out of which Mr. Eddie and the other men poured something into their glasses. Miss Nonnie had smiled when she came and had whispered, "Dessie, you're so pretty!" And Miss Bess had exclaimed, "Why, Dessie! Aren't you dressed up! Where in the world did you—" and had stopped and said, "I'm so glad you could come. Be careful not to spill anything on that pretty new dress," and had looked at Miss Nonnie as if mighty surprised, and then Mr. Ed had asked her to dance.

Now she waited for him to bring her some more refreshments. He had been real nice to her. She'd been afraid he wouldn't remember he'd seen her before—the time they ran into each other on the street. But he had. Hardly any of them dichties ever noticed her or remembered her, or bothered to speak to her even at church, cept Miss Nonnie and Miz Lowe. They and Miz Harris was the finest ladies on earth. Miz Lowe so smart and, when she was feeling good, always dancing around crazy, like they used to do out in the kentry. And Miss Nonnie, pretty and sweet and holdin her head so high; and Miz Harris. Miz Harris sho was good. She prayed ever morning a long time before she dressed, and she talked about having a clean heart and about the blessed Lord and made you feel like you was gwine die or some'in right solemn inside. And now here *she* was—But she hadn't stole it, she'd git it right back before Miss Harriet could miss it. The prettiest dress in the world! Harriet had brought it home from Atlanta and when they lifted it out of its box to

207

show Mrs. Harris, she had caught her breath and pressed her hands together until the knuckles cracked. Red silk organdie, they said it was, and it had white specks in it and fitted Harriet tight to the waist with yards in the skirt aflouncin around in the air, and it had a square neck cut low and little sleeves like butterflies blowin about, and when Harriet went to a party she wore white satin pumps with it and a white flower in her hair. Today she'd seen the dress hanging in the closet—the prettiest thing . . .

And then Miz Harris had called to her to polish the silver. She'd sat there lookin out of the window, thinkin—some'n sad, Dessie was sure. Then she said, "I'll read to you, Dessie, while you're rubbing. You know the white people are having a revival meeting and I would like for you to have some small part in it. I want you to be a good girl, Dessie, and you can't be without knowing what God means by good."

"No'm," sighed Dessie. Hit would've made you a thief to have stole that dress. Here you is thinkin of stealin a dress when Miz Harris trusts you. Miz Harris said when she hired you, "Now, Dessie, everybody who works here is trusted."

Dessie rubbed a knife until her cheeks quivered.

"It isn't necessary to rub so hard, Dessie." Mrs. Harris was searching for the chapter.

"Ya'm," breathed Dessie. She'd walk in and they'd say, "My, Dessie, that's the prettiest dress . . ."

Mrs. Harris read to Dessie about the ten virgins.

"*. . . be likened unto ten virgins which took their lamps, and went forth to meet the bridegroom.*" Her voice was just like church. "*And five of them were wise, and five were foolish. They that were foolish took their lamps, and took no oil with them: But the wise took oil—*"

"Do Reverend Dunwoodie do nothin sides preach at da meetin?"

"No, why do you ask that?"

"Case he eats a powaful lot not to git rid of it no ways sides talkin." Dessie smiled broadly at her mistress.

"Dessie," Mrs. Harris looked at her gravely, "it is wrong to criticize people. It is especially wrong to criticize one of God's servants. You are—my servant, aren't you? You work for me?"

"Ya'm," Dessie nodded loyally.

"Brother Dunwoodie works for God."

"He do?"

"Yes. In the Old Testament there is a story—I'll read it to you some time—it is about the respect which we must always show God's servants."

Dessie picked up a spoon and rubbed it slowly and very softly. Hit would've been a black sin ef you'd a stole dat dress! How come you ever thought of stealin . . . how come . . . Dessie's hand paused, suspending a fork in mid-air, her eyes grew wide, a heavy pulse began to beat in her throat. . . . You kin jes borry it . . . and bring it back termorry fore Miss Harriet gits up . . . you kin. . . .

"Dessie," Mrs. Harris abruptly laid down the Bible.

Dessie's heart flapped against her ribs like a cornered chicken.

"Dessie, tell me about your family. Your mother and father. Where are they? Did they go North?" Mrs. Harris's voice had a lonely sound in it, as if she wanted to talk to somebody.

Dessie smiled, sighed deeply, "I don know nothin atall bout ma pappy and mammy. All I knows is ma granma."

"I suppose something happened to your mother," Mrs. Harris said.

"Ya'm. Granma say—"

The door opened. Mr. Harris came in from the mill, laid aside his hat, glanced at his wife, rubbed his hands over his pink bald head as he always did when tired out, picked up the evening paper.

Dessie turned back to the black-eyed lady who'd hardly

209

noticed her husband. "Ya'm. Granma say she runned away da minute I was drapped—lit out like a greased pig." Dessie smothered a giggle with her hand. "As fur ma pappy . . ." Dessie pursed her lips, picked up the basket of silver, shook her head in eloquent silence.

"Well . . . you'd better run now and help Aunt Susan with supper."

"Ya'm." Dessie gathered up her things. "I'm much obleeged to you fo yo kindness," she said and went out, hearing Mr. Harris chuckle, hearing Mrs. Harris say, "Tom, you ought to be ashamed of yourself!"

After the party was over, Henry was coming for her. He hadn't been invited to the party, but he said he'd come to the gate and carry her home. Sometimes she believed she'd marry Big Henry. He seemed more like the folks out in de kentry than most of these here town folks. But he was bad. He sho was what Miz Harris would call bad, cause ever time he was with her he tried to take her back of a palmetto clump or some'n. She knew how to git shet of white boys quick, but sometimes she was afraid she wouldn't want to git shet of Henry . . . ef he kept on . . . like he done . . . sometimes.

Dessie straightened the neck of the red dress. She hadn't spilled a drop on it. Every once in a while she reached in with her handkerchief and wiped the sweat off of her armpits to keep from spoiling it that way. Miss Harriet would never know the difference.

Now as she waited on the back porch, she heard a noise. A whistle. And Miss Nonnie slipped out and hurried under the arbor. Dessie leaned over the porch banisters. She could hear voices.

"I can't stay now," Miss Nonnie's voice, it sounded worried, "not now."

"But it won't take long—it won't take a half hour." A man's voice.

210

"Tracy . . . I can't bear not to do what you want. You know that. I can't leave now. It's Eddie's party—he—"

"What on earth! When did a party get so important?"

"It's Ed. He hasn't had a good time at home, he and I haven't got along—if I were to leave now—" Her voice sounded in awful misery, "I can't, Tracy. Please go."

"Running me off?" The man laughed as if angry.

"Please. It's Eddie's party. Later tonight . . . Can't you come back? I'll go with you then—anywhere—"

The voice laughed again. "That's not what I want," he said. "It's a little business."

"Business?"

Inside the house you could hear Mr. Ed's voice calling, "Come on out, Sam, with Dessie and me. On the back porch. Bring a twin . . . Which one? I said a *twin*," laughing loud now. You could tell he was gittin high.

"Yes," the voice in the arbor said. "Guess it can wait."

"Yes, Tracy. And go now—"

Nonnie started back to the house. The man hesitated a moment, walked across to the cane patch path.

Ed came out on the porch. "Non?"

"Yes, Ed."

"What's the matter?"

"Nothing."

"Anybody with you?"

"No."

There was a crackle of leaves. Ed turned quickly, looked toward the cane patch.

"Ed," Nonnie was smiling into her brother's face, having quickly run up the steps and put her hand on his arm, "get your sis a glass of punch and let me stay out with you and Dessie. Won't you? It's cool out here—and the moon's lovely."

"Oh sure."

Ed looked hard at his sister, went inside the house.

211

While he was gone Dessie sat mute as a little statue gazing up at Nonnie, who was herself as still as death.

The moon was silver bright, and the ground all sprangled with black shadows, and they sat there looking at it, not saying a word, as they drank their punch.

Somebody said, "They're calling you, Dessie. Someone at the gate is calling you." So Dessie thanked Miss Nonnie for a nice time, and when she shook hands with her, Miss Nonnie's hand was like ice. And she thanked Miss Bess and said good night to Mr. Ed and ran down the walk to the gate where Big Henry was waiting.

He made as if he didn't notice she was there and that got her to giggling, and as they walked through the dark piece of road under the cedars he slipped his hand around her hips and felt for her body through the full folds of the dress, and she giggled even more and felt shamed, kind of, though she knowed she wasn't going to do nothin bad, and then she began wiggling her hips at him until she remembered the dress and that hushed her up quick. "Ef yo please, Mister Smarty, I doesn't preciate none of dat kind of attention," she said, and moved away and tried to walk uppity-like on her side of the road. But Henry grabbed her hand and pulled her toward him. "Ouch, Henry . . . don't . . . don't . . . don't scrunch my dress . . ." He'd ruin it sho, ef he kept on. "Don't scrunch my dress . . ."

"Scrunch yo dress! Well, fo cryin out loud!"

"No, Henry," as he pulled her closer, breathing on her neck now, trying to make goose-flesh rise, "no, Henry . . . please don't scrunch it, please, Henry . . . don . . ."

But Henry, mistaking her reluctance for capers, only pulled her the harder, big hand reaching around her shoulders, pressing shoulder blade, pulling in her hips closer to him, laughing deep and low. And suddenly Dessie fought him. Like a swamp cat she went after him. "Take yo hans off'n me," she screeched, "take um off! Take um—" Big

212

Henry laughed deep and with one strong pressure held her close against his body.

And then she heard it. Thin as a mosquito singing in her ear. "Oh, you've did it," she whispered. "Henry, you've did it," she sobbed.

"What I did?"

"You've tore my dress. What'll I do?"

"Honey, I'll git yo anudder, come Saddy."

But Dessie was beside herself now. "Ooooooo . . ." she moaned, and suddenly began to run ahead of him squalling, and with each step she took she squalled more loudly until Henry had to take three or four big strides and catch up with her and lay his hand across her mouth. "Now shet up! If you don, the night watchman thow you and me bof in da calaboose. Shet up now!"

So Dessie shut up, but all night in her room she cried, muffling her mouth with an old towel, for the tear was every bit of two inches under the arm, and she had nothing to sew it up with but a spool of brown cotton darning thread.

Light was breaking over the pines on the sawmill side of town when Dessie remembered Miss Belle. Miss Belle sold perfumes and toilet articles to folks on College Street to make a living, and lived in the little house left her by her family when they died, on one of the side streets where white folks lived but near the Negro Lodge and ball ground. Sometimes she sewed for the colored people too, though she liked for you to slip in the back door when you came to be fitted. Maybe Miss Belle would fix it.

Miss Belle was sure to be sound asleep, and she'd git mad as a old sow if you waked her up. Dessie would have to wait awhile. She got up, put on her work clothes, went outside and sat on the doorstep. The morning was cool and beautiful. A heavy dew had wet down the grass, and the vines lay heavy and fresh-green with the dampness. She walked slowly past the row of shacks in the north part of Colored Town, past the Lodge, across the green of the white folks' ball ground. Miss Belle's small yellow house was still closed up.

Dessie walked up and down the deserted street, saw the cooks go to work. There went the Anderson girls, Miss Nonnie so spick and span in her white uniform, Miss Bess in her blue. There went Aunt Susan—she'd better duck. Dessie ducked until Aunt Susan had safely turned the corner. There went Hernsey and the others. Lawd Jesus . . . she'd have to wake Miss Belle. She'd have to . . .

Across the street a white man was walking fast, as if in a great hurry. Mr. Tracy Deen . . . Lawd Gawd . . . in the arbor last night . . . And him ajinin da church today. He'd better be gittin home and shavin and gittin cleaned up ef he was gwine live spectable atter today.

After Dessie had knocked a long time, Miss Belle came to the door. Dessie did not wait to be asked in but ran inside with the dress, scarcely noticing Miss Belle's plump, sleepy surprise. Words rushed past her lips. "Miss Belle, please mam, fix it . . . fix it right away, please mam. I'll be so much obleeged . . ."

"But it's Sunday, Dessie. And what on earth do you want fixed? You know I don't sew on Sunday."

"Yas'm, but, Miss Belle, I gotta have it. I—" suddenly Dessie began to cry, holding the dress out to Miss Belle with both hands. "I've gotta have it," she sobbed. "Please mam . . ."

Miss Belle took the dress, found the tear, looked at the dress closely, looked hard at Dessie. "I see," she said, and smiled like a glass breaking.

"I don't sew on Sunday," she said, her little tight blue eyes boring through Dessie. She pushed a loosened curler behind her ear. "You know I don't sew on Sunday." Her plump neck looked wrinkled so early in the morning and messed up and dirty, Dessie noticed, even as she cried. "I don't like to break the Sabbath."

"Yas'm, I knows it. But I'll pay you anything you say to break it, please mam, and fix my dress fo me."

"I couldn't fix it for less than three dollars," Miss Belle said slowly, staring hard at Dessie.

*Three dollars!* That was two weeks' pay, and she had her insurance and room rent to pay—

Miss Belle's fingers crawled over the dress—white and soft and pudgy like big old worms crawling in wood. Suddenly she wanted to poke out her lips at hateful Miss Belle and flutter em at her hard, but ef she did she knowed Miss Belle'd slap her windin. She dassn't give her no sass . . .

"Yas'm," Dessie breathed a little fast. "I kin pay yo a dollar now and a dollar a week ontil it's all paid. Yas'm, I kin do it. Please, Miss Belle. I'll be so much obleeged . . ."

Miss Belle threaded her needle, took her seat by the window where the light was good, and picked up the sleeve of the dress.

Dessie sighed in blessed relief, and wiped her nose on her apron.

# FOURTEEN

EDDIE WATCHED the meeting. Night after night he came and watched the meeting. As you'd see the boys around town watch the screened box at Rainey's market, where sometimes there'd be a captured coon, or a rattler coiled in the corner, or some rabbits. You'd stand there and watch the animal, maybe feed it something. Maybe just watch. Not thinking much. Not feeling much.

And sometimes Ed didn't feel, didn't think, then sometimes he felt what he believed the white folks were feeling. Or most of them. Something you felt against your mind. Against all you knew. Against all you believed. Yet, there it was.

White girls from College Street seemed to feel it too. You watched them to see. They made you curious. You'd always wanted to know a white girl. You knew their brothers, you'd played with them as kids, sometimes gone fishing. But you never knew a white girl. You'd have to be a house boy, or cook or gardener, to know a nice white girl in Maxwell. And even to know the whores in the hotels you'd better be a bellboy.

In the middle of the congregation, close to the aisle, sat Tracy Deen. They said he had joined the church. That he joined Sunday. They said he was getting married to that Pusey girl. By his side she sat there now, pushed up close to him, kind of cuddling in public, as some little women do. She was looking up at him every few minutes and smiling. And Deen smiled back, as if he meant it. As if he meant it.

Ed suddenly felt hungry. Starved. As if he had not eaten since coming to Maxwell. He felt good. He'd go home to-night and sleep. He'd eat and then he'd sleep.

He turned away from the tent opening, went across the business section of town to Salamander's.

The café was crowded. "Stinks like the devil," he muttered, as he pushed through to a table in the rear, where a back window cooled a small area of the room.

He waited a long time without catching Salamander's attention. Old man slow, getting deaf. Needed somebody to help him with the place. Go over and tell him what you want. Or maybe stand and whistle at him—

A voice lifted above the roar of the crowd— "Let a big boy in, you!" Henry McIntosh strode into the room. Wide shoulders pushed aside the human impediment in his path, hands

216

slapped a bill on the counter, big mouth bellowed, "Give me food, old man!"

"Look at im! He done broke open the Nashnal Bank, sho. Where'd yo git ten bucks, boy?"

"Ten?" Henry laughed, deep in his belly. "Look here man. Look here!" And Henry waved a wad of bills above the shining sweaty black faces. "Ever see a hundred bucks?"

"My Gawd, no!"

"An don aim to," another voice yelled, "hit'd kill me sho to look at um—"

"Don worry—ain no chanct of yo dying fum dat." Another voice laughed. "Dat ain a way none of us'll die. Ain none of us'll die dat sweet . . . no . . . baby!"

"Count um, boy, while our moufs waters," Bill Brown's feminine voice piped high above the others.

"Sho, count um!"

"Betcha dey's countfitten," a skeptic muttered.

"Betcha he robbed old Miss Jones of her pappy's trunk. Ma uster say hit was full of confedit bills, and dey ain worth spit—"

Eddie sat down. Might as well wait. Looked as if they had old big mouth gnawing on the wrong bone this time. Ed smiled. Felt good to smile and mean it. To sit here like this, waiting for a cup of coffee and wanting it when it came.

"Spit—well, git dat spit outen yo own eye and maybe you can see," and Henry slouched over and held a bill close to the speaker's face. "How dat, huh, how dat?"

"Hit's good as Jesus," the awestruck voice whispered. For a moment there was reverent silence as the stilled room worshiped this vision of actual wealth.

But soon—

"You gon set us up, sho, ain't you, Henry?"

"Sho. Fill um up, Salamander! Fill um all up." Henry was near about busting with hospitality.

"How come you got um, Henry?"

"Wherever dey comes fum, he got um all. No use to pry aroun lookin fo scraps, is deah, Henry?"

"Ain none lef aroun nowheres, is dey, Henry?"

Henry smiled, swelled like a toad. "Not a scrap."

"I knows how he got um—" Every head turned toward Little Gabe, who until now had sat on the counter in silence. "He go up to Mr. Hah'is down at da mill. And he say, 'Mr. Hah'is, you makes a sight of money outen dis here sawmill, acuttin all dem million feet of lumber, and wif dem barrels of tuhpentine asetting out deah, gwine up to Savanny ever week, don't yo?' And Mr. Hah'is say, 'Sho boy. I makes a mighty lot of money. What kin I do fuh yo?' And den Henry say, 'Well, Boss, kin yo let me hev a hundred bucks till Saddy night? I plum run outa change and I needs a liddle snuff fuh ma old woman and a new automobile and a few other liddle things . . .' " Gabe was at his lifetime role of storytelling, and the crowd, mouths open, eyes on his face, were following every word in contented identification. "And den Mr. Hah'is he retches in his pocket and pulls out a roll of bills and wets his finger and counts off a hundard and say, 'Reckon a hundard'll do, Henry?' an Henry say—"

Henry said, in half-drunken loyalty, "Dis money come fum da Deen family. I works for the Deens. I don work at no sawmill fo no Hah'is white man. I'se de Deen's houseboy . . ."

"Sho. Hit's a liddle extry they thowed in fo good measure dis week—dat it, ain't it, buddy?"

Henry's lips swelled out, as Henry's liquor swelled his loyalty. Muttering stubbornly now, "Tracy Deen give me dis money."

"Ain't yo birfday, is it, Henry?"

"Tracy Deen give me—"

"No hit's Christmus," somebody guffawed.

"Trac—"

"Christmas gif, Henry," everybody was yelling now.

"Sho, Christmus gif," piped Bill Brown.

218

Into Henry's muddled brain entered the necessity to defend his dignity, and his employers. He slowly wiped his mouth on his sleeve, and faced the crowd. "All right, smartcats. Put dis in yo bellies and watch um swell and bust. Mr. Tracy Deen done gimme dis money cause he and me, we friens, an we'se made a bargain."

"What kind of bargain?"

Henry turned to the counter, swallowed the remainder of his third cup of whisky. "Hit's a private bargain," he giggled drunkenly, "about a girl." Rolling his eyes now, trying to leer.

"What girl?"

Henry rolling eyes now. "Oh, jes a girl. Hit's a secret!" he giggled.

"What girl? Come on—what girl?"

"Jus a purty girl what he done got into trouble."

Ed sat up as if a knife had been shoved through him.

"What's yo bargain?" Bill piped hungrily.

"I'm to marry her." Henry laughed. "Yeah man, he give me a hundred bucks, and dis big boy gwine to marry Nonnie Anderson to—"

They tried to stop him, for someone had seen Ed, but it was no use. It was no use to do anything but back out of the way as brown man came striding across the little room to black man, brown man's face like the wrath of God. "You goddam son of a bitch," breath sucking in and out in great sobs, "you damned black nigger—" Ed drove into Henry's jaw, once, twice. Henry, off his guard and utterly dumfounded to see Ed Anderson standing before him, stumbled back, hit the side of the counter and fell to the floor.

Ed turned away from the still man, stumbled out of the café. He had no more time to waste on Henry McIntosh. No more time to waste on niggers. Only Tracy Deen's face could he see, only Deen's slow, tired, sarcastic voice rang in his ears—

His breath came in short dry gasps as he ran across the street and into the alley. Behind the Supply Store he paused, leaned against the back door, tried to breathe. Blood pounded in his head, blinded him, and for a time all words were lost in his mind, drowned by simple physical sickness.

Four blocks away, across the deserted business streets of Maxwell, Preacher Dunwoodie's voice struck out at his congregation, rising, falling, like a great hammer beating against the town's conscience: "Repent . . . day of judgment . . . at hand . . . God . . . great mercy . . . one more chance . . . Turn aside . . . deaf to his pleading . . . How long . . . God's patience . . . endure . . . you . . . secret sins . . . you hiding behind . . . social position . . . pillars . . . church . . . yes, you . . . God sees . . . your heart . . . some . . . last chance . . . No more . . . will Jesus . . . your way . . . too late . . . too . . . ."

But Ed's ears were filled now with another white man's words, another white man's face . . . *hundred dollars . . . you marry her . . . make her . . . you marry her . . .*

He turned and recrossed the street, turned down Back Street, walked swiftly across the ball ground, past the cemetery, to his home. The house was dark. Nonnie and Bess were at the Livingstons', he remembered now.

Nonnie . . . he paused on the steps. It was as if she stood there before him, smiling at him, poised and gentle. So proud he'd been of her—he'd never seen a woman who could touch her. And now they'd made a whore out of her—thrown her out like garbage to a stinking lecherous low-down—

Ed's breath broke into sobs as he stood there on the steps. A decent educated Negro—her own kind—wasn't good enough for her! No! No! *She* had to have a white man, a damned no-count white—

Ed sat down on the steps and buried his face in his hands. White man filled his mind. White man scrouged his soul. White man—

220

Singing across town stopped.

She had to . . . she had to have . . . she . . .

Ed's breathing grew quiet. Sitting there on the step he felt quiet. He knew now. It was curious, after the aching trouble of the past week. Curious and pleasant to know just what you had to do.

Words chanting through his mind, again, again, again, again, hurting, had inexplicably changed into new words, bringing peace. Beating against him now until all his body sang them: *He's got to die for this—he's got to die—he's got to die—*

In ancient rhythm his body swung with the old, old song.

Ed wiped his face, went upstairs to his room, fumbled around in his suitcase until he found what he wanted, walked downstairs.

As the screen door banged after him, he whispered, "She'll be sorry—" but they were words that his ears did not hear.

# FIFTEEN

THE ANDERSON GIRLS stood up to leave. Bess laid the Spelman College catalog on the table, laughed as she said, "We've talked about teachers, courses, the place, and told you what clothes you will need. When you get there you'll both think every single thing we've said was wrong."

Each Livingston twin drew in a deep breath. The vivacious pretty one said, "You've been wonderful to us," and smoothed back her hair in imitation of Bess. And the quiet one smiled at Bess and turned and smiled at Non, and went over and slipped her arm around her mother.

"Is it worth it, Bess?" Roseanna Livingston said, her eyes filling as she tried to smile easily.

The Anderson girls were silent.

There stood Roseanna Livingston, Colored Maxwell's club-woman, Colored Maxwell's leader of its church and social affairs, Colored Maxwell's delegate to the Lodge's auxiliary, Maxwell's brown replica of the full-bosomed, pompous, full-mouthed clubwoman you'd see on College Street in any town of Georgia. Roseanna, weaving her hands and her words together in flowery speeches, speaking a little familiarly to white women's faces, tossing her head in scorn behind their backs, bending her efforts to make herself an exact copy of them—now gentled by what lay ahead of her two girls on a path which seemed to them beautiful and straight, leading on forever and ever to an exciting wonderful life where everything was going to be so . . . different. And somehow so right.

And there in that little parlor, lighted by a big kerosene lamp swinging from the ceiling, stood Preacher Livingston, who preached the Gospel on Sundays in the A.M.E. Church in his sleazy black Prince Albert coat, and on Mondays and other days did a sleazy insurance business in a room over the Pressing Club. There were the Livingstons and their twin daughters standing in the lamplight; back of the girls the reed organ; back of the preacher a round table covered with red velvet with a big Bible on it; back of Roseanna a whole life of getting ready to make her twins into ladies.

"Yes," said Bess harshly, "yes, it's worth it! Everything you have to go through now . . . and afterward." And they stood there, looking at each other, or at nothing. All of them, in the Livingston parlor. Until the Reverend Livingston said, "The lamp's smoking. Always the lamps in this house smoke!" And one of the twins.climbed up in a chair and turned the wick down, and everyone tried to laugh a little.

222

Then they went home, silent. At the door Bess said almost gently, "I know it's no use for me to say it but—if you'd go to bed now, Non . . . You look so terribly tired."

"Not quite yet," Non said.

She sat down on the steps. Feeling a little tired. Yes, a little.

The singing had stopped long before they left the Livingstons'. He might come. Not last night, nor late Saturday night. But maybe tonight. And they'd go to the top of the sand ridge where they could be alone and quiet, and maybe there, with just the warm wind stirring and the stars and the little scrub-oak trees back of them, maybe she could help him find the way back . . .

And then she looked up, and there he was at the gate.

She ran down to meet him.

"Hello," he said, and stood there, not opening the gate.

"Hello."

"Non," he said, not opening the gate. "Non, I've come to tell you—" he stopped.

"Yes, Tracy."

"Guess you heard I'd joined the church."

She nodded.

"Well," he laughed a little self-consciously, "I meant it. I mean—it wasn't just something I did, as a matter of form. Like some people." He took out his handkerchief, wiped his face. "I've never felt like this before—" he stopped again.

"As I see it," his voice had grown a little strident, "my whole life's been wrong. All wrong!"

"Wrong?"

"Yeah. Things like—" he was not looking at her. "Like this, for instance. I've been weighed down all my life by a sense of—well, I reckon you'd call it sin, maybe. Or something. I've changed, Nonnie, don't know how to tell you . . . Oh, I know so-called respectable men keep on doing things like—" he stopped.

223

"Like—" just a whisper.

"Like this—you know what I mean . . . Like— But I'm through! If I'm going straight, gotta go straight. Can't do it half way. Thought once—thought maybe I could—but I see it different now. Yesterday I joined the church and I meant it. Brother Dunwoodie's done—I know I laughed at him . . . other people have too, and then gone on their knees . . . Tell you, the man gets you. Never heard anybody who could make me feel so like a skunk, listening to him— The way I'd been living—way I've always done the family . . . Mother . . . ruining her whole— Made me realize time comes when a man must face things—see what he's doing to other people—"

It seemed the words would never stop.

"Only of course you're not like . . . some—there's—" He seemed to be searching her, the whole of her, though his eyes had not once looked her way.

Nonnie didn't breathe as she watched his face.

". . . something he wouldn't . . . understand . . . about you . . ."

Her hands pressed together until the bones ached.

"I . . . Oh well—" he stopped. Went on, "Mother's so glad, it's kind of—you see, I've always failed them. Always managed somehow to do the wrong thing— There's Dorothy . . . Nobody thinks I've been decent to her—and I haven't. Been pretty yellow, I guess, but—well, to cut it short—" He drew in a deep breath. "Today I gave Dorothy a ring. We're to be married in the fall. That means—it may sound funny after all you know of me, but I'd like to go to Dorothy with my hands clean. You—you've lots of sense—you can understand that, can't you, Nonnie?"

Nonnie tried to say something, anything. No words would come. It was as if all her life, all memory of life had been rammed down her throat so hard that she couldn't get her breath.

"About the baby," his voice was very low now, "I've fixed that."

He seemed to be waiting for her to say something.

"Fixed?" her voice could not break through a whisper.

"I've been a fool to get you in trouble like this. To tell you the honest truth I thought—you'd—know—how not to—having gone off to college—and everything—" He broke off suddenly, looked straight at her. She hoped for one wild exquisite moment that he was drunk again, he looked so strange, wetting his lips again and again as he talked, as if he were saying a speech which he didn't know the meaning of—

"But never mind," he picked up his words again, "we can't cry over that—now. Thing to do now is to save you from being talked—I've got it arranged."

"Arranged?"

"Yes. You see I'd never leave you high and dry, to face that—you know that—so— What's the matter?"

Nonnie shook her head.

"You look sick . . . What's . . ."

"I'm all right," she whispered.

"So I thought of Henry. He'd do anything for me, the old fool," he half laughed, "and he's worshiped the ground you've walked on since you were knee high to a duck. I—well, I told him about it—your condition—and he said he'd be glad to —give you the protection of a name and—"

Nonnie heard no more. She was seeing Big Henry, she was breathing his sweating stench, she was looking at his big open mouth with its upper gold teeth, feeling his hot breath on her lips, her ears rang with his deep-bellied laugh, her thigh felt his wide gripping fingers. She was remembering when she was eleven. He had met up with her on the way from school and said, swinging his books back and forth across his shoulders as he said it, "Say," he said and grinned, "say, how about fuckin with me?" And as she stared the color had beat through her face and neck. "You knows," he grinned,

225

"fuckin," and opened his pants. She had begun to run and he had run close behind her saying, "Say, what's the matter? You skeered?" Suddenly she had turned on him and whispered, not able to speak out loud, "Don't you come near me, don't you come near me!" and had begun to cry and run faster and faster toward the old empty house. "Shucks," he called after her, "whassa matter wif you? Even white gals does dat." Her mother had said that night when the miserable tale was told, "You has seen folks with lice in they haids, honey, and there's plenty of um, God knows, in this neighborhood, but it's their lousy minds I want you to hate, baby girl, and they ain't all black . . . Hate um, white or black . . . hate um . . . hate um . . ." The words attached themselves to a revival tune now and began coiling, uncoiling, coiling in her mind.

"Nonnie, are you listening— What's the matter?"

She shook her head.

"Well, he'll be here to see you tomorrow. We thought it might keep down talk to get the marriage over before anybody noticed your . . ."

The ground had tilted, and everything on it—the swamp, the old house, the graveyard, Miss Ada's, the cedars, a bunch of pink honeysuckle, old cypress, the ridge—swirled around her in slow circles. She caught hold of the fence.

"Knew you'd see it this way. Told Henry you would. He . . . well, he sort of stands in awe of you. But if he ever—if he dares touch you, you come straight to me . . . Nonnie, you've been . . . I hate like hell . . . I—here I almost forgot the damned thing—the money—two hundred—ought to help you through— If you ever need more or get into trouble . . ."

He held the package out, but Nonnie's hands were motionless on the picket fence.

"I'm damned sorry—I'd hoped—you'd—"

Nothing in her empty face, nothing in her body pressed hard against the fence could have given him hope.

226

And suddenly it was as if he had begun to see the thing through her eyes, as always she had been able to make him see. He had begun to see what he could never have borne . . . "Nonnie! God in heaven, I can't leave you like this . . . Listen . . . we'll have one more night. Tonight, honey . . . Listen . . . Tonight we'll be like old times, then it'll be easier . . . for both of us . . ." He moved toward her. Between his hands and the white splotch that was Nonnie, a lightning bug darted and was gone. He touched her rigid shoulder, touched her hair, her cheek, dropped his hand quickly.

He laid the money on the fence rail, turned, **was gone.**

Nonnie stood unmoving at the gate. Stood there, holding to the picket fence, looking across—White Town. Little night creatures flew close to her face, a bat circled her head, plunged down across her, swerved, disappeared in the dark. Far across the fields, beyond the railroad, a car chugged through the heavy sand.

Sharply, plunging two holes through the night, shots rang out. It was as if they had gone through her body, cutting her nerves awake. Now she was hearing every little sound, the whir of every insect. And as if, one by one, every light in a house were switched on, her mind grew clear. Turning she ran into the house.

Bess was kneeling in the hall, bathing little Jackie in the small tin tub. She glanced up when Non came in and stood there before her. "What's the matter?" Her voice grew sharp before the words were finished as she looked at her sister's face.

"I don't know," Non whispered.

"But what were those shots, Nonnie?"

Nonnie shook her head.

Bess put down the washcloth, left the little naked boy standing in the tub and went up to her sister. She was suddenly furious with her, and frightened. She shook her hard. "Nonnie, you do know."

Nonnie slid quietly to the floor.

With quick sharp words Bess told Jackie to dry himself. Then she dipped some of his bath water out with her hand and splashed it over Nonnie's face. There were footsteps on the porch. Turning quickly she saw Eddie standing at the door, as empty-faced as the girl lying beside her knee.

"Well, I've done it," he said, and sucked in his breath with a little nervous laugh.

Bess let Nonnie's head slip to the floor. She knew with quick nausea that the time had come for whispers. She went to the door. She drew Eddie out of the lamplight to the dark porch.

"Now what have you done?"

"Killed him."

"Who?"

"Deen."

"Tracy?"

"Yes."

Brother and sister stood in the darkness, blur facing blur, breathing heavily.

"Anyone see you?"

"No. Don't think so."

"But you don't know. Anyway, they'd know it was you . . . I've got to get you out of town." Bess did not hear herself say that.

"I'll swing a freight."

"And get caught before you're halfway to the tracks! Somebody'll find him. Where—" she found it hard to say.

"Where he dropped. I wouldn't touch the bastard."

"But *where?*"

"Near Miss Ada's."

"They'll find you—they'll come straight here." She was shaking all over. Her mind was shut fast. If she could just

228

think, she kept saying to herself, she would know what to do. It was as if all her race's knowledge of how to escape the hands of white men would offer itself to her, only for the thinking . . .

An old hound barked. Its shrill cry trickled down her body like ice water. She beat frantically on a door that would not open.

"I don't give a damn," Eddie said stubbornly.

"Oh you're such a fool!" she was hating him, and hating, grew sane. "Sam. If he's home—he'll drive you to Macon or— Come on," she commanded.

"I've gotta see Nonnie and explain."

"Explain your foot! Come—you must go—"

"I can't leave without—"

Nonnie walked slowly out to them and stood there without speaking.

Bess turned, said quickly, "He's killed a white man. You know what that means."

"Tracy?" Nonnie asked quietly.

"Yes."

Around them the black night pressed with its dead weight of three hundred years. Against that heaviness they had little strength to breathe. To the brother and sister nothing seemed important that moment except to know how Nonnie felt. They waited, each groping toward her through a thick fog of a lifetime of hating and loving and sharing.

"You must go—" she finally said, and the two listening could not find any feeling in her voice.

"Mama," Jackie piped, and turning, they saw silhouetted against the lamplight the little naked fellow peering through the screen door. "I've got to pee-pee." The simplicity of his need brought the present down with a crash upon them. Fear tore off the inertia which had bound them so strangely.

Bess said, "You'll have to wait! You can't do it now. Lord, I'd forgotten him. Come here." She picked him up, started

229

down the steps. "Come," she said to the others, and began to run. As suddenly stopped. "Money." They looked at her blankly.

"How much have you?"

"Don't know—five, six."

As if it didn't matter; as if nothing mattered. Everything left to her! Faint sounds from White Town . . . "Nonnie, you'll find my money back of Mama's picture. Get yours, wherever it is. Hurry, Nonnie!" Nonnie's running feet to Bess's straining eyes moved through the night as you run in a nightmare. "Get Jackie's bank too," she called.

"No, no," Jackie screamed, "Nonnie tant hev my pennies."

"Ssssh, baby, it's for Uncle Eddie."

"He tant hev um—he tant," and Jackie began to kick his way out of Bess's arms.

"Hush! I'll whip you!"

"No, no, no!" Jackie screamed in steady crescendo. "He tant hev um, he tant hev um, he tant—"

"Oh God, make him hush—make him—" Bess moaned. "They'll hear him—"

Eddie suddenly laughed, and at the sound of it Bess began to giggle hysterically.

"I won't take your pennies, old man, now pipe down." But now Jackie was too sleepy and uncomfortable to discontinue sobs which had added so strangely to his stature in the family. "I wants to pee-pee—I wants to pee-pee—"

"For God's sake, Bess, let the fellow down!"

"Run quick behind that bush, Son—"

"You t-tole me n-not to r-run to b-bushes lak a p-puppy—"

"Oh Lord!" Bess hurried with him behind a canna.

Nature and Jackie had come to terms when Nonnie came back, breathing hard from her running.

"How much?"

"I—haven't—"

"Count it, Non, quick!"

It was nearly twelve dollars in all.

"Won't take you to Washington, Ed?"

"No."

They had reached the gate. Nonnie stopped. She pointed to the fence. Unknowing at what she pointed, Bess turned cold, as if all the cottonmouths of civilization were coiled there to strike them . . .

Non whispered, "There."

"What?"

"The money."

Bess followed her gesture, felt along the rail until her fingers found the package. She turned slowly, looked at her sister, but Nonnie had moved away and was walking down the path. "Take the back way to Miss Ada's, Non," she called softly.

They left Jackie at Miss Ada's with few words, knowing that she would accept the child at this hour and unclothed, as simply, without question, as she accepted everything that life brought to her side door.

As they came down the steps of Miss Ada's brushing close to the old hedge to get to the front path, Bess stopped. If they went out the front way, down Miss Ada's little bottle-edged path, past the row of cedars, they'd walk by his body. They'd— "We can't go that way," she said, and saying it, compulsively she looked toward the place where she knew Ed must have done it. The moon was rising now behind the dark row of tall old trees, it would soon disclose the body as clearly as would daylight. She made herself stop staring at the trees, made herself stop wanting to go there, as she felt compelled now to do, to see this thing close, this trouble that had been in their lives so long with no naming of it by anyone. It was as if something had prowled through the woods close to you ever since you could remember, sometimes just cracking a twig, sometimes crashing hard against a tree, but you had never quite seen it, or been able to name

231

it. And now it lay there before you—dead. Dead. And you wanted, or something deep down in you wanted, to look at it a long time . . .

She turned quickly, took the back path, which threaded its way through a stretch of dense woods and on to open ground back of the cemetery. They were quickly at Sam's. The house was dark.

She ran up the steps of the porch, noticed, as she ran, that the others followed her close, as if wanting to stay near her. And something eased in her a little as she saw it. She knocked briskly at the door, feeling now suddenly that maybe she could manage it, this thing that had fallen on them, which until this moment had seemed beyond anything her mind or heart or body could accept.

She knocked again. Within the house she heard a bed squeak, a foot touch the floor heavily. Slow fumbling steps. Aunt Easter. He was out. Sam had gone somewhere . . . maybe out of town . . .

She knocked on the door again, banging loudly now in sudden panic.

The door opened. Old Mrs. Easter Perry held a lamp high above her head. She stood there in her long white night-gown and surveyed Bess from head to foot, slowly. "It's you," she said. She looked beyond Bess at the other two, back to Bess.

"Yes'm," Bess said softly. "Where's Sam? Where's Sam, Mrs. Perry?"

"He ain't here." Her high nose seemed to Bess a barricade against her.

"Where is he, please? I must see him."

"He ain't here." Lips shut tight.

"Where is he, please? It's important. Awfully important." Bess was now remembering the many times when it had not been important.

"When he gits in, he say he gwine to bed. Up last night
232

wid sick folks. All night. Dey wear him out, got no time to be foolin roun wid them what don need him."

"Aunt Easter," Bess began to plead now, "this time we need him, if anyone ever did. Tell me, please. I'll go there."

"Sam don like fo me to tell folks where he is. Say fo me to make folks leave a message and he'll—"

"Aunt Easter—there's no time for us to leave a message. Every minute counts—every—Aunt Easter, we Andersons are in bad trouble."

Aunt Easter's black somber eyes widened just enough to include curiosity, and Bess saw it and knew now that she must take the chance.

She drew the old woman just inside the door, whispered, "It's Ed. He got in trouble tonight with a white man."

"Go on," the old woman's voice pushed her into further confidence.

"White man's dead."

Under the brown thin stern face you could see the muscles tighten. She looked at Bess. "He at Sally Mason's. She having a baby—but hit oughta be here by now. Sam say Sally kin have a baby easier most women take off a nightgown."

Yes, but it could take hours! Lord God! Bess turned, forgetting to thank Aunt Easter; with the others took the path that led to the north end of Colored Town.

The shack they stopped at had all the lamps the family owned burning. Sally's sister sat on the porch with Sally's old grandma and three or four neighbor women. And inside you could hear more women talking. She'd have to take care.

Quietly Bess walked down the path, telling the others to wait beyond the house. Quietly she asked someone to let her speak to Dr. Perry, told them that her little boy was bad off, otherwise she wouldn't have come just then. "Has," she found it hard to ask, "has Sally's baby—come yet?"

"No, hit ain come yit."

"Hit ain comin right when hit come," Sally's grandma said.

"Grandma seen the signs," Sally's sister giggled, making faint fun of Grandma.

Grandma twisted her dip-stick slowly around her old gums.

Sally was moaning, you could hear her out on the porch. Screaming now, two, three times. No more.

"Ugh," muttered Sally's little sister, slim and pine-colored and pert. "Ugh," she said, and stared out into the night. "I wouldn't have one for nothing—you couldn't pay me—"

"Hit ain comin dat easy," Grandma said. "Sally oughta be hollerin mo. Tole her ma—ain nevah heerd tell no oman not ahollerin mo."

The door opened and closed. Dr. Perry walked up to Bess. She looked into his calm face. Always it was the same. You see Sam, speak to him, you quiet down. You don't know what it is, his being big, strong, patient maybe, sure of himself, seeming always to understand, to know what to do. "Sam," she said and put her hand on his arm, "Sam—Jackie's real sick." She spoke loudly enough for everyone to hear. "Can I speak to you about it? It's his bowels," she added, and felt herself begin to cry, as these untrue words about her small son fitted like a key you didn't know you owned into the door of her self-control.

"Let's go outside," Sam said quietly, and walked with her through the group of neighbors. As they started down the steps Sally's sister stood up, touched his arm. "How's Sally? Is it—is it?"

Sam said, "The baby's come. Your mama's tending it now."

"Granny," Sally's little pert sister said, and began to giggle nervously as she sat down again, "it's come. The baby's come."

"Hit ain come yit," said Granny, and spat her snuff calmly

234

into the yard. "No baby ain come right less'n her hollers. Why don't her holler?"

"Because he give her something to keep it from hurtin!" her granddaughter said crossly. She stared out with a tightening of her full lips, as one thin pale hand smoothed her straightened black hair back from her face. "I wouldn't have one for nothin," she muttered.

Bess had regained her control and briefly told Sam what had happened. Without glancing in the direction of the two—Non just out of view of the people on the shed, Ed a hundred feet farther up the road—Sam said, "Walk on up the road. I'll join you in a few minutes."

The three walked quickly and waited where there were no houses. Palmettos stretched on the left of them to the swamp and on the right, back to where shacks began again, and on to the ballground. A dim, silver-gray, flat, endless stretch of palmetto and wiregrass in the moonlight, with here and there a cypress or tall pine.

The three stood waiting, each a little apart from the other. You could hear Sam start his car. As the car lights drew near, a gaunt cow slowly rose up in the road and stood looking at it, in her lower lip a big prickly-pear dangling. Sam blew the horn, slowed for her, waited while she walked over to a palmetto clump.

The car stopped. Sam called, "I'm ready, Ed. How about it?"

"O.K."

Bess said, "Here, Ed, here's the money."

Ed put it in his pocket. He took a step toward Non. "Non . . . I . . . hope you'll forgive me— Non . . . you—"

They watched her as she swallowed and swallowed again in her effort to answer him. Then she took his hand and rubbed it softly with her fingers, suddenly turned away, stood against a tree, her back to the road and them.

"Non," he sobbed, "you've got to understand—you've—"

"Ed," Sam called, "get in the car. You have no time—you—"

"Non, you've—"

"Get in that car, you fool!" Bess pulled her brother away and to the car.

The taillight faded down the sand road, the last sound of the car was gone.

"Come, Non," Bess whispered, and began to walk toward the old Anderson place.

# SIXTEEN

DESSIE WAS SINGING softly when Henry came in, singing the song the white folks sang at the revival tent, and he sat there and let her sing as he tried to remember the evening. But soon he gave up thinking and pulled Dessie's chair close to his and put his arm around her waist.

She stopped her song.

He sat there fooling with her, exploring her dress with his big hand, and all the time he was uneasily tasting Eddie Anderson's fist, hearing his, "You damned black nigger!" And like seeing ghosts he began to see Nonnie white, not Negro but white, and he knew with sudden and startling clarity that she would no more marry him than Laura Deen would. He felt dizzy with knowledge and found it sour in his mouth. He drew Dessie to him a little roughly and kissed her; and Dessie, believing it some feminine wile of hers that had provoked this fresh amorousness, happily rubbed up against him like a little frisky heifer in its first heat.

236

"Henry," she whispered, "I reckon we'll git married, won't we?"

"Marriage," Henry said ponderously, "hit ain nothin folks kin butt into widdout . . ." Difficult going with Dessie's big solemn eyes following every word. "Folks oughta study hit out fust."

Dessie nodded in soft agreement. "Marriage is a sacred institution," she said helpfully.

"Huh?" Henry's hand faltered. He felt kind of tired and worn out. "Us kin have fun widdout—us kin—"

He gave up words and pulled her into his lap.

She slipped out and sat again in her chair. "Hit ain right," she said softly.

"Ef you loved me you'd make me feel good," said Henry feebly.

"Tain't holy love tell us gits a marriage license."

"Who been givin yo dat stuff?"

"Miz Harris. She a good woman."

"You ain't Miz Harris."

"I tryin to favor her."

"Jesus Christ, how come?"

"She my ideal." Dessie spoke with sudden sweet seriousness. And as she spoke, shed her wiles like last year's snakeskin and sat erect, gracious, hands folded in her lap.

Henry stared, unbelieving.

"Miz Harris," Dessie continued, "reads to me from the Bible. She ain't—arn't"—Dessie corrected herself quickly—"she arn't so happy but—"

"Gawd knows why—got plenty what it take."

"Whut?"

"Dough, sistah, dough."

"—but she mighty good. She reads to me from the Bible and learns me religious verses. 'Blessed are the pure in heart fo dey shall see Gawd . . . Blessed are ye when men shall persecute you and revile you an say all—' "

237

"Good Gawd a-mighty, Dessie, what's come over you?"

"She say, 'Add to yo faith virtue, and to virtue knowledge, and to knowledge, temperance, and to temp—' "

"Potracted meetin wukkin on you sho—"

"Miz Harris say the sperrit of the Holy Ghost is sho powerful. Wash away our sins in the blood of the Lamb." Dessie half crooned the words. "She reads me about the ten virgins. Five was wise and five," with sudden bright animation, "was the foolishest virgins I . . . "

Henry watched her. His big wet mouth hung open. His big black hands hung dejectedly between spraddled legs. His eyes moved over her face, to her little pointed breasts, down her body, lingered long over the curve of her little belly. "I'm hongry sho," he said abruptly and heard his words with surprise. Now that he had said them, they were true and importunate.

Dessie looked at him startled. She was hongry too.

She fixed up a mess of food, which they ate contentedly. When they finished he pulled out a bottle, took a deep swig, handed it to her. Mrs. Harris's warning, "Look not upon the wine . . . at the last it biteth like a serpent," sang through her mind like yesterday's song and was gone. She looked at Henry, smiling at her now in full-bellied contentment. Her little greasy lips pouted in doubt. He whispered, "Do it fo yo big boy."

She lifted the bottle, drank deeply, choked, coughed, batted her eyes, sneezed.

He laughed, drank of it again, reached out a big lazy hand, pulled her to him. He drew her between his legs as he sprawled in the chair and locked her within them like a vise.

She trembled. A sweet sensation of warmth crept over her. He drew her closer.

"Us can't—here," she whispered.

"Us is gwine find a big palmetto bush, honey," and,

238

laughing, Henry picked her up and went out of the door. She wiggled down, pulled down her dress primly, walked sedately by his side.

A car passed. Dessie said, "Dr. Perry's out late."

They went out by the A.M.E. Church, past the white graveyard, arms around each other, walking more slowly now, Dessie hesitating, dragged back by a conscience never long at ease. Under the cedars in front of Miss Ada's she paused. "Henry," she whispered, "us is bad to do dis!"

"Bad," laughed Henry and picked her up in his arms. "Gawd yes. Us is bad!" With his kicking, giggling armful Henry crossed the road into the palmettos.

After he had had his satisfaction Henry stretched out on the warm sand, gave one deep body-resting sigh and was almost at once sound asleep.

Not so, Dessie. Dessie sat bolt upright, hands clasped together tightly, and stared out across the dark clumps of palmetto and pines. "I hadn't ought to've did it," she whispered. "We'll git married tomorry sho," she whispered again as if in conversation with someone. "Be sho to," she whispered. Now and then her head fell forward, heavy with sleep, only to be jerked back in place by this firm, vigil-keeping visitor.

As moonlight turned slowly into a clear sharp dawn, Dessie dozed but the first ray of early sun on her body was like a hand shaking her.

"Come," she said, and turned Henry over, "hit's late! Better be goin."

They sleepily stumbled through damp grass, saying few words. Dessie said as they walked past Miss Ada's, "Henry, I reckon us'll git married now?"

Henry said, "Sho. Us will." They walked on, now under the cedars. "Some time," he added.

"But, Henry—" She stopped. She had seen it. Her hand

239

pointed slowly toward the edge of the bushes, beyond the big cedar.

Henry followed the gesture, stumbled forward. "Hit's my boy!" he cried; "Gawd Jesus!" and hushed abruptly. He knelt beside the body. Stared now at the bloodied shirt, big mouth hanging loose and open, eyes unable to leave the spot they had fastened upon. Stared as his grief was slowly soaked up by the age-old capillary pull of nigger facts, knowing now only one desolating thing. And, staring into the stiff eyes of his dead playmate, he began to feel a thousand cold eyes on him, a thousand fingers pointing, a thousand bloodhounds baying down centuries, smelling him out, him, Big Henry, from the other millions of black men . . . and they'd git him sho. Sho.

He turned, retched miserably. *They'd git him sho.*

"I ain done it," he whispered.

"Cose you ain't," Dessie whispered, and hunted for something to wipe his mouth with.

"No," he whispered.

"No," Dessie whispered, and began to tremble.

# SEVENTEEN

LAURA TURNED OVER in bed and ran her fingers softly across the screen of the window. From where she lay she could see the narrow stretch of their side lawn and the street adjoining. The big pecan tree at the corner of the house had grown limbs that stretched across her window and beyond. Lying so near, she could look up through the dark branches at the sky. Now, if she wished, she could step easily from her window to a big limb, when as a child you had to cling to the ledge until your feet obtained a safe hold on the gutter and from thence climb to the roof of the sun porch and over to the small tree. It had grown imperceptibly, steadily, sap pushing up, up, with stubborn rightness, obeying all the intricacies of an inner pattern, in its good fortune so little cramped by this house, or other trees, or Maxwell. Growing old, maturing as it grew, putting out leaves and clusters of green nuts, dropping them one by one as they ripened, taking the winter in its bare strength. She wondered if human beings could grow and mature. All the people she knew seemed not to grow through life, but merely to move from year to year, as a small child plays on a stairway, taking all its playthings with it as it goes up from step to step, not knowing what to leave behind. If you knew what to leave behind . . .

Laura moved restlessly. Lying awake, like this, did your feelings no good. It was childish to be so upset. To keep putting your finger on a sore place does the hurt no good! You opened the drawer to get the clay. It was gone. Such a little thing. You could get more clay.

*She hates what I like!* she had thought as she stood there looking at the empty drawer. It seemed now that she had been knowing this for a long time without telling it to herself. That her mother had destroyed the little clay figure, Laura took for granted. It was one of those things you take for granted. But asking herself why was like going through old trunks for something lost. She had not found the answer, though she had found other answers.

You can get more clay. But there are some things you cannot get more of. She had wanted to say something, to make a scene as Tracy sometimes did. But she had no words that could safely be used. Words that, unspoken, seem so harmless would, once said aloud, become dangerous explosives containing hidden feelings that would flame into something you dared not set free. They would begin with the little chunk of clay. They would not end there. No. That little piece of clay would merely be a lighted fuse which would lead, circuitously perhaps, but inevitably, to everything in your life that you cherished. That the clay was going to be discussed soon, Laura knew. When her mother walked in Friday night after Tracy had had words with her, it was on her face. She had sat down on Laura's bed and Laura had slowly laid her book aside, dreading the look in her mother's eyes.

"We have so little time these days to talk, Laura."

"Yes, Mother. I know."

"I miss the little Laura." Her mother had smiled, but the muscles in her throat had trembled.

"You'd want me to grow up, wouldn't you?" She'd see if she could turn it into more casual directions.

"Of course. But somehow I have an idea that you still think, and feel, even if you are grown. We used to talk about —those things."

"Yes, I know. I suppose college makes a difference. If I ever have an important thought, Mumsie, I'll tell you." That sounded so glib.

"All you think is important to me."

They sat there for a moment, neither speaking.

"Laura"—Mother had looked around the room—"do you think it wise—to go around with older women so much? After all, Jane Hardy is so much older than you. Why do you like—that type of woman? Don't you like your old friends? Don't you like Harriet and the others?"

"Yes, Mother. I like them. Very much." She'd hesitated. "Jane's fun, Mumsie. She's interesting."

"But what do you talk about? You always seem to have so much to talk to her about."

Laura tried to smile easily. "Oh, I don't know. Books, I suppose. All kinds of things."

"There're—women, Laura, who aren't safe for young girls to be with. Of course you are young and inexperienced—" Mother was finding this hard going.

For heaven's sake, what do you say now! "I've been to college, Mumsie, and things are talked about there. I think I know what you are trying to say."

"Laura, it would kill me . . . if anything—happened to you."

Her mother sat there looking at her, and Laura felt naked under the gaze.

Laura said, "It's nice that Dottie is going to marry Tracy, isn't it?"

"Yes, it is." Now Mother lowered her voice: "There're women who are—unnatural. They're like vultures—women like that." Mother's face had grown stony. "They do—terrible things to young girls."

"Oh, Mother!"

"I don't believe a woman is the right kind of woman who talks about the naked body as Jane does." How did she know that? What did she mean? Laura did not try to answer her.

"Good night, Laura," Mother said, and stood up to leave the room.

"Good night, Mumsie."

After her mother left, Laura slipped out of bed and went over to her desk. What did Mother mean? Slowly she pulled the letter drawer open, picked up Jane's letters. Yes, they did write to each other even though they lived in the same town. They had so much to say. There was so much you could say to Jane that you had never before been able to say to anyone. Laura's heart was beating heavily—she did not know why. She picked up the top letter. No, it wasn't the last she had had from Jane. Then Mother had been in her letters. Mother had read them. Mother knew Jane had posed for the figure.

Jane had talked about it in that letter. The letter was gone. Mother had it. Mother had this friendship in her hands now, like the little chunk of clay.

Laura had gone back to bed, but not to sleep.

And now again tonight she could not sleep. You waited. You knew Mother was biding her time. Waiting for what she called the "psychological moment."

That her mother had discarded her own life, as you throw away a dress you don't like, and had chosen to live hers instead, Laura knew. It was as if, having once nourished Laura within her body, she now claimed an equal right to feed upon her whom she had brought to life. And maybe she had the right. She had done so much for her, more than most girls have done for them.

Laura turned until the moonlight was bright on her watch. Three o'clock. Tracy had not come in. She could not have failed to hear those steps. Eighteen steps from her door at the top of the stairs to his door. Eighteen stealthy slow steps, every other one dragging a little, a little slur against the hall carpet; then a door would open and close softly. She had been hearing it almost since she could remember. It was late tonight, even for him. Yesterday he joined the church, gave Dorothy a ring; tonight he had not come in.

She sighed. He didn't have it in him to go straight. Always he would be doing things—like this. It was as if he had to fail—as she had to succeed. Or was she succeeding? And now he would fail with Dorothy. Poor Dottie. She would never understand him. Who did? Always she would worry over him and try to reform him, pushing him further from her with each reformation, for he'd hate her for it. And as the years passed she would give up, and her lips would wrinkle up tight over her teeth like her mother's, and she would spend more and more of her time in church work.

Once when Tracy had come in late—she had left her door

244

open and was reading in bed—he had stopped in the doorway and looked at her. She'd never forget that night although nothing happened. "What you doing?" he'd said, and smiled, and for the first time in her life she noticed how deeply blue his eyes were and somehow how sad, and his quick amused smile. His thin face had relaxed and in relaxing had grown assured.

"I'm afraid, just another book." She had closed the book and laid it aside and had smiled back at him, wanting to ask him in, feeling that maybe, this once, they could talk.

"There're other things in the world, Sis," he'd said gently, "but maybe you don't want them."

"Maybe I would want them—if I knew what they are." She knew, yes she knew. He was hinting that she should go with men, maybe get married. Men didn't like her. Thought her too smart, folks said. But maybe it was because she was a little gawky. That was the real reason, she'd always known it—a little gawky and shy.

"You aren't asking me to tell you, are you?" And he had thrown back his head and laughed softly, and his teeth had flashed in the lamplight. She realized this was the Tracy that Negro girl knew. He had come so quickly from her that he had not had time to take on the protective coloring he wore in the Deen family. "Well . . . good night," he had said, and had limped quietly down the hall to his room, leaving her feeling deprived and restless. This was the Tracy Nonnie Anderson knew. The Tracy women loved. She had often wondered why women liked Tracy—all the Miss Belles, the old maids, and the young married women, and the very old ladies. She saw it now. His gentle, affectionate manner, unhappy eyes, enough tension in his voice to make women want to soothe him. They called it his beautiful manners . . .

Why had he always failed and she succeeded? It made you, lying here like this tonight, feel that you had climbed to success by standing on his failures. It made you want to throw it all away, throw your whole life away and begin over again, and let him begin over again. Far away from Mother—and Jane.

Jane was an orphan who lived on in Maxwell teaching school, living with the Harrises, but living always alone with herself. For no one knew Jane. Folks always said, "Fine woman, Jane. But she won't let anybody know her. Fine girl, though," and had been awed by Jane's learning and Jane's book-lined walls. And then one day they had been playing tennis and suddenly had begun to talk. And you knew you could talk to Jane, you could tell her about your sculpture and your verses, about your fears and your feelings. And soon you were feeling with her a security that you had not felt since you were a little girl with your Mother. And you loved her. Yes, you loved her and wanted to be with her. And now Mother was labeling it with those names that the dean of women at college had warned you about. Yes, you knew. You knew and you did not know. Your mother knew and did not know. The dean of women knew and did not know. But you also knew if Mother made an issue, if she labeled this feeling for Jane with those names, there'd be no more feeling . . .

The moonlight picked out the roofs of the houses across the street, showing little crannies and angles one never saw in the daytime. How often she had lain there and looked out on that small segment of her town. You'd hear people drive slowly down the street; sometimes someone walking would whistle a measure of brash sound against the street's quiet breathing; sometimes across town you'd hear the colored folks singing, and the slow rise and fall of it would be as sweet to your ears as Mamie's slow deep breathing used to be when you lay against her soft breast. It would be nice to see Mamie again. Eenie had never been like Mamie to either of them. Mamie so gentle and anxious to soothe her white folks. And how Tracy had hated Laura for taking his nurse away from him! She remembered little of it, of course, save what

246

Mamie had told her later. But they said that for a long time he would eat nothing that Mamie did not give him out of her own fingers. And once he had run away and hidden behind a big pecan tree in the back yard and refused to come in and go to bed until Mamie went out and wheedled him in and put him to bed herself. Mother had let Mamie go back to nursing Tracy, and she herself had looked after Laura. Yes, the colored nurse you've loved so passionately goes away—to another job maybe or to another child. And you're supposed to forget all about her.

Down the street where Mrs. Viola Smith, the dressmaker, lived somebody must have been thirsty and stepped to the back porch for a drink. For in the stillness the rasp of the pump screamed out and caught her nerves and bit deep into them, and her heart jumped and pounded hard in her throat. Yes, somebody wants a drink of water and in the getting of it, somebody else a half block away is frightened until the body's metabolism is abruptly changed because of it. Mrs. Smith would not give up the pump, declaring no city water could equal the water pumped right there from the ground beneath her own back porch. "Yes," she'd say, and ease her snuff a little under her lip, as she knelt to chalk the hem line of your dress, "people have their likes and people have their dislikes. And city water is my dislike. I abominate city water," she'd say. Laura had always wanted to ask Mrs. Viola Smith what her likes were, but her tight sallow face as she bent over the sewing machine, or crouched close to the floor chalking your hem line, invited no such question.

There'd be no more feeling. Just another of the little messes Alma cleaned up after her daughter.

Maybe you could go away. Maybe you could go away and never come back. Never come back to Mother—and Jane. You wouldn't want it. You wouldn't want your relationship with Jane when Mother finished with it. You wouldn't —anything.

247

# EIGHTEEN

IT WAS WARM and close under the tent. No air was stirring.

People were coming in; gathering slowly, but coming. Cars had pulled up to the parking space on the edge of the field—the same field used by Ringling's Circus each winter. Early this morning a second piano had been moved in and placed on the platform where the choir sat, and now Brother Dunwoodie nodded at the two pianists, who began an ensemble playing of *Beulah Land*.

It sounded good. Yes, Brother Dunwoodie said to himself, it's all right! He had told the pianists to put a little life in it. "Jazz it up," he'd said, and laughed. "God's worth putting all we got into His work. Let's make them feel good out there," he'd said. *"We* feel good, *you* feel good, don't you?" he'd said. Yes, they felt good, the two pianists said, and wiped their faces, and cautiously lifted damp skirts from their sticky hips.

Brother Dunwoodie sat by the table on which lay his open Bible and looked over his audience. The tent was almost full. Fine crowd.

The business firms had been closing daily for the morning service. But, though they closed their doors, some of these same businessmen had not been attending the service. Now, as the revival progressed, as God's spirit began to work among the people, Brother Dunwoodie hoped to win them to more awareness of His part in their prosperity and to a greater willingness to sacrifice some of their time and money to the Lord's business. He was preaching this morning his sermon on Christian Stewardship, following it with two propositions slanted to appeal to the more solid portion of

Maxwell citizenry. For, however many mill people were converted, a revival could not be called a success in Maxwell until the prominent citizens, some of whom had drifted away from the church, were returned to the fold. Without this rewakening among the better classes—those who must, in the nature of things, be counted upon for the major financial support of the church—the isolated triumph, sensational as it was, of Tracy Deen's conversion could not put the stamp of victory upon the Lord's work in Maxwell.

Brother Dunwoodie ran his fingers through his thick black hair. There were eight citizens for whom he was praying day and night. Not only was he praying for them, but he had told them and the whole town that he was praying. He rubbed his chin and smiled. In other towns it worked. It ought to work in Maxwell.

He reviewed them in his mind: the three Rushton brothers, not one of whom had attended a service of this revival. Prentiss Reid, editor of *The Maxwell Press,* a man of great talent and influence, but an infidel who denied the existence of God; and kept Tom Paine's books on his desk, right beside the Bible. Jim Nevins, owner of two farms, and now the postmaster, but one-time keeper of Maxwell's saloon, which, praise the Lord, local option and prohibition had closed the doors of forever. Aleck Brown, dealer in hardware and farm equipment and cotton futures, in his young days teacher of a Sunday School class, now claiming to be too dad-gone tired when Sunday came (so folks said he told them last week in the drugstore) to get up and walk a block to the church. Morris Jones, cashier of the bank, member of the Baptist Church, but one who took no part in the Lord's affairs except to pay the deficit on the minister's salary. Jones could be counted on to pay the deficit— "And cheap money at that," the town wit had him saying, "long as I don't have to listen to him preach." L. D. Stephenson, member of the State Legislature, and out of town for the last five days (funny thing, way folks can think up excuses to get out of town when a revival is on)—a man worth saving for the Lord, as Tom Harris said, "for he'll sure as the world be governor some day if he keeps on buttering folks bread with the people's money way he's doing now." Last night Tom Harris had helped him make a list of Maxwell's important men—some on the side of the Lord, some not—and from them all a promise was secured to attend this morning's service—with the exception of old Cap'n Rushton, who was out at the turpentine farm, and L.D., who was in Atlanta.

And they were here, some no more than ten feet from him on the front row, others scattered through the congregation.

Brother Dunwoodie stood, touched his open Bible with the tips of his fingers. "Friends—" he paused and smiled. "I know no better way to begin the worship of our Heavenly Father this morning than to give you an opportunity to testify to His goodness to you. There're folks here this morning who God has anointed with oil, pouring His blessings upon them. Come on, folks, God's prospered you! Get up and tell what He's done for you. Some of you have loved ones who have wandered away in sin and have now come back to the fold. Give the Lord thanks for it. Don't be mean. The Lord's had to wrassle with some of these folks—yes sir! He's worked hard. Now tell Him how you feel about it."

There was a little stir through the crowd. Everyone looked at the front row, where Tom Harris's bald head gleamed in the light. Harris usually started a testimony meeting off— had a way of getting it going. Tom stood. "I've got a lot to be thankful for and I know it. All the good things that have come to me have come because of God's goodness to me. I believe when you try to do God's will that He will take care of you. I believe that, folks." Tom turned and faced the congregation. His sun-red face shone with sincerity. "A few years back, a good preacher preached to us on tithing. And I told him, 'Brother, a man can't tithe when he's got a big family to raise. He just can't afford it.' And the preacher looked at me and said, 'Tom Harris, who's giving you your mills? Who's giving you every cent you make? You mean to look at me and tell me you can't give back to the Lord what already belongs to Him? What kind of honesty is that? Don't you know,' he said, 'that God will prosper you if you show your faith by giving a tenth back to him?' Well, folks, I didn't know, but I've learned. The next year I tithed, and the mills made more money than ever in their history. Yes sir, tithing is the best investment I ever made in my life. It pays."

"Amen," said Brother Dunwoodie. and turned back to the men sitting there in front of him. "Who else is ready to tell us what God's done for him?" Old Mrs. Henson stood and quavered, "The Lord giveth and the Lord taketh away, blessed be the name of the Lord," and sat down, wiping her eyes, for Mrs. Henson had just lost her tenth child, her last-born son. Then timid little freckled-faced Mrs. Davis stood, looked at all the people, opened her mouth, but no words came. She wet her lips, tried again, but no words came, and then flushing, she ducked her head and slid back into her seat. The people smiled in sympathy, and one little girl laughed hysterically and was pinched to quietness by her mother. "You remember Moses was a man of slow words," the preacher said. "Yes sir, God hears folks who say things slow just as well as he hears those who bellow. Come on, folks, who else feels like praising the Lord?"

Others stood and said a few words, and at last there was no evading Old Culpepper, who had been jumping up at the close of each testimony, eager to make his own, but until now ignored by the preacher. "All right, Brother."

Culpepper stood and wiped his hand across his face, disfigured by the big sore that had been there for many years. He stared at the preacher as if he had forgot why he was standing, then, suddenly remembering, said, "I thank God fur lettin me git to my feet and set down again. I praise him

251

fur lettin me have five teeth to chew my meat with. Yes, Brother, I praise God fur lettin me git to my feet—"

"That's fine," said the preacher. "Praise the Lord," he added, to hush the tittering at old senile Culpepper, the church's janitor.

He picked up the Bible, laid it down again. "Friends, I have taken for my topic this morning Christian Stewardship. Chris-tian Steward-ship," he repeated slowly.

The text read, Brother Dunwoodie closed his Bible, tossed it on the table with a little flick of his hand.

He spoke rapidly, as if too much time already had been wasted. But he had hardly begun when a long and heavy freight train began its slow tortuous journey across town and past the tent. People smiled and waited, as car after car ground its weight against the rails, screeched, groaned, lessened its cries, only to be succeeded by another and another and another. No voice could be heard above that sound, and Brother Dunwoodie knew it. He stood there, a patient but tried man of God. Then suddenly he shouted, "Count them, folks! Count God's blessings, for those cars are full of God's goodness to his people!" And with a lift of his arms he brought the audience to their feet. Speaking quickly to the pianist, he led the people in *Count Your Many Blessings, Name Them One by One,* and they sang it again and again and again until the train had passed on toward its destination in the North.

He wiped his face. "Yes, bless the Lord. He's good to us. Yes! God leads you to prosperity. He says, 'Behold, look you upon this land flowing with milk and honey. It's yours!' He says, 'Help yourself. Reach out, take what you want. But remember,' He adds softly, 'remember a tenth of it is the Lord's and to be returned unto Me.' God speaks softly. A still, small voice. But some of you are bragging so loud about what you've done, how smart you are"—his voice suddenly filled the tent—"that you don't hear Him! No! You don't hear

252

Him because your hearts are like sounding brass with your boasting and your pride. 'Look at me,' you say, 'look at *my* works! Look at *my* sawmill, *my* turpentine farm . . . look at *my* cotton . . . *my* store' "—he was looking pointedly now from one to another of the town's businessmen—" '*my* bank . . . *my* big job . . . *I* did it! See!' " His voice was low now as his black eyes searched among the benches. "Some of you once worshiped the Lord . . . gave of your small earnings to His work . . . taught Sunday School . . . went to prayer meeting on a Wednesday night"—the voice underscoring words more and more heavily as it grew quieter and quieter— ". . . prayed . . . read your Bible . . . until the Lord said, *Here's a good man,* and laid His hand on your shoulder gentle-like and led you to green pastures to graze. Yes, and you waxed fat with the prosperity He gave you until—" his lips curled back into scornful smile—

Sheriff Lem Taylor entered the tent, walked down the middle aisle slowly, searching the benches. Too tall a man to do anything inconspicuously, almost at once he had the eyes of the congregation on him as he moved down to the first row, bent over and spoke to Tom Harris. Tom took his hat, tiptoed up the aisle behind the sheriff, went out of the tent.

Brother Dunwoodie hesitated only a moment, went on, "Yes, your soul is so lazy it can't worship the God that gave you everything on earth you own. Now you say you're too tired a Sunday to get up and walk a block to the church . . . too tired to climb in your car even and press your foot on the gas and turn the wheel—"

Tom Harris tiptoed in, tiptoed down the aisle to the third row, whispered to Tut Deen, who fumbled for his hat as if he could not see, followed Harris out. Folks sitting close to the aisle said his face had turned the color of bile.

People moved restlessly on the benches.

"—carry you to God's house to worship Him. A people who

253

forget their God will perish from the face of the earth. Trouble and distress—"

Hat in hand, Zeb Thompson, wearing his recently acquired city-marshall uniform, tiptoed in, started up the middle aisle, hesitated, went to the rear again, wove his way across the sawdust, and started down the far side toward the front.

Brother Dunwoodie broke off his words and looked at Zeb. "Brother, do you want something?"

Zeb was husky with embarrassment. "Yes sir. Is Mr. Pug Pusey in the audience?"

Pug Pusey turned, stared like a solemn little owl, took off his glasses, got up, started out, was halfway down the aisle, discovered his song book in his hand, went back to the bench where he had sat, laid it down, went out holding his round belly with both chubby hands. A gesture which to strangers might suggest a number of possibilities, but to his friends was an invariable sign of Pug's great mental distress.

A few boys and men at the rear went out quietly now, perceiving that the center of excitement had moved from the inside to the outside of the tent.

Brother Dunwoodie wiped his face with his big blue silk handkerchief. Began again, "Jesus spake unto the Pharisees and said—"

Someone came in, stooped over and whispered to Prentiss Reid. The editor of *The Maxwell Press* eased from his seat and slipped outside.

Brother Dunwoodie's voice beat and pounded on his congregation's ears; but women had stopped fanning, as though no longer feeling the heat, and men moved a little and ran their hands through their hair or crossed and uncrossed their legs. He had almost finished his sermon when Tom Harris came in again, tiptoed down the aisle once more, whispered to Mrs. Deen and Laura, who followed him quickly outside. You could hear a car start, chug hard in the deep sand near the tent, move on. Dorothy Pusey, sitting in the choir, turned

254

white, and those near her saw her tearing at her handkerchief with hands dripping wet.

Brother Dunwoodie ended his sermon abruptly. There would be no altar service this morning, no propositions, no names called. Whatever had happened had served to ruin completely his chance of winning over the businessmen of Maxwell. You never can tell where the devil will strike in a meeting.

He announced briefly the children's service for the afternoon. "Come out tonight, everybody, and bring along somebody with you. We are going to praise God and glorify His name"—his voice rang our defiantly—"and if the devil can't keep away from us, we'll have *him* praising the Lord too if he don't watch out." With a quick movement of both arms he brought the congregation to their feet for the benediction.

As his deep mellow *Amen* rang out, the tent was hastily emptied of men, and women turned to each other with anxious questions.

Dot Pusey pushed her way through the crowd to the outside of the tent. In the white glare people looked at her and moved back to let her pass. She asked no questions of anyone but hurried down the street and across the railroad toward College Street, pushing through words that swarmed around her—*what's happened . . . Tracy Deen . . . ssssh . . . yeah . . . shot down . . . Tracy Deen . . . ssssh . . . Tracy Dean . . . killed . . . pretty bad . . . yeah . . . watch out! . . . palmetto . . . yeah . . . Tra—*

She had crossed the business streets and turned into College when a car slowed up beside her and Jane Hardy called softly, "Dorothy," and opened the car door. Dot came quickly to the car and it moved on down the sandy street, neither of its occupants speaking again.

At the Deens' house on the corner, Dot slipped out, hurried in.

Jane sat with her hands on the wheel, as if forgetting to

255

start the car, while the little black-haired girl in her pretty green dress and floppy green hat ran across the lawn and into the house. Under the big oak tree near the veranda stood three or four men fanning with their hats, now and then mopping their faces. Once Mr. Pusey came out out on the veranda, looked at her, walked halfway down the steps, stood with his hands clasped around his stomach, turned, went into the house. Two ladies came out, talking earnestly in low tones; one stooped, picked a dead begonia leaf, wiped her eyes, went back into the house. Tom Harris hurried down College Street and into the house, came out again, motioned to one of the men under the oak trees, hurried back in.

Jane Hardy turned the car slowly, drove up College Street to the Harris home.


# NINETEEN


DESSIE RANG the bell for dinner as soon as she heard Miss Jane's car at the side entrance.

The hours had been long since she came to work and heavy with her fears. Each time the telephone rang or Mrs. Harris called her, the perspiration poured from her body. And only after Mrs. Harris and the girls and Miss Jane had gone to the morning service, and the house had grown still, did Dessie's heart slow its pounding. She had never before seen a white man dead. Never quite believed a white person could die, same as colored folks. And to die like this, to be shot down just like colored folks and left there on the side of the road, bleeding all over himself—

256

"Somebody killed him," she whispered.

*I never done it,* Big Henry said. *I never done it,* he said, and suddenly he had lifted that white man's body and dragged it off the road into the gallberry bushes farther and farther from the path, around clumps of gallberry, around clumps of palmetto, farther and farther, as Dessie stood watching him, feeling that somehow they *had* done it now, somehow now they had something to do with that yellow dead face and that stiff bloodied shirt. And in panic she had screamed, "Henry! Come back." And Henry had come back, and she had taken wads of leaves damp with dew and washed off his hands and hurried him toward White Town and the back gate of the Deen home. She had pushed him toward the house and then had run as fast as she could to the Harris back door.

At breakfast, as she served these white folks, as she passed hot biscuits from one to another of the Harris family and their preacher visitor, she listened to their talk; but no word of it touched the Deen family. No word of it touched the night and its dead. They said they had had a good service last night. Somebody said politely that five more had been converted and seven had joined the church. And Preacher Dunwoodie said, "Yes, praise God, it is a good meeting! Maxwell is still on the side of the Lord."

And then they were quiet, as the Harrises always were quiet until they had had their first cup of coffee. And she stood near the sideboard, watching them, watching the sun creep across Mrs. Harris's gray hair as it did every morning in summertime, looking at her color and her dark eyes to see if this would be a good day for her mistress.

Preacher Dunwoodie asked for another cup of coffee, and as she handed it to him he said, and smiled at the others around the table as he said it, "Some day Tracy Deen may surprise his home town by turning preacher. That boy has in his eyes the look of one called to preach Christ's gospel."

257

And Dessie dropped the cup, spilling coffee across the table-cloth and on the rug and across the sleeve of Brother Dun-woodie's coat. She ran to the sideboard for a clean napkin and sopped up the dampness from his coat, and she could hear herself breathing hard, while the family looked at each other and at her, half smiling. Her folks was good folks and never got you for things.

"It's all right," he said in a kind voice. "It's all right, Dessie."

He was a good man too, Preacher Dunwoodie, even if he et enough for two farm han's. But she was trembling so, she could hardly pick up the pieces of the cup and take them to the kitchen.

All morning she kept shaking like her old Granma, who had the palsy bad; and after the family left for church, after the big house with its wide dim verandas and its high dim rooms grew quiet and still, she crept about dusting and straightening, and every once in a while she'd sit down on a piece of the parlor furniture because her legs felt queer and weak. It was cool in here and shadowy, and you could almost believe nothing bad ever had happened in the world, as you walked about with your dusting cloth flicking the dust from settee and mantel-piece and piano stool . . . that everything was a bad dream, except the deep softness of the rug and the smooth pretty glow in the furniture and the shine of the mirror in the dusky light.

She softly tiptoed to the mantel and looked at herself in the mirror. "You is sinned," she told the brown face staring sadly back at her. "Miz Deen thought you was a good girl," she whispered to mournful eyes, "and you ain't. And you is brung all dis bad thing on yoself." She stood there looking at herself, feeling that her pain was just and sent by God, pleasuring vaguely in her penitence. And then suddenly she whirled around, for it was as if back of her own face reflected in the mirror she had seen something else—the whole white

258

race staring back at her. And she was afraid as never in her life she had been afraid. Granma had looked after her, and then Mrs. Harris had looked after her. Good folks had always taken care of her. You knew there was white folks like Miss Belle who made you want to frash yo lips at um, but there was plenty colored folks you never had no use for either. You knew white boss sometimes killed a farmhand, but you'd always thought it was a bad man, even if he was white, who'd do a thing like dat. Things like dat was like the stink from privies. You never paid no mind to it and never noticed it cept on hot damp days, and then you never noticed it for long. But now hit ain little things like some'n stinkin in a privy, hit's a whole world! Hit's being black . . . hit's jes bein *black!* She stood there in the room, holding her dusting cloth. Slowly she laid it down and looked at her hand and at the brown of her arm. She touched her skin as if she had never seen it before. Ef dey wants to be good to you like the Harrises, dey is—ef dey don want to, dey ain't. You don have nothing tall to do wid it. You jes waits . . . you waits . . . and ef you gits in deh way . . . Jesus . . . dey'll—

Aunt Susan called her to come set the table for dinner, and Dessie hurried away from the parlor that now held such bitter knowledge, and choking with the taste of it she ran into Susan's bright hot kitchen, filled with smells of browning chicken and keen fragrance of fresh sliced cucumber. She ran to Susan, who turned around from the stove, her big long fork still in her hand and the sweat streaming from her face, and said, "What you runnin from, Dessie? You'll shake de dishes off'n dat wall wif all dat scamperin around!"

And Dessie knew she couldn't talk to Aunt Susan about it. She couldn't begin to talk to her, for how could you tell her you had been with Henry all night long, how could you tell her that? Aunt Susan would think a bad girl like you wouldn't be tellin the truf bout nothin—she'd think now that maybe Henry *had* did it—

259

And Dessie began to see that sometimes folks line up by color and sometimes they line up by other things—like sins, and who is good to them, and where they work.

"You better hurry, chile, an git dat table sot."

Dessie hurried and set the table, and when she heard Miss Jane's car, after the others had come home, she rang the big dinner bell.

The Harris family gathered slowly. They were big talkers, as Dessie knew, but she had never heard them talk so much and in such hushed tones as they were using now in the wide hall which served them oftener for living room than did the double parlors. Her hand trembled as she poured the ice tea. *They've found im sho . . . somebody's found im . . .*

And now, as they entered the dining room, abruptly they hushed their talk. Mrs. Harris murmured, "Brother Dunwoodie, will you return thanks?" Dessie stepped back respectfully, slipping her other hand under the ice-cold pitcher, bowed her head. The family bowed their heads. Brother Dunwoodie raised both hands:

"For these and all thy manifold blessings to this good family we thank Thee, most Heavenly Father." He paused, went on, "We beseech Thee now to gather under the folds of Thy tender compassion our dear friends down the street, so deeply troubled today by the sudden death of their son. Comfort them, Our Father, in this their great tribulation. And may they find peace in the blessed assurance that through the mercies of Jesus Christ, Thy only begotten Son, his sins had been forgiven him, and he had been accorded salvation in Thee before Thou called him to his everlasting—"

Dessie dropped the pitcher.

"—reward. Amen."

Dessie stooped quickly to pick up the fragments and to hide her shame.

"Hot day to spill the tea," Charlie said, and smiled.

"Yassuh. I'm gettin more right now."

She dashed from the room, dashed back, mopped up the floor, hurried again to the kitchen and back with another pitcher of tea.

But the others had hardly noticed her. And no one seemed to want to eat Aunt Susan's good fried chicken or the roasting ears or the sliced cucumbers—not even the preacher. Even the preacher was quiet, when most time preachers talk, pulpit or no pulpit.

Harriet said, "It makes you feel—as we felt about Clem."

Someone said, "Clem Massey, Brother Dunwoodie, is Miss Julia's brother. Four years ago, he killed a man." And then they grew quiet, and Dessie knew all the Harrises were thinking about Miss Julia and her brother Clem—who'd about ruined her with his wicked ways, as everybody in Maxwell said—and him now in the penitentiary. Miss Julia stayed in the big house on the edge of town alone. Sometimes you'd see her walking out in the woods, and if you didn't know she was born and brought up in Maxwell you'd think she had lost her way and didn't know where to turn next.

Harriet said, "Mother, we must phone to Jacksonville for the flowers." And Mary said, "Don't get carnations. I can't bear them!" and smiled at everybody in her sweet pretty blue-eyed way.

Mrs. Harris served Mr. Harris's plate. "Put it on the stove, Dessie, until he comes. Charlie"—she looked up at her son, who was not eating much either—"don't you think maybe you should go over now to the Deens' and let your father come to his dinner?"

And then everybody left the table, having no more than tasted their ice cream; even Miss Jane who liked ice cream better than anything, Dessie knew, didn't touch hers, feeling sorry, she reckoned, for Miss Laura and Miz Deen.

Everybody left the table but Mrs. Harris. Sometimes she sat like this at the table after the others had gone. Sometimes while Mr. Harris ate a late dinner. Sometimes by herself. She'd sit there, making little marks in the tablecloth with her spoon or her finger. And Dessie would clear the table as quiet as a mouse and never say a word, and all would be so still in that oak-paneled dining room, and so still in Mrs. Harris's face. Until, after a long while, she would look up and smile at Dessie and Dessie would smile back at this lady who was always so good to her. But today she did not smile or even look at her, and Dessie felt that she had been pushed out of Mrs. Harris's world. She'd stole a dress and laid out all night with Henry, and Mrs. Harris knowed it for sho. And now they'd git im—all because she—

Dessie tripped on the rug and dropped two glasses.

"Dessie! That's the fifth dish you've broken today. What am I going to do with you, so careless a child!"

"Ya'm," Dessie said, and began to cry.

"I know you didn't mean to," Mrs. Harris added hastily, as Dessie's sobs filled the room, "but I want you to learn to be careful."

"I knows I done wrong," Dessie said, and began to sob hysterically; "I knows I done awful wrong."

She suddenly went up to Mrs. Harris and stood before her, her hands wrapping her apron into a hard knot. Maybe if she confessed her sin quick, maybe Gawd wouldn't let nothin git Henry. Hit must all be her fault and—"Miz Harris, I've sinned bad. I done some'n awful—"

"Breaking dishes isn't sinning, Dessie. I didn't mean to make you think that."

"But I've sinned bad, Miz Harris. I ain no count, I—"

Mrs. Harris laid down the spoon and looked at the crying girl. "Maybe the work's too heavy. It is a big house to keep clean, and you're young—I keep forgetting how young you are."

"No mam," Dessie's sobs began afresh. "You oughta seen

262

me, mam, in da kentry. Us has to chop all day long in da brilin sun—"

"*We,*" corrected Mrs. Harris.

"*We,* all day long—in da brilin sun. I's used to hard work. Tain't too heavy. Hit's a fine job," she smiled through her tears, while from her nose two streams dripped unnoticed over her mouth, "and I'm much obleeged to you, mam."

"Here," Mrs. Harris said hurriedly, "take this handkerchief and wipe your nose, and now go in the bathroom and wash your face, and then I'm going to give you some sulphur and cream of tartar. I know you are going to be sick."

Mrs. Harris found an old clean towel and gave it to Dessie, then went to her medicine cabinet.

Dessie sighed.

Meekly she opened her mouth and took a big spoonful of the dry mixture. She felt herself choking, but swallowed hard, and little by little she worked up enough saliva to wash it down.

"Now, Dessie," said Mrs. Harris, "when have your bowels moved?"

Dessie blinked at her questioner.

"When have you—been to the toilet?"

"Oh, no'm, I ain't used yourn. You tole me never to do dat. I runs to da privy in da back yard."

"Yes, I know. But did you have an action today?"

"Action?"

"Yes," Mrs. Harris urged, "a bowel action."

Dessie looked solemnly at her questioner, then slow comprehension lighted her face.

"Yes'm, I is," she said, "but *us* calls it—"

"*We,*" corrected Mrs. Harris, mechanically.

"*We* calls it—" she began again and suddenly paused, remembering that you don't speak of such things to white ladies. She put her hand over her mouth and smiled shamefacedly. "I does think talkin," she said, "is da confusinest thing!"

"Dessie," Mrs. Harris said slowly, as if she had not heard, "someone killed Mr. Tracy Deen last night."

Dessie swallowed hard.

"And no one has any idea who did it." Dessie did not move. "Nor why." After a moment Mrs. Harris went on. "It is strange to think that in your home town, where you know—everybody, the son of one of your friends could be killed, like this. Sometimes," her voice had grown low, and Dessie knew she wasn't talking to her now, "I almost lose courage to try to bring up four sons, decently . . . You try . . . but . . ." She stared far away, her eyes black, black. "Strange to think that—in this town where we all live together, someone knows—"

"Miz Harris," Dessie's voice was trembling, "please mam, won't you read to me a little from da Bible? I ain't feelin so good."

# TWENTY

IT WAS PAST four o'clock before Miss Sadie could get to her usual afternoon visit with her friend Belle, for the switchboard had been chattering like a nervous woman since word of Tracy Deen's death was brought to town.

She plugged in Belle's number, loosened the black disks over her ears, pushed up her pompadour from her damp forehead and briefly began to answer Belle's questions, knowing full well that Belle had been at the morning service and already knew all there was to know.

"Yes, he was shot through the stomach . . . Yes, he must have bled badly . . . Yes, of course somebody shot him, no doubt about that . . . No, no one thought it suicide . . . Must have been near eleven o'clock when the Jenkins boys found him . . . What? . . . They were out in the palmettos looking for a shoat . . . No, it couldn't have been earlier . . . Well, it took time. He walked in to town and told Lem Taylor who had to find his wife before he could leave the jail . . . No, you can't just walk off and leave a jail . . . Somebody said she was over with old Mrs. Jones and . . . Well, anyway, he thought he had to find her . . . Then when Lem got downtown he told the boys, and they had to figure out how to break the news to the family when they were at church. That made it harder . . . Well, you know you wouldn't want to burst in and announce it right in church. You'd have to think how . . . It all took time—things do—"

"Yes, I know they do," said Belle, "but, Sadie, I just don't see how anybody would want to kill a sweet-mannered boy like Tracy Deen! I just don't. Many a time, many a time," Miss Belle mourned, "I've been downtown hot and tired and ready to drop in my tracks and I'd meet Tracy and he'd say, 'Come in the drugstore, Miss Belle, and have a coke with me. You look hot,' he'd say, and smile so sweet. Now, he didn't have to do that, did he? Not really, I mean, did he?"

"No," said Sadie, "he didn't have to do that."

"Well," Miss Belle said, "I don't see how anybody could be so cold-blooded and low-down as to have killed him, as sweet-mannered as he is—I just don't see how *anybody* could even—"

It was a hot afternoon and the board had been as trying today as ever in Sadie's long experience. "He's dead, Belle, whether you see it or not, and somebody must have held the pistol that shot him."

"Why, Sadie! I never knew you to be so cross!"

"Sorry, Belle, it's been a bad day. I'm sorry if I seem cross."

265

Miss Sadie looked out of the window, wiped her mouth with her handkerchief. It was a hot day; the thermometer down in front of Brown's Hardware Store had crawled to 101 when she went home for dinner, and so close to the roof up here it must be a lot hotter. She wiped her mouth and went on with the afternoon news. "They're singing over at the tent, and it's real sweet. Children's services always seem real sweet some way."

"What they singing, Sadie?"

*"Bringing in the Sheaves*—you can hear the words plain from here."

"I don't believe you could hear the words, Sadie. It must be the tune you hear."

"Well, maybe it's the tune— There goes Nonnie Anderson now towards the tent, taking Boysie Brown. I do think Mrs. Brown does the right thing to treat Boysie like a normal child, letting him get with other children and—"

"Maybe so," Belle agreed doubtfully. "He don't look normal though, with that big head, and the other children must think something—"

"Belle," Sadie interposed quickly. "Mr. Stephenson wired Mrs. Stephenson to come to Atlanta tonight."

"You don't say! What you reckon she's going to Atlanta for, and the meeting on?"

"Well, I didn't ask her," Sadie said. "Just let Mr. Hoke give her the message."

"Now, I wonder why she's—did she seem worried or anything?"

"No. She told Mr. Hoke to wire back that she and Grace would leave on the Nine O'clock tonight."

"Sadie," Miss Belle's voice had grown mournful again, "do you really think Tracy was saved?"

"I suppose so. At least I prefer to think that he was."

"I doubt it," Belle said, "I seriously doubt that he was."

"Well," said Sadie, "it's at least in the hands of God, not ours."

"You *are* cross today, Sadie! You needn't say you aren't."

"They're embalming the body now," Sadie returned to safe facts. "They telephoned to Valdosta for a coffin— The undertaker should have got here by this time."

"What kind of casket are they getting, Sadie?"

"They decided on gray, very plain and terribly expensive. And they're getting a steel vault."

"I'm *so* glad they are! Of course, they cost a terrible lot, but you feel so much better about somebody you love in a steel—"

"All seems a sin to me, to spend so much. I—"

"It wouldn't if you lost somebody you loved— When is the funeral to be?"

"Tomorrow morning. They think it best under the circumstances not—"

"Yes," said Miss Belle, "you can understand their attitude, of course, the meeting being on and all— But to me it seems plumb—it *is* plumb indecent not to let a body get cold, so to speak, before putting it in the ground! I may be old-fash—"

"It was plenty cold," Miss Sadie assured her. "In fact, they say it's bloated something terrible with the hot weather and all, and the buzzards being so bad out near the swamp had—"

"Don't tell me another word," Miss Belle interrupted. "My stomach's turned inside out as it is, been bilious for a week now, as you know, Sadie Cone! Took three grains of calomel last night and followed with a dose of salts early this morning without its having the least effect on me—well, practically none. Don't know what I'm going to do if I keep on, can't keep a thing on my stomach. If I take more, how do I know it'd help? Probably won't— What would you do?"

"You might see Dr. Deen."

"What would he advise?"

"Well, if you were married he'd tell you you were in the family way and to start on your layette," crisply.

"Why, Sadie Cone, what on earth's come over you!" and Miss Belle began to giggle. Miss Sadie had not meant to laugh because she was completely outdone with Belle today, but the giggles were contagious, and in spite of herself she succumbed to her own off-color humor.

A call interrupted the ladies' gaiety.

The voice speaking to Miss Sadie was grave, and Miss Sadie, in quick sympathy, answered gravely, while Miss Belle strained to hear. Only silence and the click-click of electrical disturbance on this close afternoon assaulted Miss Belle's astonished eardrums. For Sadie had cut her off. Some time she was going to lose her temper with Sadie. She really was! Sadie had a way of imposing on friendship—to the limit—and she needn't expect her friends to put up with it always. She—

"That was Laura." Sadie was back on the line. "She wants me to locate Mr. Harris. It's about the pallbearers. Her father would like for him to—"

"Did she say who they were to be?"

"Yes."

"Well?"

"Don't think I ought to tell you, Belle," Sadie began teasingly, and added in a sharply changed voice, her words very low,"I can't talk any more now, you'd better hang up—" And Belle found herself cut off.

Miss Sadie quietly tiptoed to the closed door on the corridor and listened. She had been conscious of men talking outside her door for some time, but had heard no words until one of them raised his voice in sudden argument. "Well, I be goddamed if I'll rest until we find the nigger who done it and break every bone in his body."

"We know who done it."

"Who?"

"That there Henry McIntosh." The voice was certain.

268

"Listen, boys," a third voice interrupted the others, "it don't seem reasonable that he done it. He's lived with em all his life, and if he ain't got a lot of sense he's always seemed a good kind of nigger. What'd he do it for?"

"What ud any nigger do it for? They don't reason! Ain't got nothing to reason with in their caboodles. When a damned nigger gits ready to kill he kills, that's all there is to it. Traipsing back here from the war, biggety black asses. One fool in a corporal uniform passed me down the street, and I stopped him and said, 'Nigger, when you pass a white gentleman, tip that damned yankee hat you'se awearin'—and by God, he sho took it off in a hurry." Laughter.

"Crazy Carl may be makin it all up. Folks has asked him so many questions he don't know what he knows by now. What was he doing out there, anyways?"

"Diggin fishin bait. He's shore he saw a big black nigger and a nigger gal out thataways this morning."

"Been out to the bushes all night likely as not. And anyways, there's plenty of black niggers everywheres."

"Look ahere, what's come over you! Turned nigger lover?"

"When I break one's neck, want to make sure I break the right one."

There was a pause in the talk. The same voice asked, "What do the Jenkins boys have to say? They found the body—"

"Saw buzzards circling and thought maybe it was the shoat they'd lost. Went in the gallberry bushes and there the body was—swelling up."

"Well?"

"They think maybe they did see a nigger out thataways."

"Yeah—after they heard Crazy Carl say it. And what would a nigger be doing hanging around hours after he had killed him?"

"Listen— We're meeting tonight, to make plans. You be

269

there. And git them crazy notions outa yo head. You think white men worth their salt's goin to let a black damn nigger git by with—" Someone else said, "Time's come to show em a little something. That's right. Ever since they come home from the war they ain't been fit— Traipsing up North like—" Voices lowered so that Miss Sadie could hear no more. She waited until she heard them move down the stairs leading to the street. She went to the window overlooking Main Street.

It looked like Saturday. All the county seemed to be on Main Street. Milling around in groups, near the calaboose, in front of Hewitt's Grocery, at the hitching lot, down by the warehouse, across the railroad in front of Rushton's mule lot. And not a Negro in sight, save Dan on the ice wagon and Uncle Pete in front of the Supply delivery wagon.

Across the street from the window was Crazy Carl, surrounded by a group of farmers from the Shaky Pond district. Dee Cassidy was asking him questions. As they talked, Sug Rushton passed, said something low to Cassidy, who nodded his head.

The others, and she recognized Bill Talley among them, continued the questioning of Carl. And now, come to think of it, every time she had gone to the window today for a breath of air she had seen Crazy Carl, surrounded by men. Funny, she hadn't thought how unusual that was. Except for handing him a few peanuts occasionally or asking him questions to hear his silly answers, nobody paid much mind to Crazy Carl. For ten years he had pushed around in his old homemade cart. Who had made it for him nobody knew. Where he slept nights only a few knew. He ate what folks gave him—overripe bananas from the grocery stores, peanuts, a pork sandwich from Salamander's Lunch Counter. Miss Sadie brought him a pint of milk in a fruit jar every day, and some time during the day Carl would pull up the stairs, flattening his big hands against the walls of the enclosed stairway and shifting his weight up until he made the landing.

270

Just why he could not walk easily no one knew. It was a part of his craziness, they reckoned. Breathing hard, he'd come in and slobber over the milk until what wasn't on the floor was in his belly. He'd say, "Zank o Mi Ad," which she had patiently taught him to say, and pull down the stairs again. And Miss Sadie with quick, efficient, birdlike movements would clean up the mess and wash the fruit jar. Sometimes the switchboard would buzz so angrily that she would have to leave the spilled milk for a long time, which sorely tried her feelings, but she never scolded Carl. She would sit in her revolving chair at the board, the black disks clamped to her ears, and watch Carl struggle with the milk, and sometimes the muscles of her wrinkled mouth would work in little sympathetic convulsions with his; but her eyes were bright and sharp like a bird's and showed no trace of the pity she felt for this poor freak of nature. That nature played such tricks on humanity Miss Sadie took for granted. She had a theory, which she had once told Belle, that the entire Negro race was a mammoth trick which nature had played on the white race. And in her opinion the white race should accept their burden with patience. To her they were ten million Crazy Carls, though some were more ingratiating than that poor boy. Ten million Crazy Carls to be tended and fed and protected from the cruelty which Miss Sadie's eyes were sharp enough to see lay in white men's breasts.

While Miss Belle agreed that the nigger was the white man's burden, she thought Miss Sadie too hard on white men. In her experience white men were mighty good to the nigger.

Miss Sadie almost retorted that Belle's experience with men was extremely limited, but checked herself in time and changed the subject.

She stood now at the window. Carl had not come up today for his milk. She called him, told the men to send him up to take a note to old Mrs. Bailey. Her guileless voice rang clear

271

and sharp, and the men, grown a little tired of Carl anyway, sent him up.

When he came in, Miss Sadie closed the door, hunted a peppermint for him, waited while he slowly ate it.

"Where were you early this morning, Carl?"

"Ow di ohms."

"What did you see?"

Carl grinned. He knew all the answers. "Big ack nig."

"What was he doing?"

"Ki-in Acy."

"You saw him kill Tracy?"

"Ar," he nodded vigorously in affirmation.

"What nigger was it?"

"Big En-y."

Carl stood before her, proud and satisfied. A heavy flush of triumph gave his face a look of maturity. She realized with sharp surprise that Carl was a grown man, and today an important one—in his own eyes. She saw as if for the first time the long fuzz thick on cheek, running down into his grained, reddened neck, on his big spraddly hands. His heavy lips hung loose and open, showing discolored teeth, and a little saliva dripped down his chin. Miss Sadie remembered, as she studied his face, that she had never seen his chin dry. Poor old harmless Carl, she tried to say, as she had said and heard others say a thousand times; but she knew suddenly that the devil as well as God uses fools.

She said sharply, "Listen to me, Carl."

He stared at her.

"You did not see Henry kill Tracy," and she pointed her finger at him in emphasis.

"Ar." He flushed angrily, a child now whose play-pretty has been jerked out of his hand. "Ar . . . I aw En-y ki Acy."

"No, no. You dug fishing bait. You did not—you could not have seen Henry kill Tracy. Tracy had been dead for hours when you were out there."

272

Carl struck his big hands together in anger. "Ar . . . Ar . . . Ar . . ."

"Listen at me. If you say that about poor old Henry, they'll kill him. You hear? They'll cut his head off, or something bad, or burn him up—like you see them burn trash back of the Supply Store. Do you understand? Poor old Henry. You wouldn't want to hurt him, would you?"

He blinked at her, saliva slowly dripping on his shirt.

"No, you don't want to hurt Henry. I am going to tell the men down there that you were joking. *You did not see Henry* . . ." And Miss Sadie underscored the words with her clear telephone voice and pressed her lips hard.

Carl's mind had not followed the full implication of Miss Sadie's words, but he recognized in her tone an obstacle and somehow knew that in her eyes he had lost the importance which had been his down on the street.

His face turned red, and raising his arm he struck hard at her.

Only the quickness of her movement saved her from a heavy blow. Still feeling incredulous, she knew now that Carl would kill her as carelessly as she had seen him sqush flies between his big flat fingers.

He took a step toward her, arm upraised. "Ar . . . Ar . . ."

She looked around the room for something with which to fend him off. There was a revolver in her drawer which she was as afraid of as she was now of Carl. And she could not have turned it on the big slobbering fool to save her life . . . when she had fed him milk every day for ten years. Her sharp eyes darted about. In the corner was the broom. With one swift little skip she had it in her hand and was waving it in his dazed face.

"Shoo," Miss Sadie screeched, and with little sweeping movements began driving the big creature from her. He moved back in slow wonderment until he was pressed against the door. With him against the closed door, blinking at her,

273

there was no opening out of which to drive him. Round and round the wall moved Carl and Miss Sadie, big Carl breathing through his mouth, dragging his heavy feet sideways, his hands hanging loose at his side. Miss Sadie mincing, waving the broom up and down. Carl's face twisted with bewilderment, watching her every movement. Miss Sadie edging closer and closer to the door. She would pull it open and make a rush on Carl with the broom. She was getting closer and closer to it now—

Carl shouted, "Boo!" and laughed in sudden glee. Miss Sadie dropped the broom. And as she did he made a wild plunge for it, slobbering in delighted excitement. It was a game she was playing.

Fright, horror, amusement fought for possession of Miss Sadie's little pigeon breast. She knew Carl would get that broom and run her up and down the room with it until he grew tired of the play. The board was buzzing like a nest of mad wasps. She was breathing hard, and her heart was thumping as it had not done since she was a child. Sweat poured down her legs. And Carl was bearing down on her.

"Milk," she gasped. "Your milk, Carl."

He stopped. "Ar," said Carl. "Ar. Ik." The broom fell from his hands. Carl dragged his body over to the cooler, dragged out the milk, began to lap at it, choking, spitting, snuffling quantities of it down his throat. With the lap, lap and gurgle in her ears, Miss Sadie fastened on the headpiece, plugged in numbers.

"Yes," she said as quietly as she could control her breathing, "yes, I'm sorry, Mrs. Reid. I know you have waited a long time— Just a minute, there's 48 . . . No, they don't answer . . . Yes, I'm sorry, Mrs. Brown . . .Yes, I saw Nonnie taking him toward the tent a long while ago . . . Do they answer, Mrs. Pusey? . . . Oh, it was terrible, just terrible. I know they're all broken up . . . Yes, I know . . . Poor Dorothy . . . Yes . . . Poor child."

274

Carl had finished his milk. There was a puddle of it on the floor, rolling down the cracks.

She said, "Here's a penny, Carl. Go buy you some candy."

"Zank o Mi Ad." The milk made a little white line on his lip. Sweat beads hung on his forehead and in the creases of his neck.

He worked with the knob until the door opened, started his slow way down the stairs.

Miss Sadie pulled the plugs out. The board was silent. Quietly she cleaned up after Carl.

She went to the window. From the tabernacle came the sound of children's shrill voices singing *No Not One*. The service was mighty long, she thought. She saw Nonnie rolling Boysie Brown down Main. He was whimpering, and Nonnie stooped swiftly and talked to him. Miss Sadie saw white men glance at the girl's hips, saw their eyes stick like flies in syrup. Nonnie straightened up, slim in her white uniform, adjusted Boysie's pillows, rolled him on down the street toward home.

Miss Sadie found herself crying. First time she had cried since her mother died, eight years ago. She had no idea what she was crying about and promptly stopped. The hot weather maybe, or something.

Her hands were trembling when she plugged 45 to 98. She wiped her face, pushed back her dyed hair from her forehead. Plugged in 63. "Laura," she said softly, "is Henry there?"

"Yes, Miss Sadie."

"Don't let him come downtown. You'd better keep him right to the house."

"Has something—"

"They're after him."

"You mean—because of—"

"Yes. Every Tom, Dick and Harry in the county." Miss Sadie paused, went on, "Even if he had anything to do with it—we wouldn't want them to get him this way."

275

"No. Thank you, Miss Sadie. I won't let him leave the house. He didn't—do it, of course. Does Father know?"

"I don't know, honey. His office hasn't answered this afternoon."

"He's out now—somewhere. I'll tell him."

Miss Sadie looked out of the west window across the ball-ground to the swamp. Black clouds had massed up over the tree line, throwing deep shadows over the town, and by some trickery of the hidden sun clumps of palmettos stood out in startling greenness. The light, dark as the afternoon was, was so intense that she could see moss hanging from the old cypress back of the Negro Lodge, something she couldn't remember being able to see before. A low roll of thunder came from the northwest.

Miss Sadie plugged in 101 and 23. She did hope it wouldn't storm, for she was deathly afraid of lightning. She'd never told a living soul, being the operator, but lightning . . . of course, it was real silly of her . . . still, she did hope it wouldn't storm . . . much, since it was her night on the switchboard.

One-armed Ben Reid came in to relieve her for supper. "Better let me stay on for you tonight," he said, and laid a book on the switchboard desk.

"Why, Ben?"

"Oh, nothing. Thought maybe you'd like to go to the meeting." Ben was fastening the headgear on.

Miss Sadie hesitated, but not enough for Ben to see, said firmly, "No. We'd better stick to our nights as we've always done, except when we're sick. And I'm not a bit sick.

"Thank you though, Ben," she said as she started out. "I won't be long."

"Take your time, Miss Sadie."

Miss Sadie's high heels went tippy-tap briskly down the stairs.

276

# TWENTY-ONE

BESS RAN ACROSS the Stephensons' back yard and out of the gate, slamming it behind her. She stopped, thrust the thermos bottle deep within one of the shrubs, walked rapidly down Back Street.

She had figured that by five Sam would be back, maybe earlier, and it was now after five.

All day as she went about her work she had pushed Ed nearer and nearer safety as the clock's hands moved slowly from hour to hour. Five o'clock. If he made that train as they hoped, he was now in Virginia. One more full swing of those hands and he would be in New York. Lost and safe in that big place. If he had sense enough to keep his name from people—and not talk. You couldn't count on Ed. Sometimes shrewd, smart . . . Other times . . . If he got Nonnie on his mind . . . he might do anything. Give himself up—anything! To make them feel sorry for *him* now. As a kid he did crazy things—dashing across the track in front of the train, missing it by inches, scaring you to death. But he'd never have done it unless folks had looked at him. Had to have an audience.

All day she had watched the clock, and then suddenly she knew that Mrs. Stephenson too was watching it. She had been so intent on being her natural self, so busy about it, that she had not noticed until after dinner how unnatural Mrs. Stephenson was. She had not attended the morning service, and now Bess remembered that all day long she had walked back and forth, back and forth, from room to room, looking for something.

It was past three o'clock when Mr. Hoke called with a telegram, and after receiving it Mrs. Stephenson seemed not to be looking any more. She told Bess that she and Grace

277

would go to Atlanta on the Nine O'clock, that she wanted her to come every day and look after the two roomers. "Keep their rooms and air the house. You can bring Jackie and let him play in the back yard," she added, "and take the flowers, as soon as you come tomorrow morning, over to the Deens'. They'll be in on the train tonight. We'll be gone some time," she said, and stared at Bess without seeing her, "so I want you to look after things . . . Feed the chickens . . ."

Her mention of Jackie had given Bess the excuse she wanted. She quickly seized it, asked Mrs. Stephenson if she could run home for a little . . . Jackie had been ailing, a little fever . . . not much, but it kept her uneasy. She had waited until five o'clock to ask, having fixed her salad for supper and brought the two suitcases down from the storeroom. She had said the wrong thing. For at once Mrs. Stephenson asked her more questions, as though spreading Bess's small worries over her mind would cover up something which she did not want to see. And as Bess started out, she came into the kitchen and insisted upon making lemonade for Jackie, and made most of it herself, squeezing the lemons slowly—so slowly it seemed to Bess as she watched the juice trickle down those slim pointed fingers—pouring it into her own thermos bottle, asking more about him, telling Bess to take good care of him—she was fond of the little fellow, she said, and Bess must look after him—until Bess was half crazy with impatience. She'd managed to be calm all day—to wait. But now that she knew Sam must be home, she could wait no longer. She had to find out, had to see him, had to talk.

But it looked as if she could not get away from Mrs. Stephenson's kindness. To get away from Mrs. Stephenson's kindness was not ever easy. She hedged you in with it, made you prisoner and walled herself from you as the kindnesses mounted. Bess had cooked for Mrs. Stephenson seven years, but she knew about her only that she was kind. She had been

278

kind then—kind since. Always the same. Once last winter a tramp had come to the door. Bess was about to send him away, for they were busy. The Missionary Circle was meeting with them that day and they had chess pies to make for it— and Bess had one of her sick headaches too which the rich odor was not helping. And tramps are no-count white folks anyway; if colored folks can find jobs—and God knows some do—then there's no excuse for white men being out of work. So she was turning him away when Mrs. Stephenson said, "The side porch is sunny and warm. Go out there and we'll find something for you to eat. Bess, fix him a sandwich and a cup of coffee." But her voice had not changed nor had the muscles of her face moved. She was neither irritated nor sorry for him. This was what should be done and therefore was done. You had a queer feeling about it—as if Mrs. Stephenson had died some time when nobody was noticing and now nothing was left of her but good deeds blooming like little flowers on her grave. It had flashed through Bess's mind, and ever since she had caught herself watching her mistress.

Yet finally she had escaped her, and now she must make haste. It was hot and close. Bess slowed her rapid walk. Already big splotches had soaked through her uniform. She would have to change before supper. She lifted her arm. Smelled to heaven! "Pure nigger smell," she whispered, whipping herself with her compulsion to see her race through white eyes.

"Yes, nigger," she whispered as she hurried along Back Street. "It's caught up with us." It was as if the Andersons had been running away from it, getting a little whiter and whiter with each generation, running hard. But it's caught us. As it catches everybody, sooner or later. It's reached out and caught us. You can run until you're panting, but it'll catch you. Going to college won't help you run any faster— all that stuff they tell you there makes it worse. Be proud of your African heritage, they tell you! Yeah . . . music . . .

rhythm . . . all that . . . Proud! When you're pushed around through back doors, starved for decent friendliness and respect, they tell you about Benin bronzes—things like that. Sure! When you're so hurt you feel as if you're bleeding inside, you're supposed to remember that some old archeologist or somebody found that way back there in Africa your ancestors could make bronze—sculpture or something. And now you're supposed to feel fine. See? When all that matters to you or any other Negro is that your folks were slaves and you're still slaves. You can't run away from that shadow; whichever direction you turn it turns with you.

She had left the white part of the street and was crossing a patch of gallberry bushes before entering the colored section of town.

God knows, Eddie's a fool—always making you lose your temper. But he wouldn't have killed a man had it not been for his color. No. He'd have found some other way to let out his spoiledness. It wouldn't have been killing. Too tenderhearted as a kid to hurt a bug without whimpering.

And suddenly Bess was crying a little, for now she saw what lay ahead of Ed—even if he were safe, if he escaped, he'd still have to come back in his mind and look at that white man he'd killed. Sooner or later he would have to do that, and when he did, when he made that journey back, something would happen inside him and it wouldn't be good. No. God knows she didn't care about the white man being dead. She was glad. Yes, she was! Glad! But you care what happens inside your brother, even if he is a fool. You care.

She gave a quick sob and hushed for fear some passer-by would notice her.

Reckon Ed had picked up where Pap left off. Always suspecting somebody. Pap was like that. Once when they were children they had been playing in the graveyard, and she had run home to get a bottle to put lightning bugs in. She had just come around the house when she heard Pappy on the veranda saying, "He don look like my kid," voice heavy as lead, "he don favor—"

Pap in one of his glum spells. And she had drawn back half under the veranda, knowing folks don't like for children to hear things.

"He's yo's," Tillie had said. "He's all yo's. You is like as two peas in a pod. En you bof is gittin hard to live wif!" she'd suddenly added. "Eddie whining all over everywheres sence the baby come, while you is so glum . . . Hit ain good, Ernie," she added, "for chudren to be brung up round glumness. Dey need to hear folks laughin. You know dat! A spoonful of grits'll make a child healthy ef you keep him alaughin while he eats it."

"Tillie," he'd said, "I ain found nothin sence I was born dat was worf laughin over."

She saw Mama walk slowly to the edge of the veranda where Pappy stood, lay her big broad hand on his shoulder, look him straight in the eye. "Dat ain so, Ern Anderson."

"Cep you," he muttered.

"Cep me . . . and da chudren."

"Sometime I near go crazy . . . thinkin things . . . How I know dey— Dey don favor me—"

"Ern—look at me—look at Tillie! Dey is yo own. You talkin crazy! Crazy! Ever child we got is *yo own*. En they all the spittin image of you. Mean jes lak you," she added and laughed. "Mean jes like deh pa."

But Pappy hadn't laughed. He went on talking low, as if he had not heard Tillie. "Saddy night . . . I were in da store . . . buyin me a plug of tobaccy . . . back of me . . . two white men talkin . . . bout women. I warn't payin no mind till one spoke . . . spoke yo name . . . said—" He paused. Went on, "En I turned en walked out widdout lookin, for I know'd I'd kill um ef I looked . . . I'd kill um! En I been thinkin ever since I oughta killed um. A man any count woulda kill um for sayin—"

"You knows better. Ernest Anderson, you knows *no matter what,* you don *do* nothin, you hear? You don *do* nothin!"

"Tillie—you ain had no . . . traffic . . . wid . . . white—"

"Hush! I oughta slap you on da mouf—fillin yo mind full of nasness like dat. Worryin yoself crazy. Crazy!"

They both were silent after that. It was so quiet you could hear the others laughing over at the graveyard.

"Ernie," Mama's voice was gentle now and soft, "we works so hard—we don—most nights you is dead sleep time I gits shet of my housework. Let's . . . Ernie . . . me and you— Let's go inside . . . for a little—"

"Hit ain black-dark, Tillie 'oman, en da chudren—"

"The baby's sleep and the res of um is over in the graveyard wid Sammie en da others, ketchin lightnin bugs. Dey won't come tell I calls um in. Let's go, Ernie." And Tillie had led the way to her bedroom, followed slowly by Pappy, and somebody had shut the door.

Well, she wasn't over in the graveyard catching lightning bugs. She was crouched under the edge of the veranda, and she had walked, without knowing where she walked, to the big palmetto clump and flung herself down on her stomach in the sand, and the tears had rolled down her face without her knowing what she was crying about and she had whispered, "No, no, no, no, no," without knowing what she meant by such words. And when she got up after Mama called, she didn't want any supper. It was sometime in the night that she had awakened with a headache and sick at her stomach and fearing she would vomit had started outdoors to the privy, not being afraid of the dark. But as she stepped out on the shed, she heard somebody crying a little, and there sat Mama on the back steps.

"Sometime, Jesus," Ma said low, almost in a whisper, "yo Tillie think hit's time for you to he'p her a little . . . he'p her a little . . . wid things."

Seven-year-old Bess had slipped back into the house and

282

used the slop jar, and Mama had heard her and had come and put a cold rag on her face and told her, "Shet yo eyes, honey, and Mama tell you bout time her mama made her a brand-new red dress," and before she finished telling how that red calico dress was bought from a pedlar and cut out and sewed up, Bess was asleep.

Things like this come back to you . . . keep coming back all your life.

It all seemed Non's fault somehow! If she'd let that white man alone! It was as if she were hypnotized, not once thinking what it all added up to, just moving along in a world that wasn't on this earth. Of course Ed suspected! How could he help it? Plain as the nose on your face. Let that white man whistle and she'd be there. Every night at the gate, waiting. And that last night she'd been with him, he'd come so late, calling her in the arbor until Bess had turned sick with fear of Ed's hearing. She'd lain there listening . . . hearing Nonnie come softly down the steps, open the door, go outside, hearing his voice, a little loud. Drinking. Yes, you could tell that. And hours passed. Or it seemed like hours.

Bess had crept out to the back shed, and seeing no one in the arbor had sat on the doorsteps, waiting; growing sick and scared and angry as she waited, as minutes piled up into an hour. Or more. And then Nonnie was standing there before her. She must have dozed not to have heard her come up. Standing there. And Bess knew without a word being spoken that Non was hurt.

"He's hurt you." Nonnie had not seemed to hear. "Where're you hurt, Non?"

Nonnie shook her head, sat down on the step. It was the same face, yet not the same. You knew something bad had happened to her and that she'd never tell you. Never in this world tell anybody.

"I don't care if you hate me the rest of your life," Bess had said, "you're going to let me see how bad you're hurt." And

Nonnie had made no effort to stop her as Bess slipped the blouse off of her shoulders. She'd tried not to show her shock when she saw the bruise on arm and breast. But she heard herself breathing hard as she examined the places. "I'll get some iodine. Stay here." And she had run to her room sobbing a little in her fear and anger, trying to be quiet to keep from waking Ed. She'd bathed the places with alcohol, touched them with iodine, whispering, "You need a doctor—you need Sam." But Nonnie shook her head and Bess knew better this time than to urge. She tried to remember what Mama would have done, what Sam would do, for things like this. She wanted to take Nonnie in her arms—the kid needed somebody to mother her a little now—but she knew if she tried to do it she'd begin to squall at the top of her voice, and God alone knew what Non would do.

"Now," she'd said instead, "now, that's much better. I know you'll feet better soon. You're bound to. I'm going to get you a little ammonia—" As she turned to go back into the house she grew sick with a new fear. "Non . . . you're not—Are you hurt anywhere else? Tell the truth, you've got to! Are you?" Non whispered, "No." She hesitated—praying God that Non said the truth, though knowing she would never tell her—then went in for the ammonia. If she could keep doing things! But she could think of nothing else. After Non drank the ammonia, Bess stood watching her, hoping to see her begin to look better, to see her color come back instead of this gray look. She saw that Non was shaking, and she ran in and heated some water on the oil stove and fixed a bottle and made her put it on her stomach. Everything she did made her feel better, but she was afraid it wasn't helping Non much. As she watched her, she began to have the feeling that Non could die—not because her body was hurt enough to kill her but because maybe she had no reason for living. She knew it was a crazy idea. She knew whatever happened *she'd* always want to go on living, but she wasn't sure Non-

284

nie would. "Let me put you to bed," she said—as if this simple normal act would somehow hold Non to normal folks' ways—and leaned over and touched her hair, hoping she would know how sorry she felt for her, for all the times she'd fussed at her. Two slow tears rolled down Nonnie's face. She shook her head. "If you don't mind, I want to—be alone—a little—"

"Hadn't you better go to bed?" feeling as she said it that Non did not hear her—as she never heard her, really. And Bess had gone into the house, leaving Nonnie sitting there on the back doorsteps, in the cool early dawn.

That was the last time Non had been with him. As far as she knew. That night. And now he was dead. That white man was dead! She'd tried not to think about Nonnie today —what she was feeling while she nursed Boysie Brown. To think about her at any time was not easy. Your thoughts slid off like oil on glass. There was nothing to catch hold to. You felt Non had done all her growing inside, all her living there, sending out no faults or virtues like most folks whose growth has reached out toward their world; no little mannerisms of voice or body. Just a slender tall girl with skin the color of a rich eggshell, with features that made folks say, "She's beautiful"—somebody who talked softly, smiled, turned away if you came too near. She was like a quiet vague tune to which each person sets his own words. And you were never sure your words were the right ones.

You did not know how she felt, but of one thing you were sure. Non could not have that baby. They'd have to make her get rid of it. She had to! It was not fair. She had to! And yet as Bess said it over and over to herself she knew Non would not give it up. Non had never fought for things, never reached out and snatched what she wanted from the world, but when it came her way, when it fell into her hands, she held on to it.

285

When she was six years old, someone gave her a kitten. One evening, as Bess and her mother sat on the porch, Non had taken it in her arms and walked slowly down the road a little way. A passing dog saw the cat, began to bark at it. At first Tillie and Bess were not alarmed, thinking the child would let it go and seek her own safety. But Nonnie, making no cry, only backed away from the dog, gripping her kitten more closely to her. The dog's barking drew other dogs, and quickly there were six or seven dogs there, barking, jumping up at the cat, each increasing the others' greed, whipping themselves into a great excitement over one small kitten. Tillie called sharply, "Bess, go to the child!" and Bess ran toward her screaming, "Let it go, Nonnie! Drop it quick!" But Nonnie, pale-faced and tense, only held it more tightly to her as the angry dogs barked and snapped and jumped into her face. She'd taken a big stick and beat the dogs off, while Non stood there, her breath coming in sharp little gasps, the vein beating in her temple, the kitten held tightly to her body. She'd always beaten the dogs off for Nonnie, but this time Non had to—

Here was Sam's house. And now quickly Bess was in his office and talking to him. He looked as if he had not had time to change his clothes since the trip. As if he might have just come in. His satchel was on the desk. A calendar advertising Horlick's Malted Milk hung on the wall, and the sunlight now shifted brightly on it. August 21. Yes, August 21. That was today. August 20—that was yesterday. This time yesterday nothing had happened. Or not the worst had happened. It was like stringing beads on a cord. One after another after another. If the cord had broken, or a bead had been dropped or lost—that last bead would not have been strung.

She turned to Sam and looked at him. His brown face was

286

tired, his eyes yellowed and bloodshot, and he needed a shave. But it was Sam. And good to see him.

Briefly he told her of the journey. Ed had made the train in Macon—would soon be in New York. He had warned him not to communicate with them, had given him a friend's name in New York. The friend would be discreet. Everything should be all right. "How are you?"

"All right. I reckon I am. All this— I'm glad you're back."

"You look tired. Headache?"

"No. You look tired yourself. Mrs. Perry glared at me when I came in. Said you needed sleep more than you needed talk." They both smiled. "I know you do."

She ought to go now. Sam's face, so red under the brown usually, was yellow under the brown, and drawn. Her eyes moved over his desk. A prescription pad. A book—Sam didn't read much. His pipe. An old glass paper weight. An embroidered linen table runner . . .

"Sam—what's happened to us? I feel as if it's the end."

Sam smiled. "Not quite the end, maybe. I hope not." They stood there staring past each other.

"Things are bad," he went on after a moment. "You know I realize how bad. But for the time being Eddie is safe. Later — It won't be easy—when he begins to see all—he's done. But if you can just—wait, maybe—" He smiled again and rubbed his hand over his forehead and that portion of his head that was bald.

"Wait. Yes. Negroes are supposed to know how to do that. It's got me— I ought to let you sleep, and I need to get back to my work. But—last night— it— I couldn't look at Non. We went home. I didn't try to go to bed. I got rid of Eddie's things—thought it best to. I burned them."

Sam nodded. "I hoped you'd think to do it."

"I happened to open the closet in Mama's room for something, and there on the nail was Pap's overalls. One strap off the nail—you remember how it always fell off his shoulder that way." She tried to smile. "Hanging there. Fifteen years hanging there—a pair of overalls—all that was left. Work. He'd come home after work and sit at the table, glum, while Mama fixed supper . . . Always nagging at Eddie, picking on him . . . We hated him, Eddie and me . . . Glumming up everything . . . never laughing."

It's late, she thought, you got to get back to your supper, it's late. But she went on talking.

"Last night . . . looking at those overalls . . . I began to see him—" Sam looks tired. No sleep. "I burned them too. Afraid they'd find them and think them Eddie's. Ever since, I've—felt—kind of—like I burned—Pappy—all there was left of him." She was trembling a little.

"You're tired, Bess. When folks get this tired, they have feelings like that—everybody does."

"And going through things—Eddie always leaves his things all over the house, I was afraid I'd overlook something—I came across—" She swallowed, wondering what had come over her.

Sam put his hand on her shoulder. "Bess, you're tired. You've got to get back to your supper. I want you to talk, but maybe—"

"I know . . . And you're tired too. But if you don't mind, let me say it. It's—kind of—got on my mind. You see, I found a pair of Mama's old shoes. That was all, but all at once—" The light from the setting sun was on Sam's hand now, the one with the scar from the fishhook. "You see, they'd never been people to me before—and all at once standing there, they stepped out right before me, as people, not Mama and Pap. It was just a second, but I saw them so plainly—it's made me feel . . . confused . . . Children aren't supposed to see their parents quite like that." She tried to smile. "Sometimes I'm afraid . . . these headaches . . . Seems to me I think a lot of—kind of queer thoughts . . . Could they make me a little crazy, Sam? Could they?"

"You know better than that, Bess."

She looked at his brown stolid face. She always believed Sam. He couldn't know much more than she— What made her believe him, like this?

"And somehow, seeing those two things . . . hurt so. They were so poor, Sam! All their life colored folks so poor . . . working . . . Pap and Mama . . . every livelong day . . ."

"Bess, you must see the other side. You must. It's not just the Negro—"

"If you tell me white folks are poor too, I'll—I'll almost slap you!" She tried to laugh. "We've argued it so often! I know they're poor—I know all over the world people are poor—and work hard—or don't have any work to work hard at. It doesn't make it a bit easier when it's your own mother you're remembering. Going to work early every morning, coming back late at night . . . All she ever saw that was pretty or bright or soft,  things she liked, was in white folks' houses. I remember she used to talk— All her life she used to talk about some day painting the house white, splashing it 'befo and behind,' she'd say—I can still hear her—and getting her some big-size sheets. Yes. She was going to do that when she got us all through school and through college. Well—she didn't get to do either one—"

"Bess—"

"I can almost see her . . . coming down the path from Miss Ada's, that big old straw hat pulled clean down on her head to her ears, her little bundle under her arm . . . looking quick for Nonnie at the gate . . . walking slow . . . on the edge of her feet to ease her bunions—all her life, doing that. And when she was so sick at the last and I'd rub her feet to try to get a little warmth in them, they were so hard and rough, it was like—rubbing a piece of—old wore-out shoe leather . . ."

She'd said too much. If she looked at Sam now, she'd cry.

He was speaking, his slow way. "It's strange—way folks re-

member somebody. My own mother died when I was too little to remember, and I always lived round with kinfolks—
until Aunt Easter came down here to keep me straight—" He
half smiled. They all remembered the day Aunt Easter had
arrived from North Georgia and was waiting with a basket,
a trunk and a hoe, for Sam on the porch of his house. She
announced as he walked up the steps that she was his aunt,
she could prove it—which she promptly did—and had come
to take care of him. He had never seen her before, but she
had taken good care of him, ever since.

He's forgot Ella, she thought, he's forgot all about her.

"But all my life nearly I've been going the old road by
Miss Ada's to your house. All my life nearly I've been round
your mother. With Eddie, when we were boys—all my life.
And when I think of her I see her different. I see her reaching out and pulling everybody, everything, the whole world,
to her, and sort of nursing it in her big lap—all of it, good
and mean, its nastiness and its brightness, drawing it in
against her breast. Not gently—she wasn't gentle—pulling it
to her, grimly, maybe, but taking it and giving . . . what she
had. I like to remember that. I like to remember . . . way
she used to laugh until she shook all over, every inch of her
. . . and way she'd turn to us kids right in the midst of her
laughing sometimes and say, 'Mind yo manners, chudren,
wid white folks,' and draw up her mouth tight like you draw
up a tobacco pouch."

"I know. As if any white person was worth our manners!"

"She said it to protect your life. Good manners are still
best life insurance a colored person ever took out." He
smiled.

Oh how could he smile! How *could* he!

"I don't see how you take things as you do. You'd think
there was no feeling in you—no shame for your race—"

"I'm proud to be a Negro, Bess. Proud."

"Proud! You're lying. You think that's the thing to say.

Well, it isn't the thing to say to me! It's being nigger—*nigger*, Sam—that's done this to us. Oh I know Ed's crazy ways—that temper, his feeling that— I know all that. He couldn't— Sam," she looked up at him, "did Ed tell you why he did it?"

"No."

"Have you any idea?"

"No."

He's lying. He knows something.

"Have you heard anything since you got back?"

"No. But then I wouldn't."

"They've found him." She could not make herself say Deen's name.

He looked at her without speaking.

"This morning."

"I thought as much. They turned me back while ago—I'd started out to see Aunt Cyn. They'd sent in word she was dying."

"What did Aunt Easter tell them? I'm—she's old and—"

"Said I was delivering a baby. She always says that."

"Who turned you back?"

"Some white boys—hardly grown—but I didn't argue," Sam smiled quickly.

"Sam, Ed said he left him on the path. They found him in the palmettos, fifty yards from the path."

"Maybe Ed moved him."

"He said he didn't touch him. And I don't believe he would have. It's worried me . . . If they don't get Ed, they'll — What'll they do?"

"I don't know."

"They'll . . . get somebody else?"

"I don't know."

"Would we . . . keep our mouth shut . . . and let them?"

"Don't cross that bridge! You're too tired— Let's wait, let's just wait."

"Sam," she whispered, "they . . . wouldn't dare . . . get

291

Non?" She hadn't even thought of it until this minute. She was fighting sudden panic.

His face blazed with something Bess had never seen before, grew as suddenly quiet. He turned to her, spoke irritably, it seemed now to her. "Bess, you must go. You've got your supper to get, and I've some calls."

And then she told him. She would never know what made her speak. She simply said it, hearing her words before she knew she was saying them. "There's something else—Nonnie . . . she's pregnant." She spoke rapidly, did not look at him, wishing now that she hadn't said it, not today. "We've got to do something—make her—it'll soon be too dangerous—she's got to have an abortion. You'll do it, won't you?"

He did not answer her.

"You'll do it, won't you, Sam?" Why did he just stand there as if he had not heard! "She's so hardheaded!" Suddenly she was angry. Why didn't he answer her! "Says she wants it. She— We can't *let* her have it! You can see that. Anybody could see that. But Nonnie. No. She wants it, therefore—" Bess paused, turned quickly. "Sometimes I wonder if there *is* something in the Negro—Ed killing, Nonnie pregnant—what's the matter with us! Is it Negro? Is it Anderson? What is it? What's the matter with people like us!"

"White women get pregnant—plenty." His voice was harsh and angry.

"They wouldn't want it—they'd be too shamed to want it. And I don't see how any colored woman would want to bring another Negro into this world!"

"Jackie?"

"I didn't want him. I was young—he just came." She tried to laugh.

"You love him."

"Oh, I love him, but I don't enjoy him!" She added low, "And he's no bastard. I reckon I've made a mess of things. I ought to have managed her better. Even when we were little, Mama was always worrying about Nonnie and boys. Telling me to watch out for her. Never worried about me." She tried to laugh.

Sam was rubbing his hands together, turned suddenly, looked out of the window.

"Sometimes it's seemed to me, this is crazy, but it's seemed to me that Nonnie has never in her life admitted to herself that she is Negro."

Sam turned, face flushed darkly. "Maybe she's never thought about it one way or the other."

"How could she help it! When it's rubbed in your face like something dirty every day, everywhere you move."

"There's more to life than color, Bess. There's more. Lot more." He had moved to his desk now, picked up his satchel, put it down.

"Oh, how can you say it! How can we even stand here and say anything—when our color has ruined our lives—yours too. Don't say it hasn't! You go around doing good to people. It's fine for everybody but you. But you know inside you, you want something more. You'd like to be natural and easy and simple. It *would* be so simple, Sam, to be white. I'm so tired of being two people! Sometimes I get mixed up myself," she laughed shakily, "and forget which one is me—Mrs. Stephenson's Bess, or mine."

"White folks have trouble, Bess." He half smiled and touched her arm, but his eyes had a terrible look in them.

"I don't believe it! Oh, I don't believe it—not like ours."

"Trouble with themselves and the folks they love. And that's what's important to all of us."

"I don't want to believe it."

"You've got to feel sorry for them too."

"I can't. Take my hate of white folks away from me, I'd not have anything left. I'd—crumple up. Makes it a lot easier on Jack, for me to hate them." She tried to laugh, wiped her eyes instead, suddenly found her chin shaking, turned away,

293

wiped her eyes again, turned back. "Sam, what are we going to do about Nonnie? We can't wait."

He looked at her, through her, said slowly, "I would like to marry your sister."

Marry Nonnie! *Marry* her after a white man—

Always it had seemed to Bess when things got bad, snagged at her like an old saw, Sam was thinking about her. Always you'd thought, when he came over to talk, he'd come to talk to you. And it wasn't you he'd come to see—

"After this—would you even—I don't see how you *could* after thi—"

"Bess," his voice was sharp and angry, "there's something about you that makes a man sick!"

She flushed, said quickly, "I'd better go now. It's terribly late." And she had turned and left him standing there with a tight hard look on his face, as if he hated her.

It was time now for supper to be on the table. She'd have to make up something about Jackie being worse than she had thought.

She slipped quietly into the Stephensons' kitchen, turned the damper on the stove, put in some dry chips, laid a skillet on for her chicken patties, put the kettle over the hot part of the stove, hurried into the dining room with the plates. She had turned to the sideboard to get the silver when she heard Mrs. Stephenson and Grace in the adjoining bedroom.

"Mother, is it bad as—having a baby?"

"No. It won't be bad." There was silence now except for footsteps moving back and forth. Then in the same low tone, clear as if long ago strained of feeling, Mrs. Stephenson said, "Grace, is there anybody in this town, besides Mart, who knows?"

"I don't think so.

Bess quietly picked up the silver, eased over to the table, softly began laying knives and spoons on the right, forks on the left.

# TWENTY-TWO

WHEN HE FINISHED his supper, Tom Harris called Dessie into the parlor and shut the door. She came slowly, a wet dishrag wadded tight in her hand, dragging her feet across the floor as if chained to guilt.

Laura had been to see him and had gone, leaving with him the list of pallbearers and those who had offered to sit up with the body. She'd said, "We're worried about Henry. Miss Sadie called. She says they're after him. He didn't do it of course," she'd added quickly.

"Maybe he did," though he knew better.

"No," Laura spoke as if she knew. "No. He wouldn't have done it." She looks a lot like her mother, Tom Harris thought, she looks a lot like her. So sure.

"He'd have no reason for doing it," she added slowly, her gray eyes looking straight into his, her hand pushing her hair back slowly. She's about sick from all this, Tom thought, too quiet to be natural.

"There're others—who'd have more—cause." She moved her lips as if to say more, stopped. Her hand was by her side now. "Anyway, we wouldn't want Henry—hurt—even if he did do it. Not by— We've talked to Henry," she went on quickly now, "Daddy and I. He says he knew it. Says he—saw him lying on the path near Miss Ada's—says he was out with your Dessie." She half smiled and swallowed, went on, never raising her voice, holding her lips almost together now as she spoke. "They saw—him—early. And Henry—he's not very bright—it seems he dragged Tracy off—into the bushes. Said he knew they'd think he did it, said he was afraid to tell us. He cried so much, it was hard to get—words out of him—" She stopped, began again, "Daddy is—broken up." She swallowed hard, and Tom could see the muscles trembling in her cheek and throat, but she went on almost dully, "He can't get his mind on—this, very much. We haven't told Mother. I thought if you knew, perhaps—you'd—" She was looking at her father's, her whole family's longtime friend, steadily, quietly, as if unaware that she had not finished her sentence.

"Yes, I'll do something, Laura. Now run on home and try to rest. Or could you stay here and rest?"

"No. I must go. Thank you." And she went quickly down the walk to the street. Yes, she's getting more like her mother every day. So sure, and controlled. Be better if she'd break down a little.

He looked up now at the waiting girl.

"Dessie."

"Yassuh."

"Were you with Henry last night?"

"Yassuh."

"Where were you?"

Dessie gulped, looked toward the door as if praying Mrs. Harris's ears were not glued to it as hers would surely have been. "We was in my house."

"All night?"

"Nossuh."

"Did you go somewhere?"

"Yassuh."

"Where?"

Dessie swallowed hard.

"Where did you go?"

Dessie's eyes did not leave his face. "Out in da bushes."

"What were you doing, Dessie, in the bushes?" and was quickly sorry he had said it, knowing Dessie.

"Cuttin up." Her big eyes were very grave as they looked straight into his blue ones.

"Cuttin up— You mean—"

"Yassuh. Cuttin up bad," and Dessie nodded her head to confirm his worst thoughts.

"What time did you two come home?"

"Long daybreak."

"Did you see anything on the way?"

Dessie nodded again, her tongue refusing words.

"Mr. Tracy?" very low.

Her eyes grew wide with fear. She wet her lips.

Mr. Harris studied her face. "Dessie," and in his voice was the deep solemnity he had used many a time when questioning his children or about to punish them, "do you know who killed Tracy Deen?"

Dessie squeezed hard on the dishrag until drops of water spilled slowly down her dress. "Nossuh. Honest to Gawd."

He looked at her steadily, letting his eyes bore through her nervous little body.

"Honest to Gawd, Mr. Harris!" She began to sob.

"Ssssh," he said. "Does Henry know?"

"Nossuh. Nossuh! When he seen it—the—the—it—he puked up all over hisself."

"He got sick?"

"Yassuh."

"Did he wonder who'd done it?"

"Nossuh. He jes said he knowed they'd think he done it."

"What did he do then?"

"Drug it out in da bushes—offn da path."

"Why did he do that?"

"I don know, suh. He jes done it."

"What time did Henry come to you last night?"

"I doesn't own no timepiece," she said, and smiled shamedly over this deficiency, "but hit musta been . . ." She frowned, "It was atta da Nine O'clock run and da meetin was still goin high, for I was singin along wid dem." She smiled again. "On my shed," she added, "the sound comes across fine."

"What were they singing?"

"Almos persuaded, Christ to receive, almos persuaded now to believe—"

And Tom Harris believed. He knew as he looked in that brown candid face that Dessie was telling the truth. He said briskly, "Well, run along now and finish up your dishes. You're not to leave the house tonight. Make up a pallet in Mrs. Harris's room and sleep there. Tell her I said for you to."

He telephoned Miss Sadie. "Miss Sadie—you tried to locate me this afternoon?"

"Yes, about the pallbearers."

"I have that. Anything else?"

Briefly she told him about Crazy Carl.

"Nobody with a grain of sense would listen to Carl . . . Who've you seen around?"

"The usual crowd—Tracy's friends—"

"Anybody else?"

"Bill Talley, some of the Shaky Pond folks."

"Still in town?"

"Were when I went out to supper."

"I see. Well, much obliged, Miss Sadie."

Laura had got it right. Something was up—more than the hotheads.

It was about dark when he had left the office for the mile-and-a-half walk to his house. And as he crossed the railroad and passed through the narrow stretch of cypress and palmetto, a light had flashed in his face. "It's Harris," a voice had called. Another one muttered, "All right."

"What you up to, boys?"

"Checking up on the niggers."

"Mind you check on yourselves too," he laughed, walked on, stopped. "Don't go stirring up trouble in my quarters. My boys got to be on the job in the morning."

On the short-cut through the live-oak grove he had been

stopped twice. In the dark of the big oak in front of his own corner gate he was stopped again. A light flashed full in his face, was lowered. Someone walked away.

"Watch your step, boys," he had called out to the darkness. If these irresponsible whippersnappers didn't watch out, there would be trouble. Bad trouble, and they didn't have the sense to see it.

Tom stood at the telephone, his hand still on the receiver. Across the room his son Charles sat reading. No one else was in the wide hall, though he could hear Mrs. Harris moving about in her room, dressing for the service. He looked at his watch. Half-past eight. Time, after time, for church.

"Going to the meeting, Son?"

"Thought I wouldn't tonight, Dad." Charles looked up at his father, smiled, "Kind of fed up."

"Your mother's going, and the girls. Things not so quiet around. Hate for them to be out tonight by themselves. Wish you'd go, if you don't mind."

Charles laid down his book. "What's the matter with this town? Have you heard the talk?"

"Yeah. I've heard."

"Thing I don't see is why the niggers and God take it lying down."

"Son! Talk easy—your mother'll hear you." Tom rubbed his pink bald head. "It's not so simple as all that, Charlie. Not so simple." Tom sighed and stretched his legs as he sat down in his armchair. "Keep your mouth shut, keep out of it, whatever it is, and look after your mother and the girls."

"And what are you up to?" Charles laughed suddenly, went over, picked up the car keys.

Tom chuckled. "Well, I reckon I've got to put a few ducks in a row. I'll drop in to the meeting later, if I get through."

Tom stretched his legs and sighed. The house was quiet. They'd gone now to the meeting, and he could hear Dessie

299

fixing up Mrs. Harris's room and making a pallet. It'd be easy to go to sleep right here in this chair . . . not move until morning. Tired . . . day had been hot!

As soon as he had been able to leave the Deens' after dinner he had gone out to his logging camp and stayed there all afternoon. Had suddenly jumped into the cab as Old Mary was pulling out after dinner, sat there with C.B. as he guided her over the narrow-gauge track down the tricky curve, on out beyond the Rushton turpentine still, on to the new stretch of timber he'd just bought the rights to.

C.B. said, "Old Mary needs a new boiler mighty bad. Some day she's going to blow me and her to kingdom come."

"Fine old lady, but tell her to hold herself in a little longer. Money's scarce now."

"Always scarce," said C.B., "and nobody gits used to it."

Harris had gone out to the camp, feeling restless, finding it difficult to fit Tracy Deen's murder into the peaceful pattern of Maxwell. Maxwell's a good town, a quiet town, good place to bring your children up in—and he had brought up nine. Except for Saturday nights, a few razor fights, a dead nigger now and then, nothing violent ever happened in Maxwell. Things still went on in the southwest of the county that had no business going on. Niggers disappeared out on Bill Talley's place too often—dropped plumb out of sight—but you didn't have proof, and there was seldom much talk about it. What was happening to the College Street young people that made them get into such bad trouble? Four years ago Clem Massey killed a man—not here in Maxwell, thank God, in Americus—but Clem had been born on College Street and mothered by one of the finest women Maxwell ever claimed as a citizen—and Clem now in the State Farm for it and his mother in her grave, and his sister Julia with a broken heart. Now here today, in the middle of the revival, they come with news of Tracy Deen. Many a man in Maxwell knew why Tracy was killed on the Old Town road, though of course

300

the women didn't. Yes, she must have done it. That Anderson girl. Everything pointed that way. Where he was. Fact that he'd given Dorothy Pusey a ring. Quietest nigger girl in Maxwell. Too quiet. Dangerous when they're so quiet. Jealousy eats them like a disease. Best thing folks can do now is to hush it up. Get the boy buried, hush the talk. Bring that mulatto girl to trial, pretty as she is, and you'd spread a scandal from end to end of the United States—ruin the little Pusey girl, finish breaking Mrs. Deen's heart. They'd have to watch Tracy's friends. Boys like Gus, who never thought beyond their nose, likely to start something. Talking about running those Anderson girls out the county. Not so easy to run out the best Negro family the town ever had. Bound to be scandal if you tried. No, better hush it up, get folks minds on something else. Sug Rushton said he'd fix it. Hope he could. Best thing would be to get folks' minds back on the meeting, if that could be done. Looked now as if Dunwoodie might as well fold up his gospel tent and call it a bad time for the Lord. Yes sir! Looked as if the devil had straddled the town.

Tom sighed, it made you wonder about your own boys. Wonder if you had done as well by them as you might. Anne so sure her boys would never get into trouble, her boys would never— Maybe they wouldn't. Maybe they hadn't. But it was something to thank God for—not to take the credit for yourself. And there's plenty of trouble to get into, besides in Colored Town.

Well . . . he'd stepped in trouble today everywhere he turned, it'd seemed—everywhere.

Things not going well out at the camp. Not so bad maybe, but bad enough. Chain-gang crew quarrelsome, fussing about the food, one after another having run-ins with the foreman. Didn't much like the man, himself. Folks saying, half saying anyway, that he was using the sweatbox on the chain-gang niggers. Well . . . it's no good! No sense to it! If

301

you've got any guts, if you're more than a two-by-four your-self, you don't need stocks and sweatboxes to make folks do as you want em to do. Look a nigger or white straight in the eye and give him a tongue-lashing—and mind you hand his manhood back to him when you're through, finish up with something he can laugh with you about and feel good as you. Yeah. That's the trouble. Good-for-nothing trash trying to boss other good-for-nothing trash. No wonder the timers make a foreman like that yellow cracker fool fall back on sweatboxes. Nothing in himself to fall back on—that's the trouble! Well, he wouldn't have the sweatbox used in his logging camp—not when he knew it. Trouble is, you don't have time to keep up with everything. Too much to see after! Too much! There's that gang, now—forty big black bucks, a third of them lifers, and not a nigger woman within twenty miles . . . No wonder they're mean! And what can a man do about it—who's a steward in the Methodist Church with a big family of girls and boys and a wife like Anne! What ought to be done: bring a drove of black women in there once a week. Yeah. Anne would quit him tomorrow if she knew he thought such a thing. And reckon he had enough already to face his Maker with, without adding more to the list—right now.

Tom sighed.

He had come back on Old Mary's last daily trip and, sit-ting there in the cab with C.B., had looked out across acres of pine land, acres of stumps, once the prettiest virgin pine he'd ever bought the timber rights to.

C.B. said, "Bad about the Deen boy."

"Mighty bad."

"Don't reckon he was much count."

"Not much. Never seemed to catch on to—way things have to be somehow." Pretty no-count and all his life worrying his mother and Tut, never doing a thing that they had hoped he would do. Always a disappointment. A boy like that ought to have been whipped good when he was young, or made to get out and earn his own living—or something— You wonder sometimes what would have made him turn out different . . .

"Hard to see why a boy turns out like that—with a fine Christian mother like Mrs. Deen."

"Never knowed her," C.B. said, chewing slow as he eased Old Mary around the worst curve in the roadbed.

"Fine woman."

The logging train paused at the crossing, blew twice, turned toward the mill.

"There's a lot of fine Christian women in the world, C.B.," Tom said slowly.

"Reckon so." C.B. leaned out the cab and spat. "Never knowed any." He slid Old Mary slowly into the mill yard.

When he got to the office a little before dark, Tom had found Willie Echols waiting. Willie'd come to talk wages again—a living wage, he said. It was nothing new for Willie to come in to talk wages. But Tom was tired and worried. Didn't know when he'd felt so tired. Couldn't keep his mind off the Deen family. Bad time, they were having a bad time! You'd keep thinking of your own four boys. No sense to it! All right boys, the four of them. And Anne had been a good mother to them. Whatever complaint he had it wasn't that.

Willie was talking, coughing between his words. He would cough, pause, look around for a spittoon, never seem to see the one near Tom's desk, turn, spit through the window, begin talking again. Tom watched the thin face, muscles moving up and down along the jaw, eyes moving around the room, shifting from object to object, coming back to his employer's face, a little angrily.

Willie was saying, "Nobody can live on what we get, Mr. Harris, down here. Up North they get two, three times more and shorter hours. Nobody can live—"

Yes, but that's what the fool don't seem to see! Folks do live on it—and less.

303

"Men can't go on year after year working for nothing. You work all week and what you have, come Saturday? About enough to sop up on your plate a Sunday. Labor does the work—labor has a right to share in the profits. If capital won't give them, we'll—"

"Here, wait a minute! What you mean, labor and capital? You mean you and me?"

"I mean me and you—and more," Echols said, and coughed, looked around, spat out the window. "I mean labor and capital—that's bigger than me and you. I don't know how—" He paused, and his brown eyes rested on Tom's face. "I don't know exactly how, but it's bigger— Things—unions —things is goin to make it bigger, some day. Different."

And Tom had said, "It ought to be different. I don't know how it's going to, though. When you can't half the time meet your payroll, how under heaven you going to raise wages? You see, Echols," he went on, "I'm your boss; that's right. But the bank's my boss. Maybe the bank has its boss, reckon it has. None of it's easy! Hard times come, like they are now— Who starts the hard times? War in Europe this time, yes—but before this, who started it? Tell you what I want you to do. Want you to go see Dr. Deen. Have him look you over, give you a little something. You're run down. Maybe that's what makes things seem so— Here—" And Tom wrote an order to Deen and handed it to Echols.

Willie talked on and on as if it were a speech he'd learned. "Time was, labor hadn't no power. Well, labor's gittin power now. Unions is coming South. But some of us cain't wait on unions to come when we got eight children to feed. How you expect us to live? How you expect me and my nine to live?"

"I don't know. Sometimes, Willie"—Tom Harris rubbed his pink bald head and half smiled at the thin, sallow, angry face opposite him—"I don't know."

Well . . . he'd been pretty good to Willie. And it only seemed to make the man worse. Talking wild half the time

304

now. Wages, wages, wages! Rank socialist! Fool'd keep on until he'd have to get rid of him yet. Turn into a plumb Bolshevik if he kept on. Couldn't see! No sense! Didn't he know if they started trouble he could turn the whole passel of em off and fill the mills tomorrow with more—white or black? With half the country starving out on the patches and farms, didn't he know that?

And then as they sat there, the telephone had rung. And Laura was talking to him, while across from him Willie talked on. Laura, in a faraway voice, was telling him about the pallbearers—would he see about them please for her father? Laura saying something about Henry—something about people, somebody being after him.

"I'll be home in half an hour, Laura. I'll come right over," he'd told her. No, she would come to his home and wait for him, if he didn't mind. They hadn't told Mother and did not want her worried. Harris agreed, hung up the receiver, turned back to Echols.

"Up North labor's gittin things. Hit'll git it down here, bound to—"

Hookworm eats up brains fast as it eats bodies.

"Well," Tom had suddenly stood, "it's late and lot to do. Reckon we both better be getting on home. Hope your wife's well, Willie. And the children."

And Echols had just looked at him, stood up, still looking, coughed, looked around, spat out the window.

They had parted at the door—Echols to cross the track over to the white mill settlement; Harris turning toward town and home.

Tom stretched his legs. Sometimes you— Well, better get his mind on this thing now. Bill back of it. Yeah. Up to his old tricks. Looked as if it took one dead nigger a year to keep Bill's liver regulated. Time he found some other way to keep his health up. Tom picked at the rough spot near his

305

nose, thick finger working softly over the roughness as his blue eyes grew hard with thought. There were the pallbearers ... Pug ... his own son Charles ... Gus Rainey ... all the others ... Tracy's friends or his father's—not likely any of them in this. More likely the men sitting up with the corpse, who'd do the business for Bill, or help him do it. He studied the list Laura had given him. Yeah. Town folks, but Bill's friends. Most of them. More like it now! He traced the plan Bill had worked out as easily as if it had been his own. The family would go to bed. Men would sit up with the corpse and Henry would vanish in the night. That would be all. Just another black gone. Folks, womenfolks anyway, would say that Henry must have done it and run away in the night. Strange about darkies, they'd say—you never can trust some of them, no matter how long they've worked for you. And they'd be nervous about raping for a year afterward ... But the niggers would know, and picking time was near ... These lights flashing, men prowling around ... Goings-on of Tracy's friends, the hot heads ... Not amount to more than a few shots fired, or a whipped nigger. Real work was being done by Bill.

Tom sat on for a while in thought, suddenly smiled, got up, went to Jane Hardy's door, knocked softly.

# TWENTY-THREE

IN THE BRIGHT light from the electric bulbs strung up and down the aisles and around the altar rail, the thick sawdust took on a soft golden glow.

Brother Dunwoodie sat quietly watching the crowd assemble. It was an elusive and slow-settling congregation. Some would come in, take their seats, go out again. You could feel the uncertainty. At the tent openings there were more outside than in, and in the aisles they stood, loath to make the decision to stay, as loath to leave.

He looked at his watch, let it slide back into his vest pocket.

There would be no singing service tonight. Brother Dunwoodie stood, walked to the altar rail, laid his Bible upon it. His eyes moved up one aisle, down another, as if counting his congregation. In a quiet matter-of-fact voice he talked.

He began by saying that the devil had determined to break up this meeting. Things had moved too smoothly, too successfully. In all his experience he had not seen a smoother, easier revival meeting. The devil didn't sit on the sideline idly and let the Lord have everything His way. Oh no! Devil too smart for that. So Satan had been putting his wits to work. What could he do that would take the people's minds off of God? Yes, Satan schemed, and sweated as he schemed, to find a way. And he thought of a sure thing . . . Yet God had a hand in this too. For those with eyes to see and ears to hear, the terrible, heartbreaking murder of our brother who had been a lost sinner until a few evenings before was a warning, a portent. There were others in this tent tonight whose days were numbered. Tomorrow, next day, the next . . . Who could tell? Who could read the writing on the wall? For someone the Grim Reaper would come.

"Are you going to be ready?" he shouted. "Are you?" He turned suddenly to those on the back bench. The back bench was almost empty. "Are those who are not here going to be ready? Where are they tonight? How about you, Brother?" He pointed his finger at Brother Pug Pusey. "Are you going to be ready?

"Are you, Sister?" Swiftly he was pointing here, there, eyes blazing, dark mop of hair tossing as he shook his arm at the crowd. "What are you waiting for? Tonight you are sitting here, well, healthy. You think, 'He's not talking to me, he's not meaning me.' And tomorrow you may be dead. *Dead!* A still cold lump your body will be down here on the earth. But your soul will be in Eternity, facing your God, facing Him with all your sins, your evil thoughts, your black desires. What will you have to say to Him? You can't say, 'Lord, Lord, I had no chance.' You can't cry in your terror, 'If I had only known!' For you have heard His Word."

His voice deepened. "Oh, my friends . . . My heart is bleeding tonight for the unsaved of this town . . .

"You wives . . . Where are your husbands . . . ?

"You mothers . . . Where are your boys . . . ?

"Where were they last night, and the night before . . . and the night before? Do you know?"

His despairing eyes plunged into white faces straining up toward him.

In the quick stillness the croak of frogs came through the tent, bringing the night. Darkness fell on the hearts of the women of Maxwell. Dread of knowledge seeped about their ignorance of their men's lives like cold swamp water, staining complacency, chilling sheltered spirits. And they were afraid. Where were they tonight? They did not know. They had never known. Like their knowledge of Nigger Quarters, they knew of their men's lives only that which came into their homes. They did not want to know more.

Brother Dunwoodie took out his handkerchief, wiped his face slowly.

"You can hear their cries . . . the wailing of lost souls . . . as they enter an eternity of torture. Listen . . ." His voice sank to a whisper. "Listen to those cries . . . Do you hear them, you women? Oh, can you not hear them? It is needless to talk of mother love. You Christian mothers would go down into hell to save your boys' souls. Wouldn't you?

Mothers, go down on your knees to Jesus now and beg Him to soften your boy's heart, to give him a sense of sin . . . before it is too late."

One by one, women slipped the old millstone of their men's unknown sins around their necks, sank to their knees in the sawdust, whispering awkward prayers.

Brother Trimble began to sing. Without accompaniment his clear tenor voice floated through the tent asking the old, old question, "Are you ready . . . are you ready . . . are you ready for the judgment day?"

Someone began to sob. You could hear the soft weeping of women who would face the Judgment Bar of Heaven with their men's unknown sins more willingly than they would face the knowledge here on earth of what those sins might be. Softly they cried, tears falling on their hearts like cold rain.

Little Mrs. Paine was praying aloud. "God," she prayed abruptly and shrilly, "save my boy."

Brother Dunwoodie's strong *Amen!* gave impetus to the little prayer as it winged across the blazing planets to God, while Mart Paine, who sat well toward the back, ducked his head quickly as he heard his mother's voice. And the boys with him grinned at him and each other sheepishly and moved their shoulders restlessly against the back of the bench.

Mrs. Henderson laid down her hymnbook and gathered up her gloves. It was only her civic sense of duty that had made her attend the revival services. This, tonight, was too much. She smoothed down her Episcopalian bosom and walked out into the night.

Brother Dunwoodie in silence let her go halfway down the long sawdust aisle while he looked at her retreating back. And others turned and looked. And the mill people over on the far side stared at the tall, handsome, black-haired lady and at the preacher, turning their heads from one to the other,

309

as they stared. "For some," Brother Dunwoodie spoke at last, slowly, "the Gospel of Jesus is too strong meat for their po' sick souls to stummick." Mill folks tittered, and two girls stood, the better to see her, as the lady went, a little rapidly now, out of the door.

Old Mrs. Bailey, who sat next to Mrs. Henderson, seemed not to notice when she left, for as always she was looking far away, beyond the preacher, beyond the tent, as her hands played ceaselessly with her crucifix . . . and her lips moved as she breathed, "Lovely Mary, it's been so long, so long . . ."

# TWENTY-FOUR

MRS. DEEN came down the stairs, walked through the reception hall, bowed to her neighbors, stood in the doorway of the living room.

Before her, upon its stand, lay the expensive gray casket containing her son. On the piano Mrs. Pusey had placed a bowl of Cape jasmines, and on chairs and tables lay home-made bouquets and wreaths from neighbors. The casket was bare, awaiting the family's mantle of yellow roses from the Jacksonville florist. Dot Pusey had asked Laura to have yellow roses because Tracy had noticed yellow roses wherever he saw them, and the Puseys had ordered yellow roses also, a big cross of them. Dot had been a great help to the family and everyone else, doing the important things which none of the Deens would ever have thought of doing, or thought of as important. All afternoon her little green dress had swished through the Deens' spacious rooms and hallways as she told

Eenie what to have for supper; called Henry from his cabin steps where he squatted with face buried in his big black hands; took from the neighbors their offerings of flowers and custards and cake and salad; found for the undertaker the numberless articles which undertakers seem always to need. And though her chin shook when she talked, after a first brief paroxysm of grief, she had kept herself under control. It was due to her vigilance that Tracy now wore the blue suit he had always liked instead of the brown suit she had disliked and which she had intercepted just in time from the undertaker; that Tracy had on a brown-gray tie instead of the black one; that the garnet stickpin was in it; and that his hair was parted on the left side, the way he wore it. It was due to Dot's loving care that when the undertaker finished his rites Tracy looked "real natural," as the neighbors were saying; and it was due to Dot that the center chandelier had been turned off and only the wall lights burned, making a dim room in which the handles of the casket gleamed softly. And now, with everything ready for that last brash stripping-away of reticence, the last stark display of body—the high price exacted by those left behind for our eternity of privacy within the deep earth—Dottie had run across the track to her home for the rest she sorely needed.

Across the street, down at the Wilkinsons', you could hear —if you were sitting in the hall or out on the porch—hushed voices practicing the songs for the funeral. You could hear *Nearer My God to Thee,* but you heard it as the shadow of an old memory creeps along the edge of your mind. And now there was silence. You knew they were turning the pages of the Methodist Hymnal, searching for the next song. You wondered when they'd be turning the pages searching for the next song for you, and what that song would be, what tune the Quartet would use to sing you across to eternity. They had found it. You could hear Pug Pusey sing a line before the piano began—a thin tenor line.

On the other side of town three pistol shots rang out. A
yell. Somebody screamed—or you thought they did, and you
grew restless wondering if there would be trouble tonight.

But inside the house there was no sound. The talk in the
big hall had ceased when Mrs. Deen came down the stairs.
She was still standing in the doorway, as if she had forgot to
go in. She stood so long that those behind her in the big hall
grew restless. Somebody got up and moved a bowl of flowers.
Somebody else said very softly, "Cotton's dropping again—
went down two cents today." But nobody answered. Nobody
thought you ought to talk about cotton with Mrs. Deen
standing there. Nobody thought you ought to talk about
anything on earth while the tall gray-haired woman stood
there, staring across the room at her son's casket.

Alma Deen walked into the room, closed the door.

# TWENTY-FIVE

MRS. BROWN set the tub of flowers on the floor and
wiped her face. "I hear that the Philathea Class telegraphed
for a beautiful floral piece from Jacksonville." She was busy
now taking the flowers one by one from the tub. "The Baraca
Class too. Maybe I'm old-fashioned," she tied some heavy
Boston fern together, "but I still think neighbors' own flowers, fixed by their own hands, carry more real feeling—
Don't you, Nonnie?"

"Yes mam," Nonnie said . . . *Henry will look after you
and if he doesn't Nonnie you come straight to me and I'll* . . .

"Hand me that asparagus fern— Now I've always thought

312

Cape jasmine and pink roses real beautiful together— Don't you, Nonnie?"

"Yes mam," Nonnie said. . . . *but you can't be I've got to go now Mother's after me I thought you'd know how not to having gone to college and everything* . . .

"But for a man, pink seems, kind of feminine, don't it? Do hand me that tuberose, Nonnie. Ain't they sweet! Sometimes I've thought I wouldn't mind death if I could go smelling something sweet as tuberoses— Don't it—pink, I mean—for a man?"

"Yes mam," Nonnie said. . . . *you're mine you hear they can't take you away from me damn em goddam em they can't* . . .

"Now some more asparagus fern. Let's use red roses instead of pink. I think red seems much more masculine— much more, don't you?"

"Yes mam." . . . *you're mine even if you're just a little nigger you're mine and I love every inch of you how about that coming from a white man huh how about* . . .

"Now some more fern. Help me here—yes, tie it tight now. That's right. You look so tired, Nonnie—do you feel bad?"

"No, Mrs. Brown." . . . *it's Mother you see Mother* . . .

"You're so whi—so pale! It's the heat, I reckon. I've never seen a worse heat wave, have you?"

"No mam." . . . *I've decided to go straight I believe there's something in it maybe I've changed I've* . . .

"Look through the tub for some rambler buds. I cut a little of everything— Seems to me the loveliest bouquets just sort of grow as you work along with them."

"Yes mam." . . . *having gone to college and everything I thought sure you'd know how not to I've fixed it I've fixed it Henry old fool but he'll be good to you he'd better or I'll* . . .

"That's fine. Most of the ramblers are blighted now, but I did find a few buds that're right pretty. Would you put

313

them here or here? Which do you like best? Which do **you** think, Nonnie?"

"Excuse me, mam. Here, I think." . . . *you're like the old ivories on Grandma's big square piano in Macon she always kept the shades down and it was cool and dim and sometimes I'd go in when I was a little fellow they give you the works that's what they do they lay my face on the cool pale keys like this Nonnie like this . . .*

"Now another red rose. Find me a long-stem one and break the thorns off. Hate to pick up a bouquet and get stuck in a hundred places. Is that the best you can find?"

"Yes mam." . . . *and Mother'd come in and ask me what on earth I was doing Mother's always first time she ever put Laura in first time first time too it was the first time always asked you were scared you . . .*

"Now for another tuberose. Here, tie it tight, Nonnie, pull now—that's it! What would you put here? Yes, that fern is needed. How many more Cape jasmine that aren't yellowed? How many, Nonnie?"

"Five, Mrs. Brown." . . . *first time first time thought sure you going to college and everything it's Mother she nothing ever satisfies . . .*

"Nonnie, you're shaking like a leaf. You've got malaria, sure as the world! What is it, Nonnie? Are you all right, Nonnie?"

"Yes mam." . . . *he's killed a white man I thought sure having been to college God damn em they can't make me give you up mine since you were I hope some day Non you'll forgive me shucks even white gals does dat that's what you'll be concubine that's the Bible name for it there're worse and you'll hear them you'll hear . . .*

"You're having a chill right this minute! Here. Take this quinine. Take it, Nonnie! Might have known you was going to have a chill when you came this morning. Looked sick then. Take it now."

"Thank you, Mrs. Brown." . . . *he killed a white* . . .

"You sure you're not real—"

"I'm all right, mam." . . . *you smell so good to me Non I may come back late I may come it's Mother nothing I* . . .

"Well, you don't look it. Is it your sick time, Nonnie? That's bad enough, heavens knows, but the quinine can't hurt you anyway, and I don't want you coming down with a spell of something. Boysie couldn't do without you— Now one more sprig of fern and we're through. Did Uncle Pete deliver the ribbon? I phoned right after breakfast."

"Yes mam." . . . *I'm going straight from now on he's killed a white man you're mine you hear if any has one of them ever touched you tell me Nonnie have they have they it's Mother you don't know Mother she I've never seemed able to please her she always you can't think things through down here concubine concubine that's the Bible name* . . .

"White satin . . . I do love white satin. Like a baby's skin, ain—isn't it?"

"Yes mam." . . . *you wouldn't want your man cleaning spittoons that's it isn't it you would first time first time too* . . .

"My wedding dress was white satin. Papa gave me away. Shook like a leaf, we teased him so. When we named Boysie after him we didn't know then . . . We're taking Boysie to Atlanta again, Nonnie. They're going to drain some more of the water out—it's pressing against his brain, they say, that's why the poor little fellow can't walk or talk—they think it will help. Do you suppose it will, Nonnie, do you suppose— Seems like we've tried so much—"

"I hope it will, mam." . . . *he's killed a white man I hope you'll forgive me some day here's some money two hundred dollars two* . . .

"I don't know if it will or not. I have hope, then lose it. Seems like— I've never understood God doing this to us. I— Mama says I ought not question God's purpose, that His

**315**

ways are mysterious and beyond our und— I'm sorry, Nonnie, to c-cry—before y-you—like thi—this— It's—I'm up-upset— A death always up—I try—so hard—not to—give in—know Boysie's my-my cross—t-to bear—he's such a sweet b-baby—I—shouldn't—"

"He is, Mrs. Brown." ... *you can't think things out down here that's the Bible name for it there're others you'll hear them all I'm going clean from now on Dorothy a ring back to Washington to live decently I've fixed that* ...

"Do look in m-my bureau for a hankie—arid then you must take the flowers over before they wilt. I know I should do it, but since Papa died I—it upsets me—the c-coffin—and—I want you to take it, please, Nonnie."

"Yes mam." ... *it's Mother sometimes I've thought if I could please her once God damn em concubine that's one name for it you'll hear them all before before you're look at the light on your hand hold me Nonnie you're my nigger how's that you're my nigger and I love God curse them God curse I've hurt you I've well I'm glad I'm glad why should I do all the suffering why answer me that why* ...

"And, Nonnie! Speak to Miss Laura or Mrs. Deen sure, and give them my love and tell them my heart is with them, though I can't leave Boysie. He isn't well, tell them. I know it's half a story but it's better sometimes to tell a white lie than to hurt— Don't you think so, Nonnie?"

"Yes mam." ... *I can't face it the hell part of dying I can't do it I'd rather it's Mother to live decently thought being I can't I'm going straight it's Mother* ...

"I'd break down completely—the coffin—and the music— I heard them practicing last night over at the Wilkinsons'— the quartet, I mean. It brought back Papa's death so—my pillow was sopping— Hurry, Nonnie! The flowers are already beginning to droop. It must be about time for the funeral. Hurry—"

"Yes mam." ... *I'd lay my face on them so cool and dim*

*it'd be in there it did something to me like this like this like this like this like this this this this this ...*

"I'll start your dinner for you," Mrs. Brown called, and hurried to the porch, dabbing at her eyes, as Nonnie walked down the steps with the spray of red and white flowers in her arms, walked across the railroad track, down the side street to the back door of the Deen home.

# TWENTY-SIX

LAURA HAD DRESSED early and sat now in the library, inept and griefless in her thin black dress of mourning.

Beyond the wide double doors which opened into the living room, slow-gathering friends and neighbors dragged like a heavy chain, refusing her solitude. She wanted to leave her brother's funeral to Miss Belle and the Culpeppers, to the Puseys and the Wilkinsons and all these self-appointed, and kind, mourners—and go away. Somewhere there must be a place, if she could but reach it, where she could begin to find what she had lost—or never possessed. She had to feel something. Everything she respected in herself, that seemed decent and right, clamored that she begin to feel something for this brother whose name, now whispered, called forth nothing at all.

She had been awakened in the night by the words, *He's free!* winging through her mind, like something that flies across your face in the dark. And in her sleep she had turned on him, hating, and had screamed at her dead brother. Lying there half awake, she had felt confused, believing that he had deliberately died, to keep her at home. She knew she could not believe this, and yet nothing else would enter her mind. She had not slept again. And she had grown oppressed and frightened. By everything. A future that one moment seemed to have broken off at the edge of a precipice; the next, was a road stretching out in one endless, monotonous, inevitable direction; a past that she could find no return way through.

She wouldn't mind staying at home. She wanted to stay. She had lain there in bed and cried like a child, telling herself it was a dream . . . It's just a dream . . . not something real . . . you don't feel that way about him—you couldn't . . . it isn't real. And after a time, she had grown quiet.

But she had been too wakeful to sleep afterward, and lay there, seeing in her mind the neighbors sitting downstairs with Tracy. They still sat up with the corpse in Maxwell, volunteer guardians of the living against the terrible clutch of the dead, keeping them safe by cheerful talk, by the sheer magic of themselves being alive. She could see them sitting in the reception hall, doors open into the living room where Tracy lay. Men she had known all her life downtown but seldom seen in her home. And Simmie Jones—quiet, shy, timid Simmie, who, tongue-tied and afraid in the presence of the living, was at ease and calm and at home with the dead. You'd never see Sim—or if you did he would turn his head away—until someone died; and then there he would be: quietly poised, and cheerful, and talkative.

Somebody had brought over a spray of August lilies and laid them on the mantel, and earlier Mrs. Pusey had brought a bowl of Cape jasmines and put them on the piano, sweetening the room, she had whispered. And now and then someone would interrupt the talk to go into the living room and up to the coffin and back again. She knew the old ritual so well . . . And then the conversation would be resumed, and

318

as the night wore on somebody would begin to tell old Maxwell legends—she knew them all too . . . Time the black cat appeared at the window of Miss May Brown's room and with a curving leap through the air sprang upon her coffin, landing with a soft thud; only—when driven out—to appear again and again, until finally the nerves of the three young men sitting up with Miss May's corpse capitulated to these attacks upon rationality; and the gentlemen fled through the night, abandoning Miss May to a lonely vigil with her immortal soul.

Someone walking up and down in the hall upstairs. It must be Dad . . . "Poor old Dad"—and wondered why she had whispered it. She could see her mother lying quietly in her bed. She would not be asleep. No one would sleep much tonight. Yes . . . it is a good thing, if you can, to guard a family against its dead . . . against those memories that are loosened as are the seeds of decay when life leaves the body—as if all the unspoken thoughts, the hurts, the failures of the dead have been freed and, like wasps out of a broken nest, fly back to sting the living forever.

If she could go back far enough . . . there'd be a place where she would find a Tracy and a Laura who had been, maybe, fond of each other. Surely if she could get back far enough, she'd find a time when maybe they'd played together as little children and enjoyed each other. And beginning there, she could take his path and travel it until she found out why it led—where it did. And yet she knew that she did not want to do it. If she began to see it, his way, she would travel his path again and again and again, all her life, trying to understand, assuming all he had felt, hurting with his pain. No, it was easier, easier to keep on feeling resentment—or nothing. As he must always have felt toward her. Strange . . . death doesn't break off relationships . . . they're still there . . . changing with the dead, changing as the living change.

319

Sitting there in her black dress, waiting, she grew uneasy, as if she had done something wrong or should be doing something she had not done. Perhaps she should go and see about things. There must be things to be done—and here she was leaving it all to the neighbors. After all *they* weren't responsible for Tracy's death . . . after all! Why did she keep thinking that— Why did she keep on punishing herself with— When had she dreamed the thing? Last night . . . or before . . . When? Maybe it was a childhood dream . . . maybe she had made it up. She could find no point in time for it, for it seemed as familiar a part of her as her hair, or the color of her eyes, as the old rag doll she used to sleep with . . . the dream of watching Tracy drown. The slow sinking, her suspended breath, the coming together of the water, the last bubble, like a sigh . . . her indrawn breath. Sometimes the face going down was her mother's. Once it had been her own —she remembered that clearly now, it was once when— Now when was it? She had known a moment ago, and now it was gone . . .

She should leave this room and go out there. She should go out and take up the task of weaving the small threads of Maxwell custom into a cover for death's nakedness. Something to hide life's failures under. Something to hide the obscene triumph of death under . . . Drop a little clod of dirt . . . drop a tear . . . a flower . . .

When she passed her mother's room she was sitting at her desk, head bowed in prayer. Gathering strength. For what? What lay ahead of Mother that would take more strength for the doing than she had already in such depthless amount? What? What could it be now? And Laura was afraid . . . fearing the energy that was free now to turn all of itself upon her. *She hates what I like . . .*

She must have spoken aloud, for Miss Belle hurried across the crowded living room, paused, and in a stage whisper asked her if she had called. Laura shook her head in dumb denial, knowing words would bring Miss Belle inside the room and over to her chair as inevitably as a handful of corn thrown out will draw all the chickens clucking around one's skirts.

She wanted to think about her father. To grasp and hold tight to him, until once more she found a security. Out at the back of the barn now probably, piddling around with the animals and chickens. That was his way. Mother turned to God. Dad to the little rituals of earth. And she had nowhere to turn . . . no God to believe in . . . no earth to walk on that would give her strength.

Strange . . . how you can live in the house with a brother all your life and not know him. That girl Nonnie must have known him so much better than any of them. It's queer to think of a colored girl knowing your brother better than you do. Why had she killed him? Not the kind to flare up in anger. She did not look like that. He must have done something very dreadful to have made her do it. And she must have done it slowly, so sure she was doing what had to be done. No one had said it. No one ever would . . . and yet they must know . . . Mother must know . . . Dad . . . that she did it. Strange . . . you know your family . . . you think you do . . . and then suddenly it is only a fragment that you know. As if you had opened an unread book at a casual page and left it opened there for a lifetime, reading again and again that one page, as you passed casually back and forth . . .

It was almost time. It was almost time to stage that little brave mortal gesture against death. Almost time to shout aloud, "Oh, death, where is thy sting . . . grave . . . thy victory!" as a child shouts in defiance before bursting into helpless tears. For they would weep. She would weep and they, when they sang, as they would sing, those old tunes which mat about your heart and your memories in childhood and squeeze so tightly after you are grown, when you hear them. She knew that the crowd out there, the Puseys and Miss Belle, the Culpeppers and the pallbearers—all now quietly cheerful, decorously smiling and at ease, shields well up against the enemy—would fall as one man when the singing began, leveled by a common mortality.

Someone in white was standing near the library door, in the outer room, as if uncertain where to go. With a sheaf of red and white flowers in her arms. It was the Browns' maid . . . that girl! Someone was taking the flowers now, smelling them and saying how pretty, saying how sweet, walking with them into the music room.

The girl had not moved. Now Miss Belle had come over. Nonnie was speaking, softly, monotonously. "Mrs. Brown is very sorry. Little Boysie is sick today. She cannot come. She sends her love to Mrs. Deen and Miss Laura."

"Yes . . . yes . . ." Miss Belle paused, looked the silent girl over, curiosity picking at the pale face, suddenly inclined her head toward the flower-covered casket. "Would you like to see the body?" Miss Belle hissed.

Laura stood up. "Miss Belle," she called. "Miss Belle," as quietly as she could press down her voice, "please tell Nonnie to come here."

What could she say? Now that she had called her to safety, what could she say?

The girl walked in. Her thin hands were locked together until the knuckles showed white through amber skin. Her eyes looked at Laura but beyond her, as if the white girl were merely something in her line of vision.

As if she's walking in her sleep. Laura could find nothing to say. She pressed back the question, struggling to keep it from forming words that might slip through her lips. What did he do that gave you the courage? Nobody loved him much, except you, but you must have loved him. You have to love a thing—you have to love someone a great deal to kill her, don't you? You have to love and hate what you kill, a great deal, don't you—

322

"—before you can find the courage—"

She spoke the words aloud and was utterly confused at the sound of her voice. Then, perceiving that the girl had not heard—for Nonnie's lips were apart, her eyes concentrated, as if she listened to words Laura could never hear—she forced herself back into the conventional attitude of white mistress and colored maid.

"Please tell Mrs. Brown that the flowers are lovely. And tell her, please, that we are so sorry about Boysie."

"Thank you." Words effortlessly came from Nonnie's lips, but she did not move, nor did the expression of her face change.

Laura watched her. Beyond them, from the other rooms, came a chirr of voices, restrained below a level of cheerfulness but steadily increasing in volume, as though many people now were entering the house.

"It's time . . ." Miss Belle hissed from the door. "Call your mother, Laura, it's time. Brother Summers and Brother Dunwoodie are here. I've never seen so many flowers in all my life, Laura! Honey, you must come see the flowers. They're so pretty. You must come, dear. They'll comfort you so just to look at them and realize how much everybody loved—Honey, you—"

"Yes, Miss Belle, I'll come."

"Nonnie," Laura said after Miss Belle had hurried out, "Nonnie," in a smooth white voice, "that will be all."

Nonnie turned, walked quickly through the living room and out of the back door. Laura saw her pause in the strong glare of the backyard, as if she had lost her way, then turn and walk into the side street toward the Brown home.

And as she stood at the window watching her, unable to draw her mind away from this girl, she heard other voices beyond the backyard, back of Henry's cabin.

"Naw, ain't hair or hide of him here. I tell you somebody's hid him som'ers!"

323

"Maybe he's in the privy— Been there?"

"Been everwheres—barn—everwheres. Tell ye, he ain't nowheres on this place, less he's in that house."

"Can't go in there now—you know that—can't go yit—they'll be gone soon to the burying."

Two men walked out of Henry's cabin, started down the path, came as near as the lily bed, turned, went back beyond the old privy which had been left for Henry's use after plumbing was put in the Deen home.

They were still looking. She had read a story about a lynching once; she had read a story, and it had seemed more real than this. More real than that grotesque half hour last night when Jane had driven Mr. Harris to the house and he had beckoned Laura to the kitchen. They stood there talking —while Henry sat on the woodbox back of the range with his face buried in his hands. She had heard Mr. Harris's words: "Get me one of your mother's old dresses, Laura, and a big hat and veil and some powder." And when she brought the articles they had gone into the pantry and called Henry. And with the shade drawn and the door locked they had dressed him in her mother's gingham housedress and put her own big floppy leghorn hat on his head and had made him powder his tear-smeared face until it was white, and then she had tied the veil on him. All the feeling she had had was when she saw Henry's miserable reddened eyes peering out of all that white powder. And suddenly she had not known whether her body would surrender to sobs or wild laughter, though it did neither. Then Laura and Mr. Harris had walked out of the dining room with Henry between them and down the back-porch steps and around to the car at the side entrance. It was dark, and even if they had been seen, no one would have noticed anything extraordinary about the group. They had put him between Jane and Mr. Harris, and Jane had driven off to the jail, where Henry was to be hidden. That was Mr. Harris's plan. Mr. Harris had confidence in the sheriff's keeping his mouth shut—she knew Mr. Harris had had a lot to do with putting him into office, so maybe everything now would be all right. And she had not felt deeply about it, though her mind knew that this is what happens down here in our South sometimes. This is what happens. And she had wondered which of the boys and men she knew belonged to the Ku Klux Klan . . . which ones of them would take part in a manhunt. And then someone had called her and she had gone into the house.

When she now entered the other room her mother was already there, standing near the casket with her father. Both were composed and grave. Only Tut's long hands gave evidence of his perturbation as with one he smoothed the red hairs on the other. Mrs. Deen did not move. Yes, Mother would have herself under control. Mother would always be able to keep herself under control. She was nearer them now and, looking more closely at her mother, she saw a difference. Not much. A sagging of cheek muscle; just that—but enough to make Alma Deen look bewildered and old. And suddenly Laura wanted to run to her, as she had done as a child, run and pat her cheek and kiss her and kiss her . . .

Dorothy Pusey stood near by with Mrs. Pusey. Dorothy's handkerchief was already a wet little sop as she moved it, like a small white ball, restlessly from one hand to the other. Greenish circles deepened the pallor beneath her reddened eyes. She had on a black and white dress, and somehow she looked very widowed and bereaved. And as she passed her, Laura touched her arm, and knew at once that she had done the wrong thing, for Dottie buried her face in her hands and her thin shoulders shook with silent sobs.

It was time now. The pallbearers looked at each other, and at the ministers. The ministers gravely looked at the undertaker, and somehow a silent agreement was arrived at that it was time . . . it was time . . .

Slowly the pallbearers approached the casket. Little Pug Pusey hitched up his pants, blew his nose, and stooped for his share of the burden. Gus Rainey, snuffling, could not get at his handkerchief as both big strong red hands, used to heaving haunches of bloodied beef and pork, busied themselves now lifting the body of his lifelong friend. Charles Harris, grave and silent, went on the other side, and others and others, until eight men bore the burden of Tracy Deen to its grave, forever lifting its weight off of the Deen family.

Miss Belle, who had been cheerful and helpful up to now, was crying too as she filled her arms with flowers; and the other women, most of them, followed with wreaths and sprays, crosses and stars of roses and Cape jasmines and lilies, through which tear-stained, reddened faces peered as they sought their way down the steps.

There'd be no more the click of the door late at night, or at dawn the stealthy slow steps up to his room. Tracy is out late . . . Tracy's been out there . . . Manaos is on the Amazon River . . . Cape Town in Africa . . . no more than that. Statements of facts—that is all Tracy had ever been to any of them—a statement of a remote fact.

Laura fell into line behind her parents. In faltering rhythm they followed the pallbearers as the cortege moved slowly down the steps. They paused as the casket slid easily from long practice into the hearse under the porte-cochere. And standing there waiting for their car to pull up, Laura saw, hovering close behind her, Eenie, dressed in solid black and—on this hot day—with a long widow's veil draped over her straw hat; and behind her Susan, the Harrises' cook, draped as blackly and as mournfully; and just behind Susan, Dessie, wide-eyed and wan, in a black skirt, pink silk waist and a hat with roses bobbing on it. And behind them, most of the cooks and house-servants on College Street. Eenie was sobbing. Eenie, who had never liked Tracy, was sobbing, "Lawd Gawd, Lawd Gawd." Scared. Everybody's scared.

Something bad is happening, and they are not going to be left behind for it to happen to while white folks bury their dead. She wanted to smile . . . and then she too was weeping, for the dead; weeping for the living.


# TWENTY-SEVEN


THEY WAITED until the family went to the burying, Bill Talley and Dee and the others.

Maxwell lay white and hot and empty, stores closed for the funeral, and most of College Street and the side streets at the church. College Street and the side streets would follow the body to its last resting place. They would stand in the white glare of hot sand until the grave in the new lot, bought hurriedly the day before, was filled. And then there would be a slow scattering. Some would get in their cars and go home to dinner. Some would linger . . . pulling a strand of moss from a limb . . . reading old names . . . whispering, "The Browns never clean their lot." And others would empty vases of rotted water and sweep the dirt off of slabs and pull a few sandspurs, or with their handkerchief rub a date clean in wistful genuflection to their own immortality.

Down the sand roads of the county they had come. Bill and Dee, and the others. From Sug Rushton's turpentine farm, and the cotton fields . . . from Harris's sawmill . . . from a shanty back of Shaky Pond . . . and Ellatown . . . from Old Cap'n Rushton's commissary, and the logging camp. Roads threading whitely through the county, curving around oak-black lake and pond, pushing across swamp and hammock, tying its cotton and little grayed cabins, its barrels of rosin and its turpentine and tall pines, mule and church and bank, white folks and black, to Maxwell, and to each other. Down these roads they came, shadows falling foreshortened and stubby on palmetto clumps as they plodded along in the heat, hearts as slashed as the pines under which they paused now and then, bodies as drained as the sand on their feet. But white. God-white and immaculate . . . white . . . white as Jesus . . . as an unborn child's soul . . . And now they were on their way to put the nigger in his place . . . once more to put the nigger in his place.

And sometimes there was laughter, or drawled words of voices not unkind in sound and not without humor; but eyes were hard and hating as they hunted a black victim to sacrifice to an unknown god of whom they were sore afraid.

But College Street and the side streets buried their dead and then went home and ate dinner and opened their stores and the bank, the drugstore and the warehouse and the cotton gin. Tom Harris's sawmill blew its noon whistle as it always did, and the planer sounded a shrill note for one o'clock. Dan went on his afternoon route delivering ice, ringing his bell in front of hot houses, and old Uncle Pete dozed on the dray in front of the Supply Store, and Brother Dunwoodie prepared his sermon for the next service.

And some knew and some did not know that they were after him and they'd git im . . . they'd git im . . . sho . . .

Through the hot afternoon they hunted, moving quietly as moss swings in the wind, through back yard and shanty, Lodge and Pressing Club and Salamander's Cafe, and out again to privy and pigpen, stable, and barn, cane patch and ditch, into shanty . . . weaving back and forth a grotesque slow design of hate and lust and fear. There were forty men, they said, and six bloodhounds down in the swamp, but word came back that no track had been found, no scent picked up. And every tongue muttered, "He's here sho. Right here som'ers . . . and we'll git im. Bound to . . ."

In cabin and big kitchen through the hot hours, as irons thumped, thumped, fluting dainty ruffles, and oven doors creaked open and shut for bread to be lifted in and out, voices were whispering, *"Lawd Jesus . . . Lawd . . . Gawd have mercy . . . Gawd Jesus help us . . ."*

Shadows grew thin and long, and the heat lifted. Girls in crisp summer dresses went in their cars to Deen's Drug Store and parked for their afternoon cokes. Their mothers sought a breeze on the porch and sat out with their handwork or watered their pot plants. Miss Belle and the Methodist choir ladies stepped over to the church to straighten up a little after the funeral. And all through College Street and the side streets, women—fresh-bathed and powdered, in thin pretty clothes—enjoyed the cool peace of late afternoon before their men came home.

In Bob Martin's school office, little used in summer when schools were closed, sat Dee Cassidy and Bill Talley and their lifelong friend Bob, and others. Bill with his feet on the superintendent's desk, with his shoes by his chair. Dee folded up in the window, unmoving save for the slow swing of Adam's apple up and down and up again, eyes shut as if in slumber. Bill spat and wiped his lips on his sleeve and rubbed one foot against the other. Men came in, went out again, sometimes speaking to Bill, sometimes not speaking at all. Once Bob said, "Had it comin to um—traipsin North like—" And didn't bother to finish his sentence.

The sun faded from the water tower, leaving it in shadow, but lay bright on the floor of the upstairs room.

Bob said, putting down a newspaper after having read it a dozen times, "Saw Lem Taylor down at the post office while ago. Looked like he'd et a bowl of cream."

"Saw who?"

"Lem."

329

"What say?"

"Looked like he'd et a bowl of cream."

"Say anything?"

"Passed the time of day as we went by, then turned, said, 'Well, boys,' he says, 'how you comin? Find him yit?'"

Bill stretched his feet and wiggled his toes until the damp sock adhering to them had loosened. He scratched himself between the legs and wet his red full lips. Black polished eyes had not moved as he continued to stare out of the window.

The door opened. Five mill hands walked in, sprawled on chairs around the room, tired out.

"They ain't nowheres else to look. We've did the town. Ceptn the calaboose and jail—and the bank vault."

"Even done the church-houses." One of them, dried and flat as a chewed piece of cane, laughed, and picked his nose.

Bill continued to stare out of the window. "He's not in the bank vault," he said, after a time, "but I ain't so sure about the calaboose . . . or the jail . . . I ain't—" Bill jerked his head toward Dee. "You better go look after Lem . . . for a while. Take them with you," nodding toward three of the men. "Here, you, take this jack. Reckon you got your gun."

Dee giggled shrilly, not bothering with words, as he unfolded his long legs and ambled slowly out of the room.

"Well, boys," said Bill, and lifted his heavy legs off the desk, "reckon we all've got a little business over to the jail."

# TWENTY-EIGHT

"BE WITH YOU in a minute, Sam. Sit down." Tom Harris bent over the ledger on the desk. "Bookkeepers have a way of putting everything in the wrong column," he laughed, went on copying figures in his notebook.

There was no one in the office, Sam was relieved to see. Be easier to say what he had come to say.

From where he sat he could hear saws whining through big cypress logs, could see smoke pouring from the dry-kiln and smell fresh sawdust. Now Old Mary was pulling out for the logging camp. Sam watched her big wheels turn, watched C.B. give her more steam, let his eyes go with her and the empty flatcars around the bend of the track.

Maybe he'd done better to have stayed at the camp, heaving big timbers all his life. Better than fooling with folks' troubles. Try to help folks—you help somebody's stomachache, ruin his life, maybe, by doing it. Easier, a sight easier, to hold a double mule team on the run than somebody like Ed gone hell-crazy. You see what a mule's up to, or guess it. Don't know what's inside a man. What's hurting him. Like guessing what's at the bottom of Shaky Pond.

At Macon he'd put Ed on the train for New York, told him to spend a day or two there, go back to his job in Washington if he heard no more from them. Easy as that. What good to say more to a face as blank as your own heart? What good to ask why, when you already knew better than Ed knew—though you didn't know anything.

All the way through that night to Macon you'd sat by him, trying to push back the sickness inside you, as you drove on from dark town to dark town.

"Better eat something," you'd said.

"No."

And you had driven on.

Once he'd said, "I'm not sorry!" No, he wouldn't be sorry yet. Not yet.

You had driven on until you reached Cherry Street at daylight; hunted around on a back street for a cup of coffee. After that the two of you went to Union Station. He got on the train. Trying to smile was like tearing muscles, but you managed it and stood there, watched him enter an unknown future. Turned away to your own—

Turned away to what was left. For Ed, emptying that load of bullets into Deen's body, had blown all their lives to pieces. Now, before he saw the others, he had to see what was left, what they could make out of what was left. It didn't look like much. Always there'd be the nagging fear that Ed would come back, be suspected, caught; which like an ulcer in the mouth would ruin the sweet taste of everyday living. There'd be that night never spoken of again by any of them, which with black compulsive power would soak up into its silence more and more and more of their lives until nothing much but empty routines would remain.

He'd turned his car south. Started on the longest journey a man ever makes as he tried to go step by step back through his life and the lives of those nearest him, to find the place where things had taken a wrong turn. Seeking, as children seek in recapitulating play, to master a painful experience, repeating it until it can be summoned back and forth at will. And as he drove on and on from Macon to Maxwell, from fresh early dawn to blazing dead heat, trying to find a way into the past, he kept pushing back a feeling that stole through his body like a soft tune he'd never let himself listen to. It was as if he told himself, "You can't think that now . . . maybe later," though he told himself nothing.

But he had not gone far. For always as he went from year to year, opening old memories, he'd keep turning away from

332

one door that he could not make himself open, and he knew Ella was there, waiting; and some day, some time, he had to let her out, had to set her free to move back and forth in his past. But now he could not even put his hand on the knob.

He did not know why he had married her. Why he had wanted anything so cheap and poor and tawdry as Ella. He knew only that he had taken something and had thrown it away. And you don't throw a thing away that you've possessed or that has possessed you. Some of it is always there with you the rest of your life. Some time he must be willing to accept that cheapness and nastiness as a part of the life he had lived. Now he could not do it.

Yeah . . . plenty trouble. All you've got to do is to reach out and it'll drop into your hand. Plenty to kill a man easy . . . if he wants to die. To drive him plumb crazy if he wants that kind of peace. But if you don't want to use your trouble to beat other folks to death with, or yourself, if you don't want that . . . if you want to keep on living, then you got to get your trouble in your hand, squeeze down on it until there's nothing left.

Harris knocked a letter file from the desk, Sam stepped over and picked it up.

Things looked about as usual around the mill, as far as he could see. But mill hands were gathering downtown—he saw them as he drove past the courthouse—hanging around, in twos and threes. Waiting for something to happen. Anybody with half an eye could see it if he looked. Trouble was, nobody'd be looking. And unless Harris or Cap'n Rushton or some of them did something, they'd get the damn fool—though God knows he couldn't be all fool to have hidden himself so well—get him before night. Trouble about going to white folks, they always think you're exaggerating. Sure you're wrong. Sure it won't happen. Yeah, they'd get him, come dark, and the good people, the powerful people of the town would be mighty surprised, mighty sorry it happened.

333

Yeah, mighty sorry.

Tom Harris's pink bald head continued to bend over the ledger.

Ten minutes to six. Soon be knocking-off time. Soon be two hundred more let loose to swell the restlessness downtown. But you don't hurry a white man. No, you sit and wait, hat in hand, and watch the clock over the pay window tick away minute after minute after minute of a black man's chance to live, knowing it has ticked away with it your right to decency.

Last night in the Anderson parlor they had sat like this. Waiting. Listening. Trying to hear what their eyes could not see and minds had not guessed. And all around them in the darkness outside were the pad-pad of white men on the prowl, and dogs barking, and pistol shots, and once the sound of glass breaking when a stone came through the window-pane. But inside that room was a stillness that sounds could not penetrate as they sat there mutely feeling their separate ways from past to future and back again. The lamp had sputtered once, Bess got up for kerosene; and later when the deputy sheriff and his men searched the house, Bess picked up her sewing and with careful calm began embroidering. But the hours of the long night passed with no other sound from any of them. Once he thought he heard Nonnie draw in her breath sharply, but when he looked at her she was sitting as she had sat all evening, looking into the empty fire-place. Only her hands were pressed tightly together now, when before they had lain in her lap, as if not hers. She's beginning to feel, he had thought, and saying that to himself, his own body flared up as if a draft had been opened.

He had gone to them in the evening, thinking they might need him. Since Bess's words yesterday about Nonnie he had known what he would do. He would marry her. Take care of her, if she would let him. There was nothing new in Sam

Perry's taking care of people and nothing new in the satisfaction it gave him. But the music in his body stopped as if a string had snapped when Bess spoke those words yesterday. Watching Non begin to suffer was a signal for his own hurt to begin. For within this body which had seemed so lovely to him, which had seemed a sweet good thing to think about year in and year out, on long lonely trips out in the country, something to dream some day of feeling the softness of with his own hand, Nonnie was keeping a white man, and she'd keep him there . . . forever now—his child and his child's child . . .

But Sam knew, and it was a terrible thing to know, that he loved her so much, that he loved this body Deen had used and tried to throw away so much that he was willing not only to take it, but Deen with it—to have Deen's blood forever mingled with his, Deen's child forever to bear his name . . .

*You can't do it. You can't do it* . . . she wants her baby *. . . you can't do it* . . . but she wants it . . . *you can't do it* . . .

The night had seemed a long black night with that whispering in his ears . . . And he was glad when the dawn came and with it order, so that he could leave the Anderson house. And as he walked through the cool morning, breathing deep of the freshness, his world suddenly righted itself. What difference, he told himself. What difference if you can save her from shame! What difference! And he spat the bitter taste of it out of his mouth.

It was while he was eating a late dinner, for accumulated calls had kept him busy, that Little Gabe ran up the steps. And though Aunt Easter met him with her usual alacrity, her firmness to Little Gabe was a mere something to spread oiled words upon. He was soon at the table with Sam and in low whispers began to talk.

Sitting there hunched up like a light'ood knot, black scaly-gray hands which had worked in pitch pine until they

335

had taken on its texture, rubbing together restlessly now, Gabe told Sam about the café fight. And Sam Perry sat there and listened to words that lashed his pride until it had no more feeling in it.

After the tale was told, Gabe said no more. And Sam, who had listened to Gabe, sat there without answering. All this was just facts. Yes. White and Negro facts.

A hen was singing out in the yard by the window, scratching in the oak leaves. You could hear that more plainly than you had ever heard sounds before in your life.

"Sam," Gabe said, "they're after him."

Sam looked up. They were after somebody . . .

"They'll git Henry fo dark."

Yes . . . that's right, they're after Henry McIntosh. Well . . . let em get him . . . good riddance . . . let them.

Sam said, "Know where he is?"

"Nobody's seen him since noon yistiddy."

"Then maybe they got him already."

"Wouldn't nobody keep on huntin ef they did."

"What you want me to do, Gabe?" Sam spoke angrily.

The two men looked at each other a long time. Once they had worked together at the logging camp. A long time ago that had been, and Sam's way had forked off sharply since then, and he hadn't kept up with Gabe much.

"Sam, Ten McIntosh and me was out at the camp more'n twelve year together. I was three feet fum him when he got cotched in the saw belt. Holped tote him out. Me, I buried his tore-off leg." Gabe wiped his face against his sleeve. "Henry ain't no count, but it's Ten's boy. And he never kilt Tracy Deen. You know it well as me."

"Yeah, I know. But what you want me to do, Gabe?"

"Cain't let a wrong man die when you knows who done it. Cain't do that, Sam."

"What do they care about innocence, that mob? White man dead. Nigger must die."

336

"Cain't do it, Sam."

"Can't do it! Sure I can! Who are we, you and me, to decide who killed Tracy Deen! He killed himself! That's right — Ed carried out his orders—that's all he did! That's all— and Henry furnished the bullets—Henry—and all the white race—and you and me too—and plenty others. Now you tell me to be God. Weigh souls to decide who bears the extra grain of guilt. Somebody's gotta die, might as well be that damn fool as another. God knows he ought to die!"

"Sam, I don ketch on to talk like you is usin. Hit makes sense maybe, but I don ketch on. All I knows is you and me ain got no right to set here and let a mob of crazy folks git Ten's boy."

"Lord God, how can we help ourselves?"

But here he was, sicked on by Gabe like a little fice dog at his heels. Here now to humble himself before a white man to save a low-down son of a—

"Mr. Harris," he heard himself speaking.

"Be with you now in half a minute, Sam."

"If you'll excuse me, Mr. Harris, it's about Henry McIntosh."

Tom Harris copied down another figure or two, closed his notebook, came over to his desk.

"All right, Sam—now what's on your mind?"

In for a pack of lies. Better tell them quick and hope to God to keep them straight. Swiftly, Sam told him a story of Monday evening, hours spent with Henry, shooting craps, Henry sleeping at his house with some of the boys, getting up late next morning, Sam dropping him off at the Deens' back door—

"They're after him, Mr. Harris, and he's as innocent as you or me. Things are likely to be bad around here unless," Sam smiled deferentially, "you and Cap'n Rushton and some

337

of the other good white folks can do something about it. I'd be much obliged, Mr. Harris, if you could help—"

"Who's after him?"

"Mostly county folks, I reckon, some maybe from the town too—some of the hands from the still—and other places, I hear. But Mr. Cassidy and Mr. Talley back of it, folks say."

"Sam," Tom Harris spoke slowly, "that's a good story you told, gives Henry a clean slate all right. Only trouble is, it's a lie."

Sam Perry's dark brown face did not move a muscle.

Tom Harris frowned. "Wish you hadn't told it."

Sam looked steadily at the white man. "I had to tell it."

"Why?"

"Because a Negro can't afford the truth! Truth's for powerful folks. And this time I don't know all the truth. But I happen to know enough to know Henry McIntosh didn't kill Mr. Deen. And I know they're after him in the biggest man-hunt this part of the state has ever had. They'll be getting him before dark."

"No, they won't get him. Haven't had a lynching here in ten years. We're not having one today."

"But if you'll excuse me, Mr. Harris, for keeping on like this, I'm afraid we are. All day I've—"

"Sam, you know well as me who does the lynching! Riffraff! No-counts. Always no-counts! No decent white man takes part in a lynching. Well, the riffraff can't get at Henry. You know where he is?" Tom Harris's worried red face eased into a broad smile. "Know where I got him? In jail. Yeah, behind bars! Safe as a baby. Letting the law look after him. Law ought to protect innocent well as guilty—especially when nobody knows it's doing it." Tom chuckled.

"It ought to, Mr. Harris," Sam spoke slowly, "but bars break right easy when a mob's in front and a black man's behind, and secrets leak out—"

"Nobody knows he's there! That's the point. They don't

338

know he's there. They'll be giving up soon now and going back home if we sit tight. Things'll cool off in a few days and then we can let the law take its course."

"Excuse me, Mr. Harris, if I keep on. But things don't seem to be settling down. Every colored house in town has been searched this afternoon. An hour ago men were going through my back yard—they're everywhere, just not making any noise. It's different from that bunch shooting off their feelings last night. They were Mr. Deen's friends. This crowd's after something. Colored folks moving North . . . picking time . . . hands scarce . . . reckon it's about time to—" Sam tried to smile deferentially at the white man as he left the sentence unfinished.

"Funny thing . . . how folks can imagine things. Now my wife, Mrs. Harris, is always imagining things, sees the worst in every situation. Of course, it *could* happen, Sam, but there's every chance in the world that it won't."

"But that's the way lynchings come about, Mr. Harris. It's believing they won't happen, shutting your eyes and hoping—"

"I know they do—sometimes. Know if there'd been a raping, or something—some woman involved in it—it'd be different."

It'd be different . . .

Sam suddenly leaned forward. It was somebody else speaking now. Another Sam Perry had stepped up in front of him, had taken hold of things. "You know who's lynching him? It's you and me! That's right. White man and brown. Respectable white folks don't like to get mixed up in things like this. No. And respectable colored folks don't either. So we shut our eyes, you shut your eyes, I shut my eyes and—"

"You're losing your head, Sam!"

"No . . . I've lost my soul! Traded it out in the white man's commissary—for furnish. Taking white values . . . yeah. Maybe he's nothing much to get excited about. No-count . . .

sure! But he's alive, likes to fill his belly, likes the sun on his skin . . . humanity at its mudsill, I reckon . . . I don't know . . ."

Sam had clenched his fist now and was softly beating the table, brown fist catching the light as it pounded the wood. "But he stands for something—his *living* stands for something. And they'll get him. Bound to! Got to hate something and kill it. Got to! Things couldn't keep on like they are down here if you didn't kill something. To keep from killing your own kind . . ."

"Sam, I want you to stop. You're talking too much—" Harris paused, went on, "I know it's hard for an educated colored man to live in the South. Like running into barbed wire everywhere you turn. Told you that before. Told you before you'd better go somewhere else, Cuba, anywhere, where it wouldn't be so hard on you."

"I came back because my people need me. They need me right here. I came back," Sam looked up into his white friend's face and tried to smile, "because it's my home. That's enough to make a man die laughing! It's my home . . . born here . . . family born here . . . Grandparents born here . . ." He paused, stared out of the window, turned back to the white man. "It could be worked out. Slow. Yes. But it could be. Poverty's the slowest. Yes. But there're other things . . . that hurt maybe worse than poverty. It'd be such a little thing," he looked up at the white man, "to call us mister . . . It wouldn't take a penny . . . to do that . . . It oughtn't to shame you much . . . to do that." Brown fist beat the table softly, fist moving slowly up and down. "It's things like that . . . drive us crazy . . . things . . . the little things . . . that work through the skin . . . to your heart . . ." Sam's voice dropped almost to a whisper. " . . . that turn decent men, sober decent human beings, into crazy animals. You know," Sam looked up again at Tom Harris, "you can kill a man so easy . . . slit a piece of skin at his wrist, or the side of his neck, give him one tap at the back of the head . . . You can kill his soul easy as that. God . . ." brown hand beating softly, "you take it and take it and take it . . . day comes . . . you can't take any more . . ." voice had sunk to a whisper now, "can't take any more . . ." Sam stared out of the window across the tracks. "And you turn on somebody white, or on your own kind maybe . . . somebody blacker or dumber than you, or poorer . . . and tear him to pieces . . . You go crazy as hell and tear him to pieces and tear your own soul and those you love, destroying everything on earth you prize . . . every good . . ."

"Sam, I want you to stop talking! You've lost control. I want you—"

"Mr. Harris," Sam's voice was quiet, "first time in my life I interrupted a white man. I've lost control—yes. Got to say it. All my life I've bowed and scraped, for the sake of the others beneath me, I thought, who needed help. I'd do it the white way, I'd say. It's worth licking a few hands for, I'd say—God!" he breathed, "God . . ."

You could hardly hear him now. He looked across the room as if he had stopped, had long ago forgot to go on.

"It's more than starving . . . low wages . . ." the voice picked up words again, "more than Jim Crow—it's you white men . . . sucked dry as your land . . . taking our women . . . yes, taking them as . . . manure, that's all they are to you . . . dung . . . to make something grow green in your life . . . That's all they mean to you . . . My sister . . ." voice like wind beating palmetto ". . . my own mother . . . that's all . . . the woman I love . . . white man took her . . . used her . . . threw her aside like . . . something filthy and stinking . . . Why can't you leave them alone! God Jesus, why does the Negro have to bear this!" His voice grew suddenly quiet. "I know I can't drag God in. What would a decent God have to do with a thing like—"

Tom Harris stood, struck the table hard with his hand,

341

"Hush, you fool! You black damned son of a—" stopped as if a hand had caught his arm . . . Began again, "You've forgot, Sam," he said slowly, "there're things no nigger on earth can say to a white man!"

Sam stared at him, kept staring as the room rocked with those words spoken by the best friend he had ever had in the white race. And then slowly he buried his face on the table. His sobs were like somebody tearing a shirt to pieces.

Tom sat down. Moved the inkwell, opened a drawer of his desk, closed it. Looked at the Negro's bowed head. "Sam," Harris's voice was quiet now, feeling its way, "I wouldn't have thought it of you—always steady—able to keep your eyes in the middle of the road. I— Buck up, boy . . . gotta buck up now."

The black head on the table did not move.

"It's hard," Tom said after a time, "for black . . . and white. If you try to be decent . . . anywhere . . ." He sighed, tapped his fingers on the desk. Did not talk for a moment or two. "I'm going over to the jail. Maybe some of us better go straight to Talley and have it out with him. Don't think it's as bad as you think, though. He's just trying to scare em a little. I'll check with Lem first, see if everything's quiet at the jail. You go home now, pull yourself together. Get yourself together! Thing a man can't do, white or black, is to lose control. You gotta hold on . . . Never saw you lose your head before."

Sam wiped his face, stood up, wiped his face again.

"Want you to know, Sam, I'm the black man's friend. A man who tries to be a Christian has to be as fair to black as white. I believe that. But I've got to work in the setup we got down here. I'm no radical, no addle-brained red trying"— the telephone was ringing —"to turn a hundred years upside down in a minute." Tom turned to answer the phone.

"It's been a long minute for the Negro," Sam said quietly.

Harris picked up the receiver. "Yes . . . Yes'm . . . Are

342

you sure? . . . How long, Miss Sadie . . . Are you sure . . . Where they go? . . . I'm coming . . ."

He placed the receiver on the hook and looked at Sam Perry. "They got him," he said slowly.

White man, brown man, stared across the shadows of the room, across three centuries of the same old shadow.

"Drive me to the ball ground, Sam."

In silence Sam Perry drove across the tracks, down the road past the courthouse, past business streets, past Munson's Drug Store. As they turned off College Street they could hear cries, deep, shrill, cacophonous, as of a great crowd moving; and then they came upon clusters of mill women and children near Salamander's Cafe, more near the water tower, some climbing its framework.

"Let me out here," Harris said.

"I'm going with you." Sam stopped the car.

"You go straight home!" Tom Harris slammed the car door, hurried toward the crowd on the ball ground, pushing his way through the clusters of women and children, peremptorily ordering mill people out of his way.

Sam sat still.

His revolver was in the pocket of the car. It would be easy to fight his way through the outer crowd. He had his revolver . . . Surely he was man enough to take a chance . . . if he couldn't make it, what matter? Lord God . . . what matter! He'd have tried . . . shown he had a little manhood . . . *You'll make it worse for the rest of us* . . . That's what they always say . . . *you'll turn it into a race riot* . . . That's what everybody tells you . . . Manhood's for powerful folks, you can't afford it, they mean.

It was as still in the center there, a few hundred yards in front of him, as death. Death itself. You could feel it from here.

A child whimpered, "Mommy, I'm hongry—I'm hongry,"

and pulled at his mother, whose face was turned toward the crowd.

"Hush!" she said, not turning, "hush! They're burning a nigger. Don't you want to see em burn a nigger?"

A thin spiral of smoke could now be seen rising against the late-afternoon sky. A dog barked, another took up the cry, another, another, as if a great restlessness had entered into them and would not let them go.

God . . . God Jesus . . . nothing Harris can do now . . . And you sit here and take it . . . Yeah . . . beat your fist against a steering wheel, beat your life out against your own impotence.

White women eyed him curiously, and a mill child came close up to the car and stared at him. "Hit's another nigger, Mommy" he cried, and the woman said, "Shut yo mouth! He might git ye and hurt ye. Don't you know that?"

Every nigger a boogah man . . . under every white bed . . . It made you want to cry out to God. It made you want to laugh forever as you cried.

There were shouts now. You could hear shouts, and the smoke had grown black, as if oil had been added to the flames.

Sam started the car, drove slowly toward Colored Town.

He had just turned off Oak Street when he saw a Negro girl running down the road followed by a white man. He stopped the car.

"Go home, I tell you!" the white man shouted as they drew near, and now Sam recognized Charlie Harris, breathing fast, and red-faced. "Go to Mama!"

"No!" screamed the girl, and began to cry louder. "I gotta go help him, I gotta—" She stopped and faced the white boy. "I gotta go—oh, I gotta," she sobbed.

She was covered with dirt, as though she had stumbled and fallen in the road, and her hat had slid on one side of

344

her head, its three red roses toppled together in a forlorn huddle.

Charlie went up to her now and shook her hard, as if that might stop the wild sobs. "You go straight to Mama!" he scolded as he shook. "She'll look after you, Dessie—"

"I gotta help him, Mr. Charlie, I gotta—"

"You can't help him, Dessie. Nobody can help him. He's dead."

Dessie caught her breath, backed off, dirty hand against her mouth, eyes black-staring.

"Daid!" she whispered, backing off as if afraid of the bearer of this news. "He's daid." Face gray as sand, suddenly.

"Stop it, Dessie!" Charlie said again. "Now stop it. You can't act like this."

"I'll take care of her," Sam called from the car. "I'll take her."

"Caught her at the ball diamond right in the thick of the mob, running straight to where they had him . . . like a wildcat . . . Chased her this far . . ." Charlie wiped his face. "She oughtn't to be on the street. Somebody might—" He wiped his face again. "It's a bad time, Sam—and I'm sorry."

Sam bowed his head. "I'll take care of Dessie," he said quietly, and started the car.

He drove on slowly down Back Street, letting Dessie be. She sat in the far corner of the seat, biting her hand, whispering, "Burnt im . . . they burnt im up . . ."

"Where you like to go, Dessie?"

"They burnt im up," she whispered.

"Dessie!" he spoke sharply. "Where do you want to go?"

"Please sir, to Miz Lowe's . . . I'll be much obleeged." she sobbed softly, and having begun, sobbed on quietly in her corner of the seat.

He drove through a shuttered, empty, soundless Colored

345

Town to the old Anderson home. As the car made the last turn he saw the two Anderson girls sitting on the porch, stiff, unmoving, silent. Even from there you could see the smoke, could hear the dogs barking restlessly.

He stopped the car. He should go speak to them. But as he thought it he knew he could not go through with it now. Not tonight.

Dessie got out, began to run up the walk, began to run faster as she came nearer the porch with its two unmoving women. "They've did it," she sobbed, "oh, they've did it . . . they've did it . . ." and fell in a little crying heap at Bess's feet.

# TWENTY-NINE

AS NIGHT FELL, Bill Talley and Dee and the others went to their homes back in the county or to the sawmill and Ellatown. Bill and Dee driving home in the buggy out to Shaky Pond. Wheels grinding through sand, grinding through shadows and lights along road and swamp. Bill and Dee not talking, only hoofs and creak of wheels breaking the silence as the buggy moved under moss hanging low from great oaks, past ponds, past black clumps of palmetto . . . cotton fields . . . to the old house.

Lias met them at the lane to take the horses.

"Well, Lias," Bill said, "I hear they burned a nigger over to town today," voice mighty casual. Bill lifted his great weight out of the buggy.

Lias's hand fumbled for the bridle.

346

"Made a big fire, they say."

Lias had the bridle now.

"Watcha say, Lias?"

"Nothin, Mr. Bill. Yassuh—yassuh, Mr. Bill, sho must've."

Dee laughed, pulled his long thin legs from behind the buckboard, eased to the ground.

"Well," said Bill, "reckon we better get to pickin, a Monday."

"Yassuh, Boss."

"Reckon you can round up plenty hands, don't you? Won't be no trouble about gittin plenty?"

"Nossuh, Boss. Kin git all we kin use, yassuh."

Dee laughed, walked away.

Bill said, "Better put the horses up. They're wore out."

"Yassuh, Mr. Bill."

"And rub em down. They're tired. Don't like to see my horses git so tired. Damned hot weather!"

"Yassuh, Mr. Bill; thankee, Boss."


Miss Sadie went to bed early. She would like to go to sleep if she could, for there'd been little sleep for her the night before at the switchboard. And maybe sleep would help her forget what she had seen from her office window. She shouldn't have watched, but she had watched; and now her eyes were full of a black body swinging from the old cypress . . . full of the swinging and full of flames; of man's cruelty and anger. Maybe a little sleep would help her get it out of her mind, and her eyes. She turned over and pulled the sheet straight and as she did, someone knocked on her door.

It was Belle. Belle in her nightgown with a pink summer coat over her.

"You'll just have to let me sleep with you, Sadie, for I can't stay another minute in that house by myself, I'm so nervous

347

I'm ajumping all over and I got to thinking now we're likely to have a raping tonight after this, with the niggers all aroused, you know, it's really not right, Sadie, for a woman to stay alone and you need somebody with you too so I—"

"You're welcome to stay, Belle. Just crawl in and turn off the light."

Belle crawled in and turned off the light.

Sadie edged over to her side of the bed. Maybe in a moment now she'd get to sleep and—

"Wasn't it just awful!" Belle crawled closer to Sadie. "I stood there on my piazza and watched and I was so close, Sadie, that I could hear that nigger's scream, and it made my blood—"

"Let's try to go to sleep, Belle, we're both worn out." Sadie edged over nearer the rim of the bed.

"Yes, we do need sleep all right, after all we've been through," Belle agreed.

Belle pulled down her nightgown and turned her pillow over. "My, it was terrible—terrible—you know, Sadie, I'll never forget this in all my life, it's one of those things you carry with you to your gr—"

"Yes, I know. But let's try to sleep now if we can."

Belle turned over.

Sadie smoothed the sheet once more. Maybe in a minute, now, she'd go to sleep. It's hard to believe the men you've seen downtown every day—so pleasant and agreeable to you, always doing something kind for you—could do a thing like this. What was it in folks that made them cruel? What did it satisfy in them? Must be something in a person that needed to hate—to make him want to hurt somebody weaker than himself—

"And, Sadie, the flames got so high I thought for the life of me they'd touch the sky, I did, and, Sadie, you know—I smelled it, yes I did—terrible—it was just awful—just like

348

barbecue—just exactly—made me think of all the times I'd eaten—it turned my stomach inside out and—"

Miss Sadie sat straight up and faced her guest. "Hush your mouth, Belle Strickland! You hear! If you make one **more** sound tonight—if you—I'll—I'll—I'll do something bad to you—I'll—" Shocked at herself, Miss Sadie suddenly lay **down.**

Miss Belle did not move. Nor did she speak another word.


The swing on the Puseys' dark porch whined on relentlessly.

"It's the Lord's will," Mrs. Pusey said in her patient, skimmed-milk voice; "he wasn't a good boy, Dottie, and would have caused you a life of trouble. . . They found his body out to Colored Town. You know what that means."

Creak, creak—back and forth in the darkness.

"Many a woman would thank God for being spared—what you've been spared. Look at Mrs. Sug Rushton . . . Some men, Dottie, can't keep away from nigger women—can't keep away—"

Creak—creak creak—

"It's the Lord's will, Dottie. A day will come when you'll see what you've been saved from. When you're older and know what I know about men . . . you'll be thankful that God spared you from the kind of life some women have to bear. Men are hard to live with, all of them, but some men are worse than others and those that run after . . ."

But Dottie's low sobs went on, a little endless stream of sorrow threading its way between the creaks of the porch swing and Mrs. Pusey's plaintive words.


Preacher Livingston and Roseanna sat on their shed in the dark. Roseanna had sent the twins to bed early, and now she had opened the shutters and let in some air, for though she could hear the girls talking softly in their bed, they had undressed in the dark as she bade them do.

"Ned," she said, "I want to get the twins up to Atlanta, soon as we can."

"A month fo school! They can't go now, Rosie."

"I won't have them stay another minute in this place! I can't stand the worry."

Preacher Livingston turned to his wife. "There ain no runnin away from white folks, Rosie, you oughter know that well as me. There's ways to git along wid white folks if you hunts round for um. I've spent my whole life ahuntin . . . and I've found some—glad to say—I've found a few."

"I know you have," Roseanna said, and hesitated. "But they're ways we don want our chudren atakin . . . do we, Ned?" Roseanna was talking very simply now and without her airs. "We want something better for the twins than we had, don we? Sometimes I feel—" she hesitated again, "sometimes I most feel I'd rather kill them with my own hands than have them—go through," her voice sank very low, "what I've—been through . . . and other colored women like me."

Preacher Livingston moved uneasily in his chair.

"There's ways to git along, I'm tellin you! Colored folks don have to git in trouble wid white folks. Hit's their own fault when they does. There's ways. There's always been ways . . ."


From where Willie Echols and his wife Mollie sat—and their friends—under the chinaberry tree, you could see the glare of the dry-kiln, plain.

"Tom Harris musta turned out a million feet of lumber right there this summer," Lewis said, and wheeled his go-cart around to see the glow better.

"Yeah. But to hear him talk . . . when Saddy night comes, there ain't a dollar."

"Rich folks always talks hard times. You git used to it." Lewis laughed good-naturedly.

"I never have and don aim to git used to it. I aims to git a few of them dollars one of these days. What we need is to organize for a living wage. If we was to—"

Mollie laughed a deep fat laugh. "Willie's all time talkin bout organizin. I tell him he's wastin his breath. All Tom Harris ud do would be to turn him off and hire a nigger in his place."

"Oughter run the last one out the county," old Mrs. Lewis said firmly.

"Ma, you gittin kinder hard on—"

"Reckon we got one less anyway!"

"God yes! Warn't it a sight!"

"I never seen it," Mollie said. "Musta been terrible! Never could bear to wring a chicken's neck, and I knowed it ud be moren I could stand."

"I went," gray-haired Mrs. Lewis said, and her lips grew grim. "It was a turrible sight, but you coulda stood it."

Lewis laughed, and lifted a stump of a leg over the side of the go-cart where it could get the air. "I never went. Never did like to mix up in a thing like that. But Ma always said atter she seed me come outa that belt with both legs tore off she could look at anything."

Ma looked at Lewis now. "Well, you warn't no purty plaything, I tell ye that."

"It coulda been worse," Lewis said. "It shore coulda been worse. And I'm about afeared of them wild talkers as anything. Now you take Tom Harris. He done purty good by me. Give me a hundard dollars and paid my doctor bill. And I reckon he'll be givin me a job as night watchman purty soon."

351

"A hundard dollar won't buy you no new legs," his wife retorted.

Lewis did not answer at once, and when he spoke, he spoke softly. "Well, Ma, mebbe hit don do no good to talk of it."

They were quiet for a time, just sitting there resting and watching the glow from the kiln.

Echols laughed. "It was a sight, that nigger! Swingin there. Got what he deserved. What every one of em deserve. But Mollie woulda fainted dead away when he begun to smell."

"Lawd, don't talk about it!" Mollie said, and made a face. With a plump hand she eased up one of her breasts a little where it was chafed.

"Mommy, mommy, mommy, mommy," screamed a child inside the house.

"I declare! J. L.'s havin a nightmare agin! That boy bolts his rations so fas he—"

"Mommy, mommy," sobbed the little fellow as he came running out of the house and down the steps, "they'll git me . . . they'll git me . . . I seed em . . ."

"Nobody aimin to git ye! Hit's niggers they burn—they ain't agoin to burn you. Get on back with ye to bed, boy." Echols laughed, gave the boy a playful push.

Nobody had ever seen Willie in better spirits, and everybody joined in the laughter as Mollie turned the little fellow around and sent him back.

"Well," said Mrs. Lewis, "we better be agittin home and to bed ourselves. It's atter nine o'clock."

Mollie and Willie sat on for a time under the chinaberry tree, until the Nine O'clock passed.

"Late tonight," Mollie said.

"Late half the time." Willie stood up. "Never was a train to run on time. How about bed, old woman?"

"Well, I don't care if I do." Mollie pulled her two hun-

352

dred pounds out of the low cane-bottom chair and followed Will into the house.

It did not take them long to get to bed. Nor long for Willie to pull Mollie's big soft body to him.

"My!" Mollie sighed after a time, "my . . . you ain't been like this in a year!"

"Ain't felt like this in a year," Willie laughed and reached for her again.

Tom Harris sat on the south porch of the Harris home while his wife watered her pot plants. Although it was dark and long after supper, Anne was carefully watering each fern, begonia, geranium, night-blooming cereus. Slowly and carefully. And Tom knew that she was deeply troubled.

He sat in his big porch rocker as she moved from shadowy pot to pot, herself a deeper shadow.

She emptied the watering-pot on the asparagus fern, sat down near him, rocked slowly back and forth in the darkness. Tom waited, knowing Anne was trying to say something; after a time she would find slow words.

Beyond them, on College Street, a car stopped. A voice called, "Harriet!" Waited. Moved on.

"I don't want the girls to go out tonight," he said.

"They're both here. I've told them."

"Tom," Anne said, "I worry about Charlie. If one of my boys turned out—I wish you'd speak to him."

"What do you want me to speak about, Anne?"

"I don't know . . . he never goes to church—doesn't take interest in the things we've taught our children to believe in."

"Charlie's all right, Anne."

"How do you know? Sometimes I wonder if we ever know our children . . ."

"All we can do, Anne, is the best we can and trust God to do the rest. Charlie's all right. Fine boy."

"I'm a little tired," Anne was standing now, "I think I'll go to bed. Papa," she was at the door, "try to talk to Charlie."

Tom sat on the porch after Anne had gone, looking into a darkness that was too black for his eyes to see through.

Charlie came out of the house, sat down. "Hello, Dad."

"Howdy, Son."

You could hear the singing over at the tent. From the sound of it, not many people were at the meeting.

"Dad, you were right—reckless, this afternoon."

"Well . . . I don't know."

"I don't think many men would have done what you did."

"It didn't do any good."

"They might have killed you. Pretty ugly crowd."

"It didn't do any good."

"Maybe it did more than you know. Maybe some of those watching felt . . . as I did."

"I don't know, Charlie. I'm too old to know—anything."

"You're younger than any child you've got—and a better man."

"Too old to figure out things like this."

*Praise God from whom all blessings flow,*
*Praise Him, all creatures here below . . .*

"Some of the boys doing that burning, Son, were our men from the mill. Hard-working. Good to their families. Two of them stewards in Sarah Chapel."

*Praise Him above, ye heavenly . . .*

"I can't understand why they'd want to do it." Tom sighed.

*Praise Father, Son and . . .*

"So many leaving the county, it's got folks nervous—" He stopped.

"Sometimes, Dad, when I think of the South all I can see is a white man kneeling on a nigger's stomach. Every time he

354

raises his arms in prayer he presses a little deeper in the black man's belly."

"Hate to hear you say a thing like that, Charlie. There're things hard to understand about the South . . . I know. But without God, it'd be worse. Lot worse."

"Trouble is, you can't be a Christian in the South. You can't be one even if you want to, in the setup we've got down here! Everybody gouging his living out of somebody beneath him—singing hymns as he gouges—"

"It's your saying things like that, Son, that worries your mother. Know you don't mean it way it sounds. Know you mean something else. I've lived a long time, Charlie, I can't live without God. Can't live without Him," Tom's voice was a whisper. After a moment he went on, "A lynching's a terrible thing. I know it's wrong to kill a man, no matter what his color. I know you got to be fair to him. But you can't make a Negro your social equal!"

"Why?"

"You know you can't do it! Turn em loose down here and before you know it, you'd have—" Tom stopped.

"What you reckon would happen, Dad? What you reckon?"

Tom didn't answer.

The two men sat looking out into the darkness.

Harriet came from the living room where she had been reading, and slipped into a chair. "I've always wondered how a lyncher feels," she said. "Now I know."

The two men did not answer.

"Every Southerner knows, of course. We lynch the Negro's soul every day of our lives."

The men did not answer.

"In all this town no one had the courage to try to stop it."

Charlie said quickly, "Except your own Dad—"

"Son, I'd rather you didn't discuss such things with your sister."

"Oh, Dad, don't be silly! What did he do, Charlie?"

Charlie hesitated, glanced at his father, told her briefly.

Harriet sat without speaking; then quietly went over to her father and kissed his bald head.

"I was too late," Tom said softly.

No one spoke again. After a while, Tom stood. "I hope some day you young folks will find the answer. Hope some day you'll find how come it all started and what can be done about it. Well . . . think I'll turn in. Kinda tired out. Good night, Sister."

"Good night, darling."

"Night, Son."

"Night, Dad."

Brother and sister sat on in a long silence.

"Too late," Harriet whispered. "What's the answer, Charlie?"

"I don't know one. Only thing I can see for anybody with sense to do is to get out!"

"Run away . . . Nice and easy. Smart people run away. Or maybe it isn't so smart. You can't run away from a thing like this. It'll follow you all over the world."

"Right now, I have some ideas," Charles said slowly. "If I stay here twenty years, I won't have them. Now I see things without color getting in the way—I won't be able to, then. It'll get me. It gets us all. Like quicksand. The more you struggle, the deeper you sink in it—I'm damned scared to stay—" He laughed.

"Everybody's scared," Harriet went on softly. "White man's blown himself up to such a size, now his own shadow scares him. Scared to do the decent thing for fear it will only do—harm. When every day by not doing—"

The only sound on the porch was the crunch of their rockers.

"Did you see it, Charlie?"

"From the edge."

"Who did it?"

356

"Mill folks—farm folks—Bill Talley and his crowd got it going."

"Was it—pretty bad?"

"Thing that got me the most," Charlie said slowly, "was the hate on folks' faces. Even on the women's. It wasn't Henry they were hating—or any Negro. It was—I don't know. Being poor couldn't do it—"

"It might help."

He went on after a little. "Yeah, but it couldn't do it. Not that kind of hate. Some of those men were at that revival last night at the altar . . . praying to be saved. This afternoon they burned a man to ash."

"You remember—" Harriet was feeling her way now, "the time we went with Gus to Milledgeville to see his mother? We saw a man there in the asylum who said he was God— you remember? He was out in the ward—they let him go loose—putting everybody 'in their place' . . . Telling everybody where they could sit and stand and how to speak to him. They said he picked up a chair one day and almost killed a woman because she wouldn't stay where he had put her . . . The doctors called it paranoia. It doesn't seem to me white folks are very different—from him."

"All of us nuts, huh?" Charlie laughed.

"I don't think there's much difference," Harriet said. "How about giving your sister a cigarette?"

"I'm willing—but you know how Mother feels . . ."

"O.K. Pass it up." She laughed, sighed. "What would happen, Charlie," she said after a little, "if for one day here in Maxwell you and I would do the human thing? Just act human and sane and decent—for one day. Would you have the courage?"

Charles laughed. "Let's go in. You ask too many questions."

357

Brother Saunders quick-stepped until his left foot synchronized with the evangelist's.

"Of course," he said, "this trouble is bound to hurt the revival, though the crowds will pick up better than that handful tonight."

The two men walked on in silence across the business blocks and down College Street.

"I doubt though," Brother Saunders said, "that we'll get back the enthusiasm we had."

Brother Dunwoodie pulled a strand of moss from above his head, dropped bits of it on the sidewalk as they went down College Street.

Suddenly he spoke. "I don't condone a thing like this afternoon. I feel nothing but condemnation for such bloodthirstiness."

"Nor I," Brother Saunders replied. "But it doesn't do any good to criticize people—not at a time like this. Only stirs up more bad feeling between the races. It don't do to *talk* about these things. Makes them worse! Now it's always been my policy to keep out of controversies and politics. A servant of God has no business mixing in such matters. Our job is the winning of souls to Christ."

Brother Dunwoodie sighed, "And sometimes it seems to me the devil can beat us all out of sight! Well," he raised his voice to a more cheerful level, "here's my corner. Good night."

"Good night," Brother Saunders said.

It was not far from the Harrises' side gate to the porch but far enough for Brother Dunwoodie to hear his steps echo in hollow mockery the minister's words—and his own.

"Yes," he sighed, "everywhere you turn, the devil's setting a trap for you."


Sam Perry sat before his desk. He had been there all evening. And though Aunt Easter now and then came to the door she did not go in, for there was a look on Sam's face which made Easter walk softly and stay on her side of the house. Once he said, "Go to bed, Auntie, I don't want supper." And Mrs. Perry had not urged him to eat.

Someone knocked on the door, and Sam put his hand to his gun. It was only Dan, who smiled at the gesture, came in.

"I was afraid you was asleep, Sam, but I had to come. Tempy's been so nervy all night I can't do nothin with her. She screamin and takin on like she done time she went dumb, and I feared she might be going off again into one of her spells. Maybe if you'd give her some of those powders, Sam, to make her drop off to sleep—"

Sam said yes, she probably needed to sleep, and turned to prepare something for her.

Dan sat there quietly, his dark brown face sagged with fatigue, hands resting on his knees.

"Dessie's not come home," he said evenly, "but I reckon she to the Harrises'." He rubbed his hand slowly over the bald part of his head. "If she ain't, I reckon there's nothin I kin do about it."

Sam measured the powder and rolled it in little papers.

"I reckon in a time like this, better tend my own business and leave other folks' alone."

"That's right, Dan. You're dead right," Sam said. "Tend your own business and to hell with everybody else's."

"Well, I don know," Dan half smiled, "but I sorter figure long as it's hot and folks needs plenty ice and I kin go round and ring a bell and sell um ten to fifty pounds and save a little money and keep my mouf shut and tend to Tempy I'll likely stay out of trouble and git along. Least I figure it that way."

"Yes, Dan, you'll always get along, I believe." Sam suddenly smiled. "I believe you always will."

359

The air was still. Down by the branch it would be cooler, but here at the office the day's dust still lay in the air.

In one of the cabins somebody lit a lantern. One of the sick ones worse maybe, or dying. Sam Perry mighty near right. Two more had died and five more sick. Well, they'd all been stuck with that needle now, so maybe it wouldn't get worse. But what a carryin on! Thought they'd sure have to hog-tie one wench and—

Even when you try to help the darkies, they buck it. Like the privies. Never would use them. Lot rather squat behind a palmetto. A lot rather! More like children than grown people. Maybe more like animals than either. But likeable. Yeah . . .

Cap'n Rushton chuckled. Couldn't help but like the crazy fools. Reckon that's why he stayed out at the still so much. Rather be around them than most folks in Maxwell.

He laid down his pipe. Better get to bed for the little rest that was left him. He went to the edge of the shed. Everything quiet. Shacks stretched a row of shadows down each side of the road, hardly bigger than shadows made by palmetto or sleeping cows. Well, glad it was over now. Saw when he went to town yesterday that Bill was out to git a nigger. You could see it in Bill's eye. You'd seen it before. Bill had a habit of killing one off now and then. Used to say there was too dadburn many of em. String one up now and then or drop him in the pond to the gators—made the others flourish like pruning a tree. Bill took things pretty far. Did as a boy. Kill a dog easy as that if he happened to step on the dog's tail—turn on him as if the dog had done something to *him!* Remembered seeing that once. But a lynching now and then did seem to settle things . . . Bad as it was, and it was bad, it did settle things. And things needed settling. Ever since the war the niggers had been restless. He'd been dead-set against sending them to France with the A.E.F., said then, they'd get ideas the South would pay high for. God

360

knows, plenty things crawling in their heads without mixing em with the French variety! Well, the Yankees who run things in Washington didn't believe it or didn't care. Goddurn fools promised the nigger the vote if he'd go. And now the cussed idiot expected it. Restless . . . swarming North like flies to a dirty pot. Thinking because they'd strutted around in khaki and ogled French women they could eat dinner with a white man. Like as not. Yeah. Thought they had a right now to look at white girls . . . Saw one of them a Saturday on the street staring straight at a bunch of girls in a car down at the drugstore. Bound to be trouble. Just a wonder it hadn't come before. Hands short for the pickin—short at the still—short everywheres. Some of the towns had stopped letting them buy railroad tickets to the North—turning them back.

Well, he'd kept out of it himself, for a lynching wasn't to his liking. One of those things that seem necessary now and then, but you let the other fellow do it. Like sticking a pig— much as you liked your cracklin' bread, you couldn't stand a hog-killing. Just hoped they got the right nigger. Maybe they did. Maybe they didn't. More likely Tracy Deen had come to his death in another way—from things being whispered round town today. Folks were talking a little about one of the Anderson niggers. Not saying much for the sake of the Deens, but a little something. Get a woman mad enough, she'd do you in, in a minute. Now that's a boy who'd never had a chance—with a mother like Alma Deen always trying to make him fit some fool picture she had in her mind . . . And Tut too easy on Alma! Ought to take a woman like Alma and—

He eased off his shoes. Might as well let women be.

Sometimes he wondered, maybe, if he ought to tell Della what Tut had said. Trouble is—if he told her he had less than a year to live—she'd take on like he was a prize package! Make him drink that durned mess Tut had fixed up; be fixing up messes of her own prescription for him—and fret and worry until it'd be like sitting up with your own corpse every day! As it was, Della made out well enough by herself in town. If he stayed away all the time, she'd never miss him— with her club and her missionary society and her garden, and the cook's worrisome ways and Della's old uncle, so childish he couldn't even feed himself without spilling it down his clothes. Altogether, they kept Della pretty happy. But if she thought he wasn't going to live long, she'd make him stay in town, and he couldn't abide the place! Be nursing him and fixing doo-daddles—and first thing you know they'd both be at each other's throat, or wanting to be . . .

Glad he was back here where it was quiet. He'd kept as far from the ball ground today as he could, but folks told him about it. Told him about Tom Harris rushing in there, trying to stop it. Some folks are satisfied with the world as it is; some have to work themselves to death afixin it over. And Tom has always been one of the fixers. Trying to make things over. Reform. Didn't seem able to see that it's all of a piece. You take the strain off here—you put an extra strain there. Like prohibition. Tom worked himself half to death for local option, and then for prohibition—and got it. But what did he get! What you going to give a man when you take his drink from him! Take his whisky away . . . you ain't changed him a bit. He'll just have to hunt something else . . .

Cap'n Rushton fixed the mosquito net tight around his bed and lay down. As for lynching . . . There'll be lynchings long as white folks and black folks scrouge each other—everybody scrambling for the same penny.

He stretched out and groaned. Felt good to get a bed under you. Yeah. Felt good. He turned on his side to ease the hurting. Turned back. Sighed. Sometimes he wondered what it was folks mourned over when a man died. Hard to believe it was the corpse.

362

They sat on the screen porch, the three of them, saying nothing. Only their rockers crunched now and then against the floor.

Tut looked at Alma, so quiet, so composed. He'd like to go to her and put his hand on her shoulder. Like to kiss her and remind her that he was still here—to give her what comfort he could. Been a long time since he'd kissed Alma like that. A long time. He'd like to be close to her now, to share this grief with her. He knew it was harder for a woman to lose her son than for a man—and that was hard enough . . .

The air was sweet with damp honeysuckle from the near-by trellis, but Tut smelled only the heavy fragrance of wreaths and sprays. Their boy. Made of her and him, grown to a man, unknown, tumultuous, weak maybe. Yet loving and sweet. Both children seemed mighty loving and sweet, to Tut. Things they said when they were little . . . the manly things young Tracy used to do . . . way he'd trudge after you when you went hunting, keep right up to you, never complain . . . way he'd take up for his mother if he thought you were against her—and him no more than two years old . . . way he'd give his playthings to Henry . . .

Tears were rolling down Tut's face, but he didn't know it, as he lived over his life with his boy . . . seeing the good things . . . the lovable things. He was gently replacing Tracy in Alma's womb, re-creating him, making him the boy he might have been. He was seeing him in all the beauty of man's tenderest dream. Tut would never see his son in any other way.

The telephone rang. Someone needed Dr. Deen.

Laura said, "Want me to go with you, Daddy?"

"Better stay with your mother, Sister." Tut picked up his bag.

They heard the car door slam, the buzz of the starter, the rattle of wheels sliding on gravel; watched the taillight turn the corner.

Everything seemed so far away. Yesterday, last night, this afternoon, one's whole life. That which no one would have believed in, had happened—piling dream upon dream, nightmare upon nightmare, until there seemed no way to return to the past or the present or to anything one had ever known before. Yet here they sat on the porch as they had sat a thousand evenings. Here they sat—except Tracy, and Henry . . . Back of them was the dark house—the big rooms in which they had lived their life. Back of it, the cabin. Now empty. Tonight, as Laura stood on the back porch, she noticed the door of the cabin was open. Someone must remember to shut the door. Someone must remember to write Mamie.

"Mother?" Neither had spoken since his going.

"Yes, dear."

"Mummie . . . I want to tell you, I'm staying here, now."

It was as if her mother had not heard.

"I'm not going back to school—or anywhere."

"We'll see, dear." Mother's words were clear, as certain as a clock striking the hour. "Later, when I've rested, we shall plan what is best.

"I think," Mrs. Deen added after a moment, "I shall go to bed."

"You must be worn out, Mummie. Is there anything I can do?"

"No, but it's late. You won't stay up much longer?"

"No, Mother."

Mrs. Deen's steps went firmly across the porch, into the hall, faded away as she went upstairs to her room.

Laura's rocker grew still. It was as if the porch were empty, so quietly she sat.

A car passed the house, turned the corner. Somewhere down the street a voice called out "Good night," and laughed.

Prentiss Reid, editor of *The Maxwell Press,* sat late in his office. Yellow sheets of paper lay in front of him, covered with pencil marks. The town's religious skeptic, the admirer of Tom Paine, the man who fought Prohibition, who had dared raise questions in 1917 about the persecution of aliens, had drawn a blank for tomorrow's editorial. Anything you say now will do more harm than good. That's the trouble. Always the trouble! Say what you think, make a gesture— you stir up a mare's nest. Make things worse that they were before—

So they say.

He lit a cigarette; stared at the bookshelf above his desk. *Holy Bible, Common Sense, Age of Reason, Rights of Man.* Four books worn from the handling. Pages marked, words underlined, comments scribbled in the margin. There was no man in Maxwell who could with so much ease cite Holy Writ in an argument as could the town's infidel; and none who could quote whole pages from Tom Paine as casually as if from a recent talk with a friend.

*Make things worse—*

So they say. He scribbled slowly, drew a dog, carefully pointed its ears—

Better let it pass. Let the thing go! Do something on the great need for a paved road through the county. Always safe to write about roads. God! He laughed aloud, threw his cigarette into the spittoon.

Yeah ... make folks worse ... do more harm than good—

He stared into the bookshelf. Lord God—how old Paine would tell em if he were here. What an editorial he'd write! Pin the town's ears back . . .

Reid was smiling to himself . . . looking at words in his memory which a thousand readings had put there. Freedom . . . the rights of man . . . jobs . . . wages . . . human dignity . . . a free intelligence. . . .

That's the South's trouble. Ignorant. Doesn't know anything. Doesn't even know what's happening outside in the world! Shut itself up with its trouble and its ignorance until the two together have gnawed the sense out of it. Believes world was created in six days. Believes white man was created by God to rule the world. As soon believe a nigger was as good as a white man as to believe in evolution. All tied up together. Ignorance. Scared of everything about science, except its gadgets. Afraid not to believe in hell, even. Afraid to be free.

Below his window the only sound Reid heard was that of the nightwatchman talking to his dog and far away a car churning in deep sand.

And so damned poor! Out there today . . . men rarin' to kill something. Sallow, half dead with hookworm . . . hating, yeah—but out for fun too. No fun down here. Not a goddam thing to do for fun . . . Women won't even let you—

He laughed. Began to draw a box—

Money. Money would help. If it went to the folks who need it. Maybe unions could get it to them. Dammit, somebody ought to have the courage—

He slowly finished drawing the box.

Tracy . . . Used to sit there across from him. Used to read sometimes here in the office. A boy you could talk to. Not afraid of ideas. Sit here—quick to get a point, quick to tell a good story. But no good, they'd tell you. A failure. Yeah, a goddam no-count failure. Heard em say today, behind their hands, the bastards, "Terrible thing for the family, but maybe they'll see, as time goes on, that it was for the best. After all—"

Best for whom? Good riddance, sure! Sweep up the failures, get em out of sight, bury em . . . Yes, he'd sit here talking. Always looking for the joker in every idea. Afraid somebody would put something over on him. Well, God knows, somebody did. It'd be good to know exactly who it was.

Prentiss Reid lit another cigarette; stared into the wall, shrugged, wrote rapidly for a few minutes.

". . . but what's done now is done. Bad, yes. Lawlessness and violence are always bad. And this particular form smacks of the Dark Ages. It hurts business, it hurts the town, it hurts the county, it hurts everybody in it. But it's time now to get our minds on our work, go back to our jobs, quit this talking. Those who participated in the lynching were a lawless bunch of hoodlums. We don't know who they are. They ought to be punished. But who are they? No one seems to know. A prominent white citizen was killed. Justice had to be satisfied. The case should have been carried to the courts. This black should have been brought to trial. Every law-abiding citizen believes that. But the war sent back a new kind of Negro whom the South doesn't like. And Northern labor agents have made things worse with promises they have no intention of keeping. All Northern industry will do is lure our black folks away and when they no longer need them, leave the simple creatures to starve. There won't be any back-door handouts in Chicago, either—as our colored folks will soon find out. These efforts to interfere with our Southern way of doing things have made some folks nervous, too quick on the trigger. And it has made the black man forget his place. The South will never let him forget that. As long as the North interferes in our affairs, ignorant hoodlums down here will interfere with the law.

"As for Northern criticism. There will be plenty. All we can say is: if the damnyankees can handle these folks better than we who've had more than two hundred years' practice, let them try it. Lord knows, they're welcome to try it. Up there. And we might ask them how about their own gangsters? And how about East St. Louis and Chicago?"

That'll fix it, he said aloud, and laid the copy on the table. Puts right on our side. Makes us all sorry for ourselves. Well, that's what they want, and *The Maxwell Press* aims to please.

367

Prentiss Reid picked up his pencil. Began to draw a man on a sheet of paper.

And after a time Maxwell Georgia slept. As still as only the weary can be, it lay—splotched dark against flat stretches of cotton; tied to them by roads which wound their white threads through cottonfields, past black pinelands, around ponds, under great oaks, on, on, on, in the night.

Covered by darkness, Maxwell slept . . . in tired peace. The night freight chuffed up Sandy Hill, clanked its short-lived signal of commerce, passed on to the North. The moon came up above the line of pinelands in the east, slowly moved across the town, making luminous and beautiful the thin white steeples of Baptist and Methodist churches, throwing wayward bright shafts of light on roofs, glinting the railroad track, whitening the big revival tent, washing away all trace of the day and its black sin.

# THIRTY

BESS RAISED HER HEAD. Across town the light was breaking through the pines. Enough of it had sifted through the east window to waken her. She could not believe she had slept. Her mind had not been still. Flames had filled it. The smell of burnt flesh would never get out of it. The crackle of burning wood, white laughter, sharp short bark of hounds, the low continuous sobs of Dessie . . . They'd never stop, none of it would ever stop, it would never stop . . .

Bess turned her head, moved her cramped body. Her mind grew still. She must have dozed, she thought quietly. Her left arm was asleep. She rubbed it hard, tried to lift it from the table, rubbed it again until the blood sent sharp sand-prickles through it.

The room was thick with body smells and dead air. She had shut every window and locked it, obeying a crying need of nerves, not brain—knowing that nothing could keep white men out if they wanted to come in.

She looked at the others. Nonnie lay back in Tillie's old chair, hand limp on the side of it, lips parted, long black lashes deepening shadows already deep enough. Bess's mind like a slim finger touched those lashes softly, followed them in their downward curve and upward sweep. And it whispered to her, as it had done a thousand times, of Nonnie's beauty. She felt it as men must feel it, only it left her chilled, sick with the knowledge of her own plump prettiness. Her mind moved softly down the sleeping girl's body. Inside that slim body lay a baby. "A foetus," Bess whispered quickly, to stop the flood of pity that brought a sting to her eyelids— simply a mass of pulp, which could quickly be removed, were it not for Nonnie's stubbornness. No, Nonnie wanted her baby, she had said, and with those few words great obstacles had been thrown across their future as casually as an earthquake or storm does its work.

Bess's heart stiffened with the old resentment.

She turned to ease cramped muscles. Dessie lay on the floor, curled up like a brown puppy at her feet. She was breathing easily through wide-open mouth, as she had breathed all her life in sleep. Tears had streaked her dust-covered face and dried there, a little something had run from her nose and dried beneath it. Her small pointed breasts pushed up through the thin pink silk blouse, her

369

clawlike hands were clasped tight together. Dessie looked like a dirty little child who had been spanked for some badness and had cried herself to sleep . . .

Oh, God has spanked the little nigger all right, Bess thought bitterly, and tried to smile. Instead a great shattering sob rose in her throat, choked her. She knew if she gave way, if she once let herself cry, she would never stop . . . there would be no reason to stop.

She went to the windows and opened each one, pushing hard where they stuck, until each was wide open to the fresh morning air. The dark clumps of bridal-wreath were taking on a green from the increasing light, spider lilies turned white as she looked, a streak of sun touched the porch banisters, and slowly Bess hardened her heart once more.

"Time for working women to get up," she called briskly, and followed her words with a rough shake of Nonnie's shoulder, a push of her foot in Dessie's side.

Both sat up mechanically, empty-eyed, silent.

"It's late. We'd better not be late—today." Bess unbuttoned her dress, pulled it over her head quickly, fetched a basin of water and washed herself.

Like an automaton Nonnie followed every movement of Bess. The splash of cold water took the stiffness out of her face, brought to the surface a little warmth.

"Take off your waist, Dessie, and shake out the wrinkles— and scrub yourself with plenty of soap."

Dessie obediently took off the pink waist.

"Better take off your skirt too. You look kind of ratty, honey."

Dessie took off her skirt.

"I'd wash *good* if I were you. It'll make you feel better."

Dessie washed good.

Bess slipped into her blue uniform. Nonnie slipped into her white, smoothed back her hair to the plainness required of Boysie Brown's nurse.

The whistle at the sawmill blew. Six-thirty.

Dessie fastened up the pink waist and hiked up the black skirt over her hipbones. Bess laced her black arch-supporter ties, Nonnie fastened her white oxfords, Dessie wiggled into the old pair of black satin run-down-at-the-heel pumps the Harris girls had given her.

They started out, were halfway to the gate. Dessie stopped, ran back to the house.

The two sisters waited for her. They had not said a word to each other and said no word now.

The swamp was in deep shadow behind them.

Around the curve of the cemetery, past Miss Ada's old house, the town lay. The streets would be in full sunshine by the time they got to their kitchen doors. And Dan would be delivering ice.

Everything would be the same—as it always was.

A toad-frog hopped across the path. Bess pulled away a spider's web from the gate.

Dessie stumbled on the rickety steps, righted herself, came running down the path. She had gone back for her hat. It was perched on the side of her head, three red roses bobbing up and down as she walked, breasts bobbing up and down in soft unison.